SHADOW OF PASSION

"'Tis a long, lonely day. The only pleasure for me comes when the sun hides its face and you step into the shadows," Dane whispered, nuzzling the hollow of Gabrielle's neck. Then he kissed her demandingly, seeking to know more of this mystical enchantress who appeared only at night. Lying back on the bed with her encircled in his arms, Dane pulled Gabrielle's full length against him.

"No," she whispered breathlessly. "Dane, you must let me go."

Then Gabrielle vanished into the night, just as she had warned Dane she would. There was no sign that she had been there at all. And Dane was once again alone, wondering at the silhouette that had disappeared with the fading shadows. . . .

Rapture's Dream

BY CAROL FINCH

ZEBRA BOOKS
KENSINGTON PUBLISHING CORP.

ZEBRA BOOKS

are published by

KENSINGTON PUBLISHING CORP.
475 Park Avenue South
New York, N.Y. 10016

Second printing: July 1984

Printed in the United States of America

Chapter One

The vast darkened world exploded with heated waves of colors that curled and stretched upward like disfigured hands reaching out to singe the sky. The piercing screams echoed toward the horizon like a thousand wailing voices begging for mercy, but their pleas could not be answered from the distant shore. Fate had entered a dark passageway and the seamen's escape was impossible. They were destined to perish in the fire, smoke, and torrents of water that swelled about the steaming embers that had once been a seaworthy schooner.

Tortured faces rose above him before they were swallowed up by the hungry sea. The muffled cries of anguish drowned, lost forever in the murky depths.

A last, blood-curdling scream reached his ears and he thrashed wildly, encumbered by the heavy ropes that held him captive. Suddenly Dane's eyes flew open, his body glistening with perspiration, his heart pounding against his ribs. Then, gasping for breath, Capt. Dane Hampton glanced about his quiet cabin, finding nothing more than the moon's silver shadows moving across his dark room. The tormented shriek had been his own guilty voice. The reoccurring dream was as always, he mused bitterly as he flung the tangled sheets away from his broad chest. It was so vivid that he could scarcely distinguish between the horrible fantasy and reality.

Swinging his long muscular legs over the edge of his cot, he donned his breeches and strolled across the planked floor to escape from the stuffy confines of his captain's quarters. As Dane ambled toward the main deck, he inhaled the salty sea air, then paused to lean against the rail, his blue eyes scanning the sea that he loved for its beauty and despised for its cruelty.

Raking his lean fingers through his raven hair, Dane glanced toward the distant docks of London that began to appear as the sun raised its weary head from another sleepless night. Dane had mixed emotions about returning home again. There were too many forbidden memories there to haunt him. But then, the nightmares were just as frightening at sea as they were on land. With a sigh, he slumped forward, leaning his forearms on the railing as a thoughtful frown settled in his bronzed features. Life had dealt him some devastating blows, but he had survived and outwardly accepted his fate. Yet, at times, the endless memories of what had happened ate at his guts and nothing could ease the pain.

"Cap'n, yer breakfast is waitin' in yer cabin,"

Sam murmured as he moved cautiously toward Dane who was oblivious to the fact that the boatswain had strolled up behind him. "Cap'n?" The sailor's low voice was gentle. He had heard Dane's agonizing wails on too many occasions not to know what plagued him. Such a proud man should not have to endure what Dane had, Sam mused as he eyed the broad shoulders of his captain.

Dane turned toward the burly seaman. "Sam," he said in quiet greeting.

"Yer breakfast, sir." Sam was quick to note the painful flicker in Dane's sapphire eyes. "Bad night, Cap'n?" he questioned, a concerned frown etching his brows.

"Aye," came the hushed reply.

As Dane strolled across the deck in measured strides, Sam heaved a quiet sigh. The captain shouldn't blame himself for what had happened, Sam mused ruefully. He deserved more from life than to be haunted by the ghost that had become his constant shadow. Perhaps one day he could forget. It would just take time—lots of time. When the captain disappeared from sight, Sam climbed the ladder to stand beside the helmsman. The two seamen silently watched the skyline of London grow larger on the horizon.

Gabrielle sneaked down the servants' stairway, making her flight to freedom. When she met the accusing glare of her cousin, Elaine Jarmon, who stood below her on the landing, she stopped in her tracks.

"Where are you stealing off to this time, Brielle? You know Papa will be in a fit of rage if he returns to find that you've gone out again, despite his orders," Elaine reminded her as she edged a step closer and eyed her lovely cousin suspiciously.

"I'm going riding. Why don't you join me?" she queried. "I know the perfect place where we can lope the hills, unhindered by your father or anyone else. Please come." Her tone was coaxing, hoping that just once Elaine would rebel against the tyrannical man who refused to allow either of them freedom.

The delicate blonde hung her head and then shook it despairingly. "I can't. Papa forbids it and I dare not disobey him."

Elaine peered into the shimmering green eyes that were always so full of life and adventure. Gabrielle possessed all of the beauty and strong characteristics that Elaine would have dearly loved to claim as her own. Brielle had been educated well and allowed the freedom that Elaine would never know. Her exquisite face could be gentle and compassionate, or alight with pleasure. And at times it would set in grim determination if she were forced to stand her ground, which she never refused to do when she felt she had just cause. Her dark, silky hair lay over her shoulders and down her back in a thick cascade that came to life with golden highlights when kissed by the sun. Her creamy complexion was as pure and unmarred as her free-spirited soul. Brielle was the essence of beauty, Elaine mused as she stared into the emerald eyes that waited, widening in anticipation.

"I won't betray you, Brielle," she assured her. "Go on."

Gabrielle stepped down beside Elaine on the landing and touched her frail arm. "Just once, I wish you could taste freedom. You miss so much," she said, a rueful smile hovering on her lips.

"I can't. I'm afraid of him," Elaine confessed. "You take his punishment much better than I ever could." She lifted her skirt and hurried up the stairway, wishing that she were brave enough to defy her father's commands. Gabrielle had done it so many times, but Elaine knew that she would never even try. John Jarmon was far too powerful for Elaine to confront.

As Brielle listened to the sound of rustling skirts fade into silence, she shrugged hopelessly and continued on her way. After stepping out of the back door, she glanced carefully about her and trotted to the stables where Sherman had her mount waiting, out of view of the barn's main entrance.

"Lord John said 'e would not be returnin' for a couple of 'ours," Sherman informed her. A broad smile creased his dirt-smudged face as he handed the petite lass the reins. "Now be on yer way before Benton comes along and wallops me backside for lettin' ye go off again when the master said ye was to stay at the 'ouse."

"Thank you, Sherman. I would have lost my mind long ago if it weren't for you," Brielle

11

replied as she leaned over to place a grateful peck on the lad's dark cheek.

Sherman blushed crimson red. With a grubby hand, he wiped away her show of affection and staggered back. "Blimey, lady! Ye'll 'ave me smellin' of perfume. The other men will 'eckle me to death!" he gasped in embarrassment.

"Sorry, Sherm. You know you're irresistible." Her emerald eyes glistened mischievously as she glanced at the red-faced lad. "Yer me own true love, ye know," she mocked, a dazzling smile curving her mouth as she mimicked his cockney accent. Brielle stepped into the stirrup, seated herself astride her white stallion, and gazed down at Sherman. Blowing him a fleeting kiss, she winked playfully. "Farewell, me love."

"Sure, sure. Now git ye gone," Sherman scoffed as he urged her on her way with an impatient flick of his wrist.

Gabrielle whirled her steed away from the stables and cantered toward the thicket. Sherman watched until the lovely goddess vanished from sight and then smiled to himself. Although he was only sixteen, he had found true love. He could never refuse helping Brielle escape from the massive mansion on the hill. Whistling a light-hearted tune, he ambled back to the barn to finish his menial chores, unconcerned that he smelled of jasmine. The lingering fragrance reminded him of Brielle and that eased his drudgery. A contented smile played on his lips as he grabbed a pitchfork and began tossing hay to the horses.

Escaping from her uncle's domain, Gabrielle flew across the moor. She breathed a sigh of relief when she spied her corner of the prison where no one could find her. As she drew the steed to a halt, she gazed down upon the peaceful valley that had once been her beloved home. After sliding from Blanco's back she strolled toward a twisted-trunked tree that grew near the edge of the rock cliff that marked the boundary between her home and that of her uncle, John Jarmon. Symbolically this line separated the past from the present and she yearned to be a part of all the yesterdays that fondly filled her memory. Reliving those pleasant thoughts had become more satisfying than anticipating the future.

It was her eighteenth birthday and it had quickly turned into one of the most horrible days she had had to endure. John had spitefully informed her that she would have no season in London as he had promised when she had come to live with his family. That afternoon he had told Brielle that her wings needed to be clipped and that she had too many rough edges to meet the noblemen of his social circle. He had said that she would not be compatible with any of the men who were interested in finding a suitable wife because of her insolence and disobedience. John had declared that, as her guardian, he would make the necessary arrangements for marriage, when and only when he considered her to be subdued.

A heated argument between niece and uncle ensued. Gabrielle became furious when she discovered that he intended to marry her to someone that *he* considered a proper match for her. She informed him in no uncertain terms that he would not rule her life as he did Elaine's. Brielle had a mind of her own and she intended to use it. She told John that he thought all women were slaves to all men, whether they be husband, father, or master of the house.

Her poor aunt, Brielle mused sorrowfully. John had undoubtedly smothered her will to live. She had been taken to an early grave and Gabrielle could not help but blame John. He had surely driven her to it.

Another painful scene flashed before her eyes as she continued her silent reverie. During the exchange with her uncle, Brielle's temper had freed her words. She had unintentionally told that malicious man exactly what she thought of him and his tyrannical reign over his family. Before she was able to gain control of her quicksilver temper and her sharp tongue, she had called him a pompous fool who attempted to enslave her, a self-appointed god, and an oppressive dictator. When she stormed from the room, wishing she could have swallowed a few of her biting comments, John had snarled at her, his face red with rage. John had vowed that she would regret her disrespectful outburst to the man who had taken her into his home when she had no place to go.

"I'll make your life so miserable that you will wish you were dead, you ungrateful little bitch!" he screeched, wagging a stubby finger in her direction.

Gabrielle had whirled to face him, sparks

14

flashing like lightning in her stormy, green eyes. "You already have and sometimes I do, Uncle. I have lived in hell since the day I came here!" she snapped before rushing up the stairs and slamming the door of her room with such force that the entire house vibrated with its violent closing.

She squeezed her clouded eyes shut, forcing the unfortunate incident from mind. And then the vision of her parents came before her, melting her ire into sorrow as she reflected upon her life. Her mother had died when Gabrielle was nine and her father had been taken from her six months ago. She could still remember her father's words as he gazed wearily at her with his green eyes that had the youthful sparkle she had known and loved.

"Stay with John until you marry, child," he had urged in forced breaths. "Find a good, gentle man who will love you as I do and make the most of your life. Live every moment to its fullest. There never seems to be sufficient time when we look back over the passing years."

Paul Jarmon had stretched out his arm, placing Gabrielle's small hand in his own. "Our home will be cared for by my lawyer who has set up funds for the servants. If you need to see him, you will find him in Bristol. His name is Roger Saxon. I find him worthy of my trust. I'm sending you away from home so that no money-hungry scoundrels will seek to make you their wife. You are too young to deal with that sort. John will provide for you." Paul had closed his eyes, gathering his last bit of strength before bidding farewell to his lovely daughter. Looking to her once again, he attempted to memorize each delicate feature of her face. "Gabe, my beautiful angel, always remember how much I love you," he breathed as his green eyes closed for the last time.

Gabrielle had desperately squeezed his lifeless hand, attempting to force his spirit back into his body, but he was gone from her. With tears rolling down her cheeks she laid her head on his chest, deliriously sobbing her grief until she shed only dry tears for his passing.

Gabrielle attempted to put the past behind her. Gazing out over the moor, she watched the billowing storm clouds brewing. A strong gust of wind whipped about her face, drying the new tears that mourned old, unhealed wounds. The breeze whirled about her blue muslin gown as she leaned back against the tree, facing the approaching storm. Her tear-rimmed eyes lifted; she silently prayed that someday she would find the happiness for which she searched.

From a distance, a darkly clad rider gazed at her trim silhouette on which the sun streamed down, illuminating the lovely woman who was perched on the lonely hill. At an opening between the trees that lined the road, he paused to stare in awe, wondering if his imagination was again playing tricks on him. The young woman seemed immortal as the sun rays sparkled around her and then disappeared momentarily, leaving her hardly more than a blurred shadow against the twisted tree until she reappeared, the shimmering light dancing about her shapely form. As the sun faded once again, he waited anxiously for her return. But when the clouds parted, the shadows faded and the mysterious vision had vanished.

Dane Hampton reluctantly urged his buckskin forward while the illusion filled his thoughts, leaving him pleasantly warmed by what had seemed a supernatural sight. Was this yet another ghost that had come to haunt him? he mused, thinking of the frightening shadow that continued to follow him. When he heard the thunder rumbling above him, a foreboding sign, he nudged his horse to a faster pace. At the second crack of thunder, a muffled shot found its intended mark. A searing pain blazed across Dane's skull. Captain Hampton reined his buckskin to a halt, but the frightened steed snorted and sidestepped as his rider teetered precariously on his back. Dane's hand moved up to feel the wound on his forehead; he fought to keep himself in touch with reality which was beginning to fade into a hazy gray. As he slumped forward, grasping Sultan's neck, the darkness surrounded him. He slipped from the saddle, falling in an unconscious heap beside his alarmed steed. Sultan reared and then came down striking his master's thigh with a powerful hoof. The unintended assault made Dane cry out in pain before he sank into the swirling darkness.

Gabrielle left her private sanctuary with the storm following closely at her heels. She flew across the meadow in haste, hoping to return before her uncle discovered that she had disobeyed him. Through the opening in the trees she spied the riderless buckskin and quickly pulled her white stallion to a halt. If she took time to see about the steed, she was sure to be caught by her uncle who would fly into another fit of rage. If she didn't stop, some poor traveler might be forced to suffer the violent storm without protection.

Mumbling a silent curse to her misfortune, Gabrielle rode through the trees to find a man lying prostrate on the road. The wind whipped about her and the earth shook from exploding thunder as Brielle slid from Blanco's back. She crouched beside the injured man whose forehead was smeared with blood.

As the jaws of the storm swallowed them in darkness, the clouds unleashed their fury, pounding against the overhanging trees. The cold raindrops on his face brought Dane to the edge of consciousness. He opened his eyes to see a blurred vision hovering closely above him. As a jagged flash of lightning sent a streak of silver across the sky, Gabrielle gazed down into the most handsome face she had ever seen. The man had raven hair, a tanned face, and the bluest eyes, that sparkled even when dulled with pain. She caught her breath, mesmerized by the searching orbs that were full of unanswered questions.

"Can you stand, m'lord?" she questioned, quickly shaking her head to break the spell that his captivating eyes had cast upon her.

The soft voice filtered through his confused thoughts, soothing the pulsating pain in his head. Drawing from his fading strength, he whispered hoarsely, "Perhaps, if you help me." But as he tried to pull himself up, the stiffness in his thigh made him cringe and groan in agony.

Brielle tugged on his arms to bring him to his feet. Dane clutched at her shoulders to steady himself while the world spun furiously about him. As Brielle guided his booted foot into Blanco's stirrup, Dane struggled to seat himself, only half-conscious of what he was doing. He leaned forward, grasping the horse's mane as Gabrielle swung up behind him. The heavens opened up to release the rain and Brielle quickly nudged Blanco homeward. Her steed, his wide eyes darting nervously as he made his way to shelter, stepped cautiously onto the road that had turned to slippery mud. The buckskin followed him.

Against the howling wind and darkness, Brielle squinted toward the lights of the Jarmon mansion, wondering what type of reception awaited her. It was of no importance that she had played the good Samaritan for some injured traveler. Her uncle would be enraged with her disobedience; of that she was certain.

As she reined her steed to a post at the front of the house, Brielle screamed, "Simon, help me, please!"

Her voice was barely heard above the wailing gusts, but the servant heard her plea and hurried outside. Simon pulled the unconscious man from the saddle and carried him into the house. With the man delivered to safety, Gabrielle trotted to the stables to have both steeds brushed and curried before tending to her own needs.

By the time she returned to the house, she was drenched and chilled to the bone. She was met by her uncle, his thin lips displaying a subtle smile that worried Gabrielle far more than the contemptuous sneer she had expected to see.

"We put the man to bed and he has been cared for, Brielle. After you have bathed and changed, I will see you in my study. We have an important matter to discuss," he insisted as a wicked gleam filled his gray eyes.

Her brows furrowed as she carefully scrutinized John; then she brushed past him. Without uttering a word, Brielle ascended the back stairs, wondering what the conniving tyrant had in mind for her punishment this time.

After bathing and donning a fresh gown, Gabrielle stepped into the room next to hers to check on the man she had saved from the storm. Since his quarters were void of servants she walked toward the bed and peered down at Dane's ashen face. The wound on his forehead had been bandaged and he seemed to be sleeping comfortably. Brielle moved away from the still form, reluctant to go to meet her uncle. But, she glanced back over her shoulder, silently watching him for a long moment. Then she hung her head, wishing she could see those captivating blue eyes gazing up at her. Brielle opened the door to slip out into the hall, but not before Dane caught sight of her hazy shadow.

Captain Hampton's vision was still blurred; nonetheless he was certain that the image he saw was the one that had appeared before him on the hill and had hovered over him while he lay on the road. His memory was foggy and that was all he was able to recall. He did not remember how he had gotten to the house or even where it was. With the lovely vision gone from sight, he closed his eyes and sleep overtook him, leaving all of his questions yet unanswered. At least this shadowed silhouette was not as frightening as the one that usually preoccupied his thoughts, he mused drowsily.

John Jarmon was seated at his desk, holding a contract in his puffy hands, a satisfied smile curling his thin lips. The past six months with his unruly niece under his roof had constantly tested his patience. He had attempted to break her spirit, but had only succeeded the first month while she mourned the passing of her beloved father. As the pain of her loss subsided, she again became the independent, headstrong lass that she had been at home. Paul Jarmon had set aside a sizable monthly allowance for the time Gabrielle spent with her uncle. Although John had enjoyed the funds, Gabrielle had become an unpleasant thorn in his side.

After their afternoon confrontation, John had been so enraged with the sassy vixen that he had traveled to the home of the Duke of Fairleigh. Horace had been elated with John's offer and did not bat an eye at the sum John had requested for their agreement. John had returned home well-pleased with his scheme. The fact that Gabrielle had disobeyed him again and had dragged some wounded traveler in from the road did nothing to hamper his delight at having his troublesome niece off his hands.

Brielle strolled into the study, watching her uncle like a wary prey that has just confronted its pursuer. She seated herself in the chair that faced his desk, poised to break and run if the situation demanded it. With an impatient sigh she waited until John raised his head and stared at her with his cruel, gray eyes flickering with some emotion that she could not understand.

"Before we discuss an important matter that affects both of us, I want to know where you found our injured guest," John demanded, his thin brows coming together on his wrinkled forehead.

"He was on the road west of here," she replied stiffly, her gaze failing to meet his probing eyes.

"And of course you disobeyed me again and went riding unescorted, didn't you?" John sneered contemptuously.

"Obviously," Gabrielle retorted, her tone crisp and icy. "However, the man would have died out there had I not come upon him and brought him home with me," she stated in her defense as her emerald eyes locked with his gloomy, gray orbs.

"So the man owes you his life. I pity the poor wretch," he scoffed disgustedly. "Just who is he and how was he wounded?"

Gabrielle shrugged nonchalantly. "I don't know. He was unconscious most of the time and I didn't interrogate him. He needed immediate attention, not a long siege of questions," she replied caustically.

John eased back in his chair, folded his hands on the desk, and grinned maliciously. It was better that the man was unaware of who had saved him from a dreadful fate. He suppressed a smile that attempted to surface as he approached the subject of the contract.

"Gabrielle, I went to see Horace Fairleigh this afternoon. We have signed an agreement that will be of considerable interest to you. Horace and I have drawn up a marriage contract. You will soon become the Duchess of Fairleigh." He paused to watch the flashing green eyes that sought to pierce his heart with their fury. The smile he tried to suppress earlier split his face and Brielle stiffened in outrage.

"You what?" she shrieked aghast. Surely John could not be that cruel. "You know how much I despise that lecherous fop!" She clutched the arms of her chair, wishing she could clamp her fingers around John's stubby little neck.

"Of course I do, my dear. That is precisely why you're going to marry him. *You* will be miserable that *that* will make me quite happy." John chuckled as Brielle flashed him an angry glare. "I have seen the way he ogles you when he comes to call. I know you will enjoy being pawed by the dear gentleman. He wants a young virgin upon whom he can bestow all of his amorous affection. You will suit him perfectly, Brielle. If you step out of line, I'm sure you will be properly punished. Horace thinks much as I do," he assured her with a haughty smirk.

Brielle bolted to her feet and leaned over the desk, glaring into her uncle's smug face. "He's three times my age and you have no right to arrange—"

"Horace is fifty-four to be exact," John interrupted, a satanic smile hovering on his lips. "And as your guardian I have every right to find you a respectable mate. You will obey my wishes!"

John rose to his feet and they stood eye to eye, regarding each other with hatred bridging the gap between gray and green orbs.

"Damn you!" she hissed, attempting to control her quick temper; but the chore was next to impossible.

"Watch your tongue, you foul-mouthed twit!" he growled furiously, his plump face reddening at her curse.

"Damn you to hell!" she spat into his shocked face.

Lord Jarmon slapped her cheek and she reacted by leaving her own handprint on the side of his face. With a startled bellow, John slammed his fist down on the desk and muttered a string of curses at her. Gabrielle continued to glare at him with defiance spewing from her eyes.

His auburn brows furrowed into an ugly, twisted frown. "You little bitch! The sooner you're out of my sight, the better," he snarled. "The engagement will be announced next week and you will be married in less than two months. After that, I never want to lay eyes on you again. Everything associated with you sickens me. From your wedding day forward, I will no longer have a niece."

John whirled around and peered out of the window, watching the storm that whipped about the house. He had finally had the last word with his troublesome niece. She deserved exactly what she would receive as Fairleigh's wife.

Her words wrapped themselves about his stubby neck, choking him with their insult. "I find it impossible to believe that you're my father's brother. There were never two men so dissimilar. Papa was gentle, understanding, while you are spiteful, cruel, and ruthless. The Jarmons were blessed with a saint and cursed with a devil. The only reason you outlived Papa was because you will be spending eternity in the fires of hell." Her eyes sent piercing daggers at her uncle's narrow back.

Lord Jarmon spun to face her insulting glare, quickly denying her accusations. "Your father was a gutless fool who spoiled you beyond repair. You think you can say and do whatever meets your whim, but you are a woman and you cannot! One day soon you will know your proper place. Horace is powerful enough to handle the likes of you," he assured her, his plump face reddening angrily.

"My father allowed me room to breathe and to think for myself. You have suffocated Elaine and made her an empty-headed puppet who moves and talks only upon command. You don't even treat her as a human being. All you care about is yourself. You'll sell your own daughter off just as you have done with me, all for profit, as if she were some beast of burden that could expect no more from life. You are despicable!" Brielle's eyes narrowed murderously as she sneered out the question, "How much was the purse you extracted from Fairleigh so that he could acquire me as his wife, *dear Uncle?*"

John picked up the contract and shoved it at her. "See for yourself," he insisted, once again displaying an evil grin.

As she scanned the contract, Gabrielle growled furiously and then ripped the paper to shreds, letting the pieces flutter to the floor while her uncle watched, undaunted by her reaction.

"There is another copy, Gabrielle. I expected such a childish tantrum from such an uncivilized heathen." He smirked as he crossed his arms on his chest and peered haughtily at the little spitfire who was too enraged to speak. "By the way, my dear, I forbid you to see our injured guest. He has suffered enough already without having to be insulted and degraded by the likes of you."

Brielle spun toward the door, anxious to escape from his annoying presence before the angry tears that she held carefully in check betrayed her weakness. As she dashed upstairs to her room, she heard Dane cry out in anguish. She hurried into his room, despite her uncle's orders. Dane was thrashing wildly in the quilts that held him captive. Brielle eased down on the edge of the bed to calm him, attempting to smother the rage that made her tremble uncontrollably.

"You will be fine, m'lord. You must relax," she soothed in a raspy whisper that instantly drew Dane's attention.

The lantern had been snuffed out and the only light in the room came from an occasional flash of lightning and the dim coals that glowed from the hearth. As his sapphire eyes gazed up at her,

26

her anger melted and floated away with the tears that continued to stream down her cheeks. The fathomless pools of blue seemed to beckon her. For some unexplainable reason she found herself drawn to the stranger. Brielle lowered her head and pressed her lips to his, attempting to forget her troubles by losing herself to the handsome rogue. She reluctantly drew away from his yielding lips and smiled tenderly as she brushed away her tears with the back of her hand.

Dane was pleasantly surprised by the gentle kiss and the teardrops on his cheek. His vision was cloudy and he could only make out her dark form. Yet, he had the feeling that this was the same woman who had held his attention earlier that day.

"Are those tears for me?" he questioned. "Am I in worse condition than I thought?" A faint smile curved his lips as he peered up at the hazy image that hovered over him.

Her quiet chuckle sent a warm tingle down his spine. "You will be fine. The tears are of self-pity. I'm sorry you noticed them," she whispered as she gazed into the captivating eyes that drew her to him again.

Brielle was amazed at her own abandon as she lowered her head to kiss his parted lips. Dane tasted their sweetness and inhaled the lingering fragrance that floated about him, leaving him drifting on a puffy cloud of pleasure. A contented moan escaped his lips as Brielle raised her head.

Easing from the edge of the bed, she moved across the room. Dane's eyes followed her, attempting to see her clearly. But it was useless. She was still nothing more than a blurred image of mystery. After stirring the coals and placing another log on the fire to take the chill from the damp room, she came to him again. In the soft glow of the red coals, Dane saw another silhouette surrounded by dim light. He began to wonder if this was another dream, much more pleasant than the nightmare that had awakened him earlier.

Her skirt swished gently about her as she floated toward him. Dane squinted his eyes, desperately hoping to see her clearly. "Who are you?" he questioned curiously. "What happened? Where am I?"

Brielle chuckled at his rash of inquiries. "First you must tell me your name, sir," she demanded sweetly, leaving him no choice but to obey her quiet request.

"I'm Daniel Hampton. I have an estate north of Bristol. Now who are you?" he queried impatiently.

"Someone attempted to shoot you. You were brought to Lord Jarmon's home and I am your guardian angel," she teased. "If you tell anyone in this house that you have seen me, especially Lord John, you will most likely be tossed out on your injured head. 'Tis our secret, sir. I'm afraid I cannot give you my name or tell you from where I have come. All I can say is that my home is not far from where you are."

"My guardian angel?" His dark brow arched skeptically.

"But of course, m'lord. How else could you

explain being discovered in a raging storm and being brought to safety to have your wounds tended if not without the aid of an angel of mercy?" Gabrielle smiled as his hand moved up to touch her cheek.

"I was afraid this was all a dream," Dane murmured, a pleased grin softening his rugged features. "But you are warm flesh and blood. At least I have my sanity."

"Don't be so sure, Mr. Hampton," she gently rebuked as she wrapped her hand around his and drew it away from her face. "Dreams always seem to be reality while you're having them."

"How well I know," Dane mused aloud.

"'Tis only on reflection that we see them for what they are—merely a passing fantasy that has no place in life," she insisted, still speaking in nothing above a whisper.

"Dane. Please call me Dane," he corrected. "I will wake tomorrow remembering that you were here. On that you can depend, angel." He smiled tenderly at her shadowed face.

"As you wish . . . Dane," she said, acknowledging his request. "But I doubt if you will recall talking to me at all."

"Ah, but I will," he assured her determinedly. "I only wish I could see you clearly. My head wound must have affected my sight. Right now you are only a cloudy vision of loveliness." His blue eyes searched her face, warming her with their intensity.

"All the more proof that I am indeed your guardian angel who has come to visit you in a dream," she teased. "Now you must rest." Gabrielle carefully eased herself from his side.

"Please don't go," Dane begged like a small child who feared being left alone in the dark. His hand groped for hers, detaining her escape. "If this is a dream, I don't wish it to end so quickly."

"I must go. Dreams cannot last forever. We all must wake to find that the cruel world still exists," she said quietly. Tears once again clouded her eyes when she recalled her confrontation with her treacherous uncle.

Dane carefully considered her words, wondering what had caused the hint of bitterness in her whispered voice. "If you must leave, may I have one, last kiss from my guardian angel to protect me from the long, lonely night?"

Gabrielle was lured into his spell and lowered parted lips to his, hoping to forget her misfortune for a few more moments. Dane wrapped his fingers in the silky strands of hair that lay against her neck. He kissed her passionately, exploring the sweetness that he had found while he drew her against his broad chest. Brielle melted against him, surrendering to the security of his arms.

They were strangers in the darkness, needing each other's comfort. As the rain pattered against the windowpanes, the world stopped spinning to hold them suspended while they found serenity in their embrace. As a salty tear fell against his cheek, Dane pressed her head against his shoulder and inhaled the sweet fragrance of her hair.

"What troubles you, angel?" he queried as he

nuzzled his face against her ear. "May I help?"

With a muffled sniff, she attempted to dry her eyes, but they insisted on spilling more tears. "You already have, more than you know. It has been a most disturbing day," she confessed softly. "You have been the only pleasant part of it."

Brielle remained in the security of his strong arms a few moments longer, neither of them uttering a word to shatter the spell.

"I thought angels were exempt from hellish experiences," he teased, a broad smile catching the corners of his mouth.

"I'm afraid not, m'lord. At least not this one."

"But luckily there are moments like these to ease our trials," he murmured, giving her a loving squeeze.

"Yes. But now it must come to an end. I have lingered much longer than I should have. There are other obligations that require my attention," she explained as she withdrew from his embrace.

"Another man perhaps?" he queried. For some reason the idea was not to his liking. "Are you some mystical goddess whose duty requires you to search out troubled souls and console them?"

Gabrielle chuckled softly, refusing to answer his inquiry. "Good night. Sleep well, m'lord."

The silhouette seemed to float away from him to be swallowed up in the swaying shadows.

"Will I see you again?" he queried, unable to see her.

"Perhaps. If you need my assistance I will come again," she replied while Dane strained his ears to catch the quiet words that sounded so far away.

And then she was gone as quickly as she had appeared.

Dane felt a strange emptiness touch his soul, leaving him to wonder what mysterious spell had invaded his senses. There was a soothing quality in her whispered voice. Her lingering fragrance and the honeyed softness of her kisses left him yearning for her presence. He closed his eyes and sighed in confusion. The entire afternoon and evening were vague and distorted. The silhouette on the hill, the storm, the frightening nightmare, and the dark, angelic image swirled about his mind. Had reality taken another step away from him?

Gabrielle slipped into her own room, changed into her nightgown, and curled up in the cold quilts. With an unexplained warmth, she pictured a pair of sparkling blue eyes that blotted out the hard gray eyes of her uncle. She was content to sleep instead of tossing and turning, worrying about the contract her uncle had signed.

She might be forced to spend a life of misery being married to that lecherous Horace Fairleigh, but she would enjoy what little happiness and comfort she could find with Dane Hampton during his recuperation. Her uncle had her cornered and she could see no possible way to fight his decision. After their last argument, she wondered whether Lord John disliked her father to the extent that he would take his revenge out on her or whether he just despised her. Either way, the conniving fox had snared her into a trap that left him hungrily licking his chops, anticipating the misery she would suffer. There had to be a way to free herself from the contract. Gabrielle was determined to find a solution. She had two months to think of a scheme. Somehow she would defeat his treachery, she vowed to herself before fading into slumber.

Chapter Two

Gabrielle awakened the following morning, anxious to see Dane. Smiling to herself, she wondered if he had remembered having a night visitor and whether he would recognize her when she saw him in the light of day. She donned a pink muslin gown, brushed back her dark hair, and at the back of her neck tied a ribbon, which she let stream down to intermingle with the soft curls that fell to her waist. After finishing her breakfast, Brielle prepared a tray. She hurried back upstairs, a bright smile playing on her lips. It quickly faded into a scornful frown when she met Lord John in the hall. A malicious grin curled his lips and Brielle halted before him.

"Where do you think you're going with that tray?" he questioned as he leaned against the wall, crossing his arms on his protruding belly.

"I'm taking our guest his breakfast," she replied coldly, her emerald eyes sparking rebellion.

As Brielle brushed past him, Lord John grabbed

her arm. The food slid across the tray and Brielle attempted to balance it before the cup of hot tea spilled down the front of her dress.

"I told you that you would not be allowed to see him. Your intended husband would be most distressed if you were found alone in a stranger's bedroom." His gray eyes narrowed threateningly. "I'll take the tray to him. You are to stay away from him or I'll have you locked in your room," he assured her in a gritted growl.

As John pulled the tray from her hands, Brielle glared at this despicable man who seemed to spite her at every turn. God, but she detested the very sight of him.

"Someday I will find a way to repay you for your cruelty, *dear Uncle*." She sneered and then spun away, stalking to her room, trembling with rage.

"God, forgive me," she sobbed without restraint. "I hate that man!" Brielle flung herself on her bed, burying her free-flowing tears and muffled wails in the quilts until she had released all of her frustration, and felt herself only an empty shell that was incapable of further emotion. When she finally raised her head, her delicate features were as hard as stone. She was cold, unfeeling, void of any emotion except hatred. John was attempting to destroy her. Damn! She wouldn't let him! Brielle sat up on the edge of her bed, her fists clenched on her lap. She was going to find a way to have her revenge and she would not marry that letch! Lord John Jarmon would not dictate to her!

*   *   *

Lord John eased open the door to the guest room and displayed a polite smile. He was greeted by what appeared to be a look of disappointment. John attempted to ignore Dane's expression in his effort to play the role of a gracious host.

Dane's vision had been clear when he'd awakened. Although his memory was full of confused images, one thought played with his mind. He recalled a misty dream of a lovely seraph who had brought him contentment. He had expected to see her face in the morning light that streamed into the elaborate room where he had slept. Instead of viewing a beautiful goddess, he looked up to see a small, round gentleman with thin, auburn hair.

"I am Lord John Jarmon," he stated as he placed the tray on Dane's lap and then pulled a chair close to the bed to seat himself.

"My name is Daniel Hampton. I'm a ship's captain and I own an estate near Bristol," Dane replied, carefully studying the gray eyes that reminded him of those of a fox.

"I'm glad we were able to come to your aid, Captain," John said, forcing another smile. "Do you know what happened to you?"

"I don't remember much about last night. I suppose someone must have taken a shot at me and my horse must have stepped on me when I fell. Who brought me here?" Dane queried, hoping to learn the name of his mysterious guardian angel.

"We found you unconscious on our doorstep," John lied without changing expression. "But the important thing is that you are alive and will be up and about after a day or two of rest. You were indeed lucky that your head wound was not too serious."

Lord John was pleased to hear that the man was no poor vagabond. He took immediate interest in introducing him to his seventeen-year-old daughter. Elaine would be a perfect match for this handsome sea captain.

"Do you feel up to company, Captain? I would like you to meet my daughter this afternoon."

Dane smiled. Perhaps she would be the woman he had expected to see. "Yes, of course. I would appreciate some company. Could I trouble you for a bath, sir?" he asked as he settled himself more comfortably on the feather bed.

"I'll have it prepared after you have finished your breakfast," John replied as he stood up to leave. "I'll send Elaine in after lunch. Your clothes should be ready by then." He frowned thoughtfully. "Whoever took a shot at you must have stolen your saddlebag, Captain."

Dane watched the gentleman depart and then turned his attention to the tray of tea, ham, and biscuits. When the tub was filled, he arose and weaved unsteadily across the room, limping on his bruised leg. His dizziness assured him that he would not travel until the following day so he relaxed in his bath while the vision of that lovely silhouette skittered through his mind. Elaine Jarmon must have been his guardian angel. He could hardly wait to see her.

Gabrielle changed into her blue velvet riding habit before slipping down the back stairs. When she peered inside the barn, she found Sherman tossing hay to Lord John's mount.

"Sherman, bring Blanco," she requested in a hushed voice.

Brielle moved around behind the stables, out of view of the house, and awaited her young friend. When he came to her, leading the white stallion, she greeted him with an affectionate hug that set him back on his heels.

Sherman stumbled bashfully away from her embrace. "There ye go, smotherin' me with yer affections. A plain and simple 'thank ye' would do me jest as well," he squeaked indignantly as he brushed the straw from the shoulders of his tattered jacket.

"Sherman, me love," she mocked with a playful smile. "I can't 'elp meself when yer so close at 'and. Why do ye deny me an occasional 'ug or kiss? 'Tis such a small request from a forlorn maiden. One of these days some lovely lass will come along and ye'll change yer tune. Ye back away from me like I was afflicted with some 'orrible disease. I bet ye won't act like that when the love of yer life hugs ye."

"Bah!" he snorted derisively, denying her words with a shake of his head. "It ain't likely that I'll find 'er 'angin' 'round this stable." He wanted to say that he had already found the maid to please him, but he didn't dare. Gabrielle loved him as a brother and he knew it. "Now ye best be on yer way, m'lady. Benton will be back in less than an hour. Do ye wish to get caught agin today?" he queried, wondering what punishment she had suffered for her disobedience the previous evening. "By the way, 'ow's the gent?"

"He'll be all right. And thanks, Sherman." Brielle swung on Blanco's back and waved farewell before galloping away.

She reined toward her haven. Her freedom would be short-lived, but she intended to enjoy what little time she had. She dug her heels into Blanco's flanks and he quickened his pace, knowing their destination. The ground was damp and as he followed the path, mud flew up at him, causing him to side-step. Gabrielle patted his neck and leaned down to urge him on with soothing words that eased his nervousness.

When they reached the hill, Blanco came to a halt, holding his head high, his wide eyes searching the grassy slope. Brielle slid from his back, rubbed his soft muzzle, and dropped the reins, allowing him to graze. As she strolled through the grass, her mind began to form a plan of escape that would take her from her uncle's clutches.

She would never marry the Duke of Fairleigh. She would flee from this prison and return to haunt the man who sought to destroy her spirit. As she gazed out over the land that would be hers again one day, she recalled her morning confrontation with her uncle. Suddenly the idea came to her. A slow smile crept to her lips. Her uncle had actually done her a favor although he wasn't aware of it. She had thought of a simple way to gain her freedom and still have protection. Stepping back into the stirrup, Brielle reined toward the house, satisfied that she would soon be unshackled from the oppressive tyrant who brought her nothing but grief.

John stepped out of the stables as Gabrielle pulled her stallion to a halt. "I see my dear niece has defied me once again. I shall see you to your room, Gabrielle," he sneered as he yanked her from the saddle and dragged her along with him.

After he was out of earshot of the curious grooms, he spoke again in his hateful tone. "I'm going to lock you in your room, my dear. You will remain there until tomorrow evening when the duke comes to join us for supper. Maybe by that time you will be more appreciative of your company, you tiresome little bitch." His eyes narrowed to hard slits as he glared at her. "Don't expect our guest to come to your rescue. He doesn't know that you live in this house and does not remember who brought him to safety. Rather unfortunate for you," he added, a satanic smile curling his thin lips.

Gabrielle did not bother to retort. She allowed her eyes to flash her hostility to her odious uncle as he whisked her into the house. John shoved her into her room and locked the door, his loathsome chuckle filtering its way back to Brielle.

A wry smile hovered on her lips as she stared at the locked door. "You have done me another favor, Uncle. For once I have to thank you."

Later, a lunch tray was slipped into her room and the door clicked shut again. Gabrielle shed no more tears for her plight. All her crying had been done that morning. She felt nothing now but a seething hatred which she directed toward her plan of escape.

Dane's lunch was brought in to him and he gobbled down the food, hardly tasting it in his haste to dress and await the visit of Elaine Jarmon. Although there was a dull throbbing in his skull and an occasional sharp pain shooting through his thigh, he smiled broadly as the door creaked open. Lord Jarmon and a petite blonde stepped into his room.

"This is my daughter, Elaine. And this is Capt. Daniel Hampton," John introduced them with a cheerful smile.

Although he was bitterly disappointed, Dane forced a shallow smile. The young woman was mildly attractive, but she was not the shadowed angel with the silky voice that he had anticipated seeing. Elaine was pale, thin, and appeared to be as fragile as a stemmed wineglass. When she spoke in her high-pitched voice, the afternoon began to drag on until the dull pain in Dane's skull was throbbing torture. He could endure no more of this drudgery, he thought to himself. One more minute of listening to the Jarmons would send him climbing right up the walls!

"I've enjoyed the pleasant conversation, Miss Jarmon, Lord John," he said politely, lying through his charming smile, "but I fear that I am in need of rest. My strength is drained and I must be prepared for an early-morning departure. I do appreciate your company and your generous hospitality. I am greatly indebted to you, sir."

"I'm happy that we could offer our services, Captain. When you pass this way again, we would like you to stop by. Wouldn't we, Elaine?" John sent his daughter a quick, sidelong glance, urging her to chime in with him. He was disappointed that Dane showed no more than a courteous interest in his daughter, but nevertheless, John presented his guest with a smile.

Elaine ducked her head and replied shyly, "Yes, Papa. It was a pleasure to meet you, Captain Hampton." With a dainty curtsy, she excused herself from the two gentlemen and hastily exited from the room.

Lord John moved a step closer to the bed, standing stiff and erect as he gazed down at the raven-haired captain. "You are welcome to stay as long as you wish," he offered. "We are more than happy to have you with us. I'm sure my daughter would enjoy your presence in our home for a few more days so that the two of you could become better acquainted."

"You have been very gracious, but I do have business to settle at my estate. I really must leave in the morning," Dane replied smoothly. "Thank you for your invitation. You have been very hospitable."

John bowed slightly and took his leave. Dane heaved a heavy sigh of relief and shed his clothes. After scooting down in the bed, he covered his head in an attempt to close out the unpleasant memory of the afternoon. He drifted off to sleep, dreaming of the mysterious beauty he had hoped to see. Perhaps she was merely a vision conjured up by his imagination. The frail blonde whom he had just met in no way resembled his shadowed goddess. Although Elaine was a well-bred lady, Dane's guardian angel was far more intriguing. Her gentle whisper and quick wit lingered in his mind, bringing a faint smile to his lips. Perhaps his head injury had sent him into vivid hallucinations. Maybe his dreams had intermingled with reality, leaving him to wonder where truth ended and fantasy began. Surely if there was another young woman in the house John would have mentioned it.

Gabrielle waited until nightfall before packing her leather bag. All she intended to take with her into her new life was her father's pistol, a pouch of coins, two dresses, and her nightgown. Dressed in a pink muslin gown, with no undergarments to inhibit her escape, she eased open the window and straddled the sill. She quickly scanned the small cell that had held her prisoner since the morning hours. Then, leaving very few pleasant memories behind, she stepped out onto the narrow ledge and quietly closed the window behind her. As she edged along the precarious shelf, she pressed her back against the side of the stone house. When she came to Dane's window, she crouched down to open the pane, but muttered an exasperated curse. The damned thing wouldn't budge! If this plan failed, her only alternative route was a perilous jump to the ground. She did not relish the idea of breaking her neck before she had the opportunity to seek revenge on her malicious uncle.

With a determined frown she tried the window again. The pane had swelled, dampened from the rain, but finally it eased open. Brielle breathed a sigh of relief as she slipped into the dark room. After moving toward the bed, she eased down beside the sleeping form. Her heart filled with pleasure, smothering the hatred that had sustained her throughout her long day of captivity.

As Dane felt the light, taunting kisses playing on his lips, he came awake, a contented smile curving the corners of his mouth. "Ah, my guardian angel has appeared to save a tortured soul." He breathed huskily. "How did you come?" A thoughtful frown creased his brows as his hand slid up to lightly caress her arm, sending a warm quiver shooting across her skin.

"I flew in through your window, m'lord," she retorted, an unseen smile touching her lips.

"The window?" he repeated skeptically.

"Yes, m'lord. Windows are simple barriers." Her soft chuckle floated recklessly about him, tickling his senses. "But walls . . ." she added thoughtfully. "They are more difficult obstacles. Perhaps they will pose no problem for me once I have earned my wings."

"And what are the necessary requirements for that, love?" he queried, amused at her light-hearted bantering.

"'Tis a difficult task, I fear. I must bring happiness to some poor soul whose spirits have abandoned him," she replied, feigning seriousness as she studied the dark face below hers.

"Then you shall have your wings. You have

44

brought a warm flame into this darkness." Dane reached out to brush the back of his hand across her satiny cheek.

"But are you truly happy, m'lord?" Brielle whispered, still gazing at him, knowing his sapphire eyes were peering at her.

"If I were blessed with one of your tender kisses, in truth I would be content—at least for the moment," he murmured as his hand slipped behind her neck. He pulled her close, his mouth capturing her soft lips.

Gabrielle melted against his broad chest as he wrapped his arms around her waist. Again time stood still for the two strangers who had found an unexplainable attraction and comfort in their embrace. She was content to remain in his sheltering arms. Yet she could not help but wonder what possessed her to fall so quickly into the encircling grasp of this man. She knew absolutely nothing about him except that his name was Dane Hampton and that he held a strange power over her.

"'Tis a long, lonely day. The only pleasure for me comes when the sun hides its face and you step into the shadows," he whispered against the hollow of her neck.

Gabrielle nuzzled against his bare chest, reveling in the fragrance of musk that filtered into her senses. "I find little happiness in the daylight myself," she agreed softly.

"Lord John introduced me to his daughter this afternoon. I was hoping it would be you. I wanted to see you in the full light. I was bitterly disappointed," he murmured before urgently seeking her lips once again.

Leaning back in his encircling arms, she dodged his intended kiss. "You didn't tell him that you had seen me in his house, did you?" she questioned worriedly.

Dane smiled tenderly. "No, love. I took your advice and never mentioned that I had been visited by an angel. He would have thought me crazed." He placed a light kiss to her lips and then moved away. "Now that my vision has been restored, I want to see your face." Dane sat up on the edge of the bed, but Brielle halted his movement, pressing a determined hand against his hard chest.

"No, m'lord. If the room is illuminated I will disappear right before your eyes. I'm afraid I am only visible as a shadow in the darkness," she insisted as she traced her finger across his full lips.

"Why can't I see your face? I'm leaving tomorrow and I want to hold on to your tender memory. I may never see you again," he muttered, a hint of remorse in his hushed voice. The very thought of losing this mysterious goddess was disconcerting.

"I will never be far away, m'lord," she assured him. "I told you last night that if you needed me, I would always be close at hand." Her lips sought his in a tempting kiss and Dane had to drag his mouth away to pursue his question.

"Are you trying to convince me that this is only a fantasy? That I'll see you each time my imagination flies free? Will you come to me whenever I call out to you?" he questioned, a skeptical frown furrowing his brows.

"Of course, m'lord," she insisted, chuckling softly. "I came to you as a faceless shadow when you were in danger. I saw to it that you survived a raging storm. And I have come to ensure that all is well with you. 'Tis my purpose. I cannot appear to you any other way. Do you doubt your guardian angel, sir?"

Gabrielle peered up into his dark face and drew him to her as a warm tingle caused her restraints to take flight. She yearned for one, last kiss before leaving the security of his arms. Unable to resist the invitation, Dane captured her mouth, tasting the sweet nectar to which he had quickly become addicted. His passions burned a fiery path through his limbs and he crushed her to him, feeling her firm breasts boring into his bare chest. He was aroused by her flesh molded so closely to his.

His kisses became demanding, searching, as his tongue parted her lips, urgently exploring her mouth. While his heart beat wildly, his hands moved down her back to caress her hips, seeking to know more of this mystical enchantress. Lying back on the bed with her encircled in his arms, Dane pulled her full length against him, letting her feel his bold manliness that yearned for her.

Brielle could not catch her breath and began to panic as his skillful hands roamed across her flesh. Struggling against his overpowering strength, she fought the sensation that urged her to yield to his bold caresses. At last, her mind gained control of her flesh and she pressed her hands against the thick matting on his chest.

"No," she whispered breathlessly. "Dane, please let me go." She turned her head away from his scalding kisses, determined to reject his advances.

Dane was not accustomed to being denied, but something in her innocent plea made him obey. Although it was not his wont to do so, he drew away.

"You're irresistible," he sighed, reluctantly releasing his grasp on this mysterious young woman. "I'm sorry if I have offended you. When a woman comes willingly to my bed, it is easy to conclude that we both have the same intentions in mind." His tone was harsh and Gabrielle stiffened in irritation. "Now I think we've played this little game of yours long enough. The time has come to unveil your shadowed face."

Dane stumbled across the dark room to light the lantern, but Gabrielle moved quickly. Grabbing her bag, she hastened across the room and slipped into the hall while Dane attempted to illuminate the shadows, intent on revealing the face of the goddess who had haunted his dreams for the past two days.

Holding the lantern high in the air, his anxious gaze swept the room. She had vanished just as she had promised. There was no sign that she had been there at all. He was alone again and the silhouette had disappeared with the fading shadows.

Dane saw nothing, heard nothing, except a small voice within him that muttered, "You fool!" Wishing he could have been content with her request to remain unseen, he silently cursed his impatience. At least she would still have been there with him. He could have held her in his arms if he had not been so determined to see her face. Now he had allowed a refreshing breath of life to slip carelessly through his fingers. Or was she just a vivid, lifelike dream, just as his horrifying nightmares had been? A concerned frown etched his features as his gaze swept the empty room, looking from the closed window to the bed, and then to the door.

Dane had spent many years drifting aimlessly, enjoying all females who had come his way. But the one time in thirty-three years that it had been important for him to tread carefully, he had failed to heed the warning. Now he was annoyed at himself. The mysterious angel who had brought him an unfamiliar contentment had vanished and he had no idea where to search for her. She was his gentle, innocent fantasy that he had sought in his frivolous wanderings, but had never found . . . perhaps because she didn't really exist.

With a disconcerted sigh, Dane snuffed out the light, hoping that she would reappear and he could beg forgiveness for his folly. But only shadows filled his room. When he climbed back into bed and finally drifted off to sleep, the mystical vision skittered across his mind. She was there, standing against the wind on a lonely hill. She was walking toward him in a hazy blur while the red coals of the hearth glowed against her skin. She was in his arms, yielding to his passionate kiss, comforting his fears, bringing a strange contentment to his troubled soul. His angel filled his dreams, but she was never really there at all.

Dane awoke from a sound sleep and glanced about him. She had been there earlier . . . hadn't she? Dane groaned and pulled the pillow over his head. God, he couldn't even swear that she had. Maybe he had only been walking in his sleep.

Gabrielle moved through the quiet house and then dashed toward the stables. After inhaling the damp, evening air, she exhaled a sigh of relief. In a few more minutes she would be free from the prison that had held her captive for the past six months. Stepping into the barn, Brielle moved around the stalls to the tiny room of her trusted friend. As she leaned over the sleeping form in the straw bed, she gently nudged Sherman, bringing him from the depths of drowsiness.

"Wake up, Sherm. I desperately need your help," she whispered urgently.

When he heard Brielle's voice tugging at his consciousness, the lad came awake and swung his long legs over the bed. He sat up and stared at the lovely face that was etched with concern.

"What's the matter?" he queried sluggishly, rubbing his heavy eyelids.

"'Tis a long story and I haven't time for explanations. I must leave here tonight. I need the loan of some of your clothes. Please help me. Go saddle Blanco," she ordered as she pulled him to his feet.

Sherman frowned bemusedly. "Me clothes? Why would ye—"

"Don't ask. Just give me your garb and get my horse," she demanded, cutting him short.

Sherman dragged out his tattered garments and handed them to her as she had ordered. As he entered Blanco's stall, he coaxed the white stallion to follow quietly behind him.

Having stripped off her clothes, Gabrielle stuffed her gown in her pouch, wrapped a cloth around her breasts to camouflage her curves and swells, and donned the ragged clothes. She tucked her long hair up under Sherman's dirty cap, pulled it down on her forehead, and heaved a determined sigh. After grabbing Dane's saddlebag, she crept past the stalls to join Sherman outside.

"Gabe—" Sherman choked in disbelief, unable to finish uttering her name.

"Aye, sir. 'Tis Gabe at yer service," she said saucily and then giggled as the moonlight reflected the whites of his wide, brown eyes. "Stuff yer eyeballs back in yer 'ead, friend. I ain't no ghost or goblin yer gawkin' at." Gabe chuckled again as she peered at the frozen expression on Sherman's face. Grabbing his hand, she offered him the coins for taking his only other change of clothes. "Thanks fer the garb, Sherm. I'll be back one day to take ye away from this 'orrible place. First I 'ave a few thin's to attend." A stern frown settled on her face. "Ye never saw or heard anythin' tonight."

Sherman continued to stare at her, unable to believe the nasal tone, the cockney accent, and the slight, ragged form were those of Gabrielle Jarmon, the wealthy heiress.

"Good-by, Sherman. I'll miss you more than you will ever know." Brielle swung up on her stallion and reluctantly waved to her companion

51

who still stood speechlessly before her. He glanced up, surprise and sadness written on his pale face. With a muffled moan, she threw her leg over the saddle horn and hopped to the ground, rushing to Sherman with outstretched arms. They clung to each other, feeling the agonizing emptiness of losing a dear friend.

"Oh, Sherman. You are the only pleasant memory that I shall carry when I leave this miserable place," Gabrielle muttered remorsefully. She wanted to take him with her, but she knew that it would be best to come for him after her business was settled. If Sherman disappeared too, it could cost him dearly. Lord John would punish both of them unmercifully if they were caught.

"Yer takin' the sunshine from me days when ye leave, Gabrielle. I'll 'ave nothin' to look forward to from now on." Sherman suppressed the urge to cry as he hugged her close. "Now git ye gone before yer found out," he ordered bravely as he stepped away and gazed into the misty green eyes that he adored.

Gabrielle nodded as she wiped the tears from her cheeks with her dirty sleeve. With a slight sniff and a rueful smile she stepped into the stirrup. She urged Blanco into a trot, never looking back to the shadowed form she had left behind. Sherman's tear-filled eyes continued to sweep the shadows until the hoofbeats of the stallion faded in the night. Only then did he weep for the maiden who took his heart when she departed. With slumped shoulders, the lanky urchin trudged back to his straw bed, unconcerned whether the sun ever showed its beaming face again. The one true happiness that he had ever known had just been swallowed up in the darkness.

Through the eerie shadows, Brielle made her flight to freedom, trusting Blanco to care for them. With guarded steps, the steed traveled the familiar path to the hill that marked the border of Lord Jarmon's estate. Without command he stepped down between the rocks of the steep slope and edged along the creek that meandered through Gabrielle's own estate.

A short time later, riding aimlessly, her eyes clouded with unspilled tears, she came upon a grassy refuge where she could spend the night, sleeping on the cold, damp ground. With her saddle for her pillow and a gown for her quilt, she contentedly closed her eyes, believing that her present conditions were much better than those of the last six months when she had been housed under the same roof with her treacherous uncle.

Gabrielle had no doubt that living as an orphan boy, wandering the countryside, would offer her more pleasure than living as a young lady at Lord John's home. If her father had known how much misery he would cause her by merely attempting to protect her, he certainly would have made other arrangements, she thought to herself. But Gabrielle was not one to readily admit defeat. She was determined to outwit her conniving uncle. It might take a great deal of time and cause her discomfort, but she would conquer him, she vowed as her jaw set in stubborn defiance. As

Gabrielle curled up on her hard bed, Blanco whinnied softly. Brielle opened one eye and smiled up at the proud stallion who stood watch over her. Then she drifted off to sleep, thankful that she had her freedom—very little else, but she had escaped from her prison.

Chapter Three

Dane awakened as the first morning light streamed into his room, but a troubled frown settled on his handsome features. The previous evening had seemed so real and yet was so unbelievable. The mysterious angel had begun to replace the ominous shadow that had long been his midnight companion. Those painful memories had begun to fade, but now they became confused with another vision. Dane had spent many restless nights, tortured by his nightmares. Now another dreamlike fantasy was intermingling with those other ghostly visions. Had she been only another dream? Had his midnight ravings sent him sailing on an endless sea of hallucinations? Had his perilous journey carried him so far from reality's shore that he could never plot a course of return? What was happening to him? He wasn't sure he could trust his own mind.

Shaking away the confusing questions, he arose, dressed, and changed the bandage on his forehead. He gathered his composure and went downstairs to find Lord John seated alone at the dining table.

"Good morning, Captain. How are you feeling?" John inquired as he offered his guest a chair across the table from him.

"Much better. Thank you, sir." Dane seated himself and forced a faint smile of greeting for his host.

Lord John leaned his elbows on the table and peered into Dane's handsome face. "Are you married, Captain?" he questioned abruptly.

His dark brows raised acutely and then returned to their normal arch. What the hell kind of question was that? "Why . . . a . . . no. Why do you ask?"

"My daughter, Elaine, would make you a fine wife. She's seventeen and in need of a husband. I thought perhaps we could strike an agreement." His gray eyes twinkled as a smile curled his thin lips.

Dane was startled by Lord John's forwardness. He hardly knew the skinny little chit and there was nothing about her that interested him. Her father was offering her in marriage as if she were a piece of horseflesh to be bought and sold. What kind of scoundrel was Jarmon?

Masking his surprise with a shallow smile, Dane replied glibly, "Your daughter is quite attractive. No doubt she would make someone a fine wife, but marriage is the farthest thing from my mind." His tone hinted at finality and John was well aware that the captain was not likely to be persuaded otherwise.

John straightened himself in his chair, disappointed that he could not make arrangements with a ship's captain and landowner. "Well, I suppose it didn't hurt to ask," he said with a reckless shrug.

Simon entered with their breakfast and both men took their meal in silence. Dane expressed his gratitude and walked out onto the front porch to find his horse saddled and readied. Heaving a sigh of relief, he pulled his hat down over his bandaged forehead and swung up into the saddle, urging Sultan into a lope.

His mind began to wander as he rode. He pulled Sultan to a halt at the same location where he had seen the mysterious vision standing on the distant hill. Dane gazed upon the spot with anticipation, quickly recalling her image, hoping that somehow she would return. But all he saw was the empty slope with the tall grass blowing lazily in the breeze. The leaves on the twisted tree seemed to bid a silent farewell as they rustled in the wind. With a disappointed frown creasing his brow, Dane nudged his steed and trotted down the road. Fond memories of the vision clouded his thoughts and invaded his senses, bringing a faint smile to his lips. If he was going mad, at least he was doing so in a pleasant way, he thought to himself.

After an hour's ride, Dane heard a rustling in the brush behind him. He glanced back to see a small waif, sitting atop a white stallion. With the reins gathered in one hand and his free hand holding his cap on his head, the lad emerged from the thicket and galloped toward the captain.

"'Ey, mister. Wait up!" came the nasal voice that slid from low to high pitch.

Dane critically examined the tattered breeches, patched shirt, and shabby vest on the urchin. Then he peered into a pair of sparkling green eyes that were set above dirt-smudged cheeks. Dane's gaze wavered between repulsion and pity as he assessed the frail ragamuffin who looked to be nothing more than a bag of bones concealed in loose-fitting garb.

The waif's features were camouflaged by the brimmed cap that was pulled forward on his head. All that Dane could see were emerald eyes, a small nose, and a rounded chin. But of one thing he was certain: somewhere beneath the layers of dirt and grime was the face of a very young lad. A wave of sympathy engulfed him. A pity, he mused thoughtfully. Such a frail child should have been under his parents' protection. It was obvious the child needed an adult's supervision. The lad should not have been allowed to roam the countryside, left to his own devices, to make a life for himself.

Gabe was also busy surveying the muscular gentleman with the raven hair and beautiful blue eyes. Dane appeared to be a tower of strength as he sat erect on his buckskin gelding, poised like an invincible warrior who did not know the meaning of fear. His rugged features were chiseled on his face and deep lines led to those fathomless pools of sapphire which were surrounded by thick, black lashes. She sensed an inner power that no one but he could control or command. Gabe felt a strange security just being in his presence. If she had not been determined to play her charade, she would have been drooling over this dashing rogue.

Smothering her awe-struck thoughts, she resumed her role of waif. "Would ye mind if I rode a ways with ye?"

"I suppose not." Dane shrugged carelessly, his gaze sweeping the skinny wretch in final inspection.

"Well, that's a fine attitude fer ye to be takin' toward the person who dragged ye from death's doorstep and hauled ye to shelter!" the lad snapped, his chin tilting indignantly.

"*You* found me on the road?" Dane inquired incredulously. His dark brows shot up in surprise as he focused his attention on the ragamuffin. Lord, surely not, he thought to himself.

"Aye, sir," the waif assured him with an affirmative nod. "Ye were lyin' there in the mud, bleedin' like a stuck pig. 'Twas Blanco 'ere that carried ye through the storm to safety." The "urchin" reached down to pat her steed's neck before returning her gaze to the bewildered captain.

Dane arched a skeptical brow. His voice laced with suspiciousness, he said, "That is a fancy piece of horseflesh for such a poorly garbed lad to be riding. Did you steal him before hauling me to shelter?" he inquired, frowning accusingly.

Gabe's chin tilted a notch higher. "Cert'nly not!" she protested hotly. "A lady gave 'im to me. I ain't no thief." Her green eyes sparked condemnation at the captain. "Yer damned sure an ungrate-

59

ful oaf, not showin' the least bit of gratitude after what I did fer ye."

Dane ignored the insult in his effort to continue his line of questioning. "And just where does this woman live that has given you such a generous gift?" he quipped, a doubtful smile threatening the corners of his mouth.

The "lad" dropped her head, milking the captain of sympathy as she replied remorsefully. "She no longer exists. Now she's jest a fond memory to me, a warm spirit that brightens me way when all looks dark." Gabe gazed across the land, seemingly entranced by a faraway thought.

"Oh, I'm sorry," Dane offered lamely, regretting his prying question. He quickly rushed on with another, feeling rather uncomfortable. "What is your name, boy? And where is your home?"

Her gaze finally slid back to the captain, meeting his quizzical stare. "Me name's Gabe. I ain't really from no place in particular. I'm 'eaded toward Bristol. And what be yer name?" the waif inquired, preferring not to spend much time in explanation of herself.

Dane peered curiously at the skinny urchin, wondering what dark secrets he was protecting, but he did not press the lad further. "I'm Capt. Dane Hampton," he answered stiffly.

"Well, Cap'n? Do we ride together? 'Tis but a small request that I ask fer savin' yer neck. I should think ye would be a bit more appreciative. Ye didn't even bother with a 'thank ye' or nothin'." Gabe stared into his handsome face, unable to suppress the mischievous smile that grazed her lips.

"Pardon my bad manners, Gabe." Dane returned the sly grin as he bowed from atop his gelding. "I'm indebted to you, m'boy. I heartily thank you for the service you rendered by delivering me to safety. I would be most happy to have your company," he replied as he urged Sultan forward.

Gabe edged Blanco up beside Dane, observing the confident manner in which he settled himself on his horse. Reaching behind her, she unstrapped Dane's saddlebags and tossed them to him. "'Ere's yer belongin's." When the captain shot her an accusing glance, she hastily defended, "I wasn't plannin' to steal 'em. I was jest makin' sure they was safe."

Dane's brows furrowed deeper and Gabe attempted to explain, wishing she would have kept her mouth shut in the first place. "I was watchin' fer ye to come down the road so I could give 'em to ye." A sheepish smile surfaced on her grimy face. "I guess I was 'opin' fer a little company on this lonely road."

A slow smile touched Dane's lips. At least the lad was honest, tattered and filthy, but honest, nonetheless. He nodded his acceptance of the lad's explanation and Gabe breathed a constricted sigh of relief.

"Did ye figure out who took that shot at ye?" she questioned, anxious to change the subject.

"I have no idea who or why. Perhaps I was about

to be robbed when you happened along." Dane paused a moment as a thoughtful frown crossed his rugged features. "Was there by chance a woman with you that night you found me?" He cast the bedraggled waif a sidelong glance. He still had the impression that the mysterious companion who had hovered over him was a woman, not a boy. Was the lad telling the truth? Gabe seemed to know exactly what had happened that night and he *was* carrying Dane's saddlebags. Dane could not recall the incident clearly enough to deny the urchin's words.

"A woman?" Gabe quipped in a nasal squawk, glancing at the captain as if he were daft. "Nay. It was only me, and ye kin plainly see I ain't no woman." The "lad" flung her arms wide, daring the captain to dispute the fact.

"I thought I remembered seeing a woman leaning over me." Dane shrugged and continued with a faint smile, "Ah, well, perhaps it was my guardian angel." He sent the lad a quick, sidelong glance, but he was carefully studying his reaction.

"Bah. Guardian angel!" she snorted cynically. "Don't tell me ye believe in them sort of thin's?" Gabe rolled her eyes and shook her head as if the captain had just confirmed the fact that he was addle-witted. "Seems to me that the shot must 'ave scrambled yer brain. Now me"—the lad tapped his chest as a wry smile settled on his dirt-smudged features—"I only believe in thin's I kin see and touch. I don't waste me time believin' in them good fairies, angels, and such."

"Oh?" Dane arched a dark brow. "If your name

is Gabe, perhaps it is short for Gabriel. You ought to believe in angels if, in fact, you were named after one," he mocked dryly.

With a derisive snort, Gabe glared at Dane whose face seemed to light with pleasure. "Gabe ain't short fer nothin'," she protested. "It's jest Gabe, plain and simple, no more, no less."

Dane's shoulders lifted in a careless shrug. "Well, whatever the case, I am indebted to you and to Lord Jarmon for tending my wounds. I hope to repay both of you for your trouble."

Gabe winced at his words. If he knew who she really was, he would undoubtedly send her back to her dreadful prison to suffer a fate worse than death. When the "lad" urged her white stallion into a trot and rode ahead of the captain, Dane frowned at the urchin's narrow back. Gabe was a hot-tempered, unpredictable, little devil, Dane mused thoughtfully. He touched his boot heels to Sultan's flanks and proceeded at a quicker pace while his thoughts spun in confusion. Perhaps he had imagined that lovely vision on the hill. Maybe it was only a lingering image of it that had filled his mind while the lad was bending over him on the road. He didn't know exactly what he believed or what had really occurred. All he had was the young wretch's account of the incident. Oh well, Dane thought with a hopeless shrug, what difference did it make? His guardian angel, fact or fantasy, was gone and he had managed to escape with his life.

After riding quietly for several minutes, Dane's curiosity got the better of him. "What is your last name, Gabe? Where are your parents?"

"Don't rightly know," she replied, completely ignoring the first question. "I jest woke up one mornin' and found meself on me own. Ye wouldn't be needin' a 'ouseboy or a stableboy, would ye? I was goin' to Bristol to find work, but seein' 'ow I saved yer life and all, maybe ye would put me up fer a while." Gabe glanced hopefully at the gentleman in the white linen shirt and form-fitting brown breeches, careful not to dwell overly long on his striking physique.

Dane was dissatisfied with the lad's evasive answer, but Gabe's last comment brought a faint smile to his lips. Gabe was a brazen little wretch. His gaze swept the dirty-faced urchin from the top of his dingy hat to the toes of his tattered boots. "Well, I suppose I could keep you on as my valet," he offered blandly.

Gabe's green eyes lit up like a candelabrum. "Lord luv ye, Cap'n. I do appreciate it. I might be able to save yer life again someday. I jest might be worth 'avin' close at 'and in case ye meet with more trouble." A thoughtful frown spread across the smudged face. "Say, 'ow come yer a cap'n? Were ye in the king's army or navy?" she quested as she settled herself more comfortably on the hard saddle.

Dane chuckled again at the lad's candor. "No, I'm just a sea captain who transports merchandise," he explained. His gaze swung back to the dirt path. "There's a tavern up the road. Would you care to stop and eat?"

"Me belly 'as been playin' a 'ungry tune on me

ribs all mornin'. I 'aven't 'ad much to eat of late," she confessed. "I sure could use some nourishment, but I'm a little short of funds at the moment." Gabe rubbed her stomach and licked her lips as she glanced pitifully at the captain, again chiseling away at his sympathy. She played her role as if she were born to it and Dane swallowed the bait without bothering to chew it.

"I'll buy your lunch, lad," he offered and then peered curiously at the frail wretch. There was something familiar about Gabe, come to think of it. It wasn't the sea-green eyes or the cockney accent, but yet, something nagged at his mind. He still couldn't put the pieces of the puzzle together and was confused about what had happened that night on the road. Perhaps he *had* seen the skinny lad instead of a young woman. After all, he was only half-conscious. What the hell! Shrugging away the thought, Dane decided that he had dwelt on the incident long enough. He would accept the lad's story and that would be the end of it.

After dismounting, the two travelers entered the tavern and seated themselves at a table. A red-haired waitress sauntered toward them, quickly recognizing Dane. She plopped down on his lap and planted an affectionate kiss on his waiting lips. Dane's lean arms came about her hips, tarrying momentarily for a gentle caress.

"I've been expecting you for a week. Would you care to take your meal upstairs?" she questioned, a delicious smile hovering on her lips.

"It sounds like an excellent idea, my dear," he retorted with a willing grin. His hand moved upward to caress the back of her peasant blouse as his gaze boldly raked her.

Gabe's eyes narrowed and she stiffened as she watched the distressing scene. She felt like stomping from the inn, but she suppressed that urge and questioned in a resentful tone, "What the 'ell am I supposed to do while yer dillydallying upstairs, Cap'n?"

With a devilish grin curling his lips, Dane dragged his eyes off the waitress and rested his gaze on the small ragamuffin. "Surely you don't mind eating alone, Gabe. My lady friend and I won't tarry too long."

An irritated frown wrinkled Gabe's dirt-smudged face as she watched the friendly couple make their way up the creaky staircase. After they disappeared from sight the woman's merry giggle drifted down to Gabe and she muttered under her breath. However, when a tray of food was set before her, she quickly forgot her aggravation and feasted hungrily on the bread and mutton. With her hunger appeased, she wiped her face on her shirt sleeve and stepped back outside to water the horses, impatiently awaiting the captain's return. Her anger kindled into a raging blaze with each passing minute that he didn't step through the door.

In an upstairs room Dane lay entangled in the redhead's embrace, wondering why a woman who had previously sated his appetite had suddenly lost her appeal. Each time he had closed his eyes, a misty shadow hovered over him. He found himself wishing that he were holding that mysterious angel in his arms. He shook his head, attempting to free his thoughts from her spell and quickly donned his breeches. Before strolling to the chair to grab his shirt, he tossed a few coins to the naked wench who lay curled up in the middle of the bed.

She looked up at him, a rueful smile touching her lips. "What's the matter, Dane?"

He shrugged noncommittally and threw his muffled reply over his shoulder. "Nothing. I'd better be going."

"When will you return?" She pulled the sheet around her and sat up to watch him leave.

"In a couple of months . . . maybe," he replied blandly. When he had buttoned his shirt, he left the room without another glance in her direction.

The woman stared at the closed door, wondering why Dane, who was usually amorous, seemed so indifferent to her caresses. He was preoccupied with some thought that refused to allow him to find pleasure in her arms.

Dane saw no sign of the ragged urchin when he descended the stairs so he strolled outside. Gabe was sitting cross-legged in the grass, chewing on a blade of straw, his dirty face displaying an annoyed frown.

"What's the matter with you?" Dane questioned disinterestedly as he grabbed Sultan's reins.

Gabe scrambled to her feet, snorting at the ridiculous inquiry. "'Ow the 'ell would ye like it if ye were left to wait out 'ere, twiddlin' yer thumbs while some fancy-dressed fop was upstairs seekin' 'is pleasure with some little strumpet?" she quipped, her tone biting at him like a rabid dog.

67

Yanking at Blanco's reins, she swung up onto the stallion's back and glowered at the startled nobleman whose wide, blue eyes had suddenly narrowed to hard slits.

"That's enough, you dirty-faced little brat!" he thundered, wagging a lean finger at Gabe. "What I do is none of your damned business and you have no right to criticize me!"

"Yer right, Cap'n, it ain't. And it ain't none of yer business what I think either. So next time, don't ask me what's the matter unless ye want an earful. I got a tendency to say jest exactly what I think!" Gabe countered in her own irate bellow.

Dane eyed the fiery wretch for a long moment. His anger dwindled to mild amusement. "You're a bit hot-tempered, aren't you?" he concluded as he leaned his elbow on the saddle and peered up at the waif who sat astride his white stallion.

As Gabe's gaze swung to the captain, her irritation cooled and she silently cursed her outburst. "Aye, Cap'n," she admitted soberly. "'Tis one of me many faults. Ye are not me father and I 'ave no right to expect ye to be a saint. Besides 'avin' a quick temper, I don't like to be kept waitin'. I'm afraid the fuse on me temper and me patience is the same length—short. I'm sorry I snapped at ye." She ducked her head from the probing blue eyes that appraised her.

"Where is your father, Gabe?" Dane questioned, hoping to pry some information from the sprite while he was in one of his gentler moods.

"Dead," Gabe muttered as she touched her knees to Blanco's ribs, urging him down the road.

Dane followed the lad who slumped dejectedly on his steed. Neither of them had much to say as they traveled the winding road that led to Hampton Estate. Dane and Gabe were forming their opinions of each other. Although they were grateful for the services that had been rendered, there was a hint of mistrust when they glanced at each other.

As Dane led the way through the entrance to his estate, Gabe gazed at the stone home that was nestled among the trees. It was a majestic house with circling gardens which denoted meticulous care. She glanced from the mansion to the man who owned it, quickly scanning his muscular form. Dane studied his surroundings with a contented smile, but Gabe noticed a hint of pain that flashed across his face, as if he were haunted by something here that he would much rather forget. She suddenly remembered the nightmare that had awakened him the first night they had met. Her brows furrowed thoughtfully. Dane had not guarded his expression and Gabe detected his mixed emotions.

Hoping to raise his sinking spirits, she played her new role to the hilt. "Lord, Cap'n. Ain't this a fancy place ye got 'ere," she exclaimed with an appreciative whistle. "Looks to me like the king's palace fer sure, although I ain't rightly seen the real one. Why, I bet me bed in the stables will be finer than any place I've 'ad yet to rest me weary 'ead. 'Course, seein' 'ow I saved yer life and all, I would be thinkin' yer probably plannin' to put me up in me own room inside them grand walls." A hint of a smile grazed her lips as she raised anxious eyes to the captain. "I know if somebody rescued me from death's door, I'd be wantin' to show 'im me gratitude." Gabe peered steadily at the captain, scratched her nose with a dirty sleeve, and waited for Dane to comment on her proposal.

Dane could not suppress the smile that settled on his dark features. The wretch was outspoken, pushy, quick-tempered, and yet he somehow managed to be a likable sort. There was nothing dull or humble about Gabe and Dane was certain no one had ever taught the lad his proper place. Gabe would most likely say whatever came to mind. It wouldn't have mattered if he were talking to the king or his lowly servant. The lad would undoubtedly offer his honest opinion on any topic if given the opportunity.

As he thoughtfully rubbed his chin, Dane playfully mocked the lad's accent. "I s'pose since ye saved me life and all, ye should 'ave a room in the 'ouse. Like ye said before, I might be in need of yer services," he added with an amused snicker.

Gabe blessed him with a blinding smile that made Dane feel as though he had turned the pauper into a prince. "I won't cause ye a lick of trouble. Ye won't be sorry, Cap'n. I'll mind me manners when others are about," she promised faithfully.

"And what about when the two of us are together?" Dane questioned, arching a dubious brow.

"I'll try, Cap'n, but I ain't makin' no pledges on that account," she retorted as she glanced at him.

70

Throwing her leg across the saddle, she hopped to the ground, pulling her grimy hat down around her ears.

"I do hope you have a change of clothes that is more presentable than the garb you're wearing." His eyes swept the tattered ragamuffin, displaying a disapproving frown. Higgins would be incensed if he saw Gabe strolling through the front door dressed in those wretched clothes.

Gabe shot him an annoyed frown. "Now don't be gettin' particular about me clothes, Cap'n. This is all I got, except fer me bare 'ide." A slow smile threatened the corners of her mouth, her green eyes twinkling mischievously. "Since yer indebted to me, ye'll probably be wantin' to find me some of them velvety breeches and frilly shirts."

Dane rolled his eyes in disbelief. The little snip wasn't afraid to ask for anything. As he swung down from his steed, Dane leaned against Sultan to unstrap his saddlebag. His face hardened as he glared at the insolent waif. "If you bring up that incident one more time, I'll send you packing. I do not need to be reminded of your heroic deed anymore today," he warned with a hint of finality in his tone that would have silenced anyone but Gabe.

"All right, all right," she snorted as she pulled her cap down over her brows. "Lord, ye don't 'ave to growl at me, Cap'n. I was jest—"

"Enough!" Dane snapped, his eyes narrowing meaningfully.

Gabe grabbed both horses' reins and led them toward the stables, deciding not to provoke the captain further. "Aye, Cap'n," she replied with a saucy salute.

Dane grumbled to himself as he watched the urchin swagger away with a light spring in his step and a merry tune floating about him. The lad was a lively little bundle and Dane was certain that Hampton Estate would never be the same now that Gabe had set foot upon it.

"Hello, Higgins," Dane greeted as he stepped inside the door that immediately opened for him.

"Good afternoon, sir. We expected you several days ago. Did you have trouble at sea?" the servant asked with no inflection in his voice.

"No, I was waylaid on land," Dane explained before issuing an order. "Have a bath prepared for me and air out the small room next to mine. I brought a young boy home with me. He'll be staying awhile." Dane started up the stairs, but then paused and turned back to Higgins. "Send Gabe up to my room when he comes in from the stables."

Lord Hampton trudged up to his room and tossed his bags on the bed before strolling to the window to gaze over the grounds.

After stripping from his shirt, he sank down in a chair to pull off his boots and stockings. Leaning his elbows on his knees, he sighed and studied the rich carpet beneath his feet. A shapeless face appeared before him and a soft voice whispered in his ears. Lost to pleasant memories, the lovely ghost entranced him, but he bolted to his feet and impatiently paced the floor, waiting for his bath and the little urchin who had managed to brighten a dull day. Dane's head began to ache so he removed the bandage to inspect the wound. A thoughtful frown furrowed his brows as he peered into the mirror. Was he a victim of circumstance or was someone actually plotting to kill him?

Gabe had inspected the stables and found that Blanco would be well-tended, as were the rest of the fine mounts in the barn. Satisfied, she ambled to the mansion and rapped on the door. A stiff-mannered servant with cold, hazel eyes and gray hair appeared in the entrance. He surveyed the shabbily dressed waif with a perspicuous expression that incensed Gabe. She bristled at his haughtiness and could not resist putting the arrogant chap in his place.

"I may not be dressed like a prince, but I ain't no empty-'eaded twit who can't tell when 'e's bein' snubbed. I kin read yer mind like an open book, mister. Yer jest a servant 'ere jest like me," she said bluntly, forgetting her promise to mind her manners.

Higgins sucked in his breath at the urchin's audacity and then his eyes narrowed in annoyance. He was certain the little wretch needed a gag in his mouth and a swat on his young ass. Higgins was about to put the brazen guttersnipe in his place when the lad blurted out his question.

"Where's the cap'n?" Gabe pushed past the staunch servant and glanced about the entryway.

Higgins sternly corrected her. "*Lord Hampton* is in his room waiting for you."

As the servant again prepared to scold him,

Gabe sauntered toward the steps. "Which room?" She turned to see Higgins trembling with rage. It serves him right, she mused, biting back a mischievous smile.

"The south wing," he snapped harshly. "The third door on the left."

Higgins slammed the front door and Gabe jumped as the sound echoed across the tiled entryway and ricocheted off the walls. With a deliciously aggravating grin that sent Higgins' temper spewing, she pulled her sheepskin jerkin in place, flicked a piece of straw from her dirty sleeve, tilted her proud chin, and swaggered down the hall. Muttering under his breath, Higgins stalked across the entryway and disappeared into the sitting room.

Releasing a wicked chuckle, Gabe strolled up to the captain's door and rapped lightly upon it. When requested to enter, she stepped inside just as Dane was about to discard his breeches and ease into the tub. With a startled squawk Gabe whirled to face the wall and gulped over the large lump that had collected in her throat. Never before had she witnessed such a show of bare flesh and it proved to be quite unnerving.

Dane frowned, wondering why the lad seemed so shocked. After sliding down into the tub he peered over his shoulder at the waif's narrow back. "Don't tell me the sight of bare flesh offends you?" Dane snickered amusedly. "Come to think of it, that shouldn't surprise me. There seem to be very few things that *don't* offend you."

Gabe attempted to gain control of her shattered

composure after hearing the splash that assured her part of his masculine form was concealed in water.

Slowly, she turned to face his amused regard. "Well, I ain't used to seein' dudes in the raw. And with the company I bin keepin' lately, bathin' ain't bin one of our daily rituals." She defended her actions while keeping her eyes averted from the handsome rogue.

"If you are going to serve as my valet, you'll have to outgrow your aversion to bathing and, as you so tactfully expressed it, seeing *dudes* in the raw." He smirked as he grabbed the soap to lather himself.

"Per'aps me services would be put to better use in the stables, Cap'n. I think I would be more useful carin' fer a steed than a stud," Gabe added with a mischievous twinkle in her eyes. She allowed her gaze to slide to Dane for a moment and then looked away, afraid to tarry too long on his virile form.

Dane shot her a disapproving glare that brought a chuckle from the ornery wretch. "Be that as it may, Gabe, I had the room next to mine prepared. That is where you will be staying. Now come scrub my back," he demanded as he leaned foward, lifting the soap and sponge over his shoulder to the reluctant waif.

Gabe moved up behind him to do as she was ordered, her dirty face reddening from embarrass-ment. As Dane peered at the fumbling lad, he shook his head in wonder.

"You're a strange one, Gabe. One minute you're growling like a vicious wolf and the next instant you're cowering in the corner like a timid lamb. You're certainly a moody little snip."

Gabe sputtered behind him. "I told ye, Cap'n. I ain't perfect and I ain't used to waitin' on nobleman 'and and foot." With renewed vigor, she began scrubbing his back, bringing a pained screech from Lord Hampton.

Clutching the sides of the tub, Dane sat erect and then threw a condemning glare over his shoulder. "Damn it, boy. I asked you to *wash* my back, not *peel* the hide off it! There you go changing moods again. Try to be gentle, will you? Surely you didn't save my skin that night on the road just to scrub it off in this tub," he growled.

A self-satisfied grin settled on her smudged face. "I'm so sorry, Cap'n," she cooed, continuing her chore in a gentler fashion. "I should 'ave known ye noble rakes were tender-skinned. I was jest tryin' to rid ye of that feminine fragrance that's bin floatin' 'round ye all afternoon. Lord, ye smell like one of them perfumed madams that takes yer breath away when ye git downwind of 'er."

Dane stared straight ahead, attempting to ignore the snide remark. Knowing how the lad had reacted, he did not care to rehash the midday interlude. The waif seemed to intensely dislike ladies of pleasure. Dane was curious about what had caused Gabe to form such a narrow-minded attitude, but he held his tongue. In a few years Gabe would take an entirely different view on that subject, he mused with a smug grin. He would enjoy being around when Gabe's time came.

"Your room should be ready by now. Go see to

your own needs. Your bath has been prepared. See that you make use of it. And get rid of that filthy, damned hat!" The captain snapped, sending the waif a stern glance.

Gabe rinsed the captain's back and stood up behind him, drying her hands on her breeches. "Aye, Cap'n. I'll bathe, but the 'at stays where it is," she announced determinedly. "I ain't never takin' it off, not for you or even the king 'imself."

Dane raised a quizzical brow as he peered at the stubborn wretch. "What's so important about that blessed hat?"

Gabe stammered hesitantly as she stuffed her hands in her pockets and studied the carpeted floor beneath her feet. "Ah . . . welllll. I 'ad the fever last winter and me 'air fell out. When it grew back, it came in patches. I don't want nobody makin' fun of me, so I never take off me 'at," she explained, feigning embarrassment as she feasted on his sympathy.

"I'll see if I can find you another one," Dane offered. "I will tend to the matter when I finish my bath."

With a relieved smile, Gabe reached for her pouch and prepared to leave, but Dane's snicker drew her curious glance.

"I may smell like a woman, but *you* smell like a damned horse. If you don't scrub good, I'll take on the duty myself," Dane assured her, a mocking smile catching one corner of his mouth.

Gabe pulled a sour face at him and then hastily departed, shutting the door none too gently behind her. Once outside, she breathed a sigh of relief as she leaned back against the wall. She was free from her odious uncle, but playing this charade would be no easy task. She had misjudged Dane in his weaker moments. When she first met him, he had been dazed and injured. But in the light of day, she had confronted the strong personality of a dashing rogue and an authoritative lord. It seemed she was to learn more about this rake than she had anticipated. And if she were to view his sparse attire in the future, she must learn to camouflage her embarrassment. More dirt, she mused with a wry smile—a few more layers of grime on her face would hide her crimson-red complexion.

As she entered her own room, she tossed her bag in the corner and smiled appreciatively at the tub of hot water that awaited her. Only in the privacy of her own quarters could she become Gabrielle, the sophisticated heiress. She quickly shed her garb and eased into her bath. After scrubbing away the grime, she leaned back against the edge of the tub, holding her hands up in front of her for inspection. What had once been long, well-manicured nails were now short, uneven nails caked with dirt. Oh well, it was a small sacrifice. A knock at the door instantly brought her from her musings.

"Who is it?" she questioned, an annoyed frown settling on her face.

"Dane. I brought you some clean clothes. I'm coming in," he announced as he turned the knob. He was about to enter when he heard a loud yelp that halted him in his tracks.

"Nay! I ain't dressed, Cap'n," she screeched in exasperation. "Give me a moment." Gabe scrambled from the tub, pulled her hair up under her hat, rubbed the soot from the lantern globe on her face, and yanked the quilt from the bedpost to wrap herself in a tight cocoon.

"All right, ye kin come in," she snapped harshly. That had been too close for comfort. She would have to remember to lock the door in the future, she decided.

Dane entered, peering at the modest waif who stared him down with an irritated frown. "I found some clothes that might fit. They belong to one of the servant boys. And here's another hat," he said, tossing the garb on the bed.

"Thanks, Cap'n." Gabe softened her tone and then braved the questions that had been on her mind. "Jest exactly what will be me duties 'round 'ere? Will I be allowed to exercise Blanco and do I git at least one day off a week?" she blurted out in a rush, catching Dane off guard.

He regarded the presumptuous lad for a long moment and then eased down on the edge of the bed. "Are you asking me or telling me?" he inquired as his dark brows furrowed slightly.

"Both, Cap'n," she replied with a reckless shrug. "If I ain't to 'ave any time to meself, then I'll jest pack me bags and be on me way. I ain't used to bein' cooped up. I don't like it."

Dane leaned back on his arms and gazed into the emerald eyes of the high-spirited wretch who quickly pulled the quilt about him and wiggled a safe distance away. "When I am at home, you will

79

see to my needs. When I travel, you will be expected to prepare and pack my clothes. When I'm at sea, you will take your orders from Higgins. You will be required to perform any task that he requests. You will be allowed to ride in the mornings, unless you oversleep or I require your services. And you will have half a day off, once a week," he stated in a businesslike tone that anticipated no argument.

"I want an entire day and who the 'ell is 'Iggins?" she questioned, hoping to bypass another confrontation.

"Higgins is the servant who let you into the house and you will only—" Dane was interrupted by a disgusted groan from the waif. "Did you and Higgins already cross swords?" His brows came together in a condemning frown.

"Aye, Cap'n," she admitted, immediately regretting her blunt remarks to the staunch servant. "'E snubbed me like I was nothin' but a rug to wipe 'is arrogant feet on. I set 'im straight right from the start and left 'im boilin' like an over'eated teakettle. I don't think the two of us 'ave much chance of bein' compatible. I don't like the looks of that bloke."

"You'd better learn to curb that vicious tongue of yours, young man," Dane warned, wagging a finger in Gabe's face.

"I don't like bein' treated like dirt!" she protested, her green eyes flashing sparks. "That 'Iggins gives me the willies and I ain't puttin' up with 'is 'igh and mighty air."

"Now don't get your feathers ruffled," Dane

taunted, a wicked smile curving his lips. "I'll try to soothe Higgins, but you promised to mind your manners and already you have broken your word before the first day is out. I won't always be around to keep Higgins from punishing you for your insolence."

"Per'aps I'll be on me way when it's time fer ye to depart, Cap'n," Gabe muttered. She was not about to endure Higgins.

Dane surveyed the face that appeared dirtier than it had an hour earlier. "Have you already bathed?" he questioned incredulously.

"Aye, I soaked in the water jest like ye said to do," she acknowledged, nodding toward her tub.

As Dane reached over to rub a layer of grime from her cheek, she shrank away from his touch. "Soaking won't suffice. This face of yours needs a good, hard scrubbing."

"Thanks fer the advice. I'll remember that the next time I bathe," she remarked caustically. "Now if ye don't mind, I'd like to dress." Gabe expected the captain to leave, but he just sat there, looking curiously at her.

"Can't a boy 'ave a little privacy, 'round 'ere?" she quipped impatiently. Still he didn't budge. Then Gabe sent a piercing barb at him that quickly routed him from her room. "Or do ye find the company of young lads jest as arousin' as ye do red-haired wenches?"

As a mocking smile curved the corners of Gabe's mouth upward, Dane bolted from the bed as if he had been struck by lightning. He stalked to the door, grumbling a long list of curses to the snippy urchin who kept creeping beneath his skin. "Damn, but you're an irritating lad! You can take your supper in the kitchen with the other servants and you are permitted *half* a day!" he growled as he threw an annoyed glance over his shoulder and yanked open the door.

"Now don't go gettin' yer feathers ruffled, Cap'n," Gabe taunted. "I was jest jokin'."

Dane's broad shoulders stiffened as he stomped from the room. Gabrielle's chuckle floated recklessly about her as she fell against the bed to stare up at the ceiling. A pair of sparkling, blue eyes shone down upon her and she found herself wishing to confront the handsome captain as a woman instead of a spiteful waif. Dane was a rogue, extremely irresistible and attractive. It was difficult to control the direction her thoughts were taking. She had come to know both faces of the dashing Lord Hampton, but the one she longed to see was the dark image she had known in the shadows.

"Ah, Captain," she mused aloud. "I have saved your life and now you have saved me from a most distasteful existence. I will no longer suffer Uncle John's deceitful plans. It seems we have managed to do each other a great favor."

Lord John sat at his marble-topped desk, his brooding, gray eyes full of contempt. The little bitch had somehow managed to escape from her room. He was left to confront the duke, who would be infuriated by the incident. He would find that little chit and she would pay dearly for this last escapade, John vowed determinedly.

Although he had questioned the livery boy about Gabrielle's disappearance, the lad had pleaded ignorance. Sherman said he had seen nothing of the wench. John doubted that the lad spoke the truth, but there was no proof. She seemed to have vanished without a trace, taking very little with her, and John did not have the slightest idea where to begin his search.

A knock on the door and voices in the hall brought him from his pensive thoughts and he braced himself for the meeting with Horace. This was not going to be pleasant. Damn that chit! he grumbled sourly. She had caused him nothing but trouble.

"Horace, 'tis good to see you. Come in," John exclaimed, displaying a pretentious smile.

Horace Fairleigh strolled forward and peered down at the short, round gentleman. "John," he said with a slight nod of greeting. His heavy brows furrowed suspiciously as he watched John's eyes dart from side to side. Something was amiss, he concluded. "What's the matter?" he questioned, cocking his gray head to the side.

"Sit down, Horace," John requested as he eased back into his own chair. When the Duke was seated across the desk from him, John cleared his throat and plunged on with the disturbing news. "I'm afraid Gabrielle has disappeared and I have found no trace of her. Somehow she—"

"Whaaaat?" Gasping in dismay, Horace bolted to his feet. He leaned over the desk, flashing Lord Jarmon an annoyed glower. "You fool! We had an agreement. Part of your duty was to keep her securely stashed away until our marriage," he growled as his full lips curled threateningly, revealing uneven teeth. "If anyone touches Brielle our contract is dissolved. Do you understand me, Jarmon? I paid a handsome price for an untouched maiden and I'll be damned if I'll accept her any other way!" Horace wagged a bony finger in Lord John's ashen face. "You'd better find her and you had best be quick about it. If anyone lays a hand on her, I'll tear up that contract so fast that it will make your head spin. You'll return every shilling I paid you! I want that chit as my wife, but you know very well I will accept no tainted woman. Do you understand me, Jarmon?"

"We'll find her," John hastily assured him. "I will have notices posted all over the surrounding area if need be. She can't have gone far. She had limited funds. I'm sure she'll turn up before the week is out."

The duke stood erect, straightening his blue velvet jacket as he attempted to control his volatile temper. The bungling fool, he mused scornfully as he glared down at the plump gentleman. Gabrielle was the most attractive young maiden in the area and he wanted her. But he had his reputation to uphold. He was not about to be content with someone else's leavings.

"She damned well better turn up . . . untouched!" Horace growled as he spun on his heels and stalked stiff-leggedly toward the door.

When the duke exited from the study, John's breath came out in a rush. Horace possessed a hellacious temper, he thought with a smirk. It would be a stormy marriage if he and Gabrielle wed. They would be at each other's throats more often than not. What a delightful scene that would be to witness, John thought with a wicked chuckle. Gabrielle would receive exactly what she deserved from Horace. When John got his hands on that insolent little spitfire she would regret the day she had defied him. That wench had dealt him nothing but misery and, by damn, he would see her suffer for it!

Gabrielle was left alone for the remainder of the day and enjoyed the sanctity of her room. After donning her nightgown, she curled up on the soft bed, thankful that she would not be spending another night sleeping on the cold ground. She drifted off to sleep, saying a prayer of forgiveness. With all of the little white lies she had told that day, she would have burned the ear off a priest. Someday, when she had her home and her inheritance, Gabrielle vowed to repay the handsome captain for all the trouble she had put him through.

She could not explain the resentment she had felt that afternoon when Dane had left with that young woman at the inn or the security she felt just knowing that Dane was in the room next to her. She had no time to delve into her soul for answers to her dilemma or her reaction to Dane's amorous endeavors. It had been an exhausting day and drowsiness overtook her. All she wanted at the moment was to sink into the soft, feather bed.

In the dim lantern light that flickered in the study, Dane sat at his desk, his raven head bent over his ledgers, preparing a list of supplies to be ordered in Bristol. His agitation with the young lad had faded as he busied himself with the affairs of the estate. The evening was quiet and life at home seemed to be much as it had been before he had left for London. His work was interrupted by a rattling tray and Dane glanced up to see Higgins moving stiffly toward him.

"Would you care for tea, Lord Hampton?" the servant questioned in his formal tone.

"Yes, thank you." Dane took the cup, set it on the desk, and glanced back up to see Higgins still standing before him.

"Sir." Higgins paused momentarily as Dane raised a quizzical brow. "It's about that dreadful waif you dragged home. He has no respect for my authority and I simply cannot—"

Dane quickly interrupted Higgins before he had the opportunity to step across the line between master and servant. Yet, he had never given it a second thought that Gabe had jumped over the same boundary with both feet, more times in one day than Dane could even count. "The lad is an orphan who has no place to go. I know he's a defiant little beggar with a razor-sharp tongue, but with a little guidance and understanding, I think he'll come around. He has a kind heart beneath that protective shell. Have a little patience, Higgins, and give the boy a chance."

It was obvious to Higgins that Lord Hampton

intended to keep that frightful little snip in the house. He nodded reluctantly. "Yes, sir." With that, Higgins whirled around and swiftly exited from the study.

After another hour, Dane left his desk and climbed the dark stairway to his room. As he crawled into bed he heaved a weary sigh, relishing the comfort of his own quarters. His head was beginning to ache again as he lay with his arms folded behind his neck, staring into the darkness, wishing the shadowed image would come to him. Suddenly, she was above him, freeing him from his nagging discomfort, hovering so close and yet so far from reach. He tried to ignore the memory of the tender moments he had spent with her, knowing that she could have been nothing more than a dream. But yet, she had seemed so real. He could recall her soft, raspy whisper that tempted and encouraged him. Although he could have sworn that he had seen and heard her, there was no logical explanation for her existence. She had been so lovely and desirable, comforting him with her hushed words. But he could not picture her face. He had not seen the color of her eyes or hair and he could not recall the true sound of her voice. If she walked up to him in the light of day and spoke to him, he was afraid he wouldn't recognize her. There was no way to describe his elusive angel to satisfy his own calculated reasoning.

With a hopeless sigh, Dane rolled onto his side and closed his eyes. The illusion appeared to him again, confirming his belief that she was no more than a misty vision of his imagination. He had not been able to force her from his mind even when he had lain in the arms of another woman. The mystical goddess seemed to have some haunting power over his thoughts—just as the vivid nightmare had. Although this was a pleasant experience, the dream managed to preoccupy his thoughts and leave him doubting his sanity.

Gabrielle had slept soundly, but woke abruptly, wondering where she was. She bolted straight up in bed, scanning the dark room. Finally she realized that she was in Dane's home and her six-month nightmare was at an end.

With a relieved sigh she swung her legs over the side of the bed and stepped onto the cold floor. As she ambled across the room, her gaze was drawn to the starlit sky that was framed by the terrace doors. With a sudden thirst for freedom, she opened the door and strolled over to the rail, listening to the muffled sounds of the night. Inhaling the fresh air, she walked the length of the terrace and then paused by Dane's room. Drawn by the thought of his captivating blue eyes and his protective arms, she eased open the door and moved toward the bed. Gabrielle placed a light kiss on Dane's lips.

Dane awoke as another kiss brushed his lips. The sweet fragrance consumed his senses and his eyes fluttered open. He reached up to touch the soft cheek that hovered so close to his own. This shadowed vision was bathed with the scent of spring breezes and Dane smiled in pleasure.

"I cannot seem to distinguish between dreams and reality. Tell me, love, which are you, flesh or fantasy?" he murmured hoarsely.

Her chuckle floated recklessly about them and another smile softened Dane's rugged features as her soothing whisper reached his ears.

"I am only a vision shrouded in darkness, m'lord. I do not exist in the light of day. I can only appear at night, casting no more than a shadow in the dim moonlight. I have no face, no name, and no voice to claim as my own. 'Tis but a dream," she assured him.

"If that be true, then let it be a pleasant one." Dane pulled her to him, covering her honeyed lips with a passionate kiss as he wrapped his arms about her, trembling with desire when she molded herself to him.

With no more words or questions they tenderly embraced, finding a strange comfort in the darkness. Gabrielle nuzzled against the hard wall of his chest, reveling in the security of his arms, wishing that her troubled existence could be as peaceful as the few moments they shared. Reluctantly, she withdrew from his embrace and eased from his side, but Dane grasped her hand to detain her hasty flight.

"My dream is not yet complete."

"Dreams never end, m'lord, and yet, although they seem to span eternity, they last only an instant. We only wake, remembering the vagueness of drowsy thoughts. Never can we recall the fantasy from beginning to end. Perhaps if we could, it would not be a fantasy, but rather that we no longer exist."

She moved gracefully toward the terrace door,

remaining among the swaying shadows. Dane watched her go, knowing that he could do nothing to stop her. Once before he had attempted to discover her identity, but it seemed she had no intention of allowing that to happen. When he blinked, she was gone. Dane breathed a confused sigh, his dark brows furrowing thoughtfully.

Unable to resist the temptation, he donned his breeches and walked out onto the terrace, finding nothing but dark shadows skipping across the ground below him, each attempting to conceal the lovely form that had disappeared in the night. He strolled the length of the terrace, listening for some faint sound that would alert him to her presence, but she had vanished. Dane ran his fingers through his hair, letting his arm drop heavily to his side.

Was he seeing things? Was it all a fantastic delusion? He walked back to his room and climbed into bed, again doubting his sanity. It all seemed so real. And yet, it was impossible that she could appear and disappear so quickly, no matter where he happened to be. No woman could be so alluring and yield so little, leaving him satisfied with her mere presence. She was a siren who called to him from across the sea of fantasy, winging just beyond his reach. He was caught in her mysterious spell, drifting aimlessly until her gentle whisper called out to him, pulling him down into the currents of murky illusions.

Dane yearned to know the truth about the mystical goddess, and yet he was strangely content with the comforting vision he had discovered among the evening shadows. At that moment Dane would have traded all of his tomorrows for one, long, uninterrupted dream filled with her whispered voice, her breeze-kissed fragrance, and her tender embrace. Nothing he could recall could compare to his angel of darkness. She was the essence of all of the intangible qualities he desired in a woman—the breath of gentleness, the feel of velvety softness, and the fragrance of spring. She was indeed an angel, a dark, unattainable image that continued to elude his grasp. She was a free-soaring spirit, a mysterious, desirable shadow that was ever present in his thoughts. Perhaps this was his private room in hell, his just reward for what had happened because of his frivolousness. He was to know the comfort of heaven only in a dream.

Dane closed his eyes, tortured by the ghastly vision of the sailors drowning in a sea of flames and by a vision cloaked in white who hovered just beyond his outstretched arms. As he fell into a restless sleep, she was with him again, whispering ever so softly, beckoning him ever so gently. And he was following her into yet another world of fantasy.

Chapter Four

Gabrielle arose early, dressed in the fresh clothes that Dane had brought, and donned the heavy jerkin that concealed her feminine form. She hurried to the kitchen to have breakfast. The aroma of freshly baked bread floated around her, reminding her that she had skipped supper and was famished. The plump woman spied the smudged face of the young lad and smiled broadly as she surveyed the clothes.

"I see my son's garments fit you reasonably well. A bit baggy in the breeches, but not bad at all," she mused with a satisfied gleam in her coal-black eyes. "My name is Liz. And you must be Gabe."

"Aye, mum, and thank ye fer the clothes. The cap'n didn't care much fer me dirty garb. I must admit 'tis a pleasure to be wearin' such clean-smellin' garments agin," Gabe replied with an easy grin.

"Sit down, boy. You must be starved since you didn't come down to eat last night. A growing lad needs his nourishment." Liz hustled the waif into a chair and brought a large plate of eggs, ham, and biscuits. She watched with pleasure as the lad hungrily devoured his meal.

"Mum, 'tis the finest meal I've 'ad in ages," Gabe confessed. She carelessly wiped her mouth with her sleeve, taking care not to use any feminine gestures while she was being closely watched by the pert woman. "Where's yer boy?" She scooted away from the table, picked up her empty plate, and started toward the wash basin.

"Give me that. You don't have to clean up," Liz insisted as she pulled the plate from Gabe's hands and shooed the waif out the back door. "Nate works in the stables. Go down and meet him and then send him for his breakfast."

Gabe peered around the open door as the woman turned back to the dirty dishes. An impish grin split her smudged face as she winked at the woman. "Me deepest appreciation fer the food. Yer a gem, Liz. Although I ain't met Nate, I envy 'im fer 'avin' a ma like ye."

Liz smiled warmly and then waved the lad away. "Get a move on, boy. I don't have time to stand here gabbing."

Filling the crisp morning air with her light-hearted tune, Gabe ambled to the stables. She was free and alive. John Jarmon was only a bitter memory from the past. As she strolled into the barn she glanced about her, searching for a young boy about her size. Finding one who was a little larger, but resembled Liz, she swaggered toward him.

"Would ye be Nate?" she questioned as she tapped the lad on the shoulder. When the boy turned to face her Gabe smiled. "Me name's Gabe and yer ma asked me to send ye up fer yer breakfast."

The boy nodded and grinned, but did not utter a word. He anxiously gestured toward the white stallion. Still he did not speak.

After staring curiously at him for a moment, Gabe realized that the lad couldn't speak. A wave of pity flooded over her. With a warm smile she answered his unspoken question. "Aye, that's Blanco. 'E's a fine steed, ain't 'e? Anytime ye want to ride 'im, jest go right ahead, Nate. 'E needs plenty of exercise and I won't 'ave as much time to tend to 'im," she explained, as if her only concern was for the horse.

The boy's face beamed with pleasure and his black eyes danced as he clasped Gabe's hands in his, squeezing them appreciatively before trotting toward the house. With an amused grin, Gabe watched Nate depart and then saddled Blanco. After leading the steed outside, she mounted up and turned him toward the meadow. Life had taken on a rosy hue and Brielle's heart filled with an unfamiliar happiness. Her spirits took flight to soar freely among the wispy clouds that graced the sky and she said a silent prayer for her blessings.

Trusting Blanco to guard his steps, they moved at a reckless pace. Together they galloped to the far corner of the moor where the muscular stallion came to a halt at the edge of a jagged cliff that overlooked the sea. Gabe gazed at the water that sparkled with the bright sunlight. As she hopped to her feet, she left Blanco laboring and snorting from his wild run.

It was a pacifying setting and Gabe sat down cross-legged in the grass to let her mind wander out with the waves. She sat suspended in time as her soul glided with the free-flying gulls that dipped and dived toward the sea in search of their quests. As did the gulls, Gabe sought that which could feed a hunger. But the nourishment she desired was intangible. On the rocky bluff she found the strength to continue down troubled rivers, hoping to find a solution to her problem. Gabe smiled to herself as she watched the waves curl lazily against the huge boulders below. At least she was free to breathe and enjoy the beautiful surroundings without being smothered by her odious uncle.

"It didn't take you long to find your way around," came the amused voice behind her.

Gabe was startled from her pleasant musings and quickly scrambled to her feet to face Dane. He stood before her, dressed in tight, black trousers that were neatly tucked into his polished boots. His white linen shirt gaped open, revealing the dark furring on his chest, and Gabe brought quick death to her arousing thoughts. She had to learn to disguise her appreciative stares.

"'Ave I bin gone too long, Cap'n? I lost track of time up 'ere. Sorry," she mumbled as she hung her head, hoping to avoid being scolded. No doubt it would lead to a heated exchange between them. It usually did. She had no desire to break the tranquil spell that had settled over her and she was much relieved when Dane displayed a faint smile.

"No need to apologize, Gabe. I was only out for a ride myself. You've discovered my favorite spot on the entire estate," he replied, nodding toward the cliff as he strolled up beside her.

"'Tis a grand view, ain't it, Cap'n? What's it like out there?" Gabe questioned, her green eyes scanning the choppy water.

"Another world," Dane said thoughtfully. "The sea can be as gentle as a loving woman or as angry as a jealous lover. She's quite a lady, Gabe. No one will ever be able to tame her, though many have died trying."

Gabe quickly noted the flash of pain that was mirrored in his eyes and sought to distract him. "I s'pose so, Cap'n," she agreed as her gaze swung back to the sea. "Since I don't know nothin' about women or lovers, I'll 'ave to take yer word fer it." She sent him a meaningful glance and then hastily looked away.

Although Dane intercepted her insinuation, he chose to ignore it. He watched the sea wrap its arms about the jagged rocks at the bottom of the cliff and sighed contentedly. They stood together in silence for a few moments before Dane spoke, shattering the peaceful spell.

"You will have your first official duty as my valet today. I'm traveling to Bristol in the morning. I want my luggage packed. Since I will be spending the night I will need sufficient clothes for at least two days, maybe more," he explained in a businesslike manner as he clasped his hands behind his back.

Her small features were alight with anticipation as she wheeled to face him. This was the opportunity she needed, but had not expected to come so soon.

"Kin I travel with ye, Cap'n?" Her sea-green eyes pleaded with him as she peered into his rugged face.

"What would I do with you while I'm tending to business? You would spend a great deal of time waiting for me. I know how much you enjoy that," he mocked dryly. "No, I think not." He noted the disappointment that engulfed the urchin's smudged features. What was so important about journeying to Bristol? he wondered.

"Aw, Cap'n, please," Gabe begged. Rubbing her nose with her tattered sleeve, she continued, a ghost of a smile hovering on her lips. "Seein' 'ow I saved yer life and all, I should think ye would be beholden to grant this small request." Gabe watched as he shook his head negatively and persisted, "I bet if I was one of them distinguished blokes like them lords and dukes ye mingle with, ye would be bendin' over backward to repay me fer me valiant deed."

Dane scoffed at the persnickety wretch. "There are so many *small* requests you have already beseeched of me, I'm beginning to wonder if I would have been better off wasting away on that muddy road. At least I wouldn't have to endure your constant reminders that I owe you my life. If you were a true gentleman, you would accept my humble gratitude and never mention the deed again," he added, unable to resist the gibe.

When Dane smiled wryly at her, Gabe returned his grin and heartily agreed with his remark, much to the captain's surprise. "I know I ain't no proper gentleman and I got no intention of ever bein' one of them arrogant aristocrats neither. Now I ain't asked ye for much, Cap'n." Her smudged chin tilted defiantly. "Ye act like I expect to be 'anded the world on a silver platter. I won't be no trouble. I promise," she vowed, placing her hand over her heart.

"*That,* my dear boy, does nothing to relieve my fears. I've heard your empty pledges before." Dane crossed his arms over his chest as a frown gathered on his features.

Gabe stuffed her hands in her pockets and kicked at the pebbles by her feet. "Yer the lord and master 'ere," she acknowledged, "but if somebody saved me life, I would be a bit more appreciative of the deed. I s'pose dandies like ye ain't got no conscience like us common folk." One shoulder lifted in a careless shrug as Gabe threw Dane a taunting smile.

"Why you ungrateful little guttersnipe!" Dane growled, grinding his teeth as he glowered at the brazen wretch.

"Me ungrateful?" she choked in disbelief. "*I* saved *yer* life, remember? I don't owe ye a damned thing!" Her quicksilver temper flared at his illogical reasoning as she met his scornful glare.

"I put food in your hollow belly and gave you a place to sleep!" Dane bellowed.

"I dragged ye up on me 'orse and carried ye

through a storm to safety!" she shot back, her voice rising testily.

"I gave you clean clothes to put on your scrawny back!"

"I found someone to take ye in and tend yer wounds instead of leavin' ye to drown in the mud!"

"I've offered you protection and I'm the one paying the bill to feed and care for that nag of yours!" Dane countered, his tone razor-sharp.

They stood eye to eye, glaring angrily at each other while lightning bridged the gap between fiery green and scorching blue eyes. Neither was willing to back down from an adamant stand.

God, how she loved those gorgeous sapphire eyes. She could lose herself in their unbound depths. The memory of the compassionate man she had known in tender moments of darkness skipped across her mind. Slowly, a smile settled on her grimy face, revealing even, white teeth.

"I'll try me damnedest to be good, Cap'n, 'onest I will," she assured him. "I know I got a tendency to git riled a bit at times, but I sure would like to go with ye. I'll try to keep out of yer way. Why, ye won't 'ardly know I'm 'round. I'll jest blend in with me surroundin's and be as quiet as a little church mouse."

With a frustrated sigh, Dane relented. How could he refuse this poor lad his request? "All right, Gabe, I'll give you a second chance to keep your promise, but it's your last," he warned, shaking a lean finger in her face.

Gabe danced gaily about him, her face radiating

pleasure. Gathering Blanco's reins, she swung into the saddle as the startled steed pranced sideways and indignantly threw his head at his rider's sudden movement. Lifting his powerful hoofs high in the air, Blanco turned a close circle around Dane while Gabe sat perched on his back.

"'Ow about racin' me back to the stables, Cap'n?" she queried as she pulled her cap down around her ears and arched a grimy brow.

"No," he replied flatly. "If that stallion is as quick-paced as you are quick-tempered, I'd undoubtedly lose and be forced to listen to you brag about your victory all the way to Bristol."

A mischievous grin caught the corners of her mouth. "Yer right, Cap'n. Blanco is fast and I wouldn't let ye forget it if I was to beat ye."

As Gabe pressed her boot heels to the stallion's flanks, Blanco lowered his head and lunged into a full gallop. Dane watched them fly across the meadow at breakneck speed, well aware that someone in the lad's mysterious past had taught him to ride expertly. It seemed unusual for a boy from Gabe's station in life to be such an experienced equestrian, Dane mused thoughtfully. He stepped into his stirrup and followed at a slower pace, wondering why he had agreed to take that little urchin with him to Bristol.

There was a strange bond between himself and the waif even though he was reluctant to admit or verbalize his admiration. The lad was proud, independent, and headstrong. He reminded Dane of his own youthful years when he had been prepared to take on the whole world in his attempt to prove that he was worthy of respect. Gabe suffered the same growing pains that Dane had once endured. The waif would have to learn that the opinions of others were not so important as one's own opinion of himself.

Gabe returned to the stables in a light-hearted mood. Nate's broad grin awaited her as he stood watching the muscular stallion canter toward him. As Gabe slipped to the ground, she offered the reins to Nate, urging him onto Blanco's back. Once again the boy's facial expression spoke louder than any words he could have uttered.

Leaning against the stone corner post, she watched Nate maneuver the steed. Dane rode into the clearing and paused to view the scene as an appreciative smile grazed his lips as he reflected that Gabe had a way of sprinkling a little happiness into each life that he touched, except for Higgins. For some reason the two were determined to dislike each other. The urchin pretended to be cold and calloused; but he was soft-hearted, whether or not he would admit it. Gabe was not as invincible as he would have led others to believe. He had eagerly offered his only prized possession to a less fortunate lad, his actions revealing his compassion for others. Dane again smiled to himself and urged Sultan toward the barn, feeling that he had gained some insight into the personality of the scrawny waif.

That afternoon as Gabe came from the kitchen,

she heard a rap at the entrance and paused to see who had come to call. She ducked behind the stairs as Higgins opened the door for Sherman Brice.

"I brought a message fer Cap'n Hampton," Sherman said as he extended the envelope to Higgins.

Gabe's heart was thumping wildly as she waited for Sherman to depart. She would have loved to follow after Sherman, but she had to intercept that message! It was most likely about her disappearance. If the captain knew that she had run away from home, he might realize she was the woman who appeared in the darkness. Her secret had to be kept!

After Higgins went into the study to place the envelope on Dane's desk and then went upstairs, Gabe moved cautiously toward the room. She slipped the envelope inside her shirt and hurried to her own quarters. After carefully opening the envelope she read John's message.

> *Dear Captain Hampton,*
> *I hope that you arrived home safely and have recovered from your injury. I was happy to be of service in your time of need.*
> *Now, I hope that you will come to my aid. My niece, Gabrielle Jarmon, has run away from home. I thought perhaps that you might have seen a young woman traveling alone during your journey. I am most distraught by her disappearance. If you have information that would aid in my search for her, please notify me. Her*

*betrothed, the Duke of Fairleigh, and I are
most concerned about her welfare.*
                                    John Jarmon

Gabe snorted disgustedly when she finished
reading the letter and then ripped it to shreds. If it
weren't for the money John was to receive, he
could not have cared less about what happened to
her. Taking quill in hand, Gabe wrote her own
version of the letter. Having done this she sealed
the envelope, and returned it to Dane's desk.

Fifteen minutes later, Dane entered through the
front door and strolled into his office. When he
spied the note, he seated himself and read the
contents.

Captain Hampton,
    *I hope your journey home was a safe one
and that you have recovered from your
injury. I was happy to be of service to you
in your time of need. I have discovered the
name of the person who brought you to us
and I thought perhaps you would be
curious to learn his name, just as I was.*
    *A young lad, who goes by the name of
Gabe, spent the night at our stables and
related his story to one of my livery boys.
We are indebted to him for bringing you to
us.*
                                    John Jarmon

A slow smile settled on Dane's rugged features.
So it *was* the little urchin. Then a bemused frown

103

replaced his grin. If Gabe had come to his aid, was the woman of his dreams really another hallucination? No one seemed to know anything about her. The sound of footsteps in the hall interrupted his silent reverie and he glanced up to see Higgins poised in the doorway.

"I see you have found the envelope, Lord Hampton," he said, his expression remaining sober. "Would you care for tea, sir?"

"No, nothing, thank you," Dane replied as he rose from his chair and ambled into the sitting room, preoccupied with a mysterious shadow that continued to fill his thoughts.

After completing the task that Dane had requested, Gabe assisted Liz with her household chores. When Dane ordered his bath, she struggled upstairs with the hot water to fill his tub. With that accomplished, she prepared her own tub and puttered contentedly about her room, enjoying her privacy. Although she was merely a servant in Lord Hampton's home, she had more freedom than that of a well-bred young woman in her uncle's house. Her plan had worked out much better than she had anticipated. She was anxious to travel to Bristol, hoping to make some sort of arrangements for her future.

After an uninterrupted bath, she donned her gown and slipped between the sheets, seeking the comfort of her soft mattress. Gabrielle's touch with reality faded in the darkness of her room as she sought the world of unencumbered sleep.

With a startled jerk, she bolted up in bed,

listening intently for the sound that had awakened her. Waiting tensely, she heard an agonizing moan and scrambled from her bed. She dashed through the terrace door and entered Dane's room without giving her reaction a second thought. As she eased down on the edge of the bed, she brushed her hand across his head, feeling the perspiration.

Her brows furrowed in concern as she heard his gasping breaths. "What terrible ghost haunts you, m'lord?"

Her soothing voice and gentle touch calmed his fearful thoughts. Dane's eyes fluttered open to see the dark image hovering above him.

"'Tis a harboring spirit that seeks to destroy me," he murmured hoarsely. "'Tis something that I can never seem to forget. The nightmares never end." He squinted his eyes, searching the shadowed face that lingered close to his. "And I am still left to wonder if you are yet another dream. You only come to me when I sleep."

Gabrielle carefully avoided his last comment as she whispered regretfully, "I'm sorry you are threatened by your dreams, m'lord. If I could free you from the chains of your painful memories, I would. Perhaps if you tell me the cause of them, I—"

Dane reached up to her, tenderly wrapping his fingers around the back of her neck to bring her closer. He breathed a weary sigh as her soft lips melted against his. "You can help, love. Just let me hold you for a moment."

Gabrielle gingerly embraced him, her hair falling about them like a protective cape. Again their lips touched and she surrendered to the comfort she had found in the nearness of this amazingly gentle man she had come to know in darkness. Just as before, the world vanished and time ceased to exist.

Dane held her close, his frightening dream forgotten. Again the fantasy of this mysterious woman became reality. She was in his encircling arms, yielding to his embrace, answering his kisses with a desire that matched his own. His hands made their way to her firm breasts, explored their shapely form, savored and learned each curve by touch since he could not know her by sight.

Startled by his intimate caress, Gabrielle drew away. "You have a long list of sins, sir. Do not add molesting your guardian angel to it," she chided as she grabbed his hands and held them in her own. "Please don't try to take what I cannot give. I treasure these quiet moments with you. Don't spoil them."

Although Dane found it difficult to control his rising desire for her, he obeyed her request. The back of his hand brushed across her soft face; he wished he could see her in the light. "What is your name, angel? At least tell me your name. Surely no harm would come of that."

Her light chuckle twisted his senses as she replied, "You have just called me by the only name you need to know, m'lord. When I come to you, you seem to know that it is I," she reminded him in a raspy whisper. "You have yet to ask who is here when I approach. I need no other name. Your thoughts reach out across the span of time and space and call to me. I come to you when you need me.''

It was true. He had never questioned who was in his room. There was never any doubt that it was she who moved gracefully toward him from the swaying shadows. And when he needed her, she was there to comfort him, asking and expecting very little in return.

"I am not to know your name or your face, but only your tender kisses?'' he queried, arching a heavy brow. "From where did you come? How can you be so close at hand when I need you?''

"I now have my wings,'' she teased playfully. "I can appear and disappear whenever you call out to me. I travel into this realm, riding on a moonbeam, following the path of a falling star as it streaks across the sky.''

With a futile sigh, Dane abandoned his attempt to discover her identity. She talked in riddles and he would never find the answers he sought. He would never again attempt to force her to reveal herself as he had when he had raised the lantern to gaze into her shadowed face. That time she had vanished. He would not lose her again.

"I suppose you are really an ugly witch with a hideous name,'' he mocked, grinning up at the woman who was cloaked in darkness.

"Ah, m'lord, you have struck upon the truth. Only those of us who fear the light stalk the night.'' Smiling in the darkness, Gabrielle traced her index finger over his sensuous lips. "And now that you hold my deepest secret in the palm of your hand, I must leave you.''

As she started to rise, Dane pushed up on his elbow and groped in the dark for her small hand. "Don't leave me. Just let me hold you a little longer. I won't add to my list of sins. I shall act the perfect gentleman even though it is not my wont to do so," he whispered as he drew her back to his side.

"Very well, m'lord; for a few moments longer. But if I trust you, do not disappoint me," Gabrielle replied as his strong arms curled about her waist.

Leaning close to press a light kiss to his lips, Brielle melted against the hard wall of his chest. The bond between them strengthened. She was lost to the manly fragrance that encircled her senses, answering his passionate kiss with a wild desire all her own. In the dark silence, a sleeping desire was awakened, shaking her soul with its intensity. She was a nameless spirit, searching for the comfort that Dane could offer. In their warm embrace, they clung together, controlling the need to satisfy passion's calling.

They lay together in silence, not daring to shatter their peaceful moment. Dane wished to see the face of his mystical goddess who warmed his soul and Brielle wondered why her conscience was not warning her to flee. It was as if she belonged with him. No place on earth could bring her such serenity.

After what seemed only a short time, Gabrielle felt drowsiness hovering about her as she lay entangled in Dane's secure embrace. She knew that she must leave before she fell asleep in his arms. Reluctantly, she attempted to ease herself from his side.

"Don't go," he murmured, pulling her closer.

"I must, m'lord. I will come to you again when you call, but never follow me or you will close the door for the passage from my world to yours. If you disobey my request I will be unable to return to you. What we have shared will die in the darkness. If you cherish these quiet moments as I do, you will not question me; nor will you attempt to search me out. Good night, Dane," she whispered as she withdrew from the edge of the bed. "May all of your dreams be pleasant ones."

As her silhouette faded into the shadows, Dane heaved a despairing sigh. Why was he drawn to the mysterious maiden? How could she comfort his fearful dreams with only the tenderness of her whispered voice? Who was she? Why would she not allow him to know her identity? From where she had come and how could she appear so quickly? Was she really a fantastic dream? Dane scanned the shadows once again, finding no sign that she had been there at all.

"Damn," he muttered as he rolled to his side, pulling the quilts about his shoulders. "You seek to steal my heart with gentle affection. Yet, you yield nothing of yourself, except for only a few fleeting moments of tenderness. Are you my envisioned fantasy or a woman? What is your purpose? Do you desire me as much as I want you?" he questioned, expecting no answers and receiving none.

Although he was annoyed by his unsuccessful quest to make some sense of the shadowed goddess, he seemed powerless when he was in her spell. It was not like him to respond to a woman like some love-smitten pup. And yet, he could not seem to deny her whispered pleas for secrecy. He would share the cherished moments with her and wait, hoping that one night she would reveal herself to him.

She was the silhouette on a grassy slope, the angel of mercy, the mysterious goddess who came when he needed comfort. She was the passionate woman who responded to his kisses, offering the honeyed sweetness of her lips. She was right. He needed no other name to attach to his elusive seraph who appeared from the depths of darkness. He knew her by her soft reassuring whisper, her tender caresses, and her shadowed form that crept softly into his life. She brought a mystical pleasure that he never knew existed. She needed no name other than angel of love. She was as difficult to describe as the intangible term he had used to characterize her. Love? He muttered cynically. This was madness. Yes, that was what it was, a maddening experience that defied logic. Day by day, so slowly that he could not grasp it, he was losing his mind and he could do nothing to stop it. Dane determinedly shook his head, forcing all thoughts of the shadowed angel from his mind. It was all a dream. That was all it was.

Warmed by the strange emotion she had discovered, Gabrielle slipped into her room and nestled down into the cold quilts. She had sought comfort and security in Dane's embrace, but tonight she had been tempted to satisfy his passions as well as her own. She could handle the strong, commanding captain who treated her as a ragamuffin, but this gentle man who sought to deal with her as a woman left her slightly shaken. She had been hard-pressed to control him and herself as well.

As slumber wrapped its tender arms about her, Gabrielle yielded to pleasant dreams of blue eyes shining upon her. Soft eager lips sought hers, bringing a quiver of excitement. She was no longer sure who she was while she played her charade. But of one thing she was certain. The handsome face and masculine frame of Capt. Dane Hampton had aroused a sleeping spirit within her. She had refused to name the emotion his embrace had stirred. There was much she had to do to gain her home and her inheritance.

Chapter Five

After hopping from bed, Gabe bound her breasts with cloth and slipped into her baggy garb. She shrugged on her sheepskin jerkin, grabbed her brown cap, and gathered her belongings before hurrying to the kitchen for breakfast.

When Gabe strolled to the barn, Nate was returning on Blanco and she watched him trot toward her. She moved around to the side of the stables to greet Nate and held the reins as the lad dismounted, his face glowing with pleasure. Blanco affectionately nudged his mistress, but his overzealous attempt to gain her attention caused her cap to shift. Several long strands of brown hair tumbled down to her shoulders. In her haste to dress, Gabe had forgotten to pin her hair in place and the evidence of her blunder had been exposed to the unsuspecting lad.

Nate's beaming smile turned to a bewildered frown. Gabe hurriedly shoved her hair up on her head and readjusted her cap. After eying her stallion accusingly, she turned a sheepish grin to her astonished friend who could do nothing but gawk at her.

"It seems Blanco wants me to let you in on my secret, Nate," she remarked, her eyes twinkling mischievously.

Gabe led the steed farther away from the stable entrance while Nate followed behind her.

"Nate," Brielle began hesitantly, "I ran away from my uncle's home because he was going to sell me off in marriage to a man that I despise. You are the only one here who knows that I am not what I appear to be. I want no one else to know my true identity. It is important that I continue to be 'Gabe.' If Lord Hampton finds out who I am, he will send me back to my uncle. Please keep my secret." Her wide green eyes searched his dark face, hoping he could understand her plight. "I trust you, Nate. Please don't betray me."

A sympathetic smile touched Nate's lips as he took her hands in his own and held them affectionately. Although he could not reassure her with words, Brielle could read the loyalty that was mirrored in his eyes and knew that he was a devoted friend.

"Thank you." Gabe leaned over to place a grateful kiss on his tanned cheek, bringing a slight blush flooding upward from his neck. When she stepped away, she resumed her role as the waif. "And now, me friend, will ye 'elp me ready the wagon for our trip to Bristol? Me and the cap'n will be leavin' shortly. Take care of Blanco fer me. 'E needs plenty of exercise and attention as ye 'ave just seen," she added with a subtle wink.

Gabe swaggered away, leading her steed into the stables while Nate hurried up beside her, a smug grin grazing his lips. After preparing the wagon, Gabe went back into the kitchen. She grabbed the lunch that Liz had packed and swiped a fresh slice of bread before sauntering into the dining room. Dane was preparing to eat his breakfast and glanced up as Gabe appeared in the doorway.

"'Mornin', Cap'n," she greeted him, but a mouthful of bread camouflaged her words.

Dane's gaze swung to Gabe and then he frowned disapprovingly at the lad's abominable manners. He watched the waif consume the other half-slice of bread and wipe his dirty face with a dirtier shirt sleeve. Cringing, he listened as Gabe smacked his lips like a hungry mutt.

"For God's sake, Gabe. Don't talk with your mouth full of food! Your manners are deplorable," Dane chided gruffly.

Stopping short, Gabe spun to face his annoyed scowl. "I quit comparin' ye to me saintly father the first day we came 'ere, Cap'n," she snapped curtly. "I ain't any of yer kin. Ye ain't got no right to criticize everythin' I do. I'll do as I please without takin' lessons in etiquette from the likes of ye . . . if ye don't mind." Sarcasm dripped from her lips as she tilted a proud chin.

As his fist hit the table, rattling the dishes, Dane bolted to his feet and glared at the insolent wretch. "How dare you address me that way! Just who in the hell do you think you are, young man? I could have you soundly thrashed for talking to me in

114

such a disrespectful tone!"

Blue and green eyes flashed heated sparks for a long moment. Gabe quickly realized that the captain was in no mood for her taunting games and she continued at a slower pace and in a more playful tone, "Now if ye was plannin' to make me the sole 'eir of yer estate—seein' 'ow I saved yer life and all—I would do me best to act like a proper aristocrat with the gracious manners of a prince," she replied, bowing slightly before him. "But ye've bin ungrateful of me goodly deed and ye ain't offered no such proposition. I s'pose I'll jest 'ave to continue as I am—a 'ot-tempered, ill-mannered servant who ain't 'ad the proper schoolin' and other advantages of noblemen. A thousand pardons, Cap'n. I didn't mean to disturb yer breakfast." Her contagious smile eased Dane's ruffled ego.

As Dane considered the lad's words and impish grin, his irritation mellowed. He opened his mouth to speak, but Gabe had seen the firm set of his rugged features change into his businesslike countenance. She quickly guessed what he had intended to say and left his jaw sagging in amazement.

"Aye, Cap'n. I'll collect yer luggage and be waitin' in the wagon fer ye." Gabe spun away from his startled gaze and strutted across the room, but paused at the door to throw a question over her shoulder. "Anythin' else ye want me to tend to?"

"No, that will be all."

Dane rolled his eyes and muttered under his breath as Gabe exited. That cocky little guttersnipe could arouse so many different emotions in him in the short span of a few minutes! Yet Dane was left with an amused smile playing on his lips when the ornery little imp swaggered away. He always seemed to know when to ease up on his badgering and just when to interject some light-hearted comment. Dane had the strange feeling that somehow he was being maneuvered. But he had to admit that what had been a dull existence of orders given and commands obeyed had suddenly become a lively escapade. He was continuously matching wits with that arrogant ragamuffin who seemed to come and go like a whirlwind. Gabe was no one's fool and no man's slave. Dane could not help but admire his spunk. Although Dane intended to take the lad under his wing and control his fits of temper, he would never attempt to smother Gabe's undaunted spirit.

After finishing his breakfast, Dane stepped outside to find Gabe sitting on the wooden seat, staring off into space. As he climbed up beside the daydreaming lad, he took the reins and popped the horses, sending them lurching forward. With a sudden jerk of the wagon, Gabe clutched at Dane with one hand and her hat with the other. Her feet flew up in front of her, drawing a satisfied smile from the handsome captain.

"Good Gawd, what the 'ell are ye tryin' to do, send me flyin' on me ass in the back of the wagon?" she snapped scornfully as she released his arm and braced herself on the seat.

With a hearty chuckle, Dane sent Gabe a hasty sidelong glance. "I expect you to have enough sense to know that when a team of horses starts off, you have to hold on. I'm sorry I gave you credit for having any sense," he teased, his blue eyes sparkling vibrantly.

Grumbling under her breath, Gabe settled herself on the hard seat in preparation for the long journey. They rode quietly for almost an hour, each planning his day, before Gabe broke the silence with a question.

"Will I be allowed to venture out on me own while yer in Bristol?"

"That depends on what kind of adventure you have in mind," Dane replied, his heavy brows arching suspiciously as he glanced at Gabe.

Gabe shrugged off his skeptical regard. "I jest thought I might visit with some old friends," she explained blandly.

"Is that all?" he inquired, a dubious frown settling on his bronzed face. "Somehow your innocent suggestion makes me wary."

"Aye, Cap'n. That's all. I ain't plannin' to set fire to Bristol if that's what yer thinkin'," she snorted caustically.

"Well, I suppose there will be no harm in visiting your friends as long as you don't keep me waiting. I have several things to do and none of them include searching all over town for some impetuous waif who has wandered off and gotten himself into trouble." Dane eyed the lad with a hint of apprehension. Gabe's short-fused temper and stubborn pride could easily attract trouble.

"I kin take care of meself, Cap'n," she insisted, her smudged chin tilting to a confident angle. "I

117

promise not to inconvenience ye in the least. If I don't come back when yer ready to leave, jest consider that I'm stayin' fer good. I don't expect ye to turn the town upside down lookin' fer me."

Wondering if Gabe really intended to remain in Bristol, Dane studied him curiously for a moment. "All right, Gabe," he agreed with a slight nod.

The lad suddenly changed the subject, catching Dane off guard as usual. "Kin I ask ye a personal question?"

"Fire away, but I'll decide whether or not I wish to answer it."

"Fair enough, Cap'n." Gabe reached under the seat and pulled the lunch basket up on her lap. "What 'appened to yer family? Are ye an orphan like me?" she questioned bluntly as she unpacked the food and casually handed Dane a leg of chicken and a slice of bread.

"Why do you want to know that?" he queried, surprised that the waif was interested in his life or cared a fig about his past.

Taking a bite of chicken, Gabe spoke with her mouth full, knowing exactly how much it would annoy Lord Hampton. "Jest curious. And it's a long ride. We might as well talk the time away unless ye got some other entertainin' idea to keep us from gittin' bored."

Dane's dark brows furrowed as he listened to these muffled sentences, but he decided not to lecture the fiery wretch. It would serve no useful purpose. "Yes, I'm an orphan like you. I lost my mother when I was fifteen. My father remarried and I inherited a stepmother and -brother. About a

118

year ago, my father and stepmother were killed when their buggy lost a wheel and overturned, and—" Dane stopped short. He was still unable to discuss the other incident that haunted his thoughts. "Now I live alone at Hampton Estate. That is one of the reasons I have my schooner. It gives me the opportunity to get away for a while," he explained in a tight voice.

Gabe watched the pain pass through his sapphire eyes and knew just how much he had suffered from the loss of his family. "I'm sorry, Cap'n," she sympathized quietly. Gabe picked up another piece of chicken, but questioned him again before taking a bite. "I guess this ain't none of me business either, but why ain't ye married? Ye got fists full of money and ye ain't exactly ugly. Is it yer foul disposition that makes ye a bachelor?" She grinned mischievously and chomped on her poultry. After smacking her lips, she wiped her mouth with a ragged sleeve and glanced over in time to see Dane wince at her manners.

Gabe certainly didn't mince words, Dane mused thoughtfully. The lad wanted to know everything about him, but Gabe was close-mouthed when it came to talking about his own life. "You're indeed correct. It's none of your business." Gabe shrugged indifferently, seeming more interested in her chicken than the conversation, and Dane smiled wryly.

"But I'll give you the benefit of my experience and answer your question, m'boy. The only woman that I could possibly marry is unavailable to me. An unattainable star, you might say. And, in truth, I'm not at all sure I want to be tied to one set of petticoats. I like doing as I please with whomever I please, just as you do. Take it from me, Gabe. The noble ladies of court are as attractive as china dolls, but they bore me with their empty-headed chatter. They are lovely to look at, but a man cannot spend his entire life with the likes of one of them."

Dane stared straight ahead, frowning thoughtfully as he offered Gabe more of his cynical opinions. "Women are shallow diversions. I learned long ago that the best policy where women are concerned is to take what they have to offer and avoid lingering too long with any one of them."

Gabe frowned at his calloused attitude. She already knew that his actions exemplified his thoughts on the subject of women, but to hear him voice his outrageous opinions annoyed her greatly.

"Are ye tellin' me that love is an empty word, Cap'n?" she quipped as she raised a curious brow and squirmed on the hard seat.

"Love is for fools and morons who confuse that elusive emotion with passion, Gabe. I, for one, have never found a woman who possesses all of the necessary qualities that would make me confess to being a fool." He smirked arrogantly.

"And if ye ever do, Cap'n, what then?"

"Then I shall have to eat my words. But I do not expect any such occurrences," he added, his voice threaded with overconfidence.

"Neither do I," Gabe agreed with a derisive snort. "Fer if it should 'appen, ye would most certainly choke to death in yer attempt to swallow such a large mouthful of cynicism."

Dane chuckled amusedly in response to Gabe's last remark. "And now that you know about me, I want to hear about you," Dane demanded, expecting another snide comment and no pertinent information.

Gabe scanned the captain's dashing appearance and considered his harsh opinion of women. Her gaze settled on the sapphire eyes that continued to draw her attention. With a pessimistic sigh, she revealed a little of her past, since it seemed to be a time for confessions.

"Ma died when I was a small child and me pa raised me alone. I lost 'im less than a year ago. I ain't got no brothers or sisters, only a despicable relative who took me in and tried to break me spirit. 'E tried to teach me to be 'is obedient slave. Then 'e tried to sell me off when 'e found someone who could afford 'is price. I ran off and 'ave been wanderin' ever since." Gabe sat in a seething rage, unable to control the bitterness of what Lord Jarmon had intended to do to her. Suddenly his face appeared before her and she was tempted to reach out and claw his cold, gray eyes from his image.

Dane eyed the lad sympathetically, wondering how much he had suffered in his short life. It was apparent that the boy was reliving some unpleasant event as he sat with his fists clenched beside him, seeing nothing but painful visions from his past. At least Dane had found out a few of his secrets. Gabe had no place to call home and few to name as friends.

After midday the wagon rumbled into Bristol. Gabe's spirits were lifted by the bustle of activity. Staring at her surroundings, she searched the names of the shops that they passed. Finally, the name she sought appeared on a shingle in front of an office, and she carefully surveyed the building so she could return to it later.

Dane brought the team to a halt in front of a two-story establishment and Gabe glanced up to read the sign hanging on the balcony above her. Frowning curiously, she read it again. Her eyes narrowed angrily when she understood its meaning. She squelched the irritation that rose within her as she glared at the sign. *House of Squires*. Business! She growled under her breath. The damned rogue had come to seek his pleasure before seeing to business!

As Dane hopped down from the wagon and started up the wooden steps, he heard the expected sneer and scornful words behind him.

"And jest what the 'ell am I s'posed to do while yer tryin' every bed in that damned 'ouse 'til ye find the one that pleases ye most, Cap'n?" she quipped, her cockney accent heavily laden with sarcasm. "Do ye expect me to sit 'ere all afternoon, carryin' on a conversation with these two nags?" Gabe flung her arm in the direction of the steeds that stood in front of her as Dane turned to face the wagon and the annoyed lad who sat upon it.

With an expression of mock concern, Dane scratched his chin, considering the waif's caustic words. "An excellent idea, Gabe. Perhaps if you teach them to talk you can make your fortune by parading them about town. You might take up a sizable collection. Or—" Dane paused, raising his index finger as if a brilliant idea had suddenly come upon him. "If that doesn't amuse you, perhaps you could go look up some of those friends you profess to have and chat with them for an hour or so."

Dane was well aware that the lad disapproved of such establishments, but he had no intention of allowing the waif to dictate his personal life. As he wheeled around to open the door, he heard the boy muttering behind him again.

"A fine way to treat the person who saved yer miserable 'ide. I should 'ave taken yer 'orse and valuables and left ye to die on that muddy road," Gabe snarled in disgust. "It was what ye deserved."

As the door closed behind Lord Hampton, Gabe reached down under the seat to grab her pouch and then climbed down from the wagon. Although she welcomed the opportunity of seeing to her business in Bristol, she could not deny the pang of jealousy that shot through her. She could picture the dashing captain turning his affection toward the painted ladies that were waiting behind those closed doors.

"He means nothing to me. Let him satisfy his lust for every whore in that place. I don't give a damn," she grumbled as she stalked down the street.

Her own words were shallow and unconvincing. It pained her deeply to realize that she cared for Dane. He knew her only as a young lad in baggy breeches whose face was always caked with dirt and whose body was fragrant with the smell of lathered horses. Determinedly casting aside the thought of his tender embrace, Gabe searched for an alley that was piled with crates. With only meager protection to conceal her, she quickly shed her shirt and threw on the pink muslin dress she had brought with her. Within a few minutes, Gabrielle stepped out of the passageway and onto the boardwalk. With her long, dark hair flowing down her back, she held her head high. Her face was free of the dirt that usually covered her delicate features as she continued toward the office she had seen earlier. The young urchin had transformed herself into an attractive lass. No one could have believed they were one and the same. Gabe was as ill-mannered and clumsy as Brielle was refined and graceful. Their mannerisms and voices were as different as night and day. Only for an important cause had the lovely lass discarded her charade.

Gabrielle stepped into an elaborately furnished office where she was met by a handsome, gray-haired gentleman who took her hand and pressed a light kiss to her wrist.

"May I be of some service, my dear?" he questioned with a pleasant smile. His eyes quickly flickered down her shapely form.

"If you are Roger Saxon, you certainly may," Gabrielle replied, returning his grin before backing a safe distance away.

"I am. And what is your name, young lady?"

"I am Gabrielle Jarmon. Paul Jarmon was my father. I have come to seek your legal advice on a matter which concerns me greatly," she explained as she took the seat the lawyer offered to her. "I have been living with my uncle. He has received a compensation from my father's estate. I am no longer residing in his home and I wish to know if I will be permitted to collect that allowance now that he is no longer boarding me."

Brielle's gaze fell to her lap and she sighed before asking her other questions. "Is it possible to regain possession of my home without being married? Does Lord John have the right to make a marriage contract for me to whomever he pleases whether I consent or not?"

Saxon stared into Gabrielle's anxious green eyes, pondering her string of questions. "Allow me to read your father's will before we continue, Miss Jarmon."

The lawyer entered the back room and returned several minutes later. As he sat down at his desk, he folded his hands in front of him and peered solemnly into Gabrielle's exquisite face.

"I see no reason why you should not be allowed the compensation that John has been receiving. If you are not under his protection, he is not entitled to the funds. However, you have failed to tell me why you are no longer residing with him." Saxon raised a quizzical brow, but Gabrielle made no offer to explain so he continued, "As to the matter of marriage, your father clearly stated that you were not to return home until you were wed. Only then will the property be turned over to you. He obviously did not approve of your managing on your own. John Jarmon has been named your legal guardian. He has the right to arrange your marriage," he added, watching the look of dismay flow across Gabrielle's perfect features.

"And if I *never* marry I cannot inherit my own home?" she questioned quietly.

"I'm afraid that is exactly what I'm saying, Gabrielle. Your father intended that your husband manage your estate. I suppose that he naturally assumed that you would marry soon. He foresaw no problem," Roger surmised, wondering why such a beautiful young woman could be so distressed. She would have little difficulty claiming a husband.

"My uncle has arranged for me to marry the Duke of Fairleigh," Gabrielle began, but she was cut short by Saxon's bewildered gasp.

"What?" He clutched the arms of his chair, his face quickly losing color. "That man has a sordid reputation. He is almost old enough to pass as your grandfather! Why would your uncle do such a thing?"

"For spite," Brielle replied bitterly. "He despises the very sight of me. It was his way of seeking revenge. He will receive a sizable purse from the duke if we wed."

"My lord!" He choked.

"I ran away. Lord John doesn't know where I am and I wish to keep it that way. I really don't know what else to do except bide my time. My father told me to come to you if I needed help. I trust you won't betray me." Gabrielle raised her eyes in an unspoken plea that nearly melted his heart.

A long, strained moment passed between them. Saxon seriously considered her dilemma and then shrugged. "If you were some trollop, your problem would be easily solved," he said, hoping to make her realize that even in her misfortune she still had her pride. "Lord Jarmon could not persuade Fairleigh to take you as his wife, but then you would still have difficulty finding a husband. Society would frown on such behavior. In this instance, your beauty and station in life are to your disadvantage, Gabrielle. I'm sure that Fairleigh would be overjoyed with you as his wife."

Saxon leaned his forearms on the desk and focused his full attention on Gabrielle. "My suggestion is for you to avoid your uncle until you find the man *you* wish to marry. When the time comes, you can wed and the estate will be yours. Lord Jarmon will have no say in the matter. If that scoundrel comes here, I won't tell him I've seen you. I will have your allowance sent to you. I do not anticipate your having difficulty in finding your own husband. You are a very desirable young woman with a sizable inheritance awaiting you," Saxon concluded as he eased back in his chair.

"And what if Lord Jarmon has already signed a contract with Fairleigh?" she questioned demurely, her eyes slowing rising to meet the lawyer's confident expression.

"Has he?" Saxon gulped.

"Yes." Her reply was no more than a forced whisper.

"Then you must take particular care to avoid Jarmon and Fairleigh. Perhaps in time they will give you up for lost and the contract will be disregarded."

"If Jarmon comes to you, questioning why he no longer receives funds for sheltering me, what will you tell him?"

"If you are not living in his home, he cannot expect to receive compensation. I don't have to tell him that *you* are receiving the allowance; only that *he* will no longer be paid. Don't worry about it, Gabrielle. I'll handle Jarmon." Saxon attempted to sound encouraging, but he was not dealing with a fool and Gabrielle was well aware that her situation was complicated.

"Thank you, sir." Brielle produced a feeble smile. It was all she could offer at the moment. The predicament looked grim and she knew it. How could she find a desirable husband, living as a servant boy on a country estate? Or in Bristol? She dared not show her face just yet. Brielle wanted her estate and inheritance, but not badly enough to marry Horace Fairleigh. She refused to suffer the harrowing existence that would be her lot with him as her husband. God forbid!

"Could I have part of my funds now? It will be difficult for you to send them to me. I want no one to know where I'm staying and I have not yet decided on my permanent residence. I'm not sure what I'm going to do. I need time to think," Gabrielle murmured as she rose and extended her hand to the lawyer. "I do appreciate your help, Mr. Saxon."

"I don't imagine your father had any idea he would be causing you so much distress. If he had anticipated difficulty, I'm sure he would have been displeased with himself. He loved you dearly, Gabrielle," Saxon assured her, his eyes mellowing in sympathy.

"Yes, I know." Brielle forced a wan smile, but everything appeared bleak and she was far from cheerful.

After Saxon gave her sufficient funds, Gabrielle hurried outside to the street and ducked into the alley she had found to double as her dressing room. In a matter of minutes, the thin ragamuffin emerged and made her way back to the wagon that still sat empty in front of the two-story establishment.

Gabe tossed her bag under the seat and pulled herself up on the wooden bench, still pondering what Roger Saxon had told her. If she were promiscuous, her uncle would have no easy time trying to marry her off to some virgin-seeking letch. As she glanced up at the sign hanging on the balcony, Gabe almost wished that for once she was not the gently bred heiress of Jarmon Estate. What was she going to do about that contract? It seemed she was destined to live as a waif indefinitely, hoping that Fairleigh would search out some other sacrificial virgin for his wife.

Gabe heard the elaborately carved door creak open and glanced up to see Dane's virile frame fill the entrance. The sound of feminine laughter wafted its way toward her as Dane ambled outside, his handsome face splitting in a wide smile. With a disgusted growl, she looked away from Dane. She caught sight of a gloved hand holding a silver dagger. There was no time to study the assailant's face which was shadowed by a large-brimmed hat. Gabe spun toward the captain, adrenaline shooting through her veins. With the quickness of a crouched cat, she sprang from the wagon, leaping onto Lord Hampton. Gabe forced him to the porch floor as the knife sailed past, quivering as it notched firmly in the post just above their heads.

As Dane fell backward with Gabe on top of him, he growled at the sudden attack. "What the hell's the matter with you!"

When he tossed the urchin aside and came to his knees, he spied the knife. If it hadn't been for Gabe, the blade would have found its mark and Dane would have been slumped on the ground with a dagger in his heart.

Gabe rubbed her aching head that had slammed against the floor when Dane tossed her aside. Gazing up at him with irate sparks flying from her eyes, she snorted scornfully, "Damn ye, Cap'n! Yer an ungrateful dolt. That's the second time I've saved yer rotten 'ide. All the thanks I git is a knot on me 'ead. I should 'ave minded me own business and let ye take that damned blade in the 'eart. That's the one place that wouldn't draw no blood. Yers is solid rock!" Scowling at the speechless captain, she climbed to her knees.

The waif slowly struggled to her feet, dug the splinter from her backside, and brushed the dirt from her tattered breeches. Dane continued to stare at her and a ghost of a smile managed to find its way to Gabe's lips. If the captain had been wearing false teeth they would have clattered to the porch the way his jaw was sagging, she thought amusedly.

"Seems to me that everybody wants ye dead. Ye must be the envy of more than one man. Or per'aps one of yer jealous pieces of fluff thought ye spread yerself too thin in there." Gabe gestured her head toward the closed door.

After yanking the dagger from the post, she stalked back to the wagon, leaving Dane to pull himself together and follow after her. As Dane climbed up beside her, Gabe peered into his ashen face and sadly shook her head.

"Per'aps yer right, Cap'n. Ye do need a guardian angel 'overin' over ye. I'd be glad to let 'er 'ave me job. I'm beginnin' to think yer jinxed. If I'm to spend me time rescuin' ye from pistols and daggers, I think I'll find me some job less risky. Somebody wants ye dead. I'll be damned if I'm goin' to 'ang 'round to guard ye from 'em. It's liable to be me who catches the next blade. I'm too young to die. Followin' ye 'round is like 'avin' one foot in the grave."

Reaching under the seat, Gabe grabbed her leather pouch and hopped from the wagon. She had enough troubles of her own without becoming involved with a man whose life was in constant danger. Spinning back to the captain who still had not found his voice, Gabe shot him a cold glance. "If I were ye, I'd be wary of me own shadow. I wish ye luck, Cap'n. Ye'll need it." Gabe made a mocking salute, threw her pouch over her shoulder, and sauntered down the street.

While Dane watched the waif depart, he heaved a weak sigh and then popped the horses, reining them in the direction Gabe had taken. As he pulled up beside the boardwalk, Gabe arched a quizzical brow.

"Get in, boy. You have no place to go and your horse is still at the estate. You may as well ride along with me for the day." Dane peered down at the lad, a hopeful smile tracing his lips.

"Oh, 'ell," Gabe grumbled. She had forgotten about Blanco. Now that she had been reminded, she had no intention of being without her horse. Throwing her pouch in the back, she crawled up beside Dane, quite disgusted with the events of the day. "All right, Cap'n. I'll ride with ye, but if someone aims a pistol at her 'ead, I'm bailin' out fer good."

Dane hung his head as he took up the reins and murmured humbly, "Thank you, Gabe. I owe you my life. I'm sorry I was so rough with you. I had no idea what you were about when you leaped off the wagon at me."

"It ain't the first bump I ever 'ad. Ferget it. I s'pose I would 'ave done the same fer any man." She shrugged indifferently and settled herself on the seat.

Noting the cool attitude the lad displayed, Dane decided that enough had been said. Gabe seemed withdrawn as he scooted to the far side of the seat and stared into space. It seemed the weight of the world rested on the waif's narrow shoulders. Gabe was in no mood for idle chatter and Dane allowed him a few minutes before he intruded on the lad's thoughts.

"What's really bothering you. Can I be of any help?" Dane queried as he glanced at the lad whose entire body slumped discouragingly.

"Nay. Thanks jest the same. The problem is mine alone to solve—unless yer good at performin' miracles," Gabe replied absently, propping her elbows on her knees so her fists could hold her aching head.

A concerned frown etched Dane's bronzed features. "Are you in need of more money or—"

Gabe cut him short with a bitter laugh. "Money don't solve everythin' and this is one of 'em. Money was the beginnin' of this problem, but it ain't got nothin' to do with the solution," she explained, completely baffling Dane. He had no idea what the little wretch was mumbling about and Gabe was not about to go into detail.

Watching the people that lined the streets, Gabe regarded them with disinterest until Dane brought the wagon to a halt in front of a shop. Dane hopped down and motioned for her to follow him inside. After selecting the supplies needed for Hampton Estate, Gabe helped Dane load the goods and then waited ouside while Dane paid the storekeeper.

"Now I intend to buy you the best meal to be had in Bristol," Dane announced as he climbed up beside Gabe.

He whipped the horses and again they lunged forward. Preoccupied with her melancholy thoughts, Gabe was unprepared for the sudden jolt. She tumbled backward, releasing a startled squawk as she landed, sprawled among the sacks and supplies.

"Damn ye!" she hissed, her tone dripping venom as she struggled to her knees. "What the 'ell's wrong with ye?" The amusement in Dane's eyes enraged her further. "I jest saved yer good-fer-nothin' neck and ye think to repay me by tryin' to break mine! Noblemen!" she snorted cynically. "Ain't one of 'em got a decent bone in their bodies. Yer cold-'earted, calloused . . ." Her voice trailed off in a long list of inaudible curses and for the life of her, Gabe didn't know why she was being polite enough to keep them to herself.

Dane chuckled at the irate bundle of spirit who shot daggers at him with those fiery green eyes. "I warned you before, but it seems you didn't take heed. Perhaps next time you'll be prepared," he countered, a wide grin settling in the lines of his handsome face.

With an indignant growl, Gabe clambered back to the seat and plopped down beside Lord Hampton. "I swear ye did that on purpose, ye bunglin' fop! I'd like to save yer assailant the trouble and do away with ye meself! It would give me excessive pleasure to bring ye to yer knees," she snapped hatefully.

Dane threw back his head and laughed out loud. "I'm sure you will manage to put an end to me sooner or later, Gabe. I think I rather enjoy the suspense of wondering how and when."

The anger suddenly drained from Gabe's smudged features. "This ain't no laughin' matter,

Cap'n. 'Ave ye any idea who wanted ye dead or why? It was no accident today and I'm willin' to bet that ambush on the road was planned, too."

Pausing a moment to contemplate the lad's words, Dane tried to find some logical explanation, but he could not come up with one. "I don't have the slightest idea who is responsible or what they could hope to gain by my death unless I have some mysterious enemy who merely cannot abide the sight of me." With a faint smile, Dane focused his attention on Gabe's concerned face. "Let's don't dwell on it. I promised you a fine meal and you shall have it."

When they walked into the café, Gabe halted by the door, gazing at the well-dressed men and women who were seated before her. She was definitely out of place. This establishment catered to the wealthy aristocrats, not the common man.

"I can't come in 'ere. I'd stick out like a weed in a flower garden. I ain't 'ungry any'ow. I'll jest wait outside."

As Gabe wheeled around, Dane grabbed her arm, halting her hasty flight. "Nonsense, lad. You may not be dressed to meet the king, but you're just as good as anyone here. Now, haven't I heard you say something to that effect yourself?" he quipped, arching a heavy brow as he dragged the reluctant waif to the table with him. He forced Gabe into a chair where she slid down and pulled her dirty cap over her face.

When the waitress wandered toward them, she eyed the shabbily dressed urchin and was about to comment but Dane ordered their meal and sent her on her way with a silencing frown. When her plate was placed before her, Gabe picked at her food, too depressed to eat. Her appetite had vanished with her hope of being free of her uncle's grasp. There seemed no way to defeat him.

"Don't you like the food?" Dane questioned, a concerned frown gathering on his brows.

"I jest ain't 'ungry." Gabe pushed the heaping plate to the side of the table and propped her head on her fists.

After Dane had finished his meal, they traveled to a large mansion on the edge of Bristol. The great stone home was surrounded by beautiful gardens and Gabe couldn't help but stare in awe as they drove up the cobblestone path that led to the double doors. Dane was shown inside the house and returned a few minutes later with a striking, blond-haired gentleman who was almost as handsome as Dane. Gabe gazed at the two men, finding herself lost to the captivating blue eyes of both men. She could just imagine how women would drool at the sight of these two rogues. Beautiful, she mused, a faint smile threatening her mouth. That was the only word to describe them. And yet the blue eyes of the man with Dane were not as distinct as those of the captain. Shaking her head to break the spell, she resumed her role, wiping her smudged face on her dirty sleeve.

"Gabe, bring in our bags. We'll be staying the night. This is the Duke of Sheffwall," Dane said in brief introduction.

Nicholas studied the scrawny urchin, wondering why Lord Hampton was traveling with such a bedraggled pup. Gabe was quick to read his skeptical gaze. Ordinarily, she would have been incensed enough to blurt out some snide remark, but at the moment, she was in no mood to confront the nobleman, much to Dane's relief.

"I'll jest sleep in the barn, Cap'n. I don't want to be no trouble to the duke," she replied as she pulled Dane's luggage from under the seat and climbed down from her perch.

"You are welcome here, lad," Nick offered politely, aware that he had managed to hurt the lad's feelings.

Forcing a shallow smile, Gabe stepped beside the two men and shrugged casually. "Thanks jest the same, but I better—"

"Nonsense. Just grab your bag and come in, boy. Any friend of Dane's is a friend of mine. Now fetch your bag," he insisted, waving away another argument from Gabe.

When Gabe returned to the house, she was first shown to Dane's room and then to her own small quarters which was a few doors down the hall. As she stepped to the door of the study, she found Dane and Nicholas in their high-backed velvet chairs with snifters of brandy sitting between them. She peeked around the corner, hoping to draw Dane's attention without making a grand entrance.

When Dane finally noticed the waif cowering against the door casing, his brows furrowed curiously. "What is it, Gabe?"

"May I 'ave a word with ye, Cap'n?" she inquired timidly.

Startled by the sudden change in Gabe's temperament, Dane's brows furrowed acutely.

"I know it ain't polite to impose on me host, but do ye think 'e would mind if I asked fer a bath?"

"I'll have the tub in my room filled. You can bathe there. 'Tis the least I can do for the lad who saved my life," he added with a quick wink and a wide smile that spoke of fond affection for the little urchin.

As Dane reached out to pat her on the shoulder, Gabe backed away as if she had been scorched by his touch. She ducked her head as a strange tingle flew down her spine. To him, she was but a shabby waif who had wandered accidentally into his life. She had thought she could handle the dashing rogue she encountered during the day, but now she was beginning to wonder if even that was becoming too difficult. The emotions that she had allowed to appear at night were begging to seep into the day. Gabe could not allow her eyes to fill with something other than disinterest in the captain. It was too dangerous for him to touch her or even to stand close. Yet, she welcomed having him near.

"Thanks, Cap'n. I'd appreciate it," she mumbled as she hurried up the steps.

Dane frowned at the lad's strange behavior. He had been acting odd all afternoon and Dane could not fathom the cause. With a careless shrug, he dismissed the thought of Gabe and returned to his chair and his brandy.

After returning to her quarters, Gabe paced the floor, pondering her misfortune. She gathered her bag and walked into Dane's room where she found the bath awaiting her. With the door locked behind her, she inspected the terrace to ensure that no one could intrude on her privacy. Brielle stripped from her garb and settled herself in the soothing liquid, leaning back against the rim of the tub to enjoy her solitude.

For a few fleeting moments, she was a young woman again. She savored what little time she was allowed to pamper herself. Floating lazily in her bath, Gabrielle closed her eyes, letting her mind drift. It settled on a handsome, bronzed face that was framed with shiny raven hair and embedded with glowing sapphires. With a despairing moan, she stepped from the tub and pulled on her tattered breeches and shirt. Gabe hurried back to her own room to continue her toiletry. With her long hair brushed to a silky shine, she climbed into the middle of her soft bed and let her weariness dissolve into a restless sleep. The twisted, red face of John Jarmon hovered over her. His contemptuous sneer made her skin crawl with repulsion. Each time she turned from him, he appeared again, refusing to let her escape. Even in slumber she could not be free from his grasp.

"What do you think of my valet?" Dane questioned as he and Nick sat consuming the large stock of liquor.

"I think he looks like a starving bag of bones. Where in the hell did you find such a poor excuse for a human being?" the duke mocked playfully as he propped his feet up in front of him and sent

Dane a silly smile.

"He found *me* on the way back from London. He's an orphan," Dane explained, his voice slurring slightly.

"I was surprised to see you traveling with such a scrawny brat," Nick admitted with a chuckle. "He doesn't look to be worth his weight. He's so frail and undernourished. I don't see how he could be of any use to you."

"I'm sure you think it strange to find companionship with a waif, but he has a way of brightening a dull day," Dane commented tritely as he poured himself another drink. "He's managed to save my life twice. The lad seems to have a sixth sense. In the face of danger he's as quick and agile as a cat. Gabe may not look like much, but he has managed to gain my respect." Dane eased back in his chair and thoughtfully studied his glass of brandy. "The boy is cocky, quick-witted, and badgers me incessantly. But for some reason I enjoy it. At times he even becomes my conscience, daring to voice opinions that most servants would never utter to a gentleman." He peered at Nick, wondering if he could ever begin to understand the subtle friendship that had developed between the nobleman and the waif. Dane doubted it. *He* wasn't even sure why he was drawn to that insolent bag of bones.

"To each his own," Nick replied with a leisurely shrug. "I prefer the company of delectable young women." He raised his glass to toast silently the many lovely faces that passed before his eyes.

"When it comes to satisfying my basic need for

affection, I heartily agree. However, I still prefer fencing words with Gabe than stumbling through a boring conversation with the beauties of our social circle." A wry smile pursed his lips as Nick arched a heavy brow. "Of course, Monica is the exception. I don't classify her in the same category. The rest of them do little to stimulate my intellect," he added cynically.

"What's this about the lad saving your life?" Sheffwall queried. The intoxicating effect of the brandy had begun to encircle his senses and he was having difficulty keeping up with the conversation.

Dane struggled up from his stuffed chair and peered at Nick who was beginning to become a swimming blur. "Someone took a shot at me when I was returning from London." He pulled his hair away from his forehead, revealing the scar. "Gabe found me and took me to Lord Jarmon's home to be nursed back to health. If Gabe hadn't come along I might have died during the storm. And then today, when I walked out of the Squires' brothel, someone hurled a dagger at me. Gabe leaped out of the wagon, knocking me from its path. The alert little whelp has shown his worth. I owe him my life," Dane admitted humbly, although his thick tongue and lazy words camouflaged his emotion.

"Who the devil is trying to kill you?" Nick questioned, his pale-blue eyes wide in concern.

"I have no idea, but whoever it is has managed to keep track of every move I make. I can't imagine who detests me so much that they want me dead. I didn't realize I had made such a vicious enemy."

Dane mumbled as he weaved unsteadily across the room. He grabbed the back of a nearby chair to keep from stumbling forward, the room swirling about him. As he looked up at the clock on the mantel, he squinted, trying to see the hands that appeared to be waving at him. How many hours had passed since they had sat down with their brandy? And how many bottles had they consumed? Dane squinted again. The hands of the clock were still bidding him good night. Lord, he was drunk. He muttered under his breath at his foolishness.

"I think I'll call it a night, Nick. Thank you for the hospitality." Lord Hampton struggled toward the study door and braced his hands against the casing.

Peering across the dark entryway, he wondered if he could scale the long mountain of stairs without a mishap. With a determined sigh, Dane started forward, groping for the banister to pull himself upward. As he climbed the dark steps he heard a clatter and a miserable groan below him.

"Nick, is that you?"

"Yes," came the painful whisper from the darkness.

"Are you all right?" Dane moved cautiously toward the doleful sound, wishing his guardian angel would suddenly appear and come to his aid.

"I suppose so. I think 'tis only my pride that has been bruised. The rest of me is too numb to feel the pain. Just help me to my feet," Sheffwall groaned as he extended his arm to Dane.

The two men stumbled forward and said good

night before going their separate ways at the top of the stairs. Dane carefully edged along the wall and found the door to his room. As he stepped into his quarters, he shed his clothes and crawled into bed, wishing he had been less indulgent with Sheff-wall's stock of brandy. With an agonizing groan, he pulled the quilt up to his chest and stared into the blackness that swam before him. An alluring silhouette floated above him in hazy clouds, beckoning him to reach upward to touch the elusive dream that was ever present in his thoughts.

When he closed his eyes a tender voice whispered to him, soothing away all of the tension of the day. She was with him wherever he happened to be. Even in the brothel that afternoon while he had made love to a most desirable woman, the image had risen above him, denying him the pleasure he had anticipated. He was plagued by that dark face that granted him neither peace nor satisfaction. As he drifted off into an intoxicated dream, the mysterious beauty gently touched his lips, bidding him to sleep well. A contented smile curved his mouth as his broad chest rose and fell in methodic rhythm. Drowsiness encompassed him, sending him sailing across another sea of fantasy.

A cool breeze swept in from the balcony doors as Gabrielle stepped in from the shadows, moving toward the sleeping form. She had been awakened by the commotion on the stairs and had lain in bed, cursing the need to feel Dane's strong arms sheltering her from troubled thoughts. Her hand brushed across his bare chest, feeling the matting

143

of hair that trailed down his muscular belly. As Gabrielle bent down to press her lips to his, an unexplainable warmth encompassed her. She always drew strength from his nearness.

When Dane became aware of the gentle kiss, he slowly responded to her embrace, knowing who was with him. He could never be sure if this dark goddess was flesh or fantasy. His intoxicated condition only made it more difficult to distinguish the difference. Because of his vivid nightmares and the appearances of his guardian angel, he had almost given up hope of being the sane man he had once been.

"How did you get here?" His voice slurred as he reached up to touch her soft face in a long, lingering caress. He was a blind man who was learning to see with his hands. The delicate lines of her face spoke of rare beauty.

"It makes no difference how or why, m'lord," she replied in a raspy whisper.

"How did you find me here?" he persisted, ignoring her vague reply.

"Here?" she repeated quizzically. "Are you certain that *you* have not come to find *me* here?"

"Are you trying to drive me mad?" he asked, his head rolling hopelessly to the side to stare into the darkness.

She chuckled softly and then placed a light kiss on his lips. "Perhaps, m'lord. And then again, maybe you have already crossed that bridge of your own accord."

Dane focused his attention on the faceless shadow. He was sure of nothing. He could have

144

been in heaven or hell. At that moment he was too drunk to care, as long as this mysterious image was with him. "I must be mad," he admitted sluggishly, "but if you stay in my arms, it makes no difference."

As Dane's breath caressed her cheek, Brielle smiled to herself. The scent of brandy intermingled with the manly fragrance that hovered about him. "I fear you have been drinking. Are you attempting to add yet another sin to your extensive list?"

Dane's hand made a slow descent on her back and then he encircled her in his arms, a guilty smile tracing his lips. "'Twas that or molesting angels. I thought perhaps you would prefer the lesser of two evils," he murmured as an unseen smile curved his lips. "Come comfort me. I've had a very disturbing day." He pulled her onto his bare chest, inhaling her sweet fragrance bathed in the freshness of night air.

Brielle complied with his hushed request. All of her restraints took flight. She yearned for the comfort that would dissolve her anxieties. "It seems we have both had a trying day, m'lord."

Dane cocked his head to one side as she nuzzled against his shoulder, seeking the security that he could offer. "What troubles you?" he questioned softly.

"Nothing now." A contented sigh escaped her lips and she pressed a light kiss to his neck. "It seems rather ironic that a guardian angel should seek consolation from Satan's advocate, especially one who appears to be very experienced."

"And how do you know that?" Dane inquired, his brow arching in mild amusement. It seemed that she knew as much about him as she had often claimed. How could anyone know his every move unless . . . No, it couldn't be. He refused to believe that she was involved, not when she was lying in his arms, yielding to his kisses. After all, she wasn't really here at all. This was only another dream.

The thought of Dane's afternoon interlude skipped across Gabrielle's mind and she drew away. "You don't hold me with the fumbling embrace of innocence. Even I can tell the difference between a master and an apprentice," she whispered, her tone quietly accusing him of promiscuousness.

"I am but a man and I fall short of perfection," he explained, making no attempt to deny her words. "Lie down beside me and bring me the only contentment I have yet to find."

As he wrapped his arms about her waist, Gabrielle melted against him. She released a melancholy sigh and a fretful tear. She was tired of being strong and independent. All she wanted was to forget her troubles for a few brief moments, letting Dane's warm embrace protect her from the cruel world. In that small space of time nothing mattered except that they held each other. Their troubled souls merged, seeking a moment of serenity. No words were needed. There were no promises, no regrets, only an unspoken assurance that in peaceful dreams they could find contentment.

Dane's world was a hazy blur and he slipped

into an intoxicated fantasy. When Gabrielle felt him relax, she reluctantly eased from his side after placing a gentle kiss on his unresponsive lips. As she stepped out onto the terrace, she paused, bracing her arms on the railing, staring at the blackened sky that was sprinkled with glistening diamonds. Only the darkness brought contentment, she mused, releasing a weary sigh. The time she spent in Dane's arms gave her the strength to search for a solution to her dilemma.

Strange, she mused thoughtfully. Both of them possessed a double identity. Dane was stern, commanding, and authoritative during the day. But at night, he was a compassionate man who sought the same comfort for which she searched.

As she turned and walked away her soft, flowing gown clung to her, bathed in the moon's silver glow. Dane roused long enough to see her silhouette disappear in the darkness. It was a dream, he muttered to himself. His dark angel appeared from out of nowhere and then vanished in the shadows. He was going to have to get a grasp on himself, he thought drowsily. These fantasies must come to an end or he would have to be put away!

Chapter Six

Gabe took time to pin her hair securely in place and properly smudge her cheeks before facing the cooks and groomsmen. With her morning duties accomplished, she returned to the house to find Nicholas and Dane in the dining room, eating in silence.

"Good mornin', Cap'n, Duke," she greeted cheerfully. A broad grin spread across her lips as she regarded the disheveled men.

"Not so loud, Gabe," Dane groaned as he rubbed his aching head, attempting to hold it in the least painful position.

"Please spare us your pleasantries, lad. As you can see, we are not up to them yet," Nick chided and then sipped his steaming tea.

Gabe crossed her arms on her chest, carefully surveying the noblemen. A devilish thought came to mind and she quickly pursued it. She dragged out the chair beside Dane, letting it screech across the tiled floor, watching in amusement as the men cringed.

When they peered menacingly at her with their bloodshot eyes, Gabe feigned concern. "Why, Cap'n, I do believe ye and the duke are a bit under the weather. Is it some sort of malady like the one I 'ad last winter? I thought I was goin' to die. Me 'ead felt like it was swollen up to twice its size and me innards were on fire. Gawd, I ain't never—"

"Sit down and dispense with the details," Dane snapped curtly. "I'm sure you know what ails us."

"Aye, Cap'n." Biting back a mischievous grin, Gabe offered them a snappy salute and scuffled into her seat as noisily as possible, drawing glares from both men.

Dane focused his attention on Gabe's grimy face and rolled his eyes in disgust. "I swear you must have bathed in dirt and water," he muttered. "I don't think you know the meaning of the word, *clean.*"

The waif's smeared chin tilted rebelliously. "*Clean* is a luxury afforded by the idle rich," she retorted. "The common lot 'ave to work and sweat. We're used to toil and grime. That don't 'old true fer lords and dukes." As she reached for a biscuit, another impish grin caught her lips, curving them upward. She stuffed the bun in her mouth and continued, "When I own me own grand estate, ye won't see no dirt on me face. Until then I'll 'ave to scratch and claw in the dirt to make me livin'."

Dane shot the insolent wretch a condemning glower as he listened to the muffled reply. Nick chuckled to himself, watching the captain and the waif taunt each other. Dane had said the lad was a sprite little imp and Nick had to agree. Gabe seemed to thrive on mischievousness.

Before they finished their meal, Gabe scooted back in her chair, creating the same disturbing screech, and then went upstairs to gather their luggage. She descended the steps, banging their belongings against the banister. Although Dane would have preferred to strangle the lad, he bided his time, swearing to even the score later.

As they rode to Bristol, Gabe turned beside Dane and tugged on his sleeve to gain his attention.

"Cap'n, I've a favor to ask of ye. I wish to stop at the dry goods store so I kin pick up a few thin's I'll be needin'."

"We were there yesterday. Why didn't you buy your supplies then?" Dane scowled. He was in a foul mood and had not planned any stops.

"I wasn't exactly sure what I wanted yesterday," she said, her voice rising testily. "Good Gawd, Cap'n, surely ye will allow this small detour. I could 'ave spent the whole damned afternoon talkin' to those stupid nags while ye dilly-dallied in yer whore'ouse! I ain't askin' ye to wait all day on me; jest a few minutes. 'Tis a small request, seein' 'ow I saved yer worthless 'ide twice."

"All right! All right!" Dane growled as he waved his hand for silence. "We'll stop. Just quit yelling. My head is pounding and I have no desire to continue this argument." He rubbed his fingertips into his temples, attempting to relieve his throbbing head. Between the rumbling wagon and Gabe's loud, nasal voice, Dane's sensitive nerves were dancing across his skin like stabbing pins.

"Thanks, Cap'n," Gabe replied, delighting in badgering him in his misery. He was getting exactly what he deserved.

As Dane pulled back on the reins, he reached into his pocket and tossed a pouch of coins to the waif. Gabe glanced from the sack to the captain and then returned his money with a determined shake of her head.

"I don't need a 'andout. I got me own funds fer what I want to buy."

Again Dane placed the pouch in her grubby hand. "Consider this a reward for your bravery yesterday. It's my way of saying thank you. Buy yourself something with it," he urged, a faint smile grazing his lips.

She hopped down from the wagon and wheeled around to face Dane, flipping the pouch up for him to catch. "Ye gave me a roof over me 'ead and kept me from starvin'. I ask no more of ye, Cap'n."

Before Dane could argue with her, Gabe spun on her heels and leaped onto the boardwalk. Dane frowned thoughtfully. The lad wanted nothing from him except the opportunity to badger him. He accepted no money other than what he had earned from his duties. Dane was certain that what Gabe intended to buy was for someone other than himself. That was the waif Dane knew—stubborn, fiery, ornery, but extremely unselfish.

Gabe hastily purchased a set of clothes, a small gold watch, an iron shackle, and a medallion.

After stuffing the package under the seat, she pulled herself up beside Dane, settled herself on the hard seat, and prepared for their long journey.

While Gabe was daydreaming, Dane grinned wickedly, ready to have his revenge for the waif's morning harassment. With a quick pop of the reins, the wagon jerked forward, throwing Gabe back into the pile of feed sacks.

Dane chuckled victoriously and continued down the street at a reckless pace, leaving Gabe tumbling helplessly in the back of the wagon. He slowed the steeds to allow two gentlemen to cross in front of them, but he immediately regretted the courtesy. With an enraged growl, Gabe crawled up behind him and yanked the startled captain backward, sending him rolling among the supplies. With Dane flat on his back, Gabe plopped her bottom on his belly and glared into his face, her green eyes alive with indignation.

"It ain't so damned funny when yer the one who gets dumped, is it, Cap'n? The next time ye pull that trick, I swear I'll save yer mysterious sniper the trouble and cut out yer black 'eart meself!"

As quickly as she had sat on him she was scrambling onto the seat to grab the reins. With a slight nod and a pleasant smile to the two men who had stopped to watch the tussle, she spoke politely, "'Mornin' gents. Fine day, ain't it?"

Gabe slapped the horses and sent them away at a fast clip while Dane lay sprawled in the back of the wagon, too humiliated to raise his throbbing head. He decided to ride where he was until they were on open road. When there was only the countryside as witness, Dane reached up to grab a handful of the skinny urchin's shirt, pulling Gabe down with him. Although she struggled against him, Gabe was no match for his superior strength. Her main concern was keeping her cap on her head. After rolling Gabe to her stomach and jabbing his knee in her back to keep her pinned down, Dane chuckled in satisfaction.

"Now, you ornery little whelp, you are about to receive your punishment for embarrassing me in front of the whole damned town. I should have done this long ago. I'm certain that you have never had your backside paddled; otherwise you wouldn't behave as you do. It's time you were taught a little discipline."

"Don't ye dare touch me, ye blackguard!" Gabe squawked as she began squirming for escape. "If ye lay a 'and on me, ye'll regret it!"

"Ply me with no threats. Your time has come and, by God, I'm going to enjoy extracting my revenge," Dane assured her.

His hand came down, cracking the morning air and her buttocks. A self-satisfied grin settled on his handsome features as he listened to Gabe's furious yelp. After four sound swats, he released the waif and climbed onto the seat, glancing over his shoulder to ensure that there would be no further attacks by the fuming ragamuffin.

Gabe rubbed her stinging backside and grimaced in pain. Dane's blue eyes sparkled with pleasure until she threatened him again. "Ye damned seadog. I ain't never goin' to forget that!" she swore, her voice acid with anger. "Ye'll rue the day ye laid a 'and on me!"

"You just see that *you* don't forget it," Dane countered, waving a lean finger in her direction. "Next time maybe you'll think twice before you attack me. Now get up here and sit down."

"Sit down? 'Ell, me rear is too bruised fer sittin'. I'll jest stay where I am. Thanks jest the same, Cap'n," she spat, sneering as she spoke his title as if it left a bitter taste in her mouth. Jerking her head away from his undaunted smile, she raised a proud but smudged chin. "Yer damned right I'll think twice before I attack ye. And when I git even with ye, I'll make sure ye can't touch me before I kin escape."

After an hour of brittle silence, Gabe climbed back onto the seat and set her mind to solving her problem. Saxon's words kept ringing in her ears. She did not intend to spend the rest of her life dressed as an urchin; nor did she plan to marry the Duke of Fairleigh. Her foremost concern was the contract. How much time would have to pass before the duke would tear up the agreement?

A concerned frown etched her face as she pondered her choices while Dane was lost to pleasant dreams. He had come to the conclusion that the shadowed form who visited him in darkness was nothing more than a fantasy. There was simply no other explanation for it. No woman could appear from nowhere, know everything about him, and disappear without a trace, unless she was never really there at all. Her misty image was with him during the day as well as night. Dane was certain that his nightmares had sent him

154

falling over the edge of reality. Last night in an intoxicated dream, his dark angel had come to him again. With patient tenderness she had lain in his embrace, bringing him contentment. But, of course, that was impossible. How could she sneak into Nick's house and find him? He had been too drunk to know what had happened. It was time he had a heart-to-heart talk with himself. He simply could not go on believing in faceless angels!

Gabe had come to a decision during her silent reverie. Once she had plotted her course of action, her face revealed her satisfaction. There was a way to destroy the contract and her uncle's spiteful plans and she had thought of it! There was one thing that John would never have expected her to do and she would do it. The plan would send John into an enraged frenzy and she would delight in seeing the look on his shriveled face when she told him.

She glanced at Dane, wondering why he seemed so melancholy. "What's the matter, Cap'n? Are ye sorry now that ye treated me so brutally?" she quipped, her brow arching slightly.

"No, Gabe. You got exactly what you deserved," Dane insisted as he shut out the image that swam above him and focused his attention on the waif.

"Yer the one who started it! That was the third time ye threw me backward and laughed at yer own cleverness," Gabe reminded him with an indignant snort.

"Let's call a truce. I'm in no mood for quarreling with you," Dane admitted as he gazed into the vibrant green eyes of the youth; their expressiveness lifted his low spirits and brought a faint smile to his lips.

"Fine with me, Cap'n. I ain't fond of fightin', especially with a bloke who's bigger than me," Gabe retorted and then plunged on, hardly taking a breath. "I'm goin' to take tomorrow off."

Dane arched a heavy brow and studied the tilt of Gabe's stubborn chin. "What the hell ever happened to 'may I please' or 'would it meet with your approval'? Are you demanding or requesting, Gabe?"

The urchin shrugged nonchalantly. "Take it 'owever ye wish, but I'm takin' me day off. I got somethin' important to do."

"I only allowed you half a day, remember?" Dane peered at the wretch, knowing he was about to yield to the lad, but not without a struggle. Gabe deserved a full day and they both knew it.

"'Ere I've saved yer ungrateful neck twice and gettin' favors from ye is worse than tryin' to lead a jackass where 'e don't want to go! Yer the most unappreciative bloke I've ever 'ad the misfortune of knowin'." Gabe shook her head in frustration and then pulled a sour face at the captain. "Gawd, I wished I would 'ave stayed in Bristol."

"If you had your way, I would deed Hampton Estate over to you. *I* would become *your* servant. And if that weren't enough you would expect me to greet you every morning with a humble 'thank you.' Well, young man, you can have the whole damned day," Dane offered, flinging his arm in an exaggerated gesture.

A broad grin split Gabe's face and she nodded

slightly. "Thanks, Cap'n. I was plannin' on takin' the entire day any'ow. After all, I don't owe ye much. I intend to keep it that way. If I wanted to leave fer good I could, ye know. I ain't yer bond slave."

"And just where would you go? No one else would put up with your abominable manners and your fiery temper," Dane retorted with a sarcastic smirk.

A smug grin spread across Gabe's smudged face as she rearranged her jerkin and straightened herself on the seat as if she were sitting on a red velvet throne and the world was her kingdom. "Ye kin make fun of me now if ye like, but one day, Cap'n, I'll own a large estate. I'll 'ave all the money I could ever need. There will be servants waitin' on me 'and and foot. I'll 'ave a stable of fine steeds and there'll be gardens of lovely flowers surroundin' the place. Jest wait and see if I ain't right."

"I wouldn't dare dispute your word, your majesty," Dane mocked, tipping his hat to the wretch. "It will most likely be *my* estate that you have overthrown. I do believe that you have decided to drive me mad with your insolence. Once you have succeeded, you'll have me sign the land over to you while I'm in a demented state." His brows furrowed thoughtfully, wondering if in jest, he had hit upon the truth.

"Yer a clever one, Cap'n. Ye've discovered me scheme." A devilish grin found its way to her emerald eyes and Dane swallowed hard. "I'll 'ave that dreadful 'Iggins callin' me 'Lord Gabe' and

157

ye'll be stashed away in the attic, livin' on bread and water while I dine on the finest foods."

The waif spoke with so much confidence that Dane was certain that the scrawny little wretch believed every word of it. If ever a pauper would become a prince, it would be Gabe.

Suddenly, Gabe remembered the package. "Oh! I almost fergot!" she exclaimed. As she reached beneath the seat to pull the parcel onto her lap, Dane frowned curiously. After unwrapping the small box, Gabe placed its contents in Dane's hand. A delighted smile crept to her lips. "Fer ye, Cap'n. Me way of sayin' thanks fer takin' me under yer wing."

Dane dangled the chain from his fingers and studied the gold medallion. A skeptical expression settled on his bronzed features. "Why did you give me this?"

Gabe shrugged leisurely. "Ye've bin good to me. I'd be sleepin' in the streets and fightin' the rats fer me dinner if ye 'adn't given me a place to lodge. Besides," she added, sending a hasty sidelong glance in Dane's direction, "a traveler like ye needs protection. St. Christopher is an excellent companion. 'E might make me job easier. Ye've already 'ad two mis'aps. I need all the 'elp I kin git when it comes to keepin' ye out of trouble."

"I thought you said you didn't believe in guardian angels and saints," Dane reminded him, a mocking smile grazing his lips.

When Gabe peered into his sapphire eyes that mirrored fond affection, she grinned sheepishly. "I don't, Cap'n, but there ain't nothin' wrong with

158

bein' cautious.''

Dane fastened the pendant around his neck and grinned at Gabe. "Thank you for the gift. It was thoughtful of you."

When the wagon was emptied of the supplies, Gabe took the horses to the stables and was met by Nate's beaming face.

"'Ello, Nate. 'Ave ye taken good care of Blanco while I was away?''

Nate nodded affirmatively as he stepped up to help the lady from the wagon. Gabe glanced cautiously about, hoping that no one was watching the two of them.

"Please don't treat me any differently than you ever have," she gently rebuked, leaning close to his ear. "Someone might think it rather odd for you to be helping me out of a wagon."

The lad dropped his arms and backed away, waiting for Gabe to hop down. After grabbing her package, Gabe motioned for Nate to follow her around to the side of the stables. She pulled the watch out in front of Nate and then placed it in his hand.

"I wanted you to have something special, Nate," she explained as she watched Nate brush his fingers over the gold timepiece. He urged her to take it back, but Gabe would not accept it. "'Tis yours to keep. You are my trusted friend and I wanted you to have it." She dropped her head for a moment and then looked back into Nate's dark eyes. "Now I have a favor to ask of you. I'm leaving tonight," she began, but Nate shook his head, silently pleading with her. "I have to go. There is

159

something I must do and I may not return. Please have Blanco saddled and waiting for me about twelve o'clock. I'll need some food for my trip if you can manage it." Disappointment was mirrored in Nate's eyes and Gabe smiled ruefully. "If things don't work out the way I hope they will, I will be forced to return. But if they do"—she placed a light kiss on his cheek—"I'll always remember you. Please do as I ask. This is the way it must be."

As Gabe ambled to the front door, she breathed a tired sigh and stepped inside to meet Higgins' disgruntled frown. At the foot of the stairs, she turned back to see the servant still staring at her with his usual, disapproving expression.

"I didn't miss ye a damned bit neither, 'Iggins." She snorted.

The servant stiffened in outrage. "Just mind your tongue, you filthy little guttersnipe! If I had my way you'd sleep in the stables under the horses' hoofs," he snapped, waving a threatening finger toward the undaunted waif.

"If I 'ad me way, ye wouldn't be 'ere at all, 'Iggins," she sneered before spinning on her heels and stalking up the stairs.

There was something about Higgins that Gabe didn't like. Her intuition told her that he was not at all what he appeared. His hazel eyes revealed his inner soul and she found nothing there that denoted kindliness. His manners were staunch, his face cold and stern. Even his occasional smiles seemed to be forced. There was nothing pleasant about him and Gabe saw no reason to waste her time trying to be polite to him.

After seeing to her chores, Gabe sneaked up to her room for a short nap to see her through the long night that awaited her. When she started upstairs that evening with water for her bath, Dane strolled out of the study, reading a letter.

"Take that to my room," he ordered blandly. "I'm retiring early this evening. I want my bath ready when I come up."

"Aye, Cap'n," she muttered as she struggled up the steps with buckets dangling from both hands.

With his bath prepared, Gabe began carrying water for her own toiletry. After several trips up and down the stairs, her tub was filled. She was about to strip from her garb when she heard Dane call out her name.

Grumbling under her breath, Gabe went to the captain's door. "Do ye need somethin'?"

"Come in here."

Gabe opened the door and immediately sucked in her breath. Dane was barely concealed by a towel that was wrapped about his waist. She wheeled to face the wall, her face flushing crimson red. Although she was trying to mask her embarrassment she had failed miserably. His bronzed chest, covered with a thick matting of hair, his sinewy arms, and his muscular legs were arousing as well as embarrassing. Lord, he was the picture of masculinity and Gabe could not keep her thoughts from the direction they were taking. Although she studied the empty wall, she could visualize his virile frame as if it had been implanted in her brain.

Dane studied the discomfited lad and frowned thoughtfully. Why was that wretch so unnerved by the sight of another man? With a reckless shrug, Dane dismissed the thought. Gabe had probably never seen a naked man or woman in his life. But a time would come when Gabe would not bat an eye at the sight of bare flesh, he mused with a smirk.

"I left a black ledger on the desk in the study. Will you bring it to me? I want to look over a few more items before I retire." His tone was business-like, ignoring Gabe's embarrassed state.

Gathering her composure, Gabe turned to face the captain. Her emerald eyes never wavered as they locked with his deep pools of sapphire; she surprised Dane by her sudden change of mood. "Aye, Cap'n. Anythin' else? A cup of tea?" she questioned, seemingly indifferent to his appearance.

"Perhaps a brandy," Dane replied as he strolled to the commode to comb his hair.

Gabe swallowed with a gulp as the towel parted to reveal the entire length of his thigh. Where was that extra layer of dirt on her face when she needed it? "Aye," she mumbled as she rushed from the room, relieved that she had not been called upon to perform some duty that would have caused her further embarrassment.

After she had retrieved the book and poured the brandy, she took a large gulp of the liquor, hoping to calm her nerves. It only set her stomach on fire and she gasped and choked to catch her breath. When she returned with the ledger Dane had donned a blue velvet robe and sauntered forward to

162

take the book.

A faint smile reached Dane's lips as he accepted the brandy. "Thank you, Gabe. The rest of the evening is yours as well as all day tomorrow. Where are you going?" he questioned curiously.

"On one of them all-day picnics."

"Well, do enjoy yourself," Dane retorted, not believing a word the lad spoke.

"I will," she said, presenting him with a subtle smile. "G'night, Cap'n." She turned to go, but paused by the door, glancing over her shoulder.

"Yes, Gabe?" Dane queried, his heavy brow arching at the waif's hesitation. There was a hint of remorse in Gabe's eyes and Dane had the feeling that the lad would have liked to tell him the truth.

Hanging her head, Gabe shrugged noncommittally and closed the door behind her.

After returning to her room, she tossed her garments in a pile and eased down into the cool water. She shivered, wondering if it was from anticipation or just a reaction to the chilly bath.

With her hair brushed and lying about her shoulders like a shimmering cape, Gabrielle snuffed out the lantern and slipped onto the terrace. Gathering her courage she strolled barefooted across the balcony and then moved inside Dane's darkened room.

Dane had checked over the ledgers in the dim lantern light until his eyes burned and he gave up the tedious chore. He crawled into bed knowing that very soon the vision would come before him. Again he would be lost to a fantasy. The woman of his dreams would have no face, no name, and no voice. She was something his mind had conjured up to represent the perfect woman. And yet, in perfection, there was nothing distinct about her. The shadow was above him, beside him, beckoning him to reach out and touch its elusive silhouette. With a despairing sigh, Dane rolled to his side, muttering under his breath, wishing sleep would come to spare him. Dane dozed, but raised heavy eyelids when he heard the raspy whisper from behind him.

The pained expression on Dane's dark face made Gabrielle frown thoughtfully. "Is something troubling you, m'lord? May I be of help?"

"Yes, you could, but you have already discouraged me from pursuing my passions where you are concerned," he replied bitterly, staring at the shadowed vision above him.

Her velvety laughter melted his ire. How could he be spiteful to his guardian angel? A reluctant smile grazed Dane's lips as Gabrielle reached out to caress his cheek.

"I can hardly believe that satisfying your desires could be your problem, sir. It seems you have found pleasure in many arms. I fear that you have a lusty appetite."

Dane propped himself up on an elbow and tenderly stroked the satiny flesh of her arm. "Perhaps only an angel could appease the craving that I have yet to satisfy in my wanderings."

"I doubt that human or immortal could accomplish that task, m'lord. What you seek may not even exist. Is there such a thing on earth as total contentment?'' Gabrielle questioned, the playfulness vanishing from her whispered voice.

"Suppose you answer that, love. After all, *you* have claimed to be the angel, not I.'' Dane ran his hand along her shoulder to the curve of her neck, wondering why it was so dark in his room. It seemed even the moon and stars refused to aid him in his quest to know her identity, if indeed she had one.

"I have never found that of which you speak. But then I know nothing of love or passion,'' Brielle confessed, hoping that he would recall her words before this evening ended. "Is it so different from the special feeling people have for one another in quiet moments such as these?''

"It can be quite different and yet very much the same,'' Dane murmured as he pressed taunting kisses to her neck.

"You talk in circles, sir,'' Gabrielle breathed raggedly.

"Just as you do, my dark angel. My reply was no more ambiguous than any answer I have yet received from you.'' His hand slipped beneath the bodice of her gown, lightly caressing her breast.

Gabrielle held her breath. His warm kisses found her lips, savoring the sweetness of her response. As his arms came slowly about her waist, his kiss deepened, devouring the resistance that she might have mustered to draw away.

He could feel her full breasts boring into his chest and Dane desperately fought the urge to seduce her as he would have any other woman who had come to his bed. She was like a fragile flower in his arms—so delicate, so desirable, and so very mysterious. While Gabrielle's arms came timidly around his neck, Dane lay back on the bed. His hands wandered up to caress the firm mounds beneath the white gown, teasing their peaks to tautness. When his kisses traced a searing path down her neck, her pulse quickened in response to his bold touch. As the buttons on the front of her gown were adeptly unfastened, Gabrielle gasped. Her quivering flesh was covered with scalding kisses and he seemed to have twice as many hands as a normal man. They traveled over her skin like burning torches, unnerving her with their ability to draw such a wild response from her.

Reality invaded her dreamlike world and Gabrielle fought the urge to pull away from his demanding kisses. Although she knew that this was what she had intended, she was unsure she could continue. Here before her was a devil whose powers over her flesh could not be denied. His touch set raging fires blazing across her skin. She was being smothered by the experienced, exploring hands that sought to know her body as no one had.

The words that she had rehearsed came much too easily from her lips. "Make love to me, Dane. I want to know the passion that exists between a man and a woman." Her trembling hands stroked the lean muscles of his back, loving the feel of his hard flesh beneath her fingertips.

An unseen smile caught his lips. Suddenly his elusive dream was within his grasp, responding to each kiss and caress. For all of the nights she had appeared to him, this was the one that would release him from the moments of which he had dreamed. If this goddess never came to him again, at least he would remember this night as the precious space in time that he had spent with perfection. He was mesmerized by the silky softness of her flesh, by the gentle fragrance that clung to her, and by the raspy voice that had called to him from afar.

"Are you no longer the uncompromising angel who hovers just out of reach?" he murmured against her ear, his hands continuing to draw away her inhibitions. "What must I forfeit to share this moment with you?"

"I am no angel; nor am I a woman. What you hold in your arms is no more than a lost soul who has been tempted beyond its will to resist. All that matters is that I want you. I ask nothing except that you teach me the ways of love."

Her voice was a reassuring whisper that sent Dane's passions soaring. He lifted the gown from her shoulders and tossed it aside. His hand continued to explore the supple form that seemed so warm and willing beside him. "I have wanted you since the first night you came to me, calming my fearful dreams with your gentle voice. I will show you the ways of passion—not because you wish it, but because I long to possess you as no man has. I know you will disappear from me, but the memory of our night together will remain with you. You will yearn for my caress when darkness surrounds you. If another man touches you, it will be me that you remember and desire. Your faceless image has haunted me and remained in my mind no matter where I turn. You will know the torture that has plagued me. You will feel emptiness capture you when you are not in my arms. You will yearn for me alone, my sweet angel," he vowed as his hand slid across her abdomen to her inner thighs.

Gabrielle gazed up at him, torn between the passion he had evoked and the curse he had put upon her. With all the patience Dane possessed, he controlled his desires to teach this mysterious goddess the ways of love. As his bold manliness pressed against her thigh, Gabrielle squirmed to the side. A vision of a blue-eyed devil, shrouded in darkness, hovered above her. At any moment she knew she would panic and attempt to flee from his intimate embrace. The feel of their bare flesh molded together was exciting and yet so very frightening.

"Why should it be different with you than any other man?" she questioned in ragged breaths.

"I am not satisfying passion, my innocent nymph. I am fulfilling a dream. I am in no hurry to see you leave. I want to touch your heart and soul. I want you to desire me just as I desire you. What we will share, you will find with no other," he persisted as his lips captured the peaks of her breasts.

Gabrielle felt herself surrendering to his skillful touch as a new-found pleasure consumed her. Suddenly she wanted him, not because it was what she had planned, but because she wanted to know the fulfillment of a passion that had set her soul ablaze.

"Love me, Dane," she murmured as she drew his head to hers. "Don't ask for my heart, for that I cannot give. Just love me for this moment. That is all the time we have. There is no tomorrow for us to share."

"No," he insisted as he lifted himself above her, parting her thighs with his muscular hips. "I want all of you. I want you to return to me, needing me as I need you, not only tonight, but every night."

Gabrielle moaned softly as he lowered himself to her. She felt the pulsating hardness press against her tender flesh. When he thrust forward, the burning pain began to smother the wild desire that she had known the previous moment. She could never go through with it, she thought frantically. It was all too frightening. She had to escape.

"No, Dane. Please. I mustn't," she breathed in panic as she pressed a small but determined hand to the hard wall of his chest.

Dane felt her stiffen beneath him and he knew that she had spoken the truth. She had never been with a man and she was afraid to yield.

"We've come too far, and I want you as I have never wanted another woman. Surrender to me," he demanded as he gazed down into her dark face. "I will be gentle with you. You have nothing to fear. Let me love you, my sweet angel."

Gabrielle yielded to this demon, knowing that his blue eyes were burning into her, drawing her very soul from its secure resting place. She was answering his intimate thrusts, arching to meet his fiery passion.

And then they were soaring to dizzy heights where rapture held them suspended in time. There was no more pain, only a lofty, budding pleasure that she was not sure she could stand. It was nothing comparable to anything she had ever experienced. She soon found the answer she had sought earlier. Together they drifted into a dark reality as an autumn leaf falls slowly toward the earth, cradled by a gentle breath of wind. As they shuddered and clutched each other close they wished that the moment would never come to an end. Theirs had been a special instant in which they had left the world behind in a foggy mist. All that mattered was the strange contentment they had found in each other's secure embrace.

Dane held her tightly to him, knowing that he had found the ultimate end of his recurring dream. The mysterious goddess had matched his passion and evoked new responses from him that he had never expected to experience. This shadowy silhouette who had haunted his waking and sleeping hours had satisfied him as no other had. She had even been with him while he was in the arms of other women, stripping him of the pleasure he might have found, as if she were telling him that only in her embrace could he find total contentment. At last he had learned the pleasure she could bring. He was reluctant to let her go, but at least his dream had an end—a strangely satisfying, long-awaited end.

A slow smile crept to Dane's lips as he recalled her words. "'Tis but a fantasy. If your dreams end, perhaps there will be no tomorrow for which to wake." But of one fact Dane was certain—if the glorious sun raised its head to bring a new dawning day, his mysterious goddess would be there to haunt him again and again, more now than ever before.

An unexplained tear trickled down Brielle's flushed cheek and Dane felt the warm droplet against his chest. "What is it, love?"

"I don't know. Just hold me close. I'm afraid to let go," she whispered as she nuzzled her head against his shoulder.

She had expected to suffer guilt after what she had done. Instead, there was a sense of shame for not regretting any part of it. Leaving his protective embrace was a fearful thought now that she had had fulfillment in his arms.

Dane rolled to his side and gathered her in his arms, letting her weep until her tears dried. It seemed no words were needed except the ones that sprung so easily from his lips.

"Dark angel of the night, I love—"

Gabrielle immediately pressed her trembling fingertips to his lips, forbidding him to continue. "Even you cannot possibly believe what you were about to say; nor can I. You cannot pretend to love what does not really exist. What we shared was a precious memory of time past. It has no present and no future. Do not offer me meaningless words of affection. Let's remember the moment for what it was and attach no empty phrases to it. Just hold

171

me in your arms, not in your heart," she whispered softly.

Laying her head back against his sturdy shoulder, Brielle smiled ruefully as she traced her fingers across his full lips. "I ask nothing more of you and you cannot expect more of me. I know nothing of love and you have spoken only in passion. Innocence does not always indicate foolishness. Even in the darkness my eyes can see the folly of believing your empty words. I'm sure you have uttered the same phrases to many others before me and shall continue to do so after I have gone. 'Tis a ploy, m'lord, and I am well aware of it. My heart and soul must remain free for I am bound to no one."

Dane sought her honeyed lips, wishing that she would trust him enough to allow him to shower her with the words of affection that forced their way to his lips. But she would never believe him; nor would she even try.

Gabrielle answered his demanding kiss with a sense of loss. His words had warmed her heart for an instant; then she remembered what he had told her while they had traveled to Bristol and she closed her ears to the husky voice that might have touched her soul. Reluctantly, she eased from his side, searching for her discarded gown.

"Don't leave me," Dane murmured as he grasped her hand. "Spend the night in my arms. Let me see your face. Tell me your name."

"I cannot."

"Will you come again?"

"I can make no promises. I must go now."

Dane released her hand as if some strange force had compelled him to do so. Fool! His mind screamed frantically. Why are you obeying her request? Force her to reveal herself! Yet, he was powerless, entranced by the dim silhouette that faded in the darkness.

Dane rolled to his side. This dark angel had matched his passion with her own wild desire, sending him to ecstasy with each innocent kiss and caress. She had been the flame that burned within him, warming his soul, bringing him a ray of hope. No woman could compare with the faceless shadow whose fragrance lingered about him and whose raspy whisper could send shivers down his spine.

He couldn't let her go! Wrapping the sheet around him as he rose, he rushed to the terrace, searching for the dark form he had held in his arms. In the moonlit shadows that danced across the gardens, he saw her fleeing image floating gracefully across the grounds below. Where did she go each time she left his arms? Where did she stay during the day? Why had she come to him? Dane raked his fingers through his hair as he watched her silhouette vanish in the shadows. He might never know the answers to his questions.

Dane returned to his room and eventually drifted off to sleep, reliving his dream. And she was with him again, surrendering to his embrace, returning his kisses.

Gabrielle ducked beneath the low-hanging branches along the creek and smiled with relief when she heard Blanco's soft whinny. She planted a quick kiss on Nate's cheek as she took the reins and laid her pouch across the saddle.

"Thank you, Nate. You're a dear friend," she whispered. In the moonlight, Gabrielle could see the frightened expression that etched the lad's face. She attempted to reassure him with a confident smile. "I'll be just fine. Don't let anyone know about me. And if I don't come back, 'tis still our secret. Do you understand?"

Although he did not comprehend the reason for her late-night journey, Nate nodded slightly. She was too lovely and much too mysterious for him to refuse her request. Nate placed his hand over hers and squeezed affectionately as a sad smile grazed his lips.

Brielle edged Blanco along the stream and then changed into her beggar's garb. As she rode through the eerie shadows, her thoughts transported her back to the splendor she had found in Dane's arms. She desperately needed time to sort through her emotions and make some sense of it all. Gabrielle wanted to believe Dane's quiet words of love, but she had seen him come from the arms of other women and had heard his opinion of love from his own lips. She believed he had said the same phrase to every trollop with whom he had fallen into bed to pass a few pleasureful moments. He knew nothing about her, she mused scornfully. How could he expect her to fall for his empty words of love? To Dane she was only another female to conquer. But Gabrielle was afraid he had spoken one truth. She would never forget him, even in the years to come when she would be in the arms of other men. Even as she rode, she recalled his every touch and these memories sent tingles fluttering down her spine. He had branded her mind with his skillful and passionate caresses.

"Why do his eyes flash before me?" she muttered into the chilly breeze that whirled about her face.

Gabrielle was painfully aware that she had forfeited much more than she had intended to give. Although she had yielded to protect herself from her uncle's scheme she had been deeply touched by this man. Had she lost her heart to the blue-eyed rogue? Why did Dane have to be the one man she could never have? No woman could ever satisfy his unquenchable thirst for passion. All of his whispered words of affection were part of a game he played. He was a deceptive devil who sought to possess her body and soul with his experienced caresses and his murmured words of love. She steeled her heart against the tender memory that skipped across her mind. Their time together had been a necessary means to an important end. *She* had used *him* for her purpose. If not for her cause, she would never have yielded to Dane Hampton.

She pressed her legs to Blanco's ribs and the steed flew across the meadow at a reckless pace as though a blue-eyed satan with raven hair followed closely at his heels, seeking his mistress's soul. Fleeing from the tormenting memory of Dane's embrace, Brielle reined toward the road that led to the Jarmon Estate, pursued by a whispering voice that would grant her no peace.

After dismounting a considerable distance from the stables, Gabrielle led her winded steed into the trees behind the barn. She unsaddled and tethered Blanco before sneaking to Sherman's small room.

"Sherman, it's Brielle," she whispered as she nudged her sleeping friend.

The lad came awake with a start, searching the dark face that hovered above him. A broad smile split his face as he reached out to her. "I never thought to see ye agin!"

"May I stay the rest of the night with you? I don't wish to go to the house until morning."

"Ye kin 'ave me bed." Sherman tried to crawl from his straw pallet, but Gabrielle forced him back.

"I'll sleep by the window," she insisted. Her brows arched curiously. "How have you fared since I've been gone?"

Sherman shrugged noncommittally. "I've bin puttin' in me time workin' jest as always. Lord Jarmon was fit to be tied after ye left. 'E was in a frightful fury that terrified the entire 'ouse when 'e went to unlock the door and found ye gone. That old dandy Fairleigh came to call and I guess 'e and Jarmon 'ad a few 'eated words. The duke went stompin' out the door and tore off down the road with a cloud of dust at 'is 'eels. Thin's ain't bin too good 'round 'ere. If I was ye, I'd tread lightly with Lord Jarmon," Sherman urged, his features setting grimly. "Jarmon ain't one to fergit what ye did to 'im."

"If things don't go well, I may have to leave quickly. I left Blanco tied in the trees. Please care for him in the morning and have him ready in case I have to go."

"Ye don't 'ave to worry about yer stallion. Jest be careful," he cautioned as he affectionately squeezed her hand and smiled up at Gabrielle.

She pressed a kiss to his cheek and then curled up in the corner by the window. A gentle pair of arms surrounded her in her weary dreams, giving her the warmth and comfort she sought as she nestled in the prickly straw. Dane's handsome face rose above her, the same face Brielle had vowed never to see in her dreams.

Sherman snuggled into his quilt, wishing he could hold Gabrielle close, but he knew she would never permit it. It seemed the sun had risen in the middle of the night when he had awoke to find her exquisite face above him. Sherman tossed and turned in fitful dreams while emerald eyes sparkled down upon him. It was difficult to accept her sisterly fondness. He wanted much more; yet he was afraid to destroy the strong bond between them. Gabrielle would not accept his affection and it was hard to deny love's first emotion. Sherman breathed a heavy-hearted sigh and resigned himself to the fact that he could only adore Gabrielle from afar.

Chapter Seven

As the sun streamed into the small window, Gabrielle rolled over and lifted heavy eyelids to its bright light. She groaned from the stiffness that plagued her. Every muscle in her body ached. As she crawled from her straw bed and came to her feet she felt each of them cry out in agony when she forced them to move. She washed her face, attempting to revive herself, but it proved to be a difficult task. After Sherman awoke and left his niche, Gabrielle changed into her pink gown and laid out the new set of clothes she had purchased for Sherman.

Gabrielle walked up to the back door and cautiously made her way to the study where she laid the slave shackles on the desk. Seating herself in the corner by the door, she awaited her uncle, mentally preparing herself for their unpleasant encounter.

John Jarmon entered his library several minutes later and halted in his tracks when he spied the chains on his desk. "Gabrielle," he hissed between clenched teeth.

"I brought you a fitting gift, dear Uncle." Gabrielle came to her feet and strolled toward him. "'Twas the only gift that seemed appropriate when I thought of you," she mocked dryly.

John whirled toward the sarcastic voice, his plump face reddening in rage. "Where have you been?"

"Why, I've been to London to have the season that you so faithfully promised me. I was escorted by four gallant knights in shining armor who pledged eternal faithfulness to my cause," she taunted, a pretentious smile lifting one corner of her mouth.

"Answer me, you little bitch!" he bellowed as Gabrielle took a daring step toward him.

"None of your damned business," she stormed at him, her green eyes spitting fire at his petulant gray orbs.

"Horace Fairleigh has been here thrice to see if I've had news from you. The man is far too important for you to tangle with and he has a temper that surpasses yours. You have angered him and you will pay dearly," John warned, a menacing sneer curling his lips.

"I doubt that the duke will want me now, Uncle," Gabrielle replied flippantly. "I also doubt that you will be able to find another wealthy fop from your social circle who will marry me and present you with a large purse."

"And just what is that supposed to mean?" he queried, his eyes narrowing to cold, hard slits.

"I am no longer the sacrificial virgin you would have offered to Fairleigh." When Brielle saw the look of condemnation that burst upon his face, she whirled away, unable to meet his hateful snarl.

"You filthy little whore! You probably slept with every tramp from here to London and enjoyed every minute of it!" he screeched.

"But of course, Uncle. And yet, the pleasure was only exceeded by the thought of seeing your reaction." Composing herself, Brielle tilted a proud chin and turned to face John. "I was not disappointed. You have behaved just as I imagined."

"You would stoop so low, ruin your good name, just to defy me?" he growled, clenching his fists at his sides to keep from strangling her.

"I would crawl on my belly like a snake when it comes to defying you," she hissed, her eyes sparkling rebelliously. "You will never marry me to a man that I despise." Her expression changed abruptly, a devilish smile hovering on her lips. "And now if you will excuse me, Uncle, I'm going to my room to freshen up before breakfast. I cannot tell you how wonderful it is to see you again— because I know how you detest lies."

John caught her insinuation and it assured him that she had spoken the truth. She had forfeited her virginity to break the engagement. His hand snaked out and yanked her around to face him. "You may think you have defeated me, Gabrielle, but let me assure you that I will not rest until I have found a way to make you regret what you have done. I will bring you the living hell you deserve," he sneered, his eyes like hard chips of granite. "I will find a man who will be content to punish you for what you have done. There are many men who delight in cleansing the souls of sinners. I will never give up until I see you suffer for your disgraceful disobedience."

Gabrielle glared contemptuously at him. "You are demented. My father would roll over in his grave if he knew what you intend to do. No man has the right to buy and sell people as if they were dogs. I hope you burn in hell!" she snapped before rushing from the room to hide the scalding tears that clouded her eyes.

As she dashed up the stairs to her room, she paused to hear the footsteps behind her. Mistrusting his intentions, she slammed the door of her room but slipped around the corner of the hall. Her fears were confirmed when she heard the click of the lock. She peeked around the corner to see Lord Jarmon tucking the key into his vest pocket, chuckling to himself.

"There are ways, dear Gabrielle, of subduing you. Before I'm through with you, I will hear you beg to marry any man I so choose."

With a silent tear trickling down her cheek, Gabrielle turned to the stairs and quietly slipped away, her spirits plunging with each step she took. She could not possibly defeat her uncle. He would find a way to destroy her and she would wish she were dead. There would be no more attempts to return. John had just turned the key that banished her from his house.

As she fled to the stables, her heart wrenched

with pain and the tears began to flow in a steady stream. After she had changed into her beggar's garb, she relieved the rest of her anger by placing a muffled curse on the man who would have again chained her within these prison walls. Damn him! He was bent on revenge and would not rest until he had seen her tortured.

Sherman glanced up when he heard the twigs snap beside him and then frowned thoughtfully. "Did it go bad fer ye?"

"Extremely," Gabrielle muttered. "I won't be back. I can't live here. There is no way to survive John's maliciousness. I would rather live as a boy than be caught and sold by that scoundrel."

Sherman looked into the lovely face that was etched with bitterness and his eyes mirrored that same emotion. "Because of 'im, I'll never see ye agin." He groaned.

Brielle produced a feeble smile. "I'll come back for you when I'm sure what I'm going to do. I need time to think this out."

His arms came about her, clutching her to him. There were no more teasing words from Sherman. He feared this would be the last time he saw the saucy lass who had brightened his dreary existence.

Then, while his eyes filled with tears, Sherman backed away and focused his attention on Blanco. "I fetched ye some food . . . jest in case. Take care of yerself, Gabe," he managed, his voice crackling with remorse.

Gabe wiped away her own tears and swung into the saddle. Her muscular stallion pranced sideways, protesting the fact that he was to travel so soon. Gabe patted her steed's neck and blew a kiss to Sherman. There was no happiness to guide her and only misery lay behind her. She longed for the contented life she had known as a child, but it was gone like a shattered dream. Nothing had gone according to plan and Brielle could see little hope for her future.

Halting on the grassy slope that overlooked the sea, Gabe peered out over the bluff to watch the whitecaps that slapped against the jagged rocks below. As she slid from the saddle, a moment of weakness buckled her knees and she struggled to stand erect. How simple it would be to end her agony. In an instant her troubles would be over. She would not be forced to endure the cruelty that sought to destroy her spirit. But she was not a coward and she knew that she would fight with her last breath to make a new life for herself. Heaving a weary sigh, Gabe rubbed her aching backside and kicked at some pebbles, sending them tumbling down to be swallowed by the hungry jaws of the sea. If only a clever scheme would come to mind, she could grasp a ray of hope; but she was too tired to think.

Again her eyes focused on the choppy water. Pleasant visions of her childhood danced across the sea, bringing a sad smile to her lips. If someone had told her that one day she would be dressed as a ragamuffin, her face streaked with dirt, her delicate features camouflaged with grime, she would have laughed at such a ridiculous idea. But here she was, her childish dreams gone, her body covered with tattered garments instead of fine silk gowns. Where were the elaborate parties, the handsome suitors, the sounds of laughter, and the warmth of loved ones? What she could have rightfully expected by birth was only a wishful dream. She had been stripped of all that she had loved and cherished. The wealthy heiress of Jarmon Estate had died as quick a death as if she had plunged onto the rocks that lined the sea.

Dane had awakened late from his pleasure-filled dreams. A satisfied smile grazed his lips as he flipped back the quilts and stretched leisurely in his bed. After donning fresh clothes from the wardrobe closet, he turned toward the door and halted in his tracks.

The dark stains on the sheets caused his jaw to sag bewilderedly. It had been no fantastic dream. The proof was there before him. His passionate angel was a woman. Questions began to fly about in his head and he thoughtfully raked his fingers through his hair. From where had she come? Where did she go each time she fled from his embrace? Why wouldn't she reveal her name or allow him to see her face? Had the woman been connected with the attempts on his life? It had crossed his mind before, but he had chased away such thoughts. He had been so certain that she was like the vivid nightmares that haunted him—a dark image born in the recesses of his troubled mind. But now he had to consider seriously the other possibility. Both his would-be assassin and his dark angel had kept close tabs on his activities. Perhaps she was an unwilling participant whose soft heart would not allow her to commit a dastardly crime. No, surely not. Dane shook his head. He couldn't believe the worst about her. She *was* an angel, not the devil's advocate.

She came to him from the shadows of darkness, whispering softly to him, seeking comfort. Was that what troubled her? Was the thought of killing him weighing heavily on her soul? No, she had no evil intentions. She was too tender, too compassionate, too loving. But why wouldn't she reveal her face and her name if she had nothing to hide? Is that why she guarded her identity? God, how could she be so wicked? Was she a witch who was slowly weaving him in her spell, biding her time until she disposed of him in some fiendish manner? The other attempts on his life had failed. Perhaps she was waiting until she had gained his trust. Then she would strike, calling upon the haunting spirits of the night to assist her.

Muttering under his breath, Dane ripped the sheets from his bed and flung them into the corner before stalking downstairs. Perhaps Gabe would be about. At least that little wretch would preoccupy him and relieve him of his troubled musings.

As Dane sank down into his chair and poured himself a cup of tea, he glanced over at Higgins. "Have you seen anything of Gabe this morning?"

"No. And I daresay it has been most pleasant without that little devil pricking me with that pointed tongue of his," Higgins replied, never changing his rigid expression.

Dane thoughtfully studied Higgins for a moment. The man's features were obviously carved from stone and Gabe was the only one who could chisel away at his impassive countenance. "What have you got against the lad?" he demanded, arching a heavy brow.

"He is a disrespectful tramp who ought to be quartered with the horses. His kind has no place in this house," Higgins grumbled.

The cold spark in Higgins' eyes brought an amused smile to Dane's lips. The mention of the boy's name was enough to send Higgins into a state of fury. "I gave him the day off. You won't be bothered by his annoying presence. He has most likely left by now."

"I will enjoy the day," Higgins said stiffly as he spun away and exited from the room.

After a few hours of book work, Dane ambled about the grounds while he awaited dinner. There seemed to be a vast emptiness within him which he could not name. It made him restless and urged him to wander. The confusing questions that had plagued him all morning swirled about his mind as he attempted to light upon some logical explanation. Dane ordered Nate to saddle Sultan and when the lad led out the steed, his downtrodden expression caused Dane to frown bemusedly.

"Something wrong, Nate?" he questioned, searching the lad's face with a probing gaze.

Evading Lord Hampton's stare, Nate lowered

186

his head and firmly shook it.

"Have you seen Gabe this morning?"

Nate's head jerked up, wishing he could tell him why he was so distraught. Dane saw a hint of remorse in Nate's black eyes before he looked away and shook his head negatively.

With a shrug, Dane relinquished his thoughts of learning anything from Nate, and mounted Sultan. He galloped across the meadow, wondering if he was running away from or toward some unknown need. The previous evening made no sense at all. He had found contentment in the arms of a mysterious maid, her soft whisper setting his nerves on edge. He was aroused by the thought of her flesh pressed to his as they soared to new heights of ecstasy. Was she part of an evil scheme? Why had she come? Why would she yield the only thing that she alone could give without asking something in return? She asked for no binding promises or favors. Dane shook his head, trying to free himself from that faceless vision who had loved him so passionately and then disappeared into the shadows.

As the buckskin made his way along the cliff overlooking the sea, Dane spied the ragged waif standing dangerously close to the edge. He seemed so frail perched there—not at all like the proud urchin that Dane had come to know.

"I should think it would be a most painful way to go," Dane said as he swung out of his saddle, eying the lad cautiously.

Gabe stiffened at the sound of his voice, but immediately relaxed when she realized it was Dane who was behind her. Without turning to face him she shrugged carelessly. "Down there the pain wouldn't last long. Up 'ere it goes on ferever. But I ain't goin' to jump. Nobody promised me a bed of roses and I don't expect to find no pot of gold at the end of the rainbow neither. Life ain't easy, but it's all I got. I 'ave no title, no fortune, no family, but I ain't takin' the coward's way out. One day I'll 'ave what's rightfully mine," she murmured determinedly while Dane strained to catch her last words.

Gabe wheeled to face him, wishing she could run into his arms and let her troubles take flight if only for a moment. The bright blue eyes regarded her curiously. In an instant of weakness, Gabe was tempted to pull the cap from her head and tell Dane the truth. But could she trust him? No, she told herself. Dane felt an obligation to her uncle and she could not take the chance of being sent home. She forced a shallow smile and strutted toward the captain in the manner that he expected.

"What's the matter, Cap'n? Did ye miss 'avin' me 'round? Ye couldn't stand the peace and quiet in that dreary old 'ouse, could ye?" she taunted.

Dane scoffed bitterly, reluctant to admit that Gabe had hit upon the truth. Gabe's youthful spirit was the only enjoyment to be had at Hampton Estate since . . .

With a derisive snort Dane denied the lad's words. "Do you think me crazed?" he quipped. "Admitting that I missed your badgering would be as ridiculous as wishing for a broken leg. Both are painful inconveniences that I can easily live without."

"Would ye rather spend the day with 'Iggins or me, Cap'n?" A devilish smile caught one corner of her mouth as she peered up at Dane.

"Neither. Higgins is foul-tempered and you're hot-tempered. One is just as bad as the other," he countered, biting back a grin.

Gabe's shoulder lifted in a reckless shrug and then she strolled over to retrieve the bread and cheese that Sherman had packed for her. She had not taken time to eat and was beginning to grow hungry.

"Want some?" she asked, extending a handful of cheese to the captain.

Dane broke off a piece and accepted the slice of bread the waif offered to him. As Gabe stretched out on the grass to eat her meager meal, Dane squatted down beside her, his gaze sweeping out over the sea. They ate in silence, each lost in his own disconcerted musings, content with each other's presence.

Finally Gabe hopped to her feet and picked up Blanco's reins. "I'm goin' back to the 'ouse fer some rest and a bath. Them all-day picnics tend to wear a body out."

"I'll ride in with you," Dane offered blandly. "I have some more ledgers to study and they won't get finished while I'm out here daydreaming."

When they returned to the stables, Nate rushed out to take Blanco's reins, a joyful smile splitting his face. He hadn't been sure that he would ever see

Gabe again and he was elated by her return.

"Give Blanco a good rubdown, Nate," Gabe requested tiredly. "I've ridden 'im 'ard and 'e's 'ad little rest. I'm sure 'e thinks I've sorely abused 'im."

Nate nodded happily and started to the stables with the stallion eagerly trailing behind him. Dane peered from one lad to the other, noting the fondness Nate had for Gabe. It seemed Nate knew more about Gabe's activities than the captain. Dane bristled indignantly as the livery boy hurried off to obey the request of a mere servant, leaving the lord and master to tend to his own steed.

"Nate," he snapped gruffly and then softened his tone as the unfortunate lad looked back over his shoulder. "I would greatly appreciate it if you would take Sultan in with you—since you're going in that direction. That is, if you don't mind," he added, his brows furrowing in silent rebuke.

With a sheepish grin, Nate took Sultan's reins and hurried to the stables.

Gabe chuckled, her emerald eyes dancing with amusement until Dane flashed her an annoyed frown. She elbowed the captain and then scratched the tip of her nose. "Sometimes titles are mean-in'less, ain't they, Cap'n? It ain't always easy to tell the pauper from the prince by the garb on 'is back."

Dane snorted indignantly and then he reluctantly smiled as his gaze locked with Gabe's sparkling eyes. "I could almost believe that you were the son of a nobleman. Even though you have the crude manners of an uneducated waif, you carry the pride of royalty like a chip on your shoulder.''

Gabe nodded in agreement, knowing Dane had come close to the truth. "Aye, Cap'n. I do 'ave me pride. When that's all ye got to claim as yer own, ye tend to 'old on a bit too fiercely at times. And to Nate I'm more than jest a pauper," she confessed.

As she swaggered toward the house, Dane thoughtfully studied the waif, wondering what was so special about him. Gabe seemed to touch the lives of those about him, sprinkling a little happiness in dull existences. The lad had an uncanny knack for filling the emptiness that often dampened Dane's spirits.

Dane strolled into the barn to find Nate vigorously brushing Blanco while Sultan stood in his stall, not yet unsaddled. Gabe was right, he mused. The captain's title was worthless. He did not have the respect of the speechless lad as Gabe had.

Clamping his hand on Nate's shoulder, he turned the boy to face him. "You know something about our young friend, don't you?"

Nate ducked his head, standing motionless before Lord Hampton.

"There is something troubling Gabe. He is hiding from someone or something and he has lost something that he values greatly. Am I right?" Dane inquired, arching a heavy brow.

The lad continued to stare at the straw beneath his feet. He was not about to reveal Gabe's identity. It made no difference that the man who towered over him was the lord and master. Nate would guard his friend's secret even if it meant taking punishment.

It was obvious to Dane that Nate knew much about Gabe, but he wouldn't part with the confidential information. Gabe had chosen an excellent comrade. Nate wouldn't talk even if he could.

Dane dropped his hand from the boy's shoulder. "I like Gabe. If he's in some sort of trouble, I want to help. It seems he trusts you more than he does me. Can I depend on you to come to me if he needs assistance?"

Nate raised his dark eyes to meet Lord Hampton's solemn expression. As he nodded his assent, a strange, unreadable smile curved the corners of his mouth upward, causing Dane to arch a bemused brow. When Nate turned back to finish his chore, Dane rolled his eyes and stalked off to the house, wishing he knew at least half of what went on at his own estate.

With the tub full of steaming water and the door locked, Gabe shed her tattered garb and eased into her bath. As she moaned with fatigue, she closed her eyes and allowed the warm liquid to soothe her aching muscles. Her mind wandered, pausing on a vision of sparkling blue eyes, raven hair, and a tender smile. Refusing to dwell on the encounter, Gabrielle attempted to smother the exciting tingle she felt. She had no desire to tie herself to a man who was nothing more than a vagabond wandering through the countryside, seeking a moment's pleasure in any woman's arms. Their time together had only been a necessary course of action.

A knock at the door sent her scrambling to gather her clothes.

"Who is it?" she questioned as she struggled into her garb.

"I brought up your supper. Liz said she thought you looked exhausted. She insisted that you take your meal in your room."

Gabe grabbed her hat and threw herself together. After checking her appearance in the mirror, she opened the door.

Dane stood before her with a tray of food in his hands and a broad smile playing on his lips. Gabe leaned against the door, her arms folded on her chest, observing Lord Hampton with a critical eye. He was dressed in a blue linen shirt, tan breeches, and shiny black boots that she had meticulously polished. His virile form was enhanced by his trim-fitting clothes and Gabe thought it to be little wonder that women found him irresistible. He was far more handsome than any man rightfully deserved and she was having difficulty keeping her eyes from roaming over him.

"Well, what 'ave we 'ere?" she mocked dryly. "'Ave ye come to admit that we should exchange roles after all?" A devilish grin grazed her lips as she met Dane's condemning glare.

Dane stuffed the tray into her belly, forcing her to hold it, and then he bowed in feigned devotion. "I'm at your service, your lordship."

The sarcasm in his voice caused Gabe to snort

indignantly. "Thank ye, Cap'n. Yer loyalty to the one who saved yer 'ide is really touchin'. Twice I've risked me neck to save ye. All the thanks I git is yer snide remarks. It makes me wonder why I even 'ang 'round 'ere."

Dane rose to full stature and sadly shook his head. "Must you ever remind me that I'm indebted to you?"

"If I don't, ye'd fergit it." She defended herself hotly. "And I see no reason not to rub in the fact that a mere boy 'as dragged ye from death's door, not once, but twice. If ye can't take care of yerself, ye ought to be man enough to admit it." Gabe ribbed him unmercifully. Although she knew he had come to see about her welfare it was what he expected from her and she was not about to disappoint him.

"I'll deed my estate over to you in the morning," Dane offered, sarcasm dripping from his lips. "Would you like your throne dusted while I'm here, your lordship? Or perhaps you would prefer that I read you a bedtime story and tuck you in."

"I'm too old to believe in them fairy tales. And now if ye'll excuse me, I'd like to study the tedious problems of me kingdom without this chatter. Ye may take yer leave." Gabe dismissed him with an arrogant nod, but when she tried to close the door, his foot barred its closing.

"You are all right, aren't you, Gabe? Nothing serious, I hope." The teasing grin faded from Dane's handsome features as he observed the pale complexion that was camouflaged with dirt.

Gabe nodded slightly. "Aye, Cap'n. I'm jest

tired 'tis all. All I need is some rest." She lifted her gaze from beneath the brim of her cap and then slid it away, careful not to allow Dane to study her eyes too closely.

After taking her meal, Gabe drifted off to sleep, welcoming the soft mattress beneath her.

When Dane finished his work, he rubbed his eyes and returned upstairs for his bath. The tub of water was waiting just as he had ordered and he stripped from his clothes. As he eased into the bath, he wondered if the mysterious goddess would appear. And if she did . . . would he force her to reveal her identity? He must, Dane thought determinedly. His life might be at stake. As the dim light cast shadows on the wall, he pictured the lovely vision hovering above him. Her soft, raspy whisper was teasing his mind. She had taken some strange hold on his senses. Although he knew he should be wary of her, he could not seem to put her out of his thoughts.

Each night that she came to him, he had intended to discover her identity. But when he heard that gentle whisper, felt her honeyed lips on his, and held her trim form, he was powerless. The subtle potency of his dark angel caught him in a trance. Only when she had disappeared did he question himself. When she was warm and yielding in his arms, he could deny her nothing. In the past he had been in complete control of his romantic encounters. But he had allowed this faceless maid to maneuver him as if he were some senseless puppet on a string. Dane sighed discouragingly. Where could she have gone the previous night as he watched her fly across the grounds? Where was her home? Was she indeed a part of the plot to kill him? What did she want from him? Did she have a purpose? God, where were the answers? Dane muttered under his breath. He wanted to know everything about her, yet he couldn't give her up. He longed to feel her lips against his, her silky flesh pressed to his, to hear that hushed whisper that melted all of his fears.

Suddenly, the room was pitch-black. Dane was jolted from his silent reverie when the candle flame died in a surge of cold air. A chill shot down his spine as he groped in the darkness for the towel that he had laid on the chair.

"What the hell?"

His hand found the firm flesh of Gabrielle's thigh and she chuckled lightly. "You need only to ask for your towel, m'lord," she teased as she placed the cloth in his hand.

A broad smile split Dane's face. "I wondered if I would ever see you again."

"You haven't seen me at all. And I doubt that you ever will," she murmured as she leaned forward, seeking his lips in a light kiss.

"And just why is that?" he questioned hoarsely, aroused by her alluring fragrance that entangled his senses.

"Because it would serve no useful purpose to reveal the name of your guardian angel." Her hand trailed down the thick furring on his chest to the water. With a quick flick of her wrist, Brielle doused him in the face, sending him sputtering and coughing to catch his breath.

"What did I do to deserve that?" he quipped as he wiped the soapy water from his eyes.

"I was baptizing your sinful soul, sir," she teased as she nibbled at his lips.

When Dane stood up to dry himself, Brielle strolled across the room, feeling her way around the furniture, wondering if she should leave before she was tempted. Although she had vowed never to return to him, she had found herself standing at his terrace door. While she stood pondering this question, she felt Dane's muscular arms slide around her waist. He nuzzled his face in the curve of her neck, his kisses trailing down her shoulder.

The strange tingle began as it had the previous evening. Gabrielle knew she had tarried too long. She wanted the security of his embrace and his affection for as long as it would last. It didn't matter that she was one of his many lovers. At least for a time, he was hers alone.

His hands moved upward to caress her breasts through the thin fabric that covered them. "Why must my only pleasure come from the eerie shadows of darkness?" he mused aloud. "It makes the days pass so slowly when I must wait until night to find you in my arms."

Brielle leaned back against the hard wall of his chest and sighed contentedly. "I have other obligations during the day, m'lord. The world from which I come only allows me to transcend its boundaries between the hours of dusk and dawn."

Dane frowned in confusion. What type of life did she lead? "I suppose I should be grateful for the darkness then," he murmured as he turned her in his arms, no longer interested in conversation.

Gabrielle felt the medallion on his chest and an unseen smile crept to her lips as she rubbed her fingers over the surface. "What is this?"

"A Saint Christopher," he whispered against her cheek. "A gift from a friend."

"A woman, m'lord?" she queried, drawing away, as if the thought brought her discomfort.

A low rumble arose from his chest. "No, from a skinny little waif. It is useless to me because I have a guardian angel. I need no further protection."

His lips slanted across her mouth in a demanding kiss. Gabrielle responded, amazed by her own abandon. She was crushed against his bare chest and she could feel his heart rapidly beating in rhythm with her own racing pulse. His tongue searched and explored her mouth in passionate urgency while his arms lowered to her hips, pulling her to him. She quivered with anticipation, knowing that she would surrender without protest.

"You've been on my mind all day," Dane admitted in ragged breaths. "I don't understand you, but I've never stopped wanting you."

"There is nothing to comprehend. I expect nothing of you: no profession of love, no promises for tomorrow, no regrets of the past. All I ask is for tonight. Just hold me. I need your comforting arms."

Dane held her as if he were consoling a small child who was lost and confused. But then a small shadow of doubt skipped across his mind. Her request was too innocent and unselfish to be believable; yet, he couldn't resist her. As he lifted her into his arms, he moved to the bed, offering her the love and protection she desired.

As he unfastened the buttons of her gown, his hand slipped inside, gently cupping her breast. His experienced ways brought a pleasureful moan from her lips and she reveled in the wild rapture that blazed a fiery path to her soul. She caressed him, learning the feel of his muscular body beneath her fingertips, wanting to bring the same passionate response coursing through his veins.

With an urgency that pursued and captured them, they came together. Their desires, fanned by the ragged breaths, spread like wildfire across their flesh. The world about them was blazing with sparks that burned and crackled, feeding more fires that burst into flame with each intimate caress. As he lowered himself to her, Brielle welcomed his possession, his hard thrusts that sent her soaring above the charred cinders of reality. She was living and dying, unable to catch a breath, spellbound by the emotions that enveloped her. And then she was soaring, alighting on passion's lofty pinnacle, content to remain there forever.

Dane groaned and shuddered, clinging to her shadowy form, engulfed by some unexplainable tremor that surpassed physical satisfaction. His strength was drained, his passion spent. He rolled to his side and gathered her close, placing a light kiss on the velvety curve of her neck, wanting to utter the words that formed on his lips. But she didn't need to hear them. In fact, she had refused them. The phrases that all women yearned to hear were empty syllables that this one, mysterious goddess, could not comprehend. She was like no other. It disturbed him greatly to realize that he didn't really want to see her face or know her name. He had no desire to change anything about her. How could he tamper with perfection? He must accept her as she was—an angel whom he could hold only in the shadows of the night.

At the budding of dawn, Gabrielle fled from Dane's room. Alarmed at her recklessness, she returned to the room of the ragged waif with the dirt-smudged cheeks and the mischievous twinkle in her eyes.

Chapter Eight

The cramping pain that awoke Gabrielle assured her that although she charaded as a young boy, she was still very much a woman. With a doleful groan she crawled from the bed, dressed in her breeches, and made her way to the kitchen although she wished she could spend the entire day in her room. Liz took one look at the waif's pale face, slumped stature, and lifeless eyes. She quickly concluded that the lad was seriously ill.

"You climb right back up those stairs and get back into bed, young man," she ordered. "You look dreadful and I will not have you wandering about the house in your condition. I thought you looked the worse for wear last night when you came home."

"I'll be jest fine," Gabe assured her, wishing she could believe her own words. "A cup of tea and I'll be on me way to do me chores."

"You most certainly will not! You hustle yourself to your room this instant or I'll come after you with my broom. Now move!" Liz presented Gabe with a determined frown and dragged her to the door.

Gabe trudged up the stairs, wondering why it seemed to take all of her strength to scale the steps. Between the aches from her long ride and the cramping pain, she doubted her ability to remain on her feet. When she heard the click of boots above her, she slowly raised her eyes to meet Dane's concerned frown. Dane peered into the dull green eyes and ashen face that lay beneath smudges of dirt and grabbed the boy's arm, hauling him up the steps.

"It looks like you've managed to take another day off," he mocked dryly.

"I ain't tryin' to avoid me chores, Cap'n. Ye don't 'ave to pamper me," Gabe snapped, futilely attempting to free herself from Dane's firm grasp. "I'll be jest fine if ye'll jest leave me be."

"A bit touchy this morning, aren't we?" Dane quipped, a taunting smile catching one corner of his mouth.

"Speak fer yerself, Cap'n," she grumbled as Dane opened the door of her room and urged her toward the bed.

Gabe crawled onto the quilts, muffling a groan as she curled up in a tight ball, hoping to relieve the pain in her abdomen. Dane strolled over and reached down to unfasten the tattered breeches, but his hands were quickly slapped away as alarmed green eyes glared up at him.

"I ain't so sick that I can't git out of me clothes! Just leave me be!"

Dane rose to full stature, crossed his arms on his chest, and frowned at the urchin's peppery protest. "You don't have to bite my head off. I was just trying to help," he defended curtly.

Gabe softened her hateful tone and averted her gaze. "Sorry, Cap'n. As ye kin plainly see, I ain't feelin' up to snuff this mornin'. I'm sort of cross."

"Sort of?" He smirked. "That is putting it mildly. I think perhaps 'extremely irritable' would be an accurate description of your temperament."

With a weak flick of her wrist, Gabe waved him way. "Characterize me as cranky or vicious, whatever ye wish. Jest leave me be." She heaved a weak sigh and lifted her gaze to Dane. "Please, Cap'n. I don't want no fiery arguments with ye today. Jest let me die in peace."

With an anguished moan, she slid beneath the quilt and pulled it over her head, wishing he would go away and leave her to her misery. Dane stuffed his hands in his pockets, thoughtfully studied the covered form, and then descended the stairs to suffer through another breakfast taken in solitude.

By evening Gabrielle was feeling much better. She went downstairs to help Liz with her chores. After the kitchen was spotless, she ambled haphazardly through the trees that lined the grounds of Hampton Estate. When she overheard voices, Gabe moved quietly along the stream until she could catch their muffled words. Although she could not identify the voices, she could understand what they said.

"It would be easy for me to solve this problem. Why don't you give it up? Every one of your plans has failed. If you would have let me handle this from the beginning, we could have saved ourselves a great deal of time and effort," came one insistent voice.

"No. Your idea is too incriminating and would draw too much attention. There is no hurry and you know it. The more time we put between the incidents the less likely our chance of being discovered. I'll find the right moment and no one will suspect us. Just have a little patience and you will be rewarded for your trouble," the second voice requested.

"Very well then, we'll do it your way; but I don't mind telling you that my patience is wearing thin. If you don't take care of him soon, you'll find the deed has been done—my way, like it or not."

Gabrielle stood frozen to the spot, hardly daring to breathe until she heard the sound of hoofs snapping the twigs. Someone *did* want Dane dead. Neither attempt on his life had been accidental. Whoever it was kept close tabs on where he went and what he did.

Later, when Gabe entered the house, she decided to ask the captain a few questions. In the entryway Gabe came face to face with Higgins and his arrogant snub, which for once she ignored in her haste to discuss the matter with Dane. As she stepped into the study, she found Dane working at his desk, an array of papers scattered in front of him.

"Cap'n, kin I 'ave a word with ye?" she queried,

her green eyes darting nervously about her.

Dane pushed his chair away from the desk and smiled as he motioned for Gabe to come forward. "Feeling better?"

"Aye." Gabe closed the door and then walked forward, staring across the desk to meet his quizzical gaze.

"Well, what is it?" Dane's brows furrowed bemusedly at Gabe's actions.

"Welllllll," she drawled before taking a deep breath and plunging on. "I know this ain't none of me business. And I ain't got no right to pry, but I was wonderin' a—" she stammered, attempting to find a delicate way to ask her question.

"Go on," Dane insisted impatiently. "Just tell me what's on your mind."

Deciding upon the direct approach, Gabe blurted out, "I bin thinkin' 'bout them attempts on yer life. I don't think they were accidents. Who would git yer estate if ye were gone?"

Dane's brows raised acutely and then returned to their normal arch as he studied Gabe's sober expression. "I have no other relatives who would inherit the estate or the schooner. It would go to whomever I choose. I see no reason to assume that anyone is plotting to kill me for what they might gain."

"I thought ye said somethin' 'bout 'avin' a stepbrother somewhere," she prodded.

Dane scowled and clenched his fists. "My fortune would do him no good where he is."

Pain flashed through his eyes and Gabe frowned in confusion. Where could he be? Dane had only mentioned him once and had not gone into detail. Something about his stepbrother caused him misery, but Dane would never allow himself to discuss it.

"No jealous woman who 'as borne yer illegitimate child?" she queried and then thoughtfully chewed on her lip, wondering why she would make such a remark and why the idea burned at her pride. With a wry smile she dismissed the accusation, teasing wickedly, "Per'aps I'm yer brat and it's me who's plotted to 'ave ye killed. After all, it would make the perfect motive."

Dane peered at the waif, a bewildered frown gathering on his brows. "*Are* you my son?"

"Could I be, Cap'n?" she countered, her tone holding a hint of amusement.

"How old are you, Gabe?" His probing gaze carefully surveyed the lad who stood before him.

Gabe shrugged leisurely and then shook her head, making no attempt to answer his last inquiry. "I ain't yer brat. When I was out walkin' I 'eard two voices talkin' 'bout doin' away with someone and 'ow they'd find the right time and place so nobody would suspect them. I'm willin' to bet they were discussin' ye." A concerned frown settled on her dirt-smudged features as she sank down in the chair beside Dane.

Dane eased back in his chair and rested his chin on his folded hands. Who could possibly want him dead and for what purpose? It couldn't be for financial gain. It must be someone seeking revenge for something he had done. Perhaps Gabe was right. Maybe the claim of an heir was not so unreasonable. But it still left him without a name for his accomplice and would-be-assassin.

"It seems I should keep you around. I may need more protection than I realized." Dane forced a faint smile. "I'm grateful for what you have done in the past and for coming to me with this information. I intend to be more cautious in the future."

Gabe nodded slightly. "I'm glad I could be of 'elp, Cap'n." Her gaze rested in her lap, failing to meet Dane's eyes. "I may tease and banter with ye overmuch, but I don't want nothin' to 'appen to ye. Ye've done good by me and I'll 'elp ye when I kin."

As she lay awake in her bed, Gabrielle went over the conversation again in her mind, searching for something that might reveal the identity of the voices. The information had piqued her curiosity and she decided to put her own problems aside. Besides, she mused, there was no place to go. The fond attachment she felt for Lord Hampton and the preservation of his life was more important than her inheritance. In time she would solve her dilemma, but now Dane needed her.

The desire to run to his arms was overwhelming, but under the circumstances, it would be impossible. Perhaps by the end of the week she would lose her yearning for his loving embrace. She could not afford to become involved with Dane. What they had shared in the darkness was causing turmoil with her emotions and she must put an end to that before she had hopelessly lost her heart to him. Brielle hugged her pillow close and heaved a sigh. There would be no more visits to Dane's room. It was over.

Dane's mind toyed with the information Gabe had given him and then, having found no answer to the riddle, shrugged it from his thoughts. His life had been running smoothly until two months ago. Now there were three puzzles that he couldn't piece together—his mysterious goddess, the secretive lad, and the attempts on his life. He decided to call it a night, hoping that his elusive angel would appear to take him to another world of raptured bliss.

When the lantern was snuffed out, he lay in bed, but she never came to him. Dane tossed and turned beneath the quilts, wondering why she hadn't returned. Did she have something to do with the voices Gabe had heard that night?

It was the first time since the ambush that she had not come to him. Had something happened to prevent her return? In anger and frustration, Dane swore under his breath. He should have forced her to reveal herself instead of obeying her requests. He had become her pawn, an ever-willing lover to be played only when it met her whim. Her words resounded in his mind, but not in the context in which she had given them.

"Innocence does not always imply foolishness." Innocent, yes. She had been that. But foolish? Hardly, he muttered bitterly. The alluring wench had posed as a compassionate angel, but beneath that silky skin and seductive whisper lived and breathed a sorceress whose long claws pricked his soul. Her wicked laughter echoed about him; first sweet and tender, and then spiteful and cruel. She changed forms each time he reached upward or drew away, ever tempting, constantly present, never allowing a moment's peace. Perhaps she was the devil's advocate and her scheme was to drive him mad, just as the other nightmares had attempted to do. Then she would come to him one dark night to put him out of his misery.

Abandoning all hope, Dane pulled the pillow over his head, avoiding the two imaginary creatures who hovered over him. The moonlit shadows streamed across the room, moving silently over the walls to tear at his sanity. He could never face them again. There would be no lovely angel to calm his fretful dreams. She had become the cause, no longer the cure.

Gabrielle had heard his agonizing groans during the long, lonely night. Her heart wrenched, but she did not dare go to him. Never again, she thought determinedly. They each must suffer solitude and forget the moments they had shared.

Chapter Nine

The following week progressed at a snail's pace. Dane's mood became blacker with each dawning day. He seemed to wake in the morning with a permanent snarl etched on his bronzed features. He snapped at the servants for petty reasons and even Gabe was not immune to his trivial complaints. At the end of a week, even the bland expression on Higgins' face held a hint of apprehension. The servants were afraid to walk past Lord Hampton for fear of being scolded for putting the wrong foot forward. The tension in the house was becoming more than any of the hired help could endure.

While Gabe was rearranging Dane's cluttered room, he stomped inside, his face twisted in an angry scowl.

"Where's my coat?" he growled as he brushed past Gabe, knocking her onto the bed while he stalked to the wardrobe closet.

Gabe bolted up from the bed and boldly faced

him. Clenching her fists on her hips, she tilted a defiant chin, her smudged features alive with fury.

"Jest who the 'ell do ye think ye are? I swear the devil 'as taken yer soul!" she snapped, her voice rising testily. "I don't know what thorn is in yer paw and I don't give a damn. But I fer one am tired of bein' yer scapegoat. Ye've bin snortin' and growlin' 'round 'ere like a crazed beast fer a week. I ain't puttin' up with another minute of it!"

"You outspoken little snip!" His booming voice cracked like thunder as he wheeled around. "Watch your foul mouth," Dane growled, wagging a threatening finger at Gabe. "You're not old enough to use such language and I want no more of it *or* your disrespectful remarks."

"I'll talk 'owever I wish." Her proud chin tilted higher. "If ye are goin' to act like some puffed-up old buffoon, then I ain't goin' to 'ang 'round and protect ye from some maniac who wants to see ye dead. Yer miserable life ain't worth savin'," Gabe spat angrily.

"Don't again remind me of your heroic deeds, you vicious little whelp, or I'll be tempted to cut out your tongue. I've had enough of this. I'm going to the village to find comfort in some wench's arms. I'm sure you disapprove of that too, but I don't give a damn! At least she won't criticize every facet of my personality." Dane grabbed his coat and stalked toward the door, his eyes blazing like torches.

Gabe quickly stepped in front of him, barring his exit as she pressed a determined hand against his chest that heaved and expanded in angry

211

breaths. "Why don't ye take a big bottle of brandy with ye so ye kin git rip-roarin' drunk while yer samplin' every piece of fluff in town? Maybe when ye come draggin' yer ass 'ome, yer 'angover will be more pleasant than yer recent sober state," she sneered into his shocked face.

A menacing frown darkened his rugged features as Dane sucked in his breath at the lad's blunt statements. He raised a clenched fist, threatening to strike the waif who blocked his exit.

Gabe plunged on, hoping to finish before she was slapped aside. "We all got our troubles, Cap'n. Mine eat at me guts every wakin' hour. Ye seem to think, jest because ye were born to carry a title, that what affects ye should matter to the rest of us. What gives ye the right to snap at everyone 'round 'ere jest because there's somethin' troublin' ye? Ye've growled at everyone in the 'ouse all week fer no good reason. They're afraid to breathe fer fear of bein' whipped." Gabe stepped aside to let him pass, offering one, last remark. "Go a'ead and 'it me now. If ye think that one word I spoke ain't the truth, then ye kin jest lay me out on the floor. I'll never open me mouth agin."

Gabe peered up at him, wondering if he realized what a tyrant he had become. Would she feel the sting of his fist on her cheek for daring to chastise him? Dane studied the brazen wretch, well aware that he had behaved miserably, but too proud to admit it to a mere child who seemed wiser than his years. With a dark scowl, the captain lowered his fist and stomped from the room, leaving Gabe to stare at his retreating backside.

Dane stormed down the hall and out of the house, slamming the front door with such force that the stone structure shook from the explosive echo that bounced within its walls. But at that moment, Lord Hampton would not have cared if the mansion crumbled and fell in a shambles behind him.

Riding at a reckless pace toward the village, Dane escaped from the stinging words of the feisty urchin. At the tavern on the edge of town, he brought the big buckskin to an abrupt halt. The steed pranced sideways and threw his head at the harsh yank on his reins. Dane stepped from the stirrup and disappeared inside the inn to drown his troubles and seek comfort for his week-long abstinence. With a bottle of liquor under one arm and a willing wench on the other, he ascended the creaking stairs to find a room that held nothing more than a commode and a narrow bed.

Making no pretense of gentleness or love, Dane proceeded with frustrated haste to ease his desires. He fought the vision that transformed the plain-faced wench into the shadowed image of his dreams. There was no magic in the encounter and it left him pacified, but hardly satisfied. After ushering the maid out of the room, scarcely allowing her time to dress, Dane grabbed the bottle and a glass. He propped himself up on the pillows in the middle of the bed. With no other purpose but to forget everything that had any resemblance to reality, the noble lord and captain took the advice of the outspoken waif and polluted his blood with every drop of liquor it could absorb.

Raising his arm in toast to his imaginary companions, Dane saluted them over his thick tongue. "Here's to you, my deceitful little witch, and you, waif, my would-be conscience. Go drive some other man insane. Your task has been accomplished here," he muttered bitterly.

Dulled to the brink of unconsciousness, Dane mumbled several, inarticulate phrases about a goddess who turned witch before he slipped over the edge into the darkness that swam before him like a circling vulture waiting to swoop down on its prey. As his glazed eyes closed, the glass fell from his hand and crashed to the floor, shattering into pieces, as did the mysterious vision that preoccupied his thoughts.

Gabe watched the captain's hasty flight, knowing that she had dared to say much more than was fitting for her place in his household. But damn it, he had it coming, she thought scornfully. Driven by anger she rushed through her chores, muttering to herself.

"Let him go bed some homely wench or a hundred of them if that's what he wants. It makes no difference to me."

The empty words were not convincing even if she repeated them a thousand times. It *did* matter and she could not let him go alone. Despite her jealousy at what he was planning to do and an uneasy feeling that he was risking an attempt on his life, Gabe set out to follow him.

After retrieving her silver dagger and the small handgun, she galloped toward the village on the back of her white stallion. When she found Sultan tethered at the shabby inn, her eyes narrowed in concern. Gabe dismounted and paced outside, wondering whether to burst in on the captain. Finally making her decision, she pulled open the door and stepped inside the dimly lit tavern. Gabe came face to face with a large, burly man that she assumed to be the proprietor.

"Pardon me, sir," Gabe began lamely. "Me master told me to fetch 'im when it was time to ride. Could ye direct me to 'im?"

The stubble-faced man eyed her dubiously. "What's his name, boy?"

"Lord 'Ampton, sir. Cap'n Dane 'Ampton," she replied without batting an eye.

Satisfied that the lad was telling the truth, he pointed toward the stairs. "First door to the right. Go on up. He's alone now."

Heaving a sigh of relief, Gabe climbed the steps and rapped on the door. Receiving no response, she eased open the door and peeked inside the dingy quarters. Holding an empty bottle under his arm, Dane had passed out on the bed. After her concern vanished, annoyance took its place and she muttered at the still form.

"Men! Sometimes I swear the whole damned lot of them are jackasses." As she picked up his boots, stockings, and shirt she continued her degrading description of the male population. "They have no common sense at all. How the hell could any sane man drink himself into a witless stupor, knowing his body will punish him for its mistreatment? And how could they fall into bed with any available wench, never caring if the poor woman had a name or not?'' Gabe paced the floor, flashing an occasional glare in Dane's direction. "They all act like strutting cocks in a henhouse. All they want is what a woman can yield, willingly or unwillingly. Damn the whole lot of them and especially you, Dane Hampton,'' she snarled, pointing a condemning finger at the quiet form who was sprawled on the tangled sheets.

"I honestly don't know why I bother with you. You deserve just what you're going to get.'' Gabe grabbed a pitcher of water and held it above the captain's head. With excessive pleasure she doused him unmercifully. Dane awoke, sputtering and waving his hands for the shower to cease. "I christen thee, noble lord of fools. Your actions bear witness to your well-earned title, Captain Lackwit.''

When Dane came to his senses, he grumbled resentfully. "What the hell are you trying to do?'' He wiped the water from his eyes and peered up at a blurred image, attempting to focus on the face above him.

"Ain't it obvious, Cap'n?'' Sarcasm dripped from her lips as she returned to her cockney accent. "Even a feeble-minded ninny could tell a cold shower when it 'it 'im in the face,'' she mocked, a lopsided grin catching one corner of her mouth.

Dane groaned miserably when he recognized the nasal voice. "Now I'm certain that you were sent to earth for no other purpose than to torture me. You're constantly present to deflate my ego and prevent me from living a peaceful life,'' he snorted derisively. "I have often wondered if this is hell and if you're the caretaker."

Gabe tossed his boots and shirt on his belly, drawing a pained grunt from Dane when they met their intended mark. "Are ye comin' 'ome or would ye prefer to stay 'ere in this rat'ole waitin' fer the rodents to feast on ye fer supper?" Gabe looked down her nose at him, amused mockery scorning everything about him.

Rolling to the edge of the bed to don his boots, Dane mumbled an inaudible reply that Gabe did not bother to ask him to repeat. After buttoning his shirt he came unsteadily to his feet, leaning on Gabe's shoulder for support.

"Lead the way, boy," he demanded in jagged breaths. He clutched at Gabe, amazed at how much faster the world was spinning from a standing position.

Cautiously assisting Lord Hampton down the steps, Gabe moved toward the door until Dane stopped to speak to the innkeeper.

"Bring us some stew," he ordered, gesturing with an exaggerated sweep of his arm. "I want to eat before leaving."

A silly smile curved Dane's lips and Gabe rolled her eyes, wavering between amusement and irritation. Dane stumbled over a chair leg and fell onto the bench, grinning proudly as if that was exactly what he had intended. With another disbelieving shake of her head, Gabe slipped into the chair across the table from the bedraggled captain. A reluctant smile lifted the corners of her mouth as she focused her attention on him. Lord, he looked a sight, she mused. His shirt was unevenly buttoned, his hair was tousled, and his blue eyes were rimmed in red.

"If ye cap'n yer ship with the same recklessness that ye steer yer life, it's a wonder ye ain't sunk yer schooner," she declared with an intimidating smirk.

Gabe's remark did not sit well and Dane peered incredulously at the audacious wretch. "I have never in my life been ridiculed by anyone as harshly as I have by you, young man," he snorted indignantly. "Your disrespectfulness plagues me constantly. I have come to the conclusion that your family abandoned you because of your sour disposition, instead of *your* leaving them."

"Me?" she squeaked. "It was yer 'ellish temperament that started all of this. If ye 'adn't acted like a damned jackass the entire week, we wouldn't be sittin' in this filthy tavern with ye 'alf-soused. Do ye know what most likely would've 'appened if I 'adn't followed ye 'ere?"

Dane opened his mouth to reply, but Gabe allowed him no time to utter a word.

"Well, I'll tell ye, Mister 'Igh and Mighty," she insisted, leaning forward to glare into his bloodshot eyes. "Ye'd be layin' upstairs like a pigeon to be plucked. Whoever is out to git ye would 'ave easy pickin's."

Pushing forward to meet the lad's derisive stare, Dane was prepared to deny the accusation, but he swallowed his words when a bowl of hot stew was placed before him. He nodded a thanks to the waitress and waited for her to retreat before lashing out at the waif who dared to speak to him as an equal.

"I've managed to live thirty-three years without your services, brat. I can make the rest of them without your annoying presence. I don't need you or your degrading remarks," he snapped, his voice rising testily. "What gives you the right to criticize my every action? And what makes you think you're so damned indispensable? I can manage my own affairs without your following me around like my shadow! You've got a hell of a lot to learn, Gabe. And the first thing you should know is that you do not tell a nobleman how to act!" His dark brows furrowed over his cold blue eyes and he glared at the waif for a long moment before turning his attention to the steaming broth.

Gabe ducked her head like a whipped pup. She had let her guard down with Dane and had grown too fond of him. There was no way to change him and she had wasted her time trying to offer a friendship that he didn't want or need. His hateful words slashed her pride and composure. She had to bite back the tears to keep from choking on them.

"Yer right, Cap'n," she agreed in a trembling voice. "Ye don't need me and neither does anybody else." A river of tears cut a path down her dirt-smudged cheeks as she slowly raised her gaze to meet Dane's unwavering glare. "I'm sorry. I 'ad no right to say any of them thin's I did today. We ain't nothin' to each other. It wasn't me place to sit in judgment of yer be'avior. I stand corrected. Please accept me 'umble apology."

Pushing away from the table, Gabe came to her feet and muffled a sniff. "G'bye, Cap'n. Ye won't be bothered by me intolerable presence from now on. Ye kin do as ye please without me criticizin' ye. I'll gather me belongin's and be gone by the time ye git 'ome."

Gabe wheeled toward the door and dashed away. Although Dane called out to her, she ignored him, never looking back as she exited from the inn. She picked up Blanco's reins, swung onto his back, and galloped down the road. After pulling the stallion to a halt in a clump of trees, she allowed her tears to flow unchecked. She wept until her frustrations were washed away and she was nothing more than an empty shell, void of emotion. She would gather her belongings and find another place to lodge.

Heaving a determined sigh, Gabe gathered her composure and buried her fragile feelings deep in her heart. She made her way through the brush until she heard a whinny in the thicket in front of her. Alarmed, she backed Blanco away from the sound and turned him back to the open road. When she came into the clearing, she heard Sultan's hoofs pounding the road and glanced up to see Dane galloping toward her, careening precariously on the steed's back, his jacket waving in the breeze.

Digging her heels into Blanco's flanks, she darted across the road, motioning for Dane to follow her. As they disappeared into the trees a shot rang out. Dane involuntarily ducked away from the explosion that cracked the air. With icy green eyes affirming that Dane had not been hit, Gabe turned in her saddle to meet Dane's startled expression. There was no haughty, I-told-you-so smugness on her face and Gabe did not utter a word before she twisted back around in the saddle. Cautiously remaining within the protection of the trees, she traveled a good distance before reining Blanco onto the open road. Gabe kicked the stallion and he lunged forward, thundering away from the danger, leaving Dane in a cloud of dust.

Dane swallowed his pride and urged Sultan into a faster gait. Gabe had been right. He had foolishly set himself up for an ambush. The little wretch had a watchful eye for trouble and he could handle himself intelligently in the face of danger. Although he was a bit outspoken, he had Dane's best interest at heart. Gabe expected him to be the perfect example of nobility and never hesitated to let him know if he had fallen short. Dane regretted his harsh words. Gabe had only spoken the truth and Dane had been reluctant to accept the fact that he had indeed become an irascible tyrant.

When Gabe stopped at the house and hopped from Blanco's back, Dane dismounted and followed her up to her small chamber. Gabe picked up her pouch, threw it over her shoulder, and attempted to leave, but Dane blocked the door.

"I want to talk to you," Dane said quietly.

"Ain't nothin' more to say. Ye expressed yerself plain enough at the tavern. I got yer message good and clear. I ain't stayin' where I ain't welcome," Gabe insisted, her expression tight and controlled as she met Dane's determined frown.

"I want you to stay, Gabe. What I said earlier was only the liquor and injured pride talking. You were right. I've been lashing out at everyone because of something that has been troubling me. I had no business taking it out on the servants and you. What bothers me personally should not have caused me to rant and rave at the help. I have been cantankerous and I'm sorry," he apologized.

When Gabe made no remark, a hint of a smile crept to Dane's lips and he folded his arms on his chest. "If you go, who will keep me treading the straight and narrow path? No one else in this house has dared to inform me when I've stepped out of line."

Gabe, deeply hurt by his previous insults, would not easily yield to the rakish grin that settled on his bronzed features. "Yer a grown man. Ye don't need some ignorant stray tellin' ye what's right and wrong. Ye'd fare better without me underfoot," she muttered, averting her eyes from his pleading gaze. She stepped forward, but Dane again refused to let her pass, barring the exit with his broad frame. "Now if ye'll excuse me, Cap'n. I'll be on me way."

"No," Dane persisted. "You're staying here even if I have to lock you in your room until you agree to remain at the estate and accept my apology."

If Dane had been aware of her past, he would have known better than to make such a threat. Unfortunately, he uttered the wrong words. Gabe stiffened in outrage, her fiery green eyes shooting daggers at him.

"That's jest exactly what me relative tried to do

when he attempted to make me 'is slave," she snapped in raw fury. "But it didn't work for 'im and it won't work fer ye neither. I ain't goin' to be nobody's prisoner ever again!" Gabe tried to squeeze through the door, but Dane wouldn't budge. "Let me out of 'ere! I want nothin' more to do with ye!"

Dane grabbed her arms, holding her securely in place. "I'm sorry. I didn't know someone had done that to you. I'm sorry for everything else I've said and done this whole damned week." In a softer tone he continued as he eased his grip on the struggling waif. "Gabe, I like having you here. You keep life from being dull and monotonous. If you knew how much I dreaded coming home this time you would realize that I am not giving you flimsy excuses." Another thought occurred to him and a faint smile threatened the corner of his mouth. "Do you hate me so much that you would leave me to Higgins? You know what a cold disposition the man has."

Unable to contain the grin that found its way to her lips, Gabe nodded reluctantly. "The two of ye deserve each other."

"Will you stay?" Dane queried, his gaze searching her deep emerald eyes. "I'll even give you an extra day off each week."

Gabe felt herself melt beneath his warm regard. "I guess I'll stay a little longer since I ain't got nowhere to go. But this ain't permanent, mind ye," she added, her chin tilting proudly.

With a sigh of relief, Dane nodded agreeably. "Very well, Gabe. This will be your *temporary* home. Now how about some lunch? We left ours untouched."

Together they descended the stairs. The waif dined in the hall with Lord Hampton. Dane treated the lad as an equal, much to Higgins' dismay, since he was the one who was forced to serve the little guttersnipe. It took all of the patience Higgins could muster to treat the lad like a human being.

Two days had passed since the incident at the inn and Gabe feared what had happened to her. The same restlessness that had nagged at her the entire week had come again. She had hoped her desire to return to Dane's comforting arms would subside with the passage of time, but her need for him had grown stronger. Chastising herself for her weakness, she snuffed out the lantern and eased down on the edge of her bed. She peered into the darkness, searching her soul, wondering if she were the cheap tramp that her uncle had claimed. She wanted Dane. When she was with him, all seemed right. She needed those special moments to sustain her.

Ignoring her pride and determined vows never to return to his room, Gabrielle arose from the bed and moved quietly through the terrace door. She hesitated for only a moment, facing the brisk, damp breeze that foretold a coming storm. As lightning sent a jagged streak across the black sky, she stepped into Dane's room. With the thunder rumbling behind her and a flash of quicksilver from the heavens to guide her way, she walked toward his bed.

As the cool breeze rushed toward him Dane glanced to see the slim form that had appeared from nowhere. Hardly daring to believe she had returned, Dane steeled his heart against the warm tide that flooded over him. She had come out of the storm to tempt and torture him again. This time he would reject her and send her fleeing into the darkness from which she had come. She was a threat to his life and his sanity and he would tolerate no more of this torture!

The shadowy image floated toward him and waited quietly beside his bed. She was like a wild, cautious bird that would take flight if he made any sudden move to alarm her. As she eased down beside him, Brielle leaned over to place a kiss on his sensuous lips.

"I have come back to your world because I need you, m'lord," she whispered.

When Dane inhaled the sweet fragrance that hovered about him and felt the coolness of her hand on his bare chest, he was lost. All of his intentions of casting her aside died the instant her soft lips melted like rose petals on his. Whatever her motives, whatever danger he might face because of this elusive witch-angel, he needed these treasured moments. He had found ecstasy in the shadows of darkness. Neither of them could deny the wild desire that ignited the instant they embraced.

Dane groaned with pleasure, silently admitting to himself that he could never be free of her spell. His hand came up to caress the velvety cheek so close to his. "I've missed you, angel. I thought you would never return and I would never know the contentment I've found in your arms."

Gabrielle chuckled lightly. "I doubt that, m'lord. I'm sure you find much pleasure elsewhere. I accept your flattering admission with a good deal of wariness. What is your motive, sir?" she questioned skeptically. "Do you wish to win my heart and add it to your collection of those who have already been conquered by your experienced ways?"

"And what of you, my mysterious angel?" he countered. "What do you wish to claim? My heart, my life?"

"I'm not sure you possess a heart, m'lord. And I gave you back your life during the last storm," she murmured against his inviting lips. "I seek only comfort. Nothing more."

"You tell me that it was you who saved me, but a young lad also makes such a claim. Which one of you should I believe?" he questioned. The thought had constantly plagued him and only now had he dared to dispute her word.

"The first night I came to you I told you that with the help of your guardian angel you were carried to safety," she replied smoothly. "I did not say that it was I who *transported* you to safety. Without my assistance the lad would not have found you in the storm. I alerted him to your presence without his being aware that I was nearby." Gabrielle was careful not to make any connection between herself and the "waif." Her account of the incident seemed to satisfy Dane.

226

With no further questions, Dane drew her against the hard wall of his chest and Gabrielle surrendered to the storm that was brewing within her. As they embraced, the blowing rain began to patter against the windows like fingertips drumming with impatience. Their passions raged like billowing storm clouds, churning and swirling, preparing to unleash their forces upon all within their path. Dane and Brielle's desire for each other was as brisk as the wind that swept its way across the earth. Nothing could stop its flight or alter its course. The thunder rumbled, drowned by the beating of their hearts, and the lightning set fire to their emotions. The rain outside their chamber was no match for the rapturous cloudburst that raged within the confines of the room.

As Dane caressed the pliant form that lay beside him, Gabrielle reached out to run her fingers through the heavy furring on his chest. She pulled his face to hers in breathless urgency.

"Take me to heaven," he murmured as he lifted himself above her. "It's been an eternity."

Gabrielle reached out to him, gently guiding him to her, lost in the tempest of love that scattered all restraints. Then he was a part of her and she arched to meet his hard thrusts, reveling in the ecstasy that sent her soaring to towering heights. They glided among the puffy clouds, finding new pinnacles of rapture, suspended in a world that knew no time or space. As they drifted peacefully to reality they found a strange calmness that followed the storm. They lay together in the sheltering quilt of contentment. There were no words to express their feelings, no promises for tomorrow, no phrases of love; only an unspoken knowledge that what they shared had surpassed passion's pleasure.

Gabrielle wanted nothing except to remain within the gentle arms that held her close. Dane bit back the words that waited on the tip of his tongue. He resigned himself to merely holding her for as long as she would stay, asking no more questions and making no more demands.

Closing his eyes, Dane drifted into an unencumbered sleep, knowing that soon she would leave him and he would do nothing to stop her. He found it impossible to refuse this bewitching angel whatever she requested. Forever, he would remain her pawn, her willing lover when she came to him from the shadows. There would always be doubts to plague him, but they were stifled by the passion that she could evoke from him with her innocent ways.

At the dark hour before dawn, in the gentle rain that dampened the earth, Gabrielle returned to her room, warmed by the passion of a man who would never be hers except in the evening shadows. She could count upon nothing from life and accepted what was offered, not expecting her rapturous dream to last forever. Her life stood in limbo with no plans for the future. There was only this fleeting pleasure to keep her spirit alive.

In the next few weeks that followed their separation, Gabrielle frequently visited Dane. When he occasionally questioned her mysteriousness, Brielle answered in teasing riddles, making light of his inquiries. She still refused to tell him who she was, fearing that his loyalty would remain with her uncle. She would take no chance of being returned to the tyrant who sought to destroy her.

Whatever her motive, Dane would not forfeit their relationship. He was torn between his passion for this dark goddess and a desire to see the face of the woman who haunted, yet satisfied, him. The kindling flame between them grew stronger with each night they spent in each other's arms. The week Dane had endured without her was undeniable proof of his need for her. Remembering that, he would not risk losing her again.

His comforting evenings had soothed his sour mood and life at Hampton Estate had become pleasant once again. Gabe played her charade, content in the role of the high-spirited waif who had earned the captain's respect and who could say and do all of the things that would have been frowned upon if she were dressed as a gently bred young lady. Her double life allowed her to explore realms that she had never hoped to see. The thought of her inheritance was not so vivid as it had once been.

Dane strolled down the steps dressed in a black velvet jacket, breeches, and a white linen shirt. As he placed his silk top hat on his head, Gabe paused at the foot of the stairs and whistled appreciatively. His stride was confident, his appearance immaculate. He was undeniably handsome, she mused as her eyes raked him from head to toe. With those captivating pools of sapphire glowing with unbelievable depths and his raven hair framing his bronzed face, he would catch the attention of every woman who glanced in his direction.

"Ye look mighty fine in yer duds, Cap'n," she complimented with a broad smile. "I'm sure ye'll 'ave them noble ladies droolin' all over ye." Gabe propped her elbow on the banister and thoroughly raked him again. Lord, he was handsome. Luckily her eyes were already green, otherwise they would have turned that particular shade of envy.

"Thank you, Gabe," Dane replied, unimpressed by the lad's effort to compliment him. Gabe's words may have been flattering, but Dane was quick to note the undertone of sarcasm in the high-pitched voice.

"Would ye be wantin' me to travel with ye to the Brunsfords' ball?" Gabe queried, raising a hopeful smile to Dane. "I could keep ye company while ye ride."

"No. And don't start up with your usual retort about how I owe you my life," Dane ordered as he brushed past the disappointed waif.

That was to be Gabe's next argument, but Dane had heard it often enough and always expected it. She pulled a face at Dane's backside as he strolled across the entryway and disappeared out the front door. She would dearly love to accompany him. She had often dreamed of going to elaborate balls, but it seemed that she would never have the opportunity. After ambling into the study, Gabe picked up her favorite book of poetry and thumbed through it until one poem caught her attention. She read it over and over again, mesmerized by the words that seemed to describe her plight. Heaving a heavy-hearted sigh, she returned the book to the shelf and then walked to the stables to saddle Blanco. As she swung into the saddle, Nate held the reins, reluctant to let her go. Gabe had decided to follow the captain and she was not about to back down. If she couldn't enjoy being a participant at the party, at least she could watch everyone else having a good time. Besides, she mused, Dane was traveling at night and there was always a chance of trouble. If he needed her she was going to be close at hand.

"Dane!" Nick greeted him warmly as a wide smile split his handsome face. Extending a hand, Nick strolled toward Hampton who had just walked through the ballroom door.

Monica followed at her brother's heels, eying Dane's striking physique in slow, deliberate appraisal. Just seeing him always made her heart flutter excitedly. He was so irresistible, she thought to herself. She couldn't remember when she hadn't been attracted to him. It seemed he had forever been a part of her thoughts and dreams.

"Nick . . . Monica," Dane said as he shook hands with Sheffwall.

Nick glanced about, drawing a curious frown from Dane. "Where is that little bag of bones that is usually one step behind you?" he questioned, his tone laden with wry amusement.

"I left the little beggar to his own devices tonight," Dane replied glibly. "I don't think he was too happy about staying home, but at least he won't be underfoot, causing me trouble and embarrassment."

When Monica raised a questioning brow, her brother hastened to explain. "While you were in London last month, Dane came to visit. He was accompanied by a bedraggled waif. That little whelp was—"

"You can tell Monica all about Gabe when you return home," Dane interrupted as he wrapped a possessive arm about the petite blonde and led her to the dance floor. "I intend to hold this fetching lass in my arms."

Monica was all smiles. She didn't give a fig about some little wretch. All she wanted was to spend the evening with Dane.

"I'm sorry I missed you when you were in Bristol," she murmured as a shiver of excitement flew down her spine the moment Dane pulled her against his hard chest.

"So am I, love," he agreed as he gazed into her exquisite face. "How was your stay in London?"

"It would have been totally wonderful except for the ball that I attended with my aunt and uncle," she confessed, displaying another dimpled smile.

Dane arched a heavy brow. "I thought you thrived on having a vast number of suitors groveling at your feet," he teased.

Monica's blue eyes danced in amusement. "If you would have been there, I would have enjoyed

232

it much more. There are those gentlemen who are terribly exciting, such as you,'' she added with a coy smile, "and then there are others who test one's patience.''

When the music stopped, Dane led Monica through the terrace doors. He leaned back against a supporting post to view his lovely companion whose golden curls glistened in the moonlight. It seemed as though only now had he realized just how beautiful Monica was. Here was one exception to the noble ladies of court.

Gabe had wandered inconspicuously about the grounds, occasionally peering in the windows, wishing desperately to be one of the young women who danced in the crowded ballroom. The poem that she had read earlier came to mind, sending her spirits plunging to their lowest depths. It seemed that she was destined to be nothing more than she was at present—a dirty little ragamuffin whose only pleasure came from watching the aristocrats amuse themselves. Gabe sat down cross-legged in the shrubs beneath the back terrace, listening to the music that floated outside, wondering if she should return to Hampton Estate. She had expected to derive at least minimal enjoyment from the ball, but it had depressed her further. When she heard Dane's rich voice above her, she sank into the shrubs to listen to the conversation.

"And did you find some handsome gentleman to take my place, Monica?'' Dane teased with an affectionate smile.

"Of course not, Dane,'' she quickly assured him.

"You know that I only have eyes for you." Monica paused a moment and then continued in a rather distressed tone. "I spent most of the evening attempting to keep an arm's length between me and the Duke of Fairleigh. What a frightful man!"

"Don't tell me he was actually invited to the affair," Dane remarked, raising a dubious brow.

Monica scoffed disgustedly. "I doubt that anyone sent him an invitation, but he attended just the same. No one dared to turn him away at the door. The duke told me that his fiancée had run away. He was in town searching for her. Supposedly he was there to gain information as to her whereabouts, but he still managed to paw half of the women at the ball. The poor wench, 'tis little wonder that she escaped from him," Monica muttered with a shiver of repulsion.

Gabe silently agreed with the young woman. The same offensive quiver flew down her spine as she pictured the lecherous old man.

"Let me see, what was her name?" Monica began, thoughtfully touching her cheek with a dainty finger. She searched her memory, but she had been far too preoccupied attempting to elude the bungling fop. Monica could not recall the name he had uttered while he was reaching for her with that lusty glow in his deep-set eyes. The duke may have been in pursuit of his missing bride-to-be, but he had still ogled everything in petticoats. Monica had been aware of his intentions and had kept her distance. Hopelessly shaking her head, she again tried to bring the woman's name to mind. "Brianna? Brenna? Belle?" she mumbled.

"It was something like that."

Gabe held her breath, hoping that Monica would not recall the name which Fairleigh used to refer to her—Brielle. Just thinking of the sound of it as it came from his puffy lips nearly nauseated her. If her name was uttered, Dane might figure out who she was. Then where would she go? She would have to leave Hampton Estate. That was inevitable. If her uncle found her now, his punishment would be far worse than it had been the first time she had fled from his home.

Finally Monica shrugged away the thought. "I can't think of her name. I had never heard of her, but I do pity her. I'm sure I would have reacted as she did if I had been betrothed to the Duke of Fairleigh," she admitted, her nose wrinkling at the distasteful thought.

Dane chuckled at Monica's facial expression. "If the wench was engaged to Fairleigh, I doubt that she could have been much of a prize." He smirked. "She was probably after his money and later decided that no amount was worth living under the same roof with him, not to mention sharing his bed. The lady should be found. She deserves to suffer a marriage to him and his inexhaustible funds."

Gabe frowned angrily at Dane's description of her and his incorrect conclusion. It took much self-control not to bolt up from her hiding place and tell him how very wrong he was.

"And what of you, Dane?" Monica questioned, taking a step closer. "Why haven't you married? I doubt that your fiancée would flee from you."

235

Dane laid one leg over the railing and shrugged leisurely. With a blinding smile, he clasped his hands around Monica's trim waist and pulled her into his embrace. "Monica, you know Nick would never consent to *our* marriage. He knows me too well, and of course, I would have no other besides you," he assured her, smiling affectionately.

"We'll elope. My dear brother will just have to accept it," Monica bantered gaily while Gabe listened with eager ears.

Perhaps this was the woman who possessed the key to Dane's heart—Sheffwall's sister. If she was as attractive as her brother, Gabe could well imagine the way Dane was looking at her. A wave of jealousy shot through her, but she quickly ignored it. She had no claim on the captain and she had no right to be envious of his affection for Monica Sheffwall.

"Dear Monica," Dane murmured forlornly, placing a fleeting kiss on her forehead. "I love you far too much to marry you. I would only make you miserable. Such an arrangement would destroy our perfect relationship."

Monica raised glistening blue eyes, memorizing the distinct lines of his face. "I seriously doubt that, Dane. I doubt that very much."

Dane could read the sincerity in her delicate features and lowered his head to place a lingering kiss on her parted lips. Monica accepted his embrace as she always had—yielding to his touch without hesitation. A long moment passed before Dane drew away.

"Shall we rejoin the others?" he questioned

huskily. "Tarrying in the moonlight does strange things to a man who stands too close to such a tempting maid."

"I'm disappointed in your behavior, Dane," Monica chided playfully. "Your notorious reputation would have me believing that I would have to fight you off with a stick. Perhaps you don't find me as attractive as some of the women you have taken in your arms."

A rakish grin threatened the corners of his mouth as he glanced down at Monica. "On the contrary, love. 'Tis only that you demand my respect. Did you ever stop to consider that the others have not attained your prestigious position? I would not take liberties with the one whom I cherish above all others."

"You're a devil, Dane Hampton," Monica scolded, her smile belying her words. "You cast me aside and yet you make me feel as if I had won your heart."

Gabe silently agreed with Monica. He was a demon whom none could resist. And now she knew what Dane thought of his guardian angel. Dane could take her as a lover, but the one who might become his wife, he held in high esteem. Reluctantly, Gabe crawled from her hiding place and stalked toward her horse. Damn that rake! It seemed he was an eloquent flatterer. He was no better than Fairleigh. After hearing that conversation Gabe had no intention of waiting for the captain. She did not care that he might be attacked. As she rode back to the estate she vowed never to go to his room again. She meant nothing to him. He wanted to possess her, make love to her, and even whisper words of adoration just as he had done to Monica. He would say almost anything to lure a woman to his bed. Damn him!

A tear formed in the corner·of her eye and trickled down her cheek. Dane placed Monica upon a pedestal. Why couldn't it have been her? Gabe would have loved to exchange roles with Monica, if only for the evening. For once she would like to see the tender smiles Dane bestowed on a woman whom he respected. When Dane had made love to her, she could never see the emotion mirrored in his eyes or the expressions on his face. Perhaps it was better that way, Gabe thought dismally. It would only cause her pain to see no more than the flame of passion. It was over between them! No more late-night visits!

Chapter Ten

Dane sat at his desk studying his ledgers and then glanced up when Higgins, clearing his throat to gain Lord Hampton's attention, stepped into the room.

"Sir, Sylvia Berklin wishes to see you," he announced stiffly.

Dane arose from his chair and hastened to the door. "Bring her in and then have Gabe fetch some tea. I believe the lad is in the kitchen."

With an annoyed frown, Higgins made a slight bow and exited. When he returned with the sandy-haired young woman, she smiled broadly and appraised Lord Hampton's virile form.

"Hello, Sylvia," Dane greeted.

"Dane, 'tis so good to see you again. You're looking well." Sylvia took the opportunity to scan Dane's handsome face.

"How long have you been back from London?" she questioned as she settled her green silk skirts about her and sank down in the chair

Dane offered.

"About two months."

"When will you be sailing again? It seems you come and go so often that I can never keep up with you," she said sweetly.

"I'll be sailing again in a few days. We leave for Edinburgh on the twenty-seventh of the month. We will be loading cargo this week," he explained, producing a faint smile. Just seeing Sylvia again opened that sensitive wound that had never healed. It brought back too many painful memories that he was desperately trying to forget.

"I do hope you will have a safe trip," Sylvia replied, offering him another sticky-sweet smile. Then she gazed down to her lap, her expression sobering. "I was on my way to Bristol and I thought I would drop in to see you. Ah . . . ah, I'm a little short of funds."

Dane instantly came to his feet and walked to the desk. Carrying a pouch of coins, he returned to Sylvia and placed the money in her hand.

"Thank you, Dane. You have been very generous. I hope to have my business set up soon. Then I will no longer require an allowance." Sylvia rose to her feet and wrapped her arms around Dane's neck, pressing a more-than-grateful kiss to his lips.

Gabe turned the corner of the study in time to hear the woman's last comment and to see her ardently embrace the captain. Who the hell was this wench? Gabe muttered to herself. With a jealous frown masked behind several layers of dirt, she moved forward to place the tray of tea and pastries on the desk.

Sylvia critically appraised the baggy pants and sheepskin jerkin the lad wore and smirked haughtily. "Wherever did you find that filthy little wretch, Dane?" she quipped, turning up her nose at the lad.

With her fists clenched at her sides, Gabe stiffened, suppressing her urge to choke the life from this spiteful wench. She was about to express her indignance when Dane stepped between them.

"Gabe, pour Sylvia and me some tea?" Dane requested hastily. He had seen the menacing sparks in Gabe's eyes and hoped to ward off any verbal attacks.

"Certainly, Cap'n. It would be a pleasure," Gabe replied, forcing a shallow smile.

After pouring the tea, Gabe walked up to the woman. Sylvia accepted the tea with a reluctant frown, as if she were afraid she might be contaminated by touching anything the ragamuffin had handled.

"*Really*, Dane. I should think Higgins would make a more suitable servant than this scrawny little waif," she commented, ignoring the fact that the lad was standing right beside her. Sylvia's gaze observed the thin lad with nothing less than abhorrence.

Gabe wheeled away and stalked to the desk to collect the captain's cup. Dane shot her a warning look, knowing that Gabe was seething from Sylvia's biting remarks. After serving Lord Hampton, Gabe extended the tray of pastries and bowed humbly, a spiteful twinkle in her eyes.

"Liz makes the best tarts I've ever tasted. I 'ope ye'll enjoy them, m'lady." Gabe smiled devilishly as her hand tilted, allowing the cream-filled tarts to slide into Sylvia's lap, intermingling with the yards of gathered silk.

With an enraged squawk, Sylvia scooped up the sugar-coated pastries and tossed them on the platter. "You bungling twit!" she shrieked furiously. "Look what you've done. You're not fit to serve a tramp!"

Sylvia bolted to her feet and brushed off her dress, looking to Dane to reprimand the wretch for his intentional mischief. Lord Hampton could do nothing but bite back a grin, knowing that Sylvia had been justly rewarded for her snide remarks.

"I guess yer right. I didn't do much of a job of it this time. I beg yer pardon," Gabe pleaded in feigned concern while Sylvia gasped. "I'm a bit clumsy today. I'll fetch ye some more pastries."

"Just get away from me, you vicious little snip!" Sylvia screeched as she brushed past the boy, taking great care not to touch his disgusting clothes. She tilted her nose toward the ceiling and put a greater distance between the two of them. "I must be going, Dane. I do hope the next time I come to visit that you will have disposed of this ill-mannered bumpkin."

When Sylvia stormed from the room, Dane followed after her, offering a lame apology. "I'm sorry about the accident, Sylvia. Gabe is just learning to be a house servant. He only lacks experience."

Sylvia glanced over her shoulder, throwing him

242

a hasty retort. "That stray should be kept in the stables. You might as well turn your horse loose in the house. You could accomplish the same thing."

After Miss Berklin swept out of the house, fuming with rage, Dane returned to the study. Gabe was leaning back on the edge of the desk with his arms and legs crossed in front of him. With an irritated frown settling on his bronzed features, Dane opened his mouth to chide Gabe's behavior, but the lad spoke first.

"Who's the snobby wench?" Gabe quipped. "I 'ope she ain't the light and love of yer life. If she is, she ain't good enough fer ye, Cap'n."

Dane strolled over to the desk and took his seat. "Not mine, Gabe," he began solemnly. "She was my stepbrother's fiancée. They were to be married next month."

Gabe swallowed with a gulp. She had the feeling that Dane had finally decided to tell her what disturbed him.

Dane paused momentarily, his sapphire eyes mirroring pain. "The night before I was to sail I . . ." He stammered, folded his hands in front of him, and then continued quietly, "I found myself in the company of a very charming woman. I woke the next afternoon feeling as if I had been drugged. Too much liquor I suppose," he concluded with a reckless shrug. "When I arrived at the docks, the schooner had sailed without me. My stepbrother took my place. I learned later that the vessel had caught fire and all aboard had perished." Dane ducked his head recalling the torturing nightmare that haunted his mind. "He died in my place. It should have been me. Because of my frivolous escapade, Sylvia was left practically penniless and without the man she loved."

Gabe's heart went out to the captain who, at that moment, in no way resembled the strong confident rogue she knew. But the thought of Sylvia and her dreamy-eyed gazes at Dane did little to gain Gabe's sympathy.

"Seems to me that Sylvia 'as taken 'er loss a 'ell of a lot better than ye 'ave, Cap'n," Gabe scoffed.

Dane shot the waif a disapproving glance, but Gabe shrugged it off.

"Well," she defended, "I bet she ain't losin' no sleep over it like ye are."

Raising a dubious brow, Dane focused his full attention on Gabe. "And who said I was losing sleep over it?"

Gabe colored slightly as she fumbled for an explanation. "I jest figured that must be what caused them nightmares of yers. I've 'eard ye moanin' and groanin' in yer sleep more than once. I bet the 'ole 'ouse and 'alf the countryside could 'ave 'eard yer midnight ravin's."

Dane's gaze never wavered as he listened to the lad's words. He was probably right, Dane thought to himself. The entire staff was most likely aware of his nightmares. But only this impetuous urchin would dare to call his attention to it.

"I realize Sylvia had it coming, but your behavior was inexcusable. Servant boys are not to treat noblewomen with so little respect," Dane chided, his eyes drilling into her.

"I'd swear that wench is related to 'Iggins,"

244

Gabe remarked with a derisive snort. "They both got their noses so 'igh in the air they can't 'ardly tell where they're goin'." Gabe strutted across the room, mimicking Sylvia and bringing an amused chuckle from the captain.

"If you were wearing a dress of silk you could charade as Sylvia," Dane commented between chortles.

Gabe spun to face him, carelessly wiping her smudged face with her wrinkled sleeve. She did not appreciate his gibe.

"'Ow come yer payin' 'er off?" she questioned bluntly as she rested her arms on the back of the chair.

"I feel I owe her something. If I had been on that ship as planned, she wouldn't have lost her betrothed. It is little compensation for what happened." Another painful flicker skittered across his bronzed features and Gabe was quick to note it.

"It's guilt money, Cap'n, and she don't deserve a penny. The wench is playin' on yer sympathy." Gabe snorted.

Dane shot the lad a black look. "Keep your opinions to yourself."

Gabe stuffed her hands in her pockets and strolled around the chair, letting the matter drop without protest. "I was wonderin' if I could 'ave the day off tomorrow."

"Whenever you want, except Friday. I want you to help me prepare for my trip." Dane had not dared discuss the matter before now, fearing Gabe would pack up and leave.

"Where are ye goin'?" Disappointed by the news, Gabe strolled to the window and toyed with the tassels on the velvet drapes, her gaze sweeping the flower-filled garden that circled the house.

"To London. I have to transport some cargo to Scotland," he said simply.

"'Ow long will ye be gone?"

"Three or four weeks. But you still have a place here, lad," Dane assured her, smiling fondly.

Gabe shook her head determinedly. "Ye know damned well I ain't stayin' 'ere with 'Iggins rulin' the roost. One or the other of us 'as got to go and 'e's bin 'ere longer than me."

"Now, Gabe—"

Gabe waved her hand for silence, an idea forming in her mind. "Kin I go with ye?" She raised wide, green eyes to Dane. It would buy precious time and put an even greater distance between her and Lord Jarmon.

"No. I have a full crew that has been with me for years. You'd be better off here," Dane insisted as he rose from his chair.

"Ye'll be dead if I don't go, ye know. Who'll protect ye while yer travelin' to London? After all, ye owe me somethin' fer savin' yer life. The least ye could do is let me go to Scotland with ye." Gabe stared at the captain with grim determination. "I ain't stayin' 'ere with 'Iggins breathin' down me neck. I'll follow ye if ye don't allow me to go. That is, unless yer plannin' to lock me in me room," she added caustically.

Dane studied the willful lad, knowing he would try to follow along and he was not about to keep

Gabe prisoner. Leaning his hands on the desk, Dane nodded reluctantly. "Very well, I'll take you along. But you'll have to room with me. There won't be a bunk for you anywhere else unless you want to sleep on deck. We have a full crew and each man has his own bunk. I wouldn't think of turning you loose with the lot of them. One of your insolent remarks to that burly crowd and they would have you walking the plank."

Gabe considered her choices. It wouldn't be easy maneuvering around the captain, but it was better than staying at the estate with Higgins or wandering the countryside in search of other lodging.

"I like me privacy, but 'avin' ye underfoot beats the 'ell out of livin' with 'Iggins' spiteful glares," she replied, a faint smile surfacing on her smudged face.

"I want no complaining out of you. And no trouble," Dane ordered, pointing an accusing finger at the suddenly innocent-looking lad.

"From me?" Gabe quipped incredulously. "I don't cause no trouble and I ain't a grumbler like some people I know." A guiltless grin caught the corners of her mouth as she glanced at the captain.

"What!" Dane gasped in astonishment. "How can you constantly criticize me after I have just witnessed one of your troublesome scenes?"

Gabe considered his words for a long moment. She was standing on shaky ground and she had to admit that her defense was a mite weak, but she had no intention of coming right out and confessing to it. "Ye told me once that ye liked a

247

little spice in yer life. Now which is it, Cap'n? Do ye want me to be a mousy little lad who never utters a word or would ye rather I stood up fer meself and says what needs to be said?" she inquired, arching a taunting brow.

"Moderation might be a pleasant change," Dane suggested sarcastically.

"It ain't one of yer practices, Cap'n," she reminded him. "Why do ye expect a lowly servant such as meself to be a saint?" Before Dane could reply, she hurried on. "I'll take off tomorrow and 'ave yer belongin's ready fer the trip."

As Gabe swaggered out of the room, Dane stared at the lad's backside and hopelessly shook his head. He should have known Gabe would want to go along and would have found some way to sneak aboard if Dane had refused him. Gabe was so strong-willed, like a constantly moving force that had no intention of halting, no matter what the odds against him. Dane had found himself wishing that Gabe was his son. He would have been proud to claim the stripling as his own. Perhaps the boy had smudged cheeks and baggy clothes, but he was made of sturdy stuff. Gabe was indeed a prince in pauper's clothes. Clothes did *not* make the man and Gabe was walking proof of it. What lay beneath those tattered garments was a soul of silk and gold braid.

Gabe hurriedly dressed, anticipating her day of freedom. She walked to the barn, wearing a happy smile, until she met Higgins, wearing his sour frown for a morning greeting, coming up the hill.

"Where do you think you're going?" Higgins snapped hatefully.

Her eyes narrowed in annoyance. "It ain't none of yer business, but this is me day off."

"Your day off?" He snorted disgustedly, his cold, hazel eyes raking her with contempt. "You have yet to earn your keep. No one around here is allowed as much free time as you have already taken and *you* don't deserve it!"

"I think I do and I'm takin' it. Everyone 'round 'ere ought to git an extra day fer jest 'avin' to put up with yer foul disposition," Gabe snapped, her tone cold as the north wind. As she started forward Higgins yanked her around to face him.

"While Lord Hampton is away, I intend to teach you your place!" he vowed in a gritted growl. "You're going to learn to behave like a servant if I have to beat the idea into your stubborn hide."

"Like 'ell ye will, ye pompous ass!" Gabe jerked her arm from his grasp, her green eyes spewing fire. "Ye ain't layin' a 'and on me."

Higgins spurted a curse, his face reddening in rage. "You're a damned nuisance, always in the way." He raised his hand, prepared to slap the defiant smirk from Gabe's face, but his arm halted in midair when he heard the threatening voice behind him.

"Higgins! If you touch him, you've lost your job!" Dane bellowed. He stood at the corner of the house, his feet set squarely, his blue eyes burning with their own rage.

A smug grin settled on Gabe's features. "Better luck next time, 'Iggins," she chuckled.

The servant whirled away, mumbling under his breath as he stalked toward the house.

"What was that all about?" Dane questioned, his brows furrowing in concern.

Gabe's shoulder lifted in a reckless shrug. "'E said 'e was goin' to teach me 'ow to act while ye were away. 'E thought 'e could beat the idea into me and I told 'im I wouldn't let 'im touch me."

"I'll have a talk with him," Dane assured her, his jaw twitching angrily.

"I kin take care of meself. If ye take sides, 'e'll resent me even more. Jest fergit about it. We'll be gone before long any'ow." Gabe looked up to Dane whose features wore a worried frown. She grinned and elbowed him in the ribs. "I ain't afraid of 'Iggins."

When Gabe strolled inside the barn, Nate displayed a warm smile and quickly saddled Blanco. Gabe swung up onto the stallion and waved farewell before reining toward the trees. She rode with the wind whipping about her face, feeling the freedom that sent her soul soaring. Drawing strength from the sturdy steed beneath her, Gabe smiled to herself. When she came to the cliff overlooking the sea, she dismounted and allowed Blanco to graze while she stood facing the gentle waves that slapped against the rocks below. She was anticipating her sea journey. Although she could never again enjoy the security of Dane's arms, she would still be near him, masquerading as a waif.

Thinking past the trip to Scotland, Gabe had decided that she would find an apartment in

Bristol when she returned. She would find work, relinquishing her disguise as a lad. Surely by then Lord Jarmon would have given up his search. With Saxon's help she would manage. As she sat down on the edge of the bluff, dangling her legs over the side, contemplating her plans, a pair of unseen hands pushed on her back, sending her over the cliff as she emitted a frightened screech.

When Gabe released her blood-curdling scream, Blanco bolted forward, galloping across the meadow, his hoofs pounding the ground in haste. With his white mane flying about him and his nostrils flaring in fright, Blanco thundered through the trees and then halted abruptly in front of the stables. He pranced nervously until Nate stepped outside to see the laboring stallion without his rider.

Nate jumped on Blanco's back and urged him to the front of the house. He rushed inside, searching for Dane whom he found seated in the study. With a guttural screech, Nate ran to Dane and pulled on his arms. The alarmed expression on Nate's face brought Dane to his feet and they dashed out to see Blanco lathered with sweat, his eyes darting fearfully about him. Dane swung into the saddle, reining the steed toward the pasture.

Dane pictured Gabe standing dejectedly at the edge of the cliff and he headed to the bluff, wondering if the lad had decided to take his own life after all. The vision of the frail waif lying dead and mangled on the jagged rocks sent Dane's heart racing in dread anticipation. When he reached the cliff, he slid from the saddle and rushed to the edge,

251

calling Gabe's name with frantic urgency. God, he didn't want to look down, afraid of what he would find. He had already lost all of his family. Losing Gabe would be the final blow.

Gabe's fall to the boulders had been broken by a narrow ledge where several tree roots grew from between the crumbling cliff. Holding frantically to the roots, she had pulled herself up to her feet and backed against the rock wall.

She had surveyed her precarious position and found no way down and nothing but solid rock above her. She found herself wishing she were indeed the guardian angel she had claimed to be. At the moment, she wouldn't have minded being anything with wings. Unfortunately there was nothing for her to do but to hold on, hoping that someone would come searching for her when she didn't return that night.

After their morning confrontation, Gabe instantly suspected Higgins, but then another thought forced its way to mind. Perhaps whoever was after Dane had decided that she had come to his aid once too often and it was time to get rid of her. Either explanation would suffice, but one thing was certain: somebody wanted her dead.

When Gabe heard Dane calling out to her she breathed a sigh of relief and looked above her. Dane braved glancing down and said a thankful prayer when he saw Gabe clutching the tree roots.

"Are you all right?" Dane questioned in a distraught voice.

Gabe shook her head affirmatively. "Only a few bruises and scrapes," she called up to him.

"I'll have to go back to fetch a rope. Will you be able to hang on until I get back?" Dane yelled as he leaned out over the bluff, his face etched with a concerned frown.

"Do I 'ave another choice, Cap'n?" she mocked, smiling faintly at his ridiculous question.

Dane shook his head despairingly. The lad had nearly met his death and there he was, cocky as ever, returning the concerned inquiry with a snippy retort.

Dane turned, grabbed Blanco's reins, and stepped into the stirrup as the stallion galloped away.

When he returned, riding Sultan, he tied a heavy rope around the saddle horn and tossed the free end over the edge to dangle just out of Gabe's reach. He tried to back Sultan close to the edge, but the horse wouldn't budge. Although Dane coaxed the reluctant steed he remained steadfast, setting his feet to prevent any movement. Gabe reached for the rope again, but it was hopeless. If she stretched another inch she would take a headlong dive onto the rocks below her.

"Back that nag up!" Gabe barked impatiently.

Dane's face appeared above the bluff. "Sultan isn't too fond of the idea. Give me a minute," Dane snapped, anger and urgency intermingling to make his tone sharper than he intended.

Gabe snorted derisively. "Wait a minute, he says," she muttered under her breath. She glanced up at Dane. "Sure, Cap'n. Ye jest take all the time ye need. I'll jest 'ang on by me fingernails and enjoy the scenery while ye sweet-talk that damned nag," she insisted, her voice heavily laden with sarcasm.

"It isn't easy to forcefully move a thousand-pound horse!" Dane defended indignantly.

Gabe rolled her eyes in disbelief. What a fine time for an argument! Her arms were about to give out and she couldn't hold on much longer. It was lucky Dane had come along. She would have never made it until nightfall.

"Ye and that 'orse better come to terms in a 'urry or ye'll be watchin' me plunge into the sea," she shot back at him.

Dane grumbled under his breath and stalked back to Sultan. When he had retrieved the quirt he gave Sultan a swat, hoping to remind the steed who was boss and who was beast. Again Sultan balked and again Dane struck him. Finally the steed stepped back and Gabe grabbed the lifeline. With it securely bound around her waist, Gabe called out for Dane to pull her up. Placing her feet against the rock wall, Gabe moved upward until she reached out to Dane's hand and he hauled her to safety. Once on firm ground she collapsed to her knees, heaving a heavy sigh. She raised a bruised but thankful face to Dane.

"Thanks, Cap'n. It seems that now I'm only two up on ye," she remarked, a wry grin etching her smudged features.

Dane ignored her bantering and proceeded with his question. "How did this happen? Did you—"

Gabe cut him short with an indignant snort. "'Ell no, I didn't jump if that's what yer thinkin'. I was pushed from behind while I was sittin' there lookin' out over the sea. If I 'ad bin standin', I would 'ave fallen all the way to the bottom. Luckily, I jest sort of slipped off.''

A worried frown gathered on his brows as he studied Gabe's bruises and scrapes. Gabe had come dangerously close to death. ''Perhaps you would be better off if you left here for good. I don't want to jeopardize your life, Gabe.''

''I'll jest be more careful in the future. I got no intention of leavin' 'till I'm ready. Nobody's goin' to *scare* me off,'' she assured him as she scrambled to her feet and brushed off her breeches.

Gabe pulled the rope from the saddle and then patted Sultan's neck. ''Thanks fer 'aulin' me up. Do I git to ride back with ye or are ye makin' me walk?'' she questioned over her shoulder.

Dane swung into the saddle, offering the waif a helping hand. Gabe grabbed him around the waist, careful not to press too close. She clutched at Dane as Sultan galloped to the house, nearly tumbling her off his back.

''Damn it! Slow this nag down, Cap'n!'' Gabe squawked angrily. ''Me backside is bruised enough as it is. Another spill may render me eternally crippled.''

Dane obliged as he sent the waif a mischievous grin. ''Are you getting soft, Gabe?'' he teased, his dark brows arching in amusement.

''No, I ain't soft, jest sore. Ye think ye'd feel any better than me if ye bounced off them hard rocks?'' she quipped resentfully.

''I probably would have broken every bone in my body at least twice,'' Dane admitted with a chuckle.

When they rode up to the stables, Nate was waiting with a relieved smile. He reached up to pull Gabe down in front of him, hugging her affectionately.

Gabe pushed away from his embrace and adjusted her hat before letting her gaze slide to Dane. "I'm fine, Nate. Cap'n said ye were the one who alerted 'im. Thank ye."

Dane eyed Nate curiously, wondering why he was so devoted to a boy who was younger. There seemed to be more than just friendship between them. The captain had difficulty analyzing the emotion that flickered in Nate's coal-black eyes.

Gabe returned to the house and started up the steps. When she spied Higgins' perfidious smirk she stalked toward him.

"Did you meet with an accident, *boy?*" Higgins hissed the last word insultingly.

"Ye should know, ye cowardly ogre," she sneered, her eyes narrowing accusingly.

Higgins took a bold step forward, a contemptuous glare darkening his cold features. Gabe shot him a challenging glower as they stood only inches apart. When Dane opened the front door, the conversation that had only begun came to a screeching halt. Gabe and Higgins spun away, still fuming from their short, but fiery confrontation.

When Gabe was in her room with the door locked behind her, she shed her clothes and washed her scrapes and bruises. After changing into clean garb, she mended her garments.

That done, a lunch basket dangling from her hand, she strolled the gardens and then settled down by the creek to eat her meal. In these peaceful surroundings, with only the chatter of birds and the trickling stream as companions, she heaved a troubled sigh. Was it Higgins who had pushed her? Or was it Dane's would-be assassin?

Gabe pulled the silver dagger from her boot and hurled it at a tree. The handle hit the bark and bounced back toward her, landing in the grass.

"Damn," she muttered with a hopeless shake of her head. "I can't even hurl a blade at a motionless tree and make it stick. Pitiful, damned pitiful."

"All you need is some practice and a little instruction," came the amused voice from behind her.

Gabe jerked in alarm and fumbled for the handgun she carried in her baggy pants. After her close encounter she was almost afraid of her own shadow. She turned the gun on Dane and then quickly dropped her hand, returning the weapon to its concealed resting place.

"Sorry, Cap'n," she apologized meekly. "I seem to be a bit more cautious of late."

"So I see," Dane remarked dryly as he ambled over and bent down to retrieve the knife. "Would you like to learn to use this blade with a little proficiency?"

Gabe smiled and nodded eagerly. Dane showed her how to hold the knife and then lightly flicked his wrist, sending the blade hurtling through the air. It dug into the tree and quivered with the force of his accurate throw.

"Now you try it," he urged, extending the knife to Gabe.

Gabe copied his movement as best she could, but only accomplished another futile attempt.

With a chuckle, Dane turned mocking sapphire eyes to her. "You throw like a girl. I can see that no one has taught you much about preserving your life. And you said you could take care of yourself," he reminded her with a caustic snort.

Gabe grumbled at his choice of words. "Ye don't need to be so insultin', Cap'n. I'm doin' the best I kin."

After more instruction from Dane and several practice throws, Gabe finally managed to stab the tree in the general area at which she had aimed.

With a sense of accomplishment, Gabe grinned up into the bright blue eyes that always melted her heart when she wasn't guarding it closely. "Thanks, Cap'n." Averting her gaze she turned away and went to retrieve the dagger.

"You're welcome, Gabe. But I have one favor to ask of you," Dane commented, a somber expression settling on his bronzed features.

Gabe yanked the knife from the tree and sauntered back to Dane. "What is it?" she queried, preoccupied with what Dane had taught her.

"The next time your quick temper breaks loose, don't pull your knife on me," he requested as a taunting smile grazed his lips.

Returning the grin, Gabe sashayed toward him. She put the point of the knife against his chest which was laid bare by his gaping shirt. "Don't ever git me riled and ye'll 'ave nothin' to fear," she warned, her green eyes sparkling mischievously.

Before Gabe had time to react, Dane grabbed her wrist, spun her around, and held the blade to her throat. He chuckled merrily at her startled expression. Although Gabe knew he was merely playing, the feel of his arm around her sent a tingle flying down her spine. She panicked.

"Let me go!" she insisted, her voice cracking with impatience.

The grin on Dane's face was transformed into a bemused frown. He released the belligerent waif who twisted away and then whirled to face him. "I wasn't going to hurt you, Gabe," he said in a soft tone.

Ducking her head from the captain's steady gaze, Gabe kicked her foot at the grass, uprooting a small clump. "I know ye weren't. But I don't like to be 'eld down. It makes me nervous," she explained, fumbling for an excuse for her queer actions.

Dane crossed his arms on his chest, studying the waif closely, wondering what incident from his past had surfaced as they struggled against each other. One moment Gabe was cocky and daring and then in the next instant he was cowardly backing away as if he expected to be beaten or attacked. Dane was certain that he would never understand Gabe unless he knew the story of his secretive past. But Gabe would only forfeit bits and pieces of his background when he was forced to it. Although Dane knew the stripling liked him, he had never gained Gabe's trust. The only one who had been allowed that privilege was Nate.

Gabe could read the captain's mind, but she could offer him only small consolation. "Someday, Cap'n, ye'll know the whole of it. I'll answer all the questions that must be flyin' 'round yer 'ead, but not now. The past 'as got to remain a carefully guarded secret or me life won't be worth livin'. There are some merciless scoundrels who would delight in torturin' me fer what I did if they could git their 'ands on me. I ain't about to let that 'appen. Only time will solve me problem; not yer title or yer money. I'm afraid ye'll jest 'ave to wait 'til I'm ready to explain and I ain't ready yet."

With a muddled frown gathering on his brows, Dane extended his hand to return Gabe's knife, amazed at how easily the lad had guessed what he was thinking. "If you're in some kind of trouble, I want to help. If you would only trust me—"

Gabe cut him short as she returned the dagger to her boot and snorted bitterly. "Ain't nothin' ye kin do. Like I told ye before, this is not yer problem. I appreciate yer offer though."

"Then why have you confided in Nate, a mere livery boy? I would surely be of more assistance than he," Dane persisted, his voice laced with resentment.

A wry smile caught one corner of Gabe's mouth. "'Tis only by accident that Nate knows what 'e does. 'E 'appened to be at the right place at the right time. But Nate don't know the full story. Besides," she continued with a careless shrug, "Nate aren't goin' to tell nobody and 'e ain't powerful enough to force me to do somethin' that I don't want to do."

Dane relinquished his attempt to gain information from Gabe. There was nothing he could say to convince the stubborn little wretch to confide in him. Dane could not fathom the meaning of Gabe's remarks. "Very well, Gabe. Have it your own way. You usually do. I won't press you. But remember, if you need me I'll always be here to help you. You have given me assistance on a number of occasions and yet you don't trust me enough to tell me what's troubling you." Dane turned away, paused, and then glanced over his shoulder. "I'm going to the house. Are you coming?"

Gabe opened her mouth, confession on the tip of her tongue, but she bit it back. She just couldn't take the chance of being sent home. "No. I'm goin' to stay out 'ere awhile longer," she mumbled as she studied the grass beneath her feet.

Gabe wandered aimlessly along the creek, lost in troubled thoughts. After practicing with her dagger until she could throw with a respectable amount of accuracy, she went back to the house to take supper with Liz and Nate.

The night before they were to leave, Brielle bathed and dressed in her white gown. She had vowed never to return to Dane's room after hearing his conversation with Monica. But knowing that this would be the last time she could nestle in his strong arms, she could not resist saying good-by to the tender man she knew in the darkness.

As she stepped into his room, she squinted, trying to make her way toward the bed. When she

261

sank down, she realized that Dane wasn't there. With a disappointed sigh, she arose and moved toward the door. Suddenly, she was grabbed and pulled against a hard, muscled chest. Her alarmed cry was muffled by a crushing kiss and she instantly melted against the virile form that held her in a tight embrace.

"Were you trying to scare the life out of me?" she queried as she dragged her lips away from his devouring kiss.

"Is it possible to frighten the life from an angel? I thought you were immortal, love," he mocked as he led her toward the bed.

"Immortal in the sense that part of me remains behind each time I leave you," she murmured.

"That's comforting to know." Dane drew her into his arms and lay back on the bed, inhaling the sweet scent that started his senses reeling. "I thought perhaps you had forgotten me. You have not come to me for more days than I care to count."

"I have many obligations, m'lord. I cannot always be with you. My life is complicated and my time is never my own—except during the witching hour," she whispered before placing a fleeting kiss on his eager lips.

A flooding tide of emotion swept over them, carrying them down the river of desire. Dane caressed her velvety skin and Gabrielle relaxed beneath his skillful touch. His hands worked magic with her, drawing forth a fervent passion that only he could appease. His mouth covered the peak of her breast and she gasped as a wild tremor flew down her spine. Her hand slid down his back, brushing lightly against the rippling muscles that flexed and eased beneath her touch. Another moan of pleasure escaped her lips as he traced scalding kisses over her body. His caresses roamed over her body, learning each curve and swell. He brought her to sensual heights that demanded fulfillment, leaving her breathlessly anticipating their union.

Dane lifted himself above her, staring into the dark face below his. As he came to her, thrusting deeply, seeking ultimate depths of intimacy, they were swirled by desire into the passion that carried them beneath reality's surface. Undercurrents of rapture left them clinging frantically to each other, drowning in emotions that set nerves on edge. They were swept to rippling falls that plunged them downward. And then they were one, cradled on a tranquil pool below passion's cascade, safe and secure in each other's embrace.

Brielle lay in his arms and nuzzled against his sturdy chest, wishing she would never have to leave. Dane seemed to be the only stable force in her chaotic world. Forgetting what they shared would be no easy task. He had taken her to the heights and depths of passion, leaving her wanting for nothing. Gabrielle treasured these moments with him, knowing tonight would be the end of her pleasureful lovemaking.

As Dane pressed a tender kiss to her forehead, he moaned drowsily. His strength was drained, his passion spent, and his desire for this dark angel only momentarily appeased. He could not seem to get enough of her. She had become an addiction, a need that he continued to crave. He would be gone an eternity. Would she be here when he returned? Their time apart would be endless agony, he mused as he placed another lingering kiss on her moist lips.

"I must leave tomorrow, love. Will you find another to take my place?" he questioned as his hand brushed her tangled hair away from her face.

"Will you seek another's arms when we are apart?" she countered in a raspy whisper. "I have asked nothing of you in the past. I demand no pledge for the future. Tomorrow is uncertain. I can make no promises to you and you will offer none to me." Gabrielle traced her fingers across his sensuous lips, wishing she could look deeply into his eyes. Would there be remorse mirrored in those pools of blue? No, she thought to herself. Dane thrived on passion and he could find it anywhere. "You are a man and I am no fool. There were many loving arms to bring you comfort before I came to you. There will be others to take my place."

"But I—" he began in frustration.

Gabrielle cut him short, pressing her fingers to his lips. "There is nothing more to say except that we have no place in our lives for empty words and broken vows."

"Will you come back to me when I return from the sea?"

Gabrielle hesitated a long moment, thoughtfully chewing on her bottom lip. How could she say good-by to him without succumbing to tears. She must never allow him to know how he affected her.

"I've got to know," Dane persisted as he lifted himself above her, peering into her shadowed face.

"'Tis over, m'lord." Her hand slid about his

neck, toying with his thick hair. "Perhaps in another time and place we will meet again. Then I can tell you all. No longer will I be forced to travel in darkness, stealing blissful moments that were not rightfully mine to claim. When you see me for what I am, you will understand. But, please, trust me now. This is how it must be if I am to survive in the world from which I came," she pleaded quietly.

Brielle attempted to squirm away, but Dane pulled her closer. "Don't leave me," he breathed.

"I must. Don't make me regret ever coming here. If you force me to stay or attempt to learn who I am you will destroy all of the fond memories that I treasure. 'Tis all I have." Her voice cracked as she muffled a sniffle, annoyed with herself for showing emotion. "Please don't take these memories away from me. They are precious and few."

How could he refuse her quiet plea? He could not bring himself to turn her against him. Perhaps she would return if he didn't press her. Dane rolled to his side and placed a passionate kiss on her parted lips, his arms crushing her so tightly against him that Brielle was unable to breathe.

"Each time darkness surrounds me, I'll think of you. In a month I will return. Each night I will wait for you to come to me," he murmured against the hollow of her neck.

Gabrielle eased from his side and slipped the gown over her head as she moved away from his bed. "I cannot, m'lord. You seek the impossible," came her distant whisper. "Saying good-by to you is my own private torture. I feel as if I am leaving part of myself behind. If you can find it in your heart to remember me with fond affection, then I can go in peace, knowing that what I have forfeited was not in vain, but rather a gift of pure emotion."

"If you feel something for me, tell me before you go," Dane sighed in exasperation. "Do you cherish what we shared above all else?"

She winced at his pointed question. Did he want her as another conquered trophy?

"We are like two ships that have passed in the night. We were both drifting on a troubled sea. You have eased my pain with your comforting arms, but now we must go our separate ways. Yes, m'lord, I cherish these moments because they came in times that saved me from despair. I will always be grateful to you for that."

As a cool breeze swept into the room Dane felt emptiness engulf him like none he had ever known. Grateful? Was that all she felt for him? "You asked for nothing and you promised nothing," he muttered to the lingering vision that floated above him. "Yet you have taken all that I might have claimed. I will never be able to rout you from my mind."

As he tossed and turned, begging for sleep, her elusive image came to him again, denying him slumber until the early hours before dawn. A hollow ache nagged at him as he dreamed of the dark goddess who had tempted and taunted him, yet satisfied him as no other had. But there was still no face and no name. Now she was gone and he would never know the feel of her soft flesh pressed to his.

Chapter Eleven

After Dane and Gabe had traveled throughout the morning, Dane stopped at an inn for lunch.

Tossing a few coins to Gabe, Dane preceded the lad through the door. "I won't be gone long. Get yourself something to eat."

As he disappeared behind the wooden door, seeking the pleasure of a red-haired wench, Gabe hung her head and shook it despairingly. "So quickly does he seek another's affection," she muttered scornfully. Clutching the coins in her fist, she drew open the door. "All of your tender words were lies. You're no different than any other man. A woman is quickly forgotten when the outstretched arms of another maid take her place. Damn you, Dane Hampton."

While Gabe picked over her food, she tried to convince herself that she had expected this from him. He was not bound to her and she could not condemn him for what he was doing. After all, she knew there would be others to share his passion.

Unfortunately, she would have the painful experience of knowing about each and every one of them.

If Gabe had not felt the need to put more time between herself and her uncle, she would have fled from the inn. But the time she would be at sea was precious. Sooner or later John would realize that she would never return. Hopefully, by the time they disembarked in London, he would have done just that.

After an hour, Dane descended the stairs to see Gabe sitting in the corner, his head propped on his hand, stabbing his fork at his food.

"Are you ready?" Dane questioned as he stood peering down at the lad who refused to acknowledge his presence.

"Aye," Gabe muttered as she rose from her chair.

Their journey to London was long and quiet. Gabe was in no mood for idle chatter. Although Dane attempted to make conversation, he finally gave it up with an indifferent shrug.

When they stopped for the night, Gabe was allowed her own small room and she was thankful for her privacy. It might be the last time in a long while that she could slip back into the role of a young woman. She appreciated what little time she had.

Although she could not deny the fond memories that lingered in her mind, the pain of knowing what Dane had done that afternoon was impossible to ignore. He was a proficient lover. In the shadowed darkness he could make her feel as though she were the only woman in the world who could arouse him to wild passion. No doubt it was the same with every woman he touched, she mused bitterly. She reminded herself that she had known from the beginning that his heart was chained to a woman he could never possess. Gabrielle had carried a dim light of hope, but it had been smothered that afternoon.

With determined thoughts she vowed to enjoy Dane as a friend and companion, expecting and receiving nothing more than she would from Nate or Sherman. She had suffered many disappointments in her short life. And yet, she had overcome them all. One man would not bring her to her knees and hold her captive with an emotion that should never have been allowed to grow. It was her own fault. She could not blame Dane no matter how easy it would have been to condemn him. He had told her that he did not offer any more than passion to a woman. He had given her the comfort and security she needed. It was she who had yielded to him, to negate the marriage contract. She continued to rationalize, but words didn't stop the aching loss she felt in her heart. Was it pride that caused her hurt? She crawled into bed, pulling the quilts tightly about her to protect herself from the cold, lonely chamber. It must be her pride, she thought tiredly. That was what led her to believe that Dane cared for her. The shame of what she had recklessly done nipped at her conscience, but she would survive, she vowed determinedly. She would not be conquered by her emotions. Time would heal the pain, just as it had covered the tender wounds of her past. Tomorrow was another day and Gabrielle Jarmon no longer existed. It was just as the poem had claimed, she mused drowsily.

Tomorrow, the ill-mannered, high-spirited waif with the quick tongue and teasing words would emerge. That would be the end of her relationship with Dane Hampton. That was the same thing she had told herself the previous evening. How many nights of repetitious vows would pass before she could accept it as truth? That was another question for which there was no easy answer.

As Gabe and Captain Hampton made their way through the streets of London, Gabe lost herself to quiet musings. She watched the elegantly dressed men and women strolling down the boardwalks. If her father had lived, she would have been among them, enjoying parties, meeting eligible bachelors. She imagined herself dressed in fine silk gowns, leaning on the arm of a handsome rogue with captivating, blue eyes, raven hair . . .

Gabe shook her head, shattering the whimsical vision. If she was going to forget Dane Hampton she could not allow herself time to daydream.

Dane arched a curious brow. The young lad sat atop his white stallion, rattling his head. "What the hell's the matter with you, boy?" he inquired, an amused smile threatening the corners of his mouth.

Gabe returned the grin, shrugging carelessly. "Aw, nothin' really, Cap'n. I was jest picturin' meself duded up in me finery, rubbin' shoulders with them noblemen."

"How did you look?" Dane queried, his smile widening to encompass his bronzed features.

"Like a jackass fitted with a cravat and stockin's."

"Come now. I thought you had a rather high opinion of yourself," Dane mocked dryly. "I remember your sitting in the wagon on the way back from Bristol, telling me that one day you would own half of England. Your last remark doesn't sound like the Gabe I know."

"I guess I jest started seein' thin's as they are," she muttered disheartenedly. "I'll never be more than I am right now."

As they made their way to the wharf, Gabe marveled at the vessels that lined the harbor. There she was in a man's world, and yet, many of the boats had some derivation of femininity painted on their bows—*Sea Nymph, Ocean Princess, The Mermaid.*

Gabe eyed one fishing craft called *Fable's Folly* and burst out laughing.

"What do you find so amusing?" Dane quipped, arching a heavy brow.

"The names, Cap'n." Gabe smirked, her eyes dancing merrily. "It seems since the beginnin' of time the downfall of many a man was a woman. And 'ere these sailors 'ave entrusted their lives at sea to a woman. Seems to me that they're askin' fer trouble."

The captain threw back his head and laughed heartily at the boy's logic. "I do believe you have a point. I think I will change the name of my schooner as soon as we step aboard."

271

"Jest what is the name of yer tub, Cap'n? I 'ope you picked a name more sophisticated than *Fable's Folly*."

"*The Sea Goddess*," he announced proudly.

Dane's gaze slid to Gabe, daring him to poke fun. The waif made an unsuccessful attempt to bite back her amusement. No longer able to control the giggle, Gabe yielded to coughing chuckles.

"Well, it's not as bad as *Fable's Folly*," Dane defended, his voice laced with indignation.

Gabe nodded slightly. "Ain't as bad," she agreed between snickers, "but it ain't too good neither."

Dane dismounted in front of his schooner and extended his arm. "Here before you is my ship, soon to be renamed the *Sea Wind*. Does that meet with your approval?"

Gabe hopped from Blanco's back and thoughtfully studied the vessel. "It beats the 'ell out of floatin' 'round with some imaginary goddess. Besides, I don't believe in such thin's."

Dane turned toward the plank and grumbled under his breath. "Neither do I. She turned out to be a deceitful witch who haunts me night and day."

"What ye say, Cap'n?" Gabe could not make out his words and she hastened her step to catch up with him.

"Nothing," Dane replied as he grabbed Gabe's arm. "Watch your step."

When they climbed on board, Dane started up the main deck, throwing an order over his shoulder to the waif. "Go below and find Sam.

Tell him I want to see him on the quarter-deck."

Gabe thoughtfully studied the captain's broad backside, amazed at the sudden air of authority he had acquired once he'd set foot upon the wooden planks of the *Sea Wind*. She spun away, grumbling to herself as she followed the steps into the musty hull to search for a sailor named Sam.

Gabe saw several rough-looking seamen stacking crates. She loudly cleared her throat, hoping to gain their attention. Since no one acknowledged her presence, she bravely stepped forward while her shadow backed away cowardly.

"Which one of ye gents is Sam?" she shouted over the noise of crates scraping across the planks.

Four stubble-faced sailors paused to peer menacingly at the brazen lad who stood impatiently before them.

"What are ye doin' down 'ere?' came the gruff voice of the burly man who stepped before Gabe, scowling as he scanned the lad's skinny frame.

"The cap'n sent me. I'm lookin' fer Sam. The cap'n wants to see 'im," Gabe explained, returning the sailor's bold gaze.

"I'm Sam. Jest who the 'ell might ye be?" he questioned harshly.

Gabe's chin tilted to a proud angle. "Me name's Gabe. The cap'n agreed to take me on. I'll be sailin' with ye."

Sam scoffed at the wretch in the baggy breeches. "Yer so scrawny that one gust of wind would blow ye away. We ain't playin' nursemaid to some barely weaned pup."

"I kin take care of meself. If I blow overboard, it

273

ain't no concern of yers." Gabe's eyes hardened as she met Sam's black look.

Slowly, Sam's bushy brows arched in amusement. Then he glanced over his shoulder at the three men who stood behind him, as if confirming his next action. Gabe was not about to spend the entire voyage being ridiculed by these rugged sea dogs. She had decided to take her stand here and now. With her arms crossed on her chest, her feet askance, her green eyes carried a challenging spark that made Sam snicker.

"Mighty sure of yerself, brat." Sam smirked as he reached out with a hairy arm and snatched Gabe up off the floor. He clutched Gabe to his chest and chuckled over his shoulder at his captive audience who were guffawing in unison.

Their smiles faded when the boy bit into Sam's arm, elbowed him in the gut, and kicked at his shins. With an agonized growl, Sam hurled the waif away. Grimacing in pain, he grabbed his injured arm. Gabe landed with a thud and rolled away, whipping her dagger from her boot, holding it behind her back. As Sam's eyes narrowed murderously, he stalked toward her like a frothing beast that was about to rip his small prey to shreds. Gabe released the knife as she came to her knees. It quivered in the dead silence and stuck in the supporting beam, only inches away from Sam's heaving chest. Although Gabe was as surprised as the rest of them when the blade met its intended mark, her expression remained grim and determined. The four men turned wide, disbelieving eyes to the waif who came cautiously to her feet.

"That blade could jest as easily bin in yer 'eart, friend. I didn't come 'ere lookin' fer no fight, but if that's what ye want, I ain't about to disappoint ye. I know I ain't too big and not nearly as strong as ye blokes, but I'll work 'ard and try me damnedest to do all the jobs ye give me. I ain't afraid of trouble or duties and I'm ready fer both," she insisted, her steady voice managing to camouflage her fear.

She waited tensely, hoping Sam would reconsider tearing her to pieces. A ghost of a smile grazed the sailor's lips as he reached over to yank the knife from the beam. His heavy brows wore a muddled frown as he studied the blade.

"I once knew a man who carried a dagger like this one. I was tempted to slit 'is miserable throat with it. Instead, I left 'im a scar to remember me by," he mused aloud as he turned the knife in his big hand.

Gabe gulped hard, fearfully awaiting her fate. Farewell world, she said to herself. She had seen her last sunset. What a place to die . . . in the bowels of a ship. Sam moved a step closer and grabbed a handful of her shirt, twisting it around his calloused hand. A wicked grin curled his lips as he laid the stiletto against Gabe's neck. Gabe's breath caught in her throat and she said a quick prayer. Sam flicked his wrist, grasping the blade in the palm of his hand, and extended the handle toward the wide-eyed wretch.

"Yer all right, friend," he admitted with a sly wink. "Ye ain't bigger than a mite, but ye got the courage of a lion."

Gabe accepted the dagger from Sam's out-stretched hand and forced a feeble smile. "Thanks, Sam. I'd rather call ye friend than enemy. Yer big as a bull and twice as stout," she added with a nervous chuckle.

The other men gathered around them and Gabe relaxed when the seamen grinned fondly at her.

"If anybody gives ye trouble, lad, jest give us a call. We'll set them straight. That is if ye need any 'elp," Tom Bates teased, his eyes twinkling merrily. "Jest what else 'ave ye got tucked in them baggy clothes of yers?"

"I believe I'll jest keep that secret until some other bully tries to push me 'round," she replied, a mischievous smile settling on her smudged face.

Sam and Gabe went back to the deck and climbed the ladder to the quarter-deck where Dane waited with a worried frown.

"What took you so long?" he queried, looking from one to the other.

Sam grinned and rubbed his stubbled chin. "Well . . . Cap'n, we 'ad a bit of a disagreement and 'ad to line out a few thin's first," he explained with a chuckle.

Dane focused his attention on Gabe and snapped accusingly, "Don't tell me you've already had trouble with the crew. You promised to mind your manners. I knew I shouldn't have brought you along."

Gabe shrugged noncommittally as her gaze swung out over the water.

Wrapping an arm around Gabe's shoulder, Sam smiled fondly at her. "'E won't be 'avin' no more

276

trouble with us now," he answered for the waif. "Besides, 'e ain't the one who started it. Now what was it ye wanted to see me about?"

It seemed that neither of them was going to relate the incident. As Dane studied the two of them, he noticed the teeth marks on Sam's arm. Broken flesh and dried blood marked the edges of the wound. The only two conclusions that he could draw were that Sam had been bitten by a mad dog or a scrawny little hellcat. It wasn't difficult to decide which. Gabe had taken on the toughest man on the schooner and had somehow managed to make him his friend.

Dane dropped the subject, prepared to see to business. He dismissed Gabe with an order. "Go fetch our bags and take them to my cabin." He pointed in the direction of his quarters and Gabe's eyes followed his extended arm.

Turning back to Sam, Dane questioned him about the cargo that had been loaded and what remained to be delivered. He strolled across the deck with the boatswain, leaving Gabe to do as she was ordered.

In high spirits Gabe scurried down the ladder, walked the length of the deck, and trotted down the plank to retrieve their belongings. With the bags under her arms, she turned to see a poster board filled with notices. A drawing caught her eye and with sickening dread she walked over and stared at the paper, confirming her worst fears.

REWARD: FOR INFORMATION AS TO THE
WHEREABOUTS OF GABRIELLE JARMON.

Beneath was a small sketch, a likeness of her. Gabe ripped the notice from the board, wondering if Lord Jarmon had hung her picture all over London.

"Damn him!" she muttered under her breath. "He will stop at nothing to destroy me."

Gabe crumpled up the paper, stuffed it in her pouch, and stalked back up the plank. When she returned from the voyage, she was going to begin searching for a suitable husband, just as Saxon had suggested.

She was in need of a man who would agree to some sort of financial arrangement. The marriage would be quick and the man must be willing to take a used woman for a wife. Gabe decided the marriage would be no more than a contract. She would return to her home while her husband took up residence anywhere except with her. A wall of ice had thickened around her pained heart. She would never again be hurt by a man. She had no hope of finding a man she could love. Her future husband could keep as many mistresses as his heart desired if he could afford them. Gabe only wanted her home and her fortune. That had become her only objective. She had closed the door to her emotions and sought to rule herself with cold, calculated reasoning.

After finding the captain's cabin, Gabe decided that it needed a thorough cleaning. She set about turning the niche upside down, shaking out the dust, and making the room livable. With the sheets aired, the room rearranged, Gabe stood back to view her accomplishment. Dane strolled inside to find his quarters immaculate. He glanced around the spotless room before focusing his attention on the lad.

"I don't remember ever seeing this cabin so clean," Dane commented with an approving smile.

"It looked to be an excellent breedin' place fer rats before I started," she snorted. "I got an aversion to them nasty varmints. If I'm to be beddin' on the floor, I don't want none of them rodents fer me bed partner." Her nose wrinkled distastefully at the thought.

"We'll rig up a hammock in here so you won't have to sleep on the floor," he offered, gesturing toward an empty corner.

"Thanks, Cap'n. I'd appreciate it," Gabe murmured as a grateful smile creased her lips. "Now what about a tub? I don't mind dirty clothes, but I got used to 'avin' me 'ide clean. Can we find a small one 'round 'ere fer bathin'?"

Dane peered at the wretch in amazement. "We are on board a shipping vessel bound for Scotland. This is not one of London's fashionable hotels. You'll have to wash yourself in the basin like all of the other sailors," he snapped.

"Well, I ain't askin' fer no brass tub," she defended hotly. "Jest somethin' big enough to sit in. After all the times I've saved yer 'ide I should think ye could 'ave a little consideration fer mine! The least ye could do is 'ave a look-see." She paused a moment and arched a taunting brow. "Come on, admit it, Cap'n. Ye wouldn't mind soakin' in a tub either, would ye?"

Dane glowered at the waif until Gabe broke into a smile. "I bet Sam or Tom would 'elp me find one," Gabe insisted. "They told me that if I 'ad any trouble 'round 'ere to jest give a 'oller. Who knows, they might even consider mutiny if it's ye that's causin' me the 'ardship."

"If you and Satan had an argument I've often wondered if you could persuade him to your way of thinking. I am about to come to the conclusion that you could." Dane snorted derisively.

"Nay." Gabe crossed her arms on her chest, meeting Dane's sapphire eyes. "'Tis the devil who stands before me and 'e ain't yielded yet."

Dane chuckled and then shook his head. He always had the strange feeling that somehow Gabe was playing a game with him. The little imp knew just when to turn on one of those blinding smiles and what to say to melt Dane's ire. How could one so young be so skilled in maneuvering him?

"Very well, we'll find you a tub, but this is not Hampton Estate and we are not allowed all the luxuries you have come to expect."

"I ain't askin' fer luxuries," she defended as she put out her chin. "I only asked fer an occasional bath. Good Gawd, ye act as if I'd jest asked ye—"

Dane waved his hand for silence. "I do not wish to discuss it further. This conversation is ended. I'm going up on deck," he said flatly and then wheeled around and stalked from the room.

By late afternoon, Dane had the ship in order and Gabe had her hammock and tub. With the day's business concluded the captain and the waif walked to a small café on dock street. After their meal they found a stable for their horses and returned to the wharf.

The sun had set on the cobblestone streets of London and fog had settled on the city, wrapping it in misty darkness. Only the dim light of lanterns guided them along the pier. Gabe shuddered as the evening chill hovered on her shoulders. A silver reflection caught Gabe's eye and her footsteps halted when she heard a muffled click from the crates that were stacked on the docks. Gabe dived at Dane's feet as he walked on ahead of her.

With a surprised yelp Dane fell down on the dock and was about to curse the wretch for his mischievousness when a shot sailed past him. Scrambling to his feet, Dane pulled a pistol from his coat and hurried toward the crates, but all he heard was the sound of someone escaping in the shadows.

"Sorry, Cap'n," Gabe apologized breathlessly as she came up behind him. "There was no time for explanations. I 'ope I didn't 'urt ye."

"How did you know there was someone there?" Dane questioned bewilderedly. "I didn't see or hear anything."

"I jest 'ad this funny feelin' while we were walkin'. Then I saw the barrel's reflection," she replied as she started up the plank.

Dane peered incredulously at her shadowed form. His vision of Gabe in the darkness reminded him of someone far away who had come to comfort him. Emptiness filled his heart and the fantasy returned to haunt him in the silence of the foggy night.

Standing alone on deck Dane whispered to the ever-present spirit that hovered above him. "You are a witch, no longer an angel. What you offered to me was a temptation, which, once given, was quickly snatched away, leaving me searching to find another to compare to you. But none can. 'Tis like holding a sunbeam in the palm of my hand, unable to do anything but watch it vanish before my eyes. Your presence was just as devastating as your absence. You were the light that guided me through the shadows. Now I grope blindly, wondering if your true intention was to take my soul, leaving me but an empty shell. I cannot seem to find another whose passions satisfy me as yours have.

"You would not give your name or show your face. Yet you come to me, offering that which only you could give, making no demands on me. The unspoken bond has chained me to your memory. 'Perhaps in another time and place,' you whispered." Dane laughed bitterly. "But I know I will never see the face of the angel that tortures me. You have come and gone. I know not where to search for you."

With a despairing sigh, Dane ambled to his cabin. There would be no shadowed goddess awaiting him, only an ornery little waif. When Dane entered the room he found Gabe stretched out in his hammock, his hands folded behind his head, his feet crossed at the ankles.

"Does your bed suit you, your lordship?" Dane quipped as he swept his hat from his head.

"'Tis better than some places I've laid me weary

'ead," Gabe replied casually. "It beats the 'ell out of fightin' them rats fer me pillow on that cold floor."

Dane sailed his hat across the room. When it came to rest on the end of the bed, he turned back to Gabe, assuming his role as captain of the *Sea Wind*. "Tomorrow I want you to acquaint yourself with this ship. You will be the errand and cabin boy. The galley is on the lower deck and you will bring our meals to our cabin. Sam will serve the morning meal at first light. After that, it will be one of your duties."

With his hands clasped behind his back, Dane sauntered toward the waif who watched him with a seemingly disinterested gaze. "Are there any questions?" Dane asked as one dark brow arched.

"Jest one, Cap'n." Gabe paused, frowning as if she were about to delve into some serious matter.

"Well, what is it?" Dane questioned impatiently.

Gabe cocked her head to the side and peered up at the captain who towered above her hammock. "Do I git to sleep 'round 'ere or must I listen to ye ramble on 'til dawn?" Gabe rolled onto her side, squirming in her nest, a devilish grin hovering on her lips.

Whaaapp!

Dane's palm found its target—Gabe's backside—sending the cocky little imp swaying in his rope bed. "I thought perhaps your brattish lordship would enjoy being rocked to sleep."

Gabe grimaced at the stinging pain on her buttocks and glared over her shoulder at the

283

wicked grin that curled Dane's lips. "Don't fall asleep, Cap'n. I'll be layin' 'ere thinkin' of a way to git even with ye fer that. When the idea comes to me, ye'll be sorry." Her spiteful hiss reminded Dane of a coiled snake that was about to sink its fangs into human flesh.

"You try any pranks and I'll cast you overboard as soon as we put out to sea," Dane warned, shaking a lean finger in Gabe's face.

"Don't make any vows that a stiff corpse can't keep," she retorted flippantly.

Casting Gabe an annoyed frown, Dane stalked to the other end of the room.

"G'night, Cap'n. Enjoy yer sleep," she taunted with an evil chuckle.

After snuffing out the lantern, Dane shed his clothes and crawled into bed. The dark image floated above him, taunting and teasing him with its closeness. Then those same blackened faces that cried out in agony rose before him. But this time, one face was recognizable. It was his own horror-filled features. Sailors were climbing all over him to save themselves. He was being trampled, fighting to keep his head above water. A faceless shadow appeared above him and he reached out to grasp her small hand. But he could not touch her and he was sinking. She floated away, leaving him to die in the murky depths.

Gabe lay awake planning her revenge. When she heard Dane's methodic breathing she tiptoed to the basin and dipped up some water. Just as she lifted her hand, preparing to douse him, Dane groaned and reached out to clutch her to his chest. The water trickled over both of them and Gabe lost her balance. She let out an enraged squawk when she was suffocated by Dane's viselike grasp.

When he was showered with water and heard the screech, Dane bolted up in bed. The light from the porthole revealed Gabe's alarmed face and Dane instantly released the struggling waif.

"What the 'ell are ye' tryin' to do?" Gabe snapped at the bewildered captain.

"I was having a nightmare," he confessed as he wiped the water from his face. "I thought you were—"

With a derisive snort, Gabe cut him short. "I know what ye thought I was; some 'ussy comin' to crawl in bed with ye."

"How did I get all wet?" Dane questioned as he propped up on his elbow. "The dreams are becoming more realistic each night."

"Seems yer tub sprung a leak, Cap'n." Gabe smirked.

Dane grumbled under his breath, remembering the lad's vengeful vow. "Go to sleep, brat," he snorted as he pulled the sheet over his head.

"'Ow kin I sleep with ye rantin' and ravin' like a banshee in the middle of the night? I think I'll go sleep on—"

"Get to bed!" Dane snapped with so much finality in his bellow that Gabe jumped as if she had been stung.

"I'm goin'! I'm bein' 'auled off to Scotland, caged with a loon. Gawd, what a trip this is goin' to be. I'll probably be strangled to death in me sleep," she muttered as she stalked to her hammock.

"Damn it, will you be quiet!" Dane growled, his

voice bouncing off the walls to nip at Gabe's heels.

Gabe hopped into her rope bed, muffling a chuckle. She should have been more sympathetic about his nightmare, but she couldn't resist harassing him.

With great pride Dane scanned his ship from bow to stern. The cargo was loaded and all was in order. He was anxious to be out to sea, away from the fluttering throngs of civilization. A clamor below him brought him from his silent reverie and he peered over the rail to see Sam climbing to the quarter-deck.

"The 'atch is locked and everythin' is ready fer tomorrow, Cap'n." Sam's face split in a broad grin. "The crew will be takin' their shore leave now . . . if that's all right with ye."

"Fine. Just make sure they all arrive back on board in one piece. They are your responsibility," Dane reminded him.

As Sam leaned his elbows on the railing, he looked over at the captain. "Do ye mind if we take yer cabin boy 'long with us and show 'im a good time?"

Dane arched a skeptical brow as he peered at Sam. "Why have you taken such a liking to the lad? I thought you didn't scoop young birds under your wing."

"The boy 'as spunk. Ye don't see many like 'im. 'E took me on and never batted an eye."

"Exactly what happened that day?" Dane queried curiously.

Sam chuckled and scratched the end of his nose.

"I was given 'im a rough time about bein' a scrawny bag of bones. Then I grabbed 'im off the floor and 'e buried 'is fangs in me arm. When I threw 'im across the planks 'e came to 'is knees and sailed a dagger at me. Fer a minute I thought I was a dead man, but he stuck the blade in the beam beside me. 'E said 'e didn't want no fight, jest a little respect."

Dane grinned, picturing Gabe scaring the wits out of Sam. "He's a brazen little scamp," he agreed. "He's saved my neck more times than I care to count."

"Where did 'e come from? 'E ain't one to answer pryin' questions."

"I know little about him. He's been just as tight-lipped with me. All I know is that he's running away from somebody."

"Well, 'ow about it, Cap'n? Does Gabe go or stay?"

Dane frowned thoughtfully. "I don't think I want to turn Gabe loose in London. He's not old enough to enjoy the ladies."

"Jest 'ow old is 'e?" Sam questioned, arching a bushy brow.

"I don't know that either. My guess is twelve or thirteen," Dane concluded blandly. "He may be a little older than that, but with all that dirt caked on his face, it's hard to say for certain. I think he needs a few years before you start hauling him with you."

Sam nodded and then turned to leave. Pausing, he glanced over his shoulder at Dane. "'Ave ye ever seen the dagger the lad totes?"

A confused frown gathered on Dane's brows. "I've seen it. Why do you ask?"

"It looks jest like the one Eric Dristol carried. I'd swear it could be the same one. Thought ye might be interested to know," Sam said quietly.

Dane's brows rose sharply and then returned to their normal arch. "You're sure about that?"

"Damned sure," Sam replied solemnly. "Dristol pulled it on me once. I nearly slit 'is throat with it. I got a good look at it then."

"Thanks, Sam," Dane muttered, a troubled frown settling on his features. "Take the crew and enjoy yourselves."

The captain opened the door of his cabin to find Gabe placing their evening meal on the table.

"'Evenin', Cap'n," the waif said with a nonchalant smile.

Dane nodded a greeting as he shed his coat and walked to the commode to wash for supper. As he poured water into the basin, he threw a question over his shoulder. "Sam wondered if you wanted to go into town with the crew. Would you like to see the inside of a brothel?"

Gabe stopped her chore and frowned at the rakish smile on Dane's lips. He knew better than to ask such a ridiculous question. "I ain't interested in them bits of fluff that ye and Sam take a fancy to," she replied, her voice rising testily. "I ain't got the urge to go chasin' them perfumed madams and ye know it!"

"I told him you were too young for an education." He chuckled as he dried his hands and turned to face Gabe.

"Me 'earty thanks to ye, Cap'n," she mocked dryly. "Now kin we eat before these cool sea rations git any colder?" Gabe picked up a strip of dried beef and then let it clank against the porcelain plate, wrinkling her nose at the unappetizing meal that awaited her.

Dane's shoulder lifted in a reckless shrug. "You could be eating steak with the rest of the crew. You can bet their meal will be more appealing than ours."

After their meal, Dane collected his jacket and prepared to depart. The derisive snort behind him made him pause at the door.

"I s'pose yer off to visit the brothel. Enjoy yerself."

"Actually," Dane began as he reached for the doorknob and casually leaned upon it, "I have to stand watch while the other men seek their pleasures."

"I'll take yer duty fer ye. I'd 'ate to keep ye from some wench's arms, knowin' 'ow ye thrive on that sort of attention."

"That's terribly considerate of you, Gabe." A wry smile parted Dane's lips. "Knowing how you feel about brothels, I'm surprised you would make such an offer, even if it was a bit sarcastic."

Gabe began clearing the table. "I told ye before that I didn't expect ye to be no saint. I'm tryin' to keep from meddlin' in yer affairs. I don't approve of yer antics, but that makes no difference to ye. I'm tryin' to remain impartial," she added, shooting him a quick, sidelong glance.

"A man has his needs, Gabe. The day is coming

289

when you will see things from my point of view."

Gabe turned to face the captain, a mysteriously wicked smile playing at the corners of her mouth. "Ye ain't never goin' to catch me chasin' after a bit of muslin. And ye kin quote me on that, Cap'n. Ye'll never 'ave the chance to say 'I told ye so,'" she insisted.

Dane threw back his head and laughed out loud as he opened the door. "We'll see about that, Gabe. I only hope I'm around when the time comes for you to eat your words. You might be the one who chokes on that mouthful of cynicism instead of me."

Gabe hurled a cup against the closed door. "The hell I will, my lord Capt. Dane Hampton," she snapped in her own sophisticated voice. "You are a fool. I have pranced around right under your nose for more than two months. You have never once guessed the truth. When I am the heiress of Jarmon Estate, you can bet you will see me for what I am. Then you will know the full extent of your folly. You will rue the day you ever laid eyes on me!"

As she squatted down to clean up the broken teacup, Gabe mumbled a curse to Dane's name each time she placed a sliver in her hand. She should reveal her identity just to spite him. It might be worth the cost if she could see the look on his face when he realized that his guardian angel was the scrawny brat in baggy breeches.

"Were you getting lonesome in that dingy room?" Dane teased as he strolled up beside Gabe who was leaning against the railing, staring at the sea.

"Aye. I was 'opin' fer some pleasant conversation, but I see Sam and Tom ain't back yet," she retorted caustically.

"Thank you, Gabe. You're certainly a complimentary little chap," Dane snorted disgustedly.

"Ain't I though," she agreed, casting him a quick glance.

Turning back to gaze at the water, Gabe was caught, trapped by the vastness that lay before her. Her mood suddenly became pensive as she looked up to the myriad of stars that splattered the black velvet sky. Wordsworth's poem came to mind as it had on several occasions. The words seemed to float from her lips with such ease that Dane was bewildered by her recitation.

"She dwelt among the untrodden ways
  Beside the springs of Dove,
A maid whom there were none to praise
  And very few to love:

"A violet by a mossy stone
  Half hidden from the eye!
Fair as a star, when only one
  Is shining in the sky.

"She lived unknown, and few could know
  When Lucy ceased to be;
But she is in her grave, and, oh,
  The difference is to me!"

Although the poem was spoken with an uneducated accent, Gabe had given so much meaning to the words that Dane felt a wave of sympathy flood over him.

"Who was she, Gabe?" Dane asked quietly. "Who was this woman you mourn? Is she the one who owned that white stallion?"

Gabe shrugged carelessly. "It don't matter now. She's gone and no one cares but me." As she pushed away from the rail, she glanced at the captain's concerned frown. "G'night."

The lad ambled away, his head bowed, his hands stuffed in his pockets. It seemed Gabe had grown more distant since they had left Hampton Estate. Dane could not fathom the change in his behavior. There were times in the past that he and Gabe had shared some close moments. Now Gabe kept to himself and there was always a hint of sadness, even in his smiles.

With a hopeless shrug, Dane walked the deck, waiting for the crew to come aboard, singing their sea chanteys and exchanging fabricated tales of their adventures. Although he could not enjoy holding a woman in his arms, he could remember a night not so long ago when he had held an angel in his embrace. His consolation was that he had touched perfection. Bah! Dane muttered under his breath. She was a witch sent to torment him. He was only kidding himself to believe otherwise. Damn her! She had made a fool of him.

Chapter Twelve

"'Ow long before we're out to sea?" Gabe questioned as she prepared the table and sat down to their morning meal.

"A couple of hours."

"Good; the sooner the better," she remarked as she bit into a hard biscuit and then held it away to study it carefully.

Dane chuckled at Gabe's distressed expression. "Don't you take to our food rations?" he taunted her, arching a heavy brow.

Gabe shrugged and tried the biscuit again, talking with her mouth full. "It reminds me of eatin' tree bark. They're both tough and tasteless."

With the table cleared, Gabe hurried to the deck to watch the crew open sails. Each seaman handled his task so easily that Gabe marveled at their efficiency. The main sails stretched toward the sun and the canvas sucked and popped in an occasional gust of wind. The schooner cut through the whitecapped waves, sending Gabe's stomach lurching in nautical rhythm. As nausea overcame her, Gabe crawled down the ladder and wove toward the taffrail to rid herself of the breakfast that had not been appetizing in the first place.

Dane chuckled in amusement as he watched Gabe part with his meal. The lad had been under the impression that a sea voyage was comparable to a Sunday picnic in the park. He had just discovered how very wrong he had been. Gabe had learned his first lesson about the sea and there would be more to come.

Gabe spent most of the day in the cabin, trying to overcome her seasickness. After telling herself that she was fine and only half-believing it, she struggled back on deck to face Dane's amused regard.

"Well, your lordship, have you enjoyed your idle time in your suite?" Dane taunted, his sapphire eyes glistening down at her.

"Don't look at me like that," she snapped. "I s'pose the first time ye went to sea it never bothered ye."

"I honestly don't remember," he admitted with a nonchalant shrug.

"Old as ye are, ye probably can't remember back that far." Her mocking grin brought back a little color to her ashen face.

"Even seasickness has no effect on your sharp tongue. I do believe it can cut to the quick. Have you been filing it to a finer point?" Dane snorted.

"I may be sick, but I ain't dead. As long as I kin

breathe, I'll be able to think of barbs to needle ye with.''

"Am I to be forever plagued by your vicious gibes? You delight in heckling me. Indeed, I think you thrive on it.''

"Not ferever, Cap'n. I'll be leavin' ye after this trip. Ye won't be bothered with me no more,'' she informed him as she allowed her gaze to swing out over the sea.

"Where are you going?'' he questioned, a hint of remorse in his tone.

Gabe shrugged noncommittally, refusing to answer his inquiry. "The sky 'as a strange color out 'ere on the sea,'' she said thoughtfully. "'Tis like nothin' I've ever seen.''

"There's a storm brewing,'' Dane explained as his gaze followed hers over the water.

Dane's senses seemed to come alive as he scanned the sea and Gabe could feel his strength that lay in repose. It seemed Dane was no longer preoccupied by the looming shadow that had come to haunt him. She studied his striking profile for a long moment, drawing confidence from his self-assured manner.

"'Ow kin ye tell there will be a storm?'' she questioned curiously.

"By the color of the sky and by a feeling that develops with experience,'' Dane replied, smiling faintly.

Gabe arched a skeptical brow. "Pish-posh,'' she snorted. "There ye go believin' in them thin's ye can't touch and feel.''

"Nevertheless you will know what it is to suffer a storm at sea," Dane assured her confidently.

The thought of having Gabe vanish from his life brought a strange sadness to Dane. He had grown accustomed to that dirty face and those lively green eyes. He was going to miss Gabe. The ornery little waif had made life an escapade.

Gabe glanced up to see the fond affection mirrored in Dane's gaze. A blinding smile spread across her lips. She knew what he was thinking. At least he cared for her in some small way. "Now don't git soft on me, Cap'n. I told ye this wasn't no permanent arrangement. I 'ave to be on me way sometime or 'nother."

Dane stiffened, amazed at how easily Gabe had read his thoughts. His face darkened as he peered at Gabe's mocking grin.

"That's better," Gabe retorted, winking subtly. "Fer a minute there I thought ye were goin' to offer to deed 'Ampton Estate over to me jest to git me to stay."

"Go fetch some tea and take it to my cabin," Dane snapped, his eyes narrowing sternly.

Gabe came to attention, presented him with a saucy salute, and swaggered away. "Aye, Cap'n," she called over her shoulder.

"Ornery little brat," Dane muttered, but there was no malice in his tone. A faint smile threatened the corners of his mouth as Gabe cast him another glance and grinned wickedly.

As Dane had promised, the wind unleashed its fury on the schooner and the ship pitched and rolled on the angry swells. Gabe struggled to keep her stomach, groaning miserably as the hammock swayed and rocked. She climbed from her bed and edged along the wall.

"Are you all right?" Dane questioned when he heard Gabe's agonizing groan.

"I'm sure ye'll be pleased to know I think I'm dyin'," Gabe muttered as she frantically searched for the chamber pot.

With a low chuckle, Dane swung out of his bed, donned his clothes, and left the lad to suffer his agony in privacy. It was over an hour before Gabe regained her composure and walked into the companionway. Steadying herself with her arms on the walls, she made her way to the galley to fetch the captain's breakfast.

Since the captain had not returned, Gabe climbed to the main deck to call him to breakfast. Seeing him at the wheel, she yelled up to him through the whistling wind. Finally, Dane heard her and looked down to see Gabe holding her hat on her head.

"I'll be down later," he hollered over the clapping of the sails. "Get back inside and for God's sake, hold on to the rail with both hands!"

Gabe turned, lowered her head, and trudged back toward the steps, still using only one hand for support. As the waves slapped against the hull, the vessel pitched rapidly. The pounding rain had dampened the railing and the planks and Gabe lost her balance. She was thrown against the wall, her head slamming into the wood. The world spun furiously about her as her knees buckled, leaving her in an unconscious heap on the deck.

"Gabe!" Dane screamed as he witnessed the lad being thrown against the wall.

Seeing no movement, Dane scurried down the ladder and knelt beside the lifeless form. Holding the lad in his arms, he moved along the wall to the steps and hurried to his quarters. After laying the stubborn wretch on his bunk, Dane fumbled in the darkness to find the lantern.

"You and that damned hat!" Dane growled at the unconscious waif. "If you would have held on to the rail instead of that filthy cap, this wouldn't have happened. It's your own fault. You just keep doing as you damned well please no matter what the consequences."

Dane reached for the drenched hat on Gabe's head, but paused, knowing the lad would wake in a fit of rage if his cap was removed. Feeling Gabe's cold forehead, the captain decided to get the boy out of his clothes and under the warm quilts before he caught his death. Dane knew Gabe would be infuriated by that too; yet, he could not risk letting him lie there chilled until he roused to disrobe himself.

When Dane had removed the jerkin and unbuttoned the shirt he found the lad wrapped in cloth from his chest to his waist. He peered at the bandage, a concerned frown gathering on his brow. What wound was Gabe protecting?

A moment of doubt caused Dane's eyes to narrow suspiciously as he studied Gabe's face. The pounding rain had cleansed the boy's small features. Dane stared bemusedly at the smooth complexion that was devoid of dirt. A long, frantic moment passed while Dane wrestled with the thoughts that flew through his mind.

"Oh, good God!" he gasped, nearly swallowing his tongue. "It *can't* be."

Reluctantly, Dane pulled the cap from Gabe's head, allowing a cascade of brown curls to tumble free. The dawn of realization hit him like a bolt of lightning and his jaw sagged bewilderedly. The frail, thin face of the young waif was transformed into the delicate features of a lovely young woman. Dane had been so preoccupied with his night-mares and his troubles that he had never once guessed that Gabe could have been his angel of mercy.

Dane reached out to brush his hand across her cheek, noticing the long, sooty lashes that rimmed her eyes. There was usually so much grime on her features that he could have sworn Gabe had no lashes at all. They had been camouflaged with dirt, just as were her delicate lines.

God, how could he have been so blind? She had been laughing at him all this time, watching him play the fool. She had been his shadow and he had never seen the connection between the angel and the waif. No wonder she had been so upset when he visited the brothels. Now he understood why she had been so modest in his presence. She had never allowed him to see her face or hear her voice. For good reason, Dane mused with a scornful smirk. Now he knew why the lad always kept to himself, wore such baggy clothes, never removed his cap, and was never seen without dirt-smudged cheeks.

How could such a lovely young woman transform herself into such a spunky ragamuffin? How could two completely different personalities be housed in the same body? Their voices, their appearances, and their mannerisms were totally dissimilar. And yet, they were one in the same.

Dane slipped the wet shirt from her shoulders, loosened the cloth, and removed her breeches. She was just as beautiful as he had imagined she would be. All of the questions that had plagued him in the past vanished when he gazed at Gabe; but now there were new riddles to be solved. He still had no idea who she was, what she was running from, and why she was masquerading as a boy. She was just as mysterious as before; but now the angel had a face—a soft, exquisite face, dark hair, and bright green eyes that could twinkle with mischievousness.

A knock at the door sent Dane scurrying to cover the young woman. He moved to the door, steadying himself against the furniture along the way. After glancing back to ensure that her form could not be recognized, Dane swung open the door.

Sam stood anxiously before him. "The 'elmsman said Gabe was 'urt." He peered around Dane to see the covered boy who lay motionless on the bunk and the color drained from his cheeks. "Lord, 'e ain't dead, is 'e?" Sam choked out.

"No, just chilled to the bone. I'm trying to warm him as best I can," Dane explained, fidgeting nervously.

Sam stepped inside to have a closer look, but Dane clamped his hand on the boatswain's shoulder, halting his steps. "Why don't you go fetch some hot tea," he suggested. "I'll let you see the boy when he rouses."

"Aye, Cap'n." Sam reluctantly turned to leave. "Yer sure 'e's all right? Seein' 'im covered from 'ead to toe with a blanket makes 'im look like a stiff corpse," he muttered disconcertedly.

"He'll be fine," Dane assured him. "You'll see those green eyes twinkling up at you before you know it. Now, how about the tea?"

"I'm goin'," Sam insisted as he strained his neck to take one last look at Gabe. "Sure wish ye'd uncover 'is 'ead. It gives me the willies seein' 'im like that."

"I will," Dane grumbled impatiently. "I didn't know you were so superstitious."

As the footsteps faded in the companionway, Dane closed the door and then eased down on the edge of the bed. Reaching down to brush the silky strands away from her face, he felt the knot on Gabe's head.

"Whoever you are, my mysterious witch-angel, you will have to pay dearly for playing me for a fool. I will not quickly forget the times you have taunted me with your charades. It will give me great pleasure to seek my revenge." Dane chuckled to himself. If this wench thought she could get the best of Dane Hampton she was in for a surprise.

Gabe's eyes slowly fluttered open to see that the storm had ceased and the sun was streaming through the porthole.

"Cap'n," she began as she focused her eyes on

301

Dane. "What 'appened?"

"You fell and hit your head, but you'll survive," he replied, a wide grin splitting his face.

Gabe felt her head. When she found the tender knot she carefully examined it with her fingertips and then realized her cap was gone. Quickly jolted to her senses, she sat straight up in bed. The quilts slid from her neck, exposing her breasts to the captain's eager gaze.

Gabrielle squealed in indignation and frantically clutched at the quilt. "Where are my clothes? What have you done?"

"Your garb was drenched, my dear," Dane replied, smiling rakishly. "I took the liberty of disrobing the poor waif I knew as Gabe."

Gabe blushed crimson red beneath his lusty stare. Then her green eyes flashed with the fury Dane had often seen in them. "How dare you! You had no right to—"

"How dare me?" he repeated incredulously. "How the hell was I supposed to know my cabin boy was not a boy! You had no right to mislead me, young lady," he snapped, waving an accusing finger in her face. "I should have your lovely neck for that. Now I want some answers and I want the truth; not just the bits and pieces of vague explanations you usually dish out."

"The truth about what?" she quipped, her voice acid with anger. "You have already seen the bare facts. What more could you possibly want?"

"I want to know who you are and why you're disguised as a waif. That will do for starters," he snorted derisively as he placed his arms on either

302

side of her hips. "I want to know exactly what you've been up to and why. And if I find that you are lying again, I will personally torture you until the entire story flows from those deceptive lips, *angel*." The hiss of his voice made Gabe wince uncomfortably.

Never before had that endearment sounded like a curse. Gabrielle searched his rugged features, wondering if she could trust him now that he knew the full extent of his folly. It was apparent that he was annoyed with her. The evidence was in his harsh voice and the icy hue of his eyes. She was in no position to bargain with the devil, but that had never stopped her before; and it would not stop her now.

"If I tell you, I must have your solemn promise that you won't send me back to the hell from which I escaped. Without your word as a gentleman, I won't explain anything. You can torture me to death if you like, but I will refuse to talk," she declared, her eyes flashing their usual determination.

Dane rubbed his stubbled chin while he considered her ultimatum, letting her stew for a few minutes.

"Well, damn it!" she cried impatiently. "Make up your mind!"

"Are you sure you want my word as a gentleman?" he mocked dryly. "I have rarely been accused of being one, especially by you."

Wrapping the sheet about her, Gabe attempted to rise from the bed, but he grabbed her shoulders and pressed her back to the pillow.

"Very well, my dear, you have my word. Now start at the beginning and don't leave anything out," he demanded before he rose from the bed and retrieved a chair.

Brielle took a deep breath, organized her thoughts, and began, "My name is Gabrielle Jarmon and I—"

"Jarmon?" He choked. "Not one of Lord John's daughters?"

"Certainly not!" she scornfully corrected. "I am his niece, but I would have preferred to be no kin at all to that blackguard."

"Why didn't you tell me who you were when you first came to my estate?" he questioned, a muddled frown gathering on his brows.

"I was afraid you would feel obligated to my uncle after he nursed you back to health. I could take no chances because I could never return to his home. You said yourself that you were indebted to him. Now, if you will allow me to continue without interruption—" Brielle arched a delicate brow and eyed him with considerable annoyance.

"Please do go on, Gab . . . rielle," he insisted, a wry smile catching the corners of his mouth.

"When my father died this past year, he requested that I stay with my uncle until I was married. Papa thought I was too young to manage my home. He wrote a will forbidding me to return to my own estate until I was wed. Uncle John was to be financially reimbursed for my presence in his home."

When she first began to speak in her soft, raspy voice, Dane was spellbound. He could only stare at

304

her in amazement. Gone was the nasal tone and the cockney accent. Her smooth, articulate speech brought back memories of nights when he had heard her comforting whisper. He marveled at the abrupt change in her voice. She had perfected her disguise with such skillfulness that Dane was mesmerized.

Brielle peered curiously at him, wondering why he wore such an odd expression, but she continued with her explanation. "Papa thought I would be unable to handle the fortune hunters who might try to win my heart. Therefore, I was entrusted to my uncle's care.

"My uncle and I did not get on well. He is a tyrant and would allow me no freedom. When I didn't conform to his expectations of the subservient woman, we began to quarrel often. He refused to allow me to leave the house, but I did so whenever I could sneak away," she added with a rebellious sparkle in her eyes.

"On my eighteenth birthday we had our worst argument. Uncle John informed me that I would have no season in London. He said I was uncivilized and would not make a suitable wife for the men in his social circle. I lost my temper and told him exactly what I thought of him and his domineering reign."

Dane chuckled, imagining that fiery argument, but quieted immediately when Brielle shot him a silencing glare.

"After our heated words, my uncle left the house and I went riding despite his orders. That was when I found you on the road," she reminded him glibly.

"When I returned, my uncle informed me that he had signed a marriage contract with the Duke of Fairleigh."

"Good God!" Dane interjected. "*You* were the woman who ran away from the duke?"

"Yes," Brielle affirmed, displaying a sarcastic smile. "I'm the money-hungry wench whom you referred to while you and Monica Sheffwall were conversing at the Brunsfords' ball."

Dane sputtered, recalling his conversation with Monica. If Gabe heard the whole of it, she was probably fit to be tied. "And just where were you hiding? I distinctly remember telling you to stay home."

"You did, but I followed you anyway. I was sitting in the shrubs below the terrace while you and Monica were tarrying in the moonlight." Her brows furrowed, assuring him that she had not missed any of the conversation.

"Do go on, Gabe. I am curious to hear the rest of your story," Dane urged hurriedly. No wonder his angel had not reappeared for several days after what she had overheard. It was a wonder she returned at all.

"I was to be the sacrificial virgin," Brielle said scornfully. "Fairleigh wanted a wife and my uncle wanted to be rid of me. Uncle John forbade me to see you, saying that I was betrothed and could not be seen in the company of another man. That's why I only came to you at night and asked you not to tell anyone that you had seen me. The day before you left, John locked me in my room to ensure that

I would be there when Horace arrived. John planned to leave me in my quarters until the following evening. I crawled through the window and then escaped through your room."

Dane shook his head in disgust. Gabrielle had just confirmed his belief that John Jarmon was not what he seemed.

"The next day I caught up with you. You know most of what I did during that time, except for two incidences. When the letter from my uncle arrived at your house, I rewrote my own version; his letter asked your help in finding his runaway niece. The day you were visiting your harlots in Bristol I went to see my father's lawyer." Brielle shot Dane a cold glance that made him squirm in his seat. He did not need to be reminded that Gabe had waited each time he had come from the arms of other women. "I was hoping Mr. Saxon could help, but he said I was bound to the will and that John could make a marriage contract without my approval."

"Did you say Saxon? Roger Saxon?" Dane interrupted, his brow arching acutely.

"Yes. He jokingly commented that if I were a trollop, John would have difficulty forcing me into marriage. No nobleman would want a tainted woman for a wife."

Dane's eyes narrowed at her last remark. So that was why she had given herself to him. She would stop at nothing to ruin the contract with Fairleigh. Yet, there had to be more to it, Dane mused thoughtfully. She had responded too willingly, too passionately.

"So you came to me with an ulterior motive." A

skeptical smile hovered on his lips as he bent his gaze to Gabe.

Brielle bristled, knowing he believed that was not the only reason she had yielded to him. "Yes," she said flatly. "You were convenient and as likely a candidate as any other man. It would have made no difference. Of course, there is no reason to explain that to you. Since you stumble from one bed to another without being too particular, I'm sure you understand explicitly."

"Thank you, my dear." Dane smirked, his blue eyes twinkling wickedly. "For a moment I was about to assume that you seduced me because you found me irresistible."

His roguish smile caused Brielle to frown in irritation. "Perhaps your other lady friends might find you so, but I, for one, do not," she snapped curtly. "For once, dear Captain, it is you who have been used by a woman, but not necessarily for pleasure."

Dane chuckled and leaned back in his chair to cross his arms on his chest. "If I am to believe that you speak the truth, then why did you come to me again? If that was your purpose, that first night would have been your last visit. It only takes one encounter to render a maid no longer a virgin."

Gabe colored hotly at his remark and then summoned her composure. "I came to fill the lonely nights when I wanted to forget my troubles. As I said before, Captain, you were easily accessible. I had noticed on several occasions that you were always happy to accommodate. Now, may I continue or do you wish to question me further, sir?"

"Do proceed." His mocking smile assured her that he didn't believe a word she spoke on that subject.

"I went back to see my uncle when you gave me my first day off. I told him I was no longer suitable for the duke and he flew into a rage. He vowed to find someone else who would be just as horrible as Fairleigh." A thread of contempt laced her voice as she tried to smother her anger. Just thinking of John had the power to infuriate her. "I had planned to stay, but my uncle tried to lock me in my room again and I returned to your estate. When we came to London I found a notice that offered a reward for information about me. I had hoped he would give me up for lost, but it seems he is obsessed with seeing me wed to some pervert like Fairleigh."

Gabe heaved a heavy sigh. "That is about all there is to tell. It has been a rather unpleasant few months."

"And just what do you intend to do? Stay in hiding forever?" Dane questioned, his eyes roaming her with an all-consuming gaze.

"I had hoped that by the time we returned to London John would end his search and had decided to go to Bristol to find a job. Mr. Saxon gives me an allowance and I can live modestly as either Gabe or Gabrielle. That depends on my uncle's perseverance."

"Perhaps I can help you." Dane sat up straight in his chair, prepared to offer his suggestion, but Gabe cut him short.

"Not unless you know some man who will agree to wed me for financial gain. When I marry, Jarmon Estate will again be mine. That is where I will spend the rest of my days. My future husband may live wherever he chooses, as long as it isn't with me."

"If that is the type of husband for whom you search, you will have difficulty." Dane grinned at Gabe's disgruntled frown. "You are extremely attractive and very desirable. To that I can attest," he added with a devilish wink. "What man in his right mind will allow that lovely body of yours to go to waste?"

Gabe glared furiously at him. "You are despicable," she stormed. "Perhaps I will not have an easy time of it, but I did not escape from my malicious uncle only to be tied to another tyrant. I would rather live as a waif than suffer a husband who tries to dominate me."

Dane bit back an amused grin. "You are extremely cynical for one so young."

"No more than you," she countered. "And why shouldn't I be? Since my father died I have been associated with three men—Uncle John, you, and that dreadful Higgins. My uncle treats me as if I were nothing more than his slave. You use women to satisfy your lust, and Higgins considers the entire human race to be two stations below him."

"Now that's unfair," Dane protested, his temper flaring at her degrading description.

"Is it?" Her amused mockery scorned everything about him. "I remember your telling me that noblewomen were nothing more than empty-headed dolls, lovely to look at, but frightfully boorish. You said you would never marry because one woman could never satisfy you." Gabrielle bestowed a disarming smile on the sputtering captain as she painfully reminded him of one of his callous remarks. "I have seen you fluttering over the countryside, alighting on various doorsteps for only one purpose. I am not so naïve as to believe that you were merely indulging in conversation." Her eyes narrowed into an accusing frown. "And I was there on each occasion, waiting for you to return. I know damned well how you passed your time. When it comes to women, your appetite can only be described as gluttonous!"

Dane bolted to his feet, ready to argue the point, but a knock at the door stifled his comments. With a growl, he glanced at the door. "Who is it?"

"'Tis me, Cap'n. 'As the lad come 'round yet?" Sam questioned.

Gabe and Dane exchanged frantic glances. She reached for the lantern to put some soot on her face, grabbed her hat, and then squirmed down in the quilts. When Gabe nodded, Dane opened the door, displaying a controlled smile.

"Come in, Sam. Our young friend is awake."

The boatswain pushed his way into the room, carrying a tray of tea and biscuits. "I 'ad the cook re'eat yer tea. Ye were still out cold the last time I was by to check on ye."

"Thank ye, Sam. Jest set it down. I'll try some later."

Sam sank down in the vacated chair, carefully studying the lad. "Are ye feelin' better?"

311

"I got one 'ell of a 'eadache, but I'll live," Gabe assured him as she sent a discreet glance to Dane who was peering over Sam's shoulder.

"Ye jest take it easy the rest of the day, boy. I'll take care of yer duties," Sam offered, grinning broadly.

"Thank ye. I'll be up and 'round tomorrow." As Sam rose to full stature, Gabe winked up at him. "And ye were right, Sam. One gust of wind jest about blew me away. Next time I go out in a storm, I'm goin' to anchor meself down."

The boatswain's eyes twinkled in amusement. "See that ye do, lad. I've grown fond of yer scrawny form and that ugly mug of yers. I would 'ate to see ye washed overboard."

Dane choked back a laugh. If Sam knew he was talking to the heiress of Jarmon Estate, he would have felt like the same kind of fool Dane had been. When Sam exited, Gabe pulled the cap from her head and propped herself up on an elbow, careful not to expose herself to Dane's leering gaze. Since he had discovered who she was, his eyes had roamed over her, unnerving her with their intensity. She was not accustomed to being ogled so blatantly and it was annoying.

"Would you be so kind as to hand me my pouch," she requested, her voice cold and brisk.

As she pulled out a clean pair of breeches from her bag, the crumpled paper fell to the floor. Dane retrieved it and read it.

"Do you plan to collect the reward?" she questioned hesitantly.

Dane ambled over to the wash basin and

returned with a towel. After folding the notice, he stashed it in her pouch and then reached beneath her chin to wipe the grime from her face. "No, Gabe. I am not turning you over to your uncle. I am disappointed to think that you would have expected such a reaction. I am wounded to the quick by your low opinion of me," he replied as his hand lingered on her cheek.

Gabe slapped his hand from her face and took up the chore herself. Dane was being perfectly charming and she was desperately trying to ignore him.

"I have the solution to your problem," he said simply.

"And what brilliant scheme do you have in mind?" she quipped, sarcasm dripping from her lips. "I have already considered every possibility and have dismissed every one."

"You can marry me. 'Tis a simple but effective solution."

"You?" She gasped in disbelief. "The man who said marriage was for fools and morons?"

Dane braced his arms on either side of her hips, his face only inches away from her tempting lips. "You have misquoted me, Miss Jarmon," he insisted, his voice like a soft caress. His eyes rested on her mouth and Gabe drew away, certain that he meant to kiss her. "I said *love* was for fools and morons. *Marriage* serves various purposes. It may be for financial gain, a pact between two noble families, or to perpetuate the family name."

Gabe peered warily at him. "And just why would you propose to wed me?"

Dane allowed a hint of a smile to graze his lips. "In my case, I am bound to take the woman whose virtues were compromised. If you are pregnant, the child must have a father." His brow arched slightly as he focused his attention on Gabe. "Unless, of course, there were others who shared your affection."

"How dare you suggest such a thing!" she snapped in raw fury. "What do you think I am? Some strumpet like—"

Dane pressed his fingers to her lips, silencing her outburst. "And also because I owe you my life. I have the opportunity to repay you for the times you rescued me from catastrophe."

After studying Dane for a long moment, she nodded in agreement. "Very well, Captain. We will wed. When my funds are restored to me I will have Mr. Saxon deposit a considerable sum in your account."

The captain waved his hands in frustration. "The terms of this arrangement must be discussed. We will be married and we will live in the same house," he insisted.

"I will do as I please and live in my own home," she protested, her voice rising testily. "I have no intention of limiting your amorous activities. I should think those terms would meet with your approval."

"They don't! If I am to marry, I plan to have a wife to show for it. You will live with me!" Dane leaned forward, glaring at her defiant expression.

"Then I must decline your offer. You are just like my uncle. You have not taken into consideration what would be best for me. I would rather masquerade as a waif than to wed a man whose frivolous wanderings would make me the laughingstock of England. At least if I were in my own home I would not be subjected to such harassment."

"And you must always have things your way! You are spoiled! Your stubbornness would put a jackass to shame!"

"And your lust for women would embarrass a strutting cock!" She spat.

They glared at each other, making mental lists of insults, but a knock at the door brought the argument to an abrupt halt.

Dane scowled at the second intrusion. "What is it now?"

"Yer wanted at the 'elm."

"We will continue this later. Now get some rest," Dane barked as he stalked toward the door.

"Whatever ye say, Cap'n," she mocked dryly.

Dane snorted derisively as he slammed the door behind him. It seemed he was forever backing down to that stubborn lad or lass. He wasn't even certain which one she was: the cocky waif or the passionate angel. She could play either part as if she were born to it. Yet, she seemed to prefer the role of the spirited urchin who constantly goaded his ego. Somehow he would have his own way when it came to this marriage, he vowed determinedly. Separate houses, ha! She hadn't heard the last on that subject!

Gabe strolled across the deck and paused to

watch the setting sun. A wave of vibrant colors spread across the horizon and she marveled at the beauty that lay before her.

"Who would you like to stand as witness at the wedding?" Dane queried, startling her from her silent reverie.

Gabe turned a bemused frown to the captain. "Is it so important to make such a decision today?"

"We will be married tonight and—"

"Tonight?" she repeated incredulously.

"As captain of this ship I can marry us. I see no reason to wait until we return to London and risk confronting your uncle." When Gabe made no comment, Dane continued, smiling faintly, "After all, it is to your advantage that we marry as soon as possible. If my unknown assailant succeeds, you will not only inherit *your* home, but *mine* as well. You will be one of the wealthiest women in England. Of course, I would expect you to play the bereaved widow for at least a month," he mocked.

Gabe suddenly became serious. "I have no desire for your fortune. Nor do I wish to see you dead. If I did, I could have stepped aside on several occasions and let it happen. I have badgered you unmercifully because it was part of the role I played. I don't want to see you hurt."

"But now you have more to gain," he reminded her. "Only a fool would refuse the offer. Of all the roles you have played, that has not been one of them."

"'Tis an important consideration, Cap'n." She rubbed her face with her sleeve in the reckless manner that the waif often used, drawing a disapproving frown from Dane. "Sam and Tom will be the witnesses. I think we kin trust the two of them."

"The ceremony will take place at eight o'clock." When Gabe tilted a defiant chin, he grinned sheepishly, "if that meets with *your* approval, of course."

"Fine, Cap'n. Now if ye'll excuse me, I will prepare meself for this important occasion." The sarcasm that dripped from her lips made Dane roll his eyes in irritation.

As Gabe swaggered away, Dane grumbled under his breath. There was going to be a marriage and it would be the way *he* wanted it. That woman was not going to manipulate him ever again. They were headed for a collision and someone would have to yield. By damn, it wasn't going to be him, not this time!

Chapter Thirteen

When Dane entered his room, he stopped in his tracks, mesmerized by the picture of loveliness before him. A soft blue gown clung to her shapely form, accentuating each swell and curve. Its low neckline exposed the fullness of her breasts to his hungry gaze. Her creamy skin glowed with a golden hue against the lantern light. The scene reminded him of the silhouette he had seen on the hill and a sea of fond memories flooded over him. Brielle's hair was swept up on her head, revealing the trim column of her neck that seemed to beg for his kisses, and it was all Dane could do to keep from devouring her. Was this the same skinny urchin with the dirt-smudged cheeks?

"You're going to make a very lovely bride," he breathed appreciatively, his eyes raking her all over again. "Mmm, very lovely indeed."

Gabrielle was unnerved by the boldness of his gaze and promptly presented her back to him. "Save your flattery, Captain. Our agreement said nothing about your being complimentary or pleasant and I certainly don't expect it."

"For Sam and Tom's benefit I think we should act considerably more than formal, my dear," he snorted as he tossed his jacket on the bunk.

"Very well, my love," Gabe purred in mock affection. "While they are present I shall portray the love-smitten maiden who cannot take her eyes off their captain."

"That will be the most difficult role you have yet to undertake." Dane smirked caustically. "I cannot wait to witness your performance. Shall I save my applause until the audience leaves and the curtain drops?"

Gabrielle sauntered toward him, a wry smile creeping to her lips. After slipping the linen shirt from his shoulders she traced her fingertips over the hard wall of his chest. "You might be surprised by my theatrical ability, m'lord," she murmured seductively. "Even though it is only an act, I assure you that no one will guess my true feelings for you, my frivolous rogue."

"And what are your true feelings?" he inquired.

Her sweet smile was in direct contrast to her biting words. "You, m'lord captain, are a scoundrel of the worst sort. Your lust is ordinarily found in a beast twice your size."

Dane returned her charming smile. "And you are a vicious, deceitful witch whose heart is chiseled from stone."

"Just as long as we understand each other," Brielle replied as her arms slid over his shoulders.

As her fingers toyed with his raven hair, she

pulled his head to hers, reaching up on tiptoe to place a tempting kiss on his lips. Brielle melted against him, using every technique she had learned from her experienced instructor. Dane's arms encircled her waist, crushing her to him. He tasted the sweetness that recalled shadowed memories. A spark of passion bridged the gap between them and Brielle felt herself losing control. Her heart was running away with itself. She leaned back as far as his embrace would allow and stared into the captivating eyes that gazed ravishingly upon her.

"Was that convincing enough?" she questioned huskily.

A devilish smile curled his lips, setting his sapphire eyes aflame. "Surely you can play your charade with more enthusiasm," he taunted. "Sailors have a perceptive eye. They will see through your game in a minute. Perhaps we should practice one more before they arrive."

"If you insist," she muttered, an annoyed frown settling on her exquisite features.

Dane's lips came swooping down in urgent reply. He pulled her up off the floor, searching the softness of her flesh as his tongue parted her lips. Brielle could play her games if she wished, but he would not be denied the treasure that he held in his arms. Although Brielle tried to feel nothing, she could not ignore the tingle that swept through her limbs. Her senses reeled in confusion; her body yearned for his caress. Her emotions were being tossed about like a wave on an angry sea. No matter how she tried she could not escape from them. His scalding kisses melted her resistance and she knew that she must withdraw before all was lost.

"Does that display meet with your approval?" she questioned as she squirmed from his grasp.

"That kiss would bring the devil to his knees," he assured her, a broad smile splitting his face.

"Then why are you still standing?" she mocked. "I thought you were the Prince of Darkness disguised as a sea captain."

Dane was not allowed to retort. A rap at the door again interrupted them. "Come in," he called before returning his lusty gaze to the dazzling beauty in his arms.

When Sam and Tom saw their captain holding a shapely young woman their eyes widened bewilderedly. Shock registered on their faces as Gabe turned to face them, displaying a deliciously mischievous smile.

Strolling gracefully toward them, she giggled at their frozen expressions. "Good evening, gentlemen."

"Gabe?" Sam choked. "Gawd, I wouldn't 'ave believed it if I 'adn't seen ye fer meself."

Gabe fluttered her eyes coyly. "Why, Sam. How could you think it would be anyone else. I look the same in my breeches or a dress. You just never paid enough attention to me to notice."

"'Ardly," he sputtered. "The only thin' that gave ye away was yer green eyes. I've never seen another pair that ornery shade of green."

The two men turned questioning gazes from her to the captain, impatiently awaiting an explanation.

Dane shrugged on a fresh shirt and grinned slyly. "Gabe and I are going to be married," he announced. As Brielle came back to him, his eyes followed her until she had curled her hand in the crook of his arm. Dragging his gaze from Gabrielle, he focused his attention on the sailors who were eying the lady with hungry stares. "You two will stand as witnesses for us. You are the two men Gabe trusted above all others. No one else aboard this ship is to know her identity. I expect you to keep an eye on her while she is on deck. But *please* keep your leering gazes to yourselves or the rest of the crew will think the two of you have been too long at sea. Is that understood?" he asked, frowning meaningfully.

Sam and Tom reluctantly raised their eyes to meet the captain's stern expression and then nodded affirmatively.

During the brief ceremony, Gabrielle gazed devotedly at Dane, assuring the witnesses that she was by no means an unwilling participant. When the ritual ended, Brielle wrapped her arms about Dane's neck and eagerly awaited his kiss. She leaned against the hard wall of his chest, enjoying the strong arms that encircled her waist. When Dane finally released her, Sam and Tom grinned and raised their glasses in toast.

"May ye find 'appiness together. But from the looks of thin's, I'd say ye already 'ave," Tom concluded.

Gabrielle wrapped her arm around Dane's waist and laid her head against his shoulder. "There is no other place I'd rather be than with the captain."

When she raised her eyes to Dane, he lowered his head to taste the sweetness of her inviting lips. He intended to seize every opportunity she offered, no matter how pretentious she might have been.

As Dane raised his head, he glanced to Sam. His eyes darted to the hammock and then to the door. Sam caught the unspoken command and his lips curved in a knowing smile.

"I guess we better git back to our duties." He strolled over to the rope and untied it as he spoke over his shoulder. "Ye won't be needin' this, so I'll jest toss it out," he offered, coughing on a chuckle.

Gabrielle stiffened angrily, knowing she could do nothing to prevent losing her bed without drawing the sailors' curiosity. When she shot Dane an accusing glare, he merely displayed a devilish grin and shrugged innocently.

When the men exited from the room, Brielle's charming smile turned into a sneer. She jerked away from Dane and put a greater distance between them. "You seem to think you are so very clever, Captain. Now just where do *you* intend to spend the night?" she snapped harshly.

Dane gestured toward his bunk. "That, my dear wife, is the captain's bed and I am the captain," he insisted, lightly tapping his chest. "It seems you are the one who has to make a choice of sleeping accommodations. You can sleep with your husband or you can bed down on the floor with the rats. Knowing how stubborn you are, I certainly do not presume to make your decision for you. If you come to my bed it will be by your own choice."

"I don't know which rodent would cause me the most distress," she hissed in annoyance.

"Make up your mind, Gabe. And be quick about it. It has been a long day and I'm ready for bed." He stripped off his shirt and sank down on the bunk to pull off his boots.

His leering gaze raked her from head to toe, leaving no doubt what he intended if she decided to sleep with him.

Gabrielle growled in irritation and quickly snuffed out the light before Dane undressed in front of her. "You leave me little choice, Captain. But we have an agreement and I intend to keep it. I will sleep with you." Brielle winced when Dane chuckled victoriously. "But that's *all* I will do with you," she assured him, her voice crackling with defiance.

She fumbled in the darkness, trying to struggle with the ties on the back of her gown. Her fingers had turned to thumbs and she had no success with her chore. "Will you please unlace this confounded dress?" she muttered as she moved toward the bed. "I may as well take advantage of *some* of your services now that we are married."

She cautiously eased onto the bunk, frightened of him for the first time. Dane's hand leisurely caressed her back as he loosened the strings and pulled the gown from her shoulders. Sitting up behind her, he slid the dress down to her waist. His arms drew her against his bare chest to fondle the full swell of her breast. Although Brielle squirmed

324

frantically, Dane held her in place, pressing arousing kisses along the curve of her neck.

"I know what you have in mind and it is out of the question. I may be your wife, but I'll be damned if you'll add my name to your list of willing strumpets," she hissed, her tone livid with anger.

"Why do you begrudge me this night? There was a time when you came to my bed without regret," he murmured hoarsely.

"That was before—"

Dane did not allow her to finish as he turned her in his arms and captured her mouth in a scalding kiss. "You took the marriage vows, saying you would stay with me for better or worse. Consider this however you wish, but I will not be denied what is rightfully mine." His hand lowered to caress her abdomen and Gabrielle twisted in his arms, dodging his kiss. "I'm surprised how quickly my angel of mercy has turned into a spiteful witch."

"I have no intention of playing your devoted wife," she snapped as she pressed a small but determined hand to his chest.

Dane's patience was at the end of its fuse. "I intend to have my way and you might as well adjust to the idea," he growled as he roughly pulled her to him.

His mouth swooped down on hers, taking her breath away with his demanding kiss. Brielle shivered as he ripped the chemise from her flesh and cupped her breast. He was like a satanic spirit who refused to let her resist him. Brielle felt herself becoming clay in the hands of a master craftsman. The world was exploding in raging fires and she was lost to all except the need to seek fulfillment in the arms of the only man who had brought her ecstasy.

He explored every inch of her flesh, deliberately rousing her to the limits of her sanity. She returned his kisses and wrapped her arms about his back, wanting to mold herself to him. And then he moved above her, thrusting deeply while a wild, unceasing wave of rapture flooded over her. Dane's ragged breath was warm against her neck and she could feel his heart thudding furiously against her breasts, matching the pace of her own racing pulse. The fires of passion singed their souls and they took flight, gliding away from the blaze. On rapture's pinnacle they nestled together, content and safe in each other's embrace.

Gabrielle's eyes were clouded with tears and she cursed her faltering willpower. With a sniff she turned her head away from his tender kiss, ashamed of what she had done after vowing never to experience his love-making again. She was no better than he was. Her thirst for passion was as great as his and she had fallen into his bed to quench her own lusty desires. How could she have been so weak?

"Did I hurt you?" Dane frowned in concern as a steady stream of tears rolled down her cheeks. "If I did, I'm sorry. It was not my intention."

Gabrielle squirmed away, wrapped the sheet about her, and sat up on the edge of the bed. Dane reached up to brush his hand across her back in a leisurely caress.

"Would a true marriage be so miserable for you, Gabe?" he questioned huskily. "I have grown accustomed to your bright eyes and your quick wit. Who knows? You might even come to like me if you gave yourself half a chance."

"That's what I'm afraid of," Gabrielle replied with a muffled sniff. Her remark drew a bemused frown from Dane and Gabe smiled ruefully. "I might become the jealous wife who demands that you cease finding affection with other women. We would quarrel often and I would never trust you when you went out without me. I would only end up loathing the sight of you. As it is now, I can accept you for what you are without trying to change you."

"I need no other women if I have you to satisfy my needs. But I must admit that my demands on you would be very time-consuming," he added, with a rakish smile that only confirmed Brielle's belief that he would say and do anything to get what he wanted.

"You have an unappeasable appetite. How long will it be before your eyes began to stray?" she questioned cynically.

"That depends on your effort to keep me faithful." He traced his hand along the curve of her neck and then pulled her back against him. "You will be the only woman I need unless you refuse to share my bed."

Gabrielle dodged his intended kiss and held him at bay. "Don't lie to me, Dane Hampton," she snapped angrily. "You seem to forget that I have been your constant shadow these past two months. The last time we were together you acted as though you regretted our parting. The next afternoon found you at the inn, mounting the steps with the same intention for that wench who hung on your arm. Love and devotion are empty words to you. 'For fools and morons,' you said. Well, I do not intend to be categorized in that class either!"

Dane growled in frustration. "We were not married then. *You* were the one who wanted no promises, not I," he reminded her harshly. "I never expected to see you again. What would you have me do, become a monk or lead a chaste life for some unknown lover who wouldn't allow me to see her face? Your last words were, 'It's over and done,' remember?"

"I certainly didn't expect you to grieve, but you didn't have to fly to some other wench's bed so quickly!" she cried in anguish. "I treasured those moments I spent with you and I was in no hurry to see the memories fade. But you . . ." Her voice carried a sarcastic hiss. "You took it in stride, noble martyr that you are. Not even a full day had passed before you crawled into another bed, you rogue!"

Gabrielle pushed away from him, wishing to be anywhere except in his arms. Dane's hand sneaked out and yanked her back to the bed. He pinned her to the bunk and stretched out on top of her to hold her in place. "If you would just let me explain, you stubborn witch!"

"I don't want to hear any more of your lies. Let me up!" she stormed at him.

"You're going to listen and we are going to settle this here and now, madam!" he thundered as he glared down at her, his face only inches from hers. "The first time you came to me I thought you were only a fantasy. I thought my imagination was playing tricks on me again. I could not even begin to describe you. Never had I seen your face or the color of your eyes or hair. I didn't even have a name to attach to you except the one you had given— angel." He laughed bitterly. "There was a better term, my dear. It was 'witch.' You played your torturesome game with me, making me think that I had surely lost my sanity."

Gabrielle stopped struggling as she listened to his hateful words. She had tried to comfort him, but it seemed she had made him despise her.

Dane eased his grip on Brielle when she relaxed, but he continued none too gently. "I sought to free myself from your illusion in other women's arms, but your image tormented me each time. When I tried to put you out of my mind, your shadowed spirit only grew stronger. For a time I thought you had something to do with the attempts on my life. When you finally returned to my arms, I had decided to send you away, but I was powerless to resist you. I couldn't deny my need for you and I finally accepted you as you were—a wild, untamed soul whom I could only know in darkness. I became your pawn, your lover, asking nothing but the passion we shared," he reminded her cruelly. "I did not come to you, my lovely witch. You were there because of your own whimsical need. We

329

played the game by *your* rules. But now, I am in command and it is *I* who will make the demands. If I want to make love to you, I will. You are my wife and the privilege is mine."

Dane roughly slanted his mouth across her quivering lips. His manner was so forceful that Brielle could barely breathe beneath his hungry kiss. As he parted her thighs with his muscular hips, Brielle whimpered, afraid of the demon who towered over her. She stiffened as he entered her. She tried to push him away, but Dane was not to be refused.

"Don't deny me," he demanded as he drove into her. "I want your heart and soul. I won't be satisfied until I possess all of you. I will haunt you day and night until you admit that I am the only man who can claim you."

As passion consumed him he forgot all except the wild pleasure that coursed through his veins. His mind was filled with burning desire. He could think of nothing but those green eyes that could sparkle so wickedly. He wanted to hear her utter words of affection, but they didn't come. He was a man obsessed, driven by revenge. She would become his slave, his pawn, as he had once been for her. He wanted to strangle the words from her lips, force her to admit that she was his possession. As he shuddered against her, he cursed himself for his own weakness. He had gained nothing. Dane lifted himself from her and turned away, as if the sight of her annoyed him.

Gabrielle's eyes were wide with alarm and confusion. This was not the man she thought she knew. Now he seemed bent on revenge and she trembled frightenedly. How could he have misunderstood her intentions? She had played a game with him only to keep her identity a secret. She had never meant to hurt him. She had yearned for his tenderness and had gone to him for comfort. She could *not* give her name or show her face. Her life had been at stake. Couldn't he understand what she had been through?

"Dane," she whispered, biting back the tears, "I never meant to hurt you. I . . ." She stopped, in doubt about her own feelings; Brielle didn't know exactly what she wanted to say. How could she make a confession to a man who moments before had been like a demon who sought to draw her life from her body.

Dane laughed without humor. "Sorry for what? Sorry that I discovered who you were? You, the deceitful witch who would stop at nothing to destroy the contract with Fairleigh? You, the vicious waif who delighted in harassing me? Save your apology, Gabe," he growled. "No longer will I play the meek lover or sympathetic friend. I am not your puppet; nor will I ever be again."

Easing from the bed, Gabe donned her garb and hurried up the steps to the deck. Charading as a waif had given her a taste of freedom that left her wanting some unattainable goal. It was a longing to find herself and some purpose for her life. But, she didn't know what she really wanted. She still yearned to be loved and protected as she had been when her father was alive. Brielle leaned her elbows on the rail and rested her chin in her hands.

Do I seek more than I am rightfully allowed? Have I found what I want? Am I too stubborn to admit it? What beckons me? Some evil force that bids me to search the unknown?

With a heavy-hearted sigh she gazed across the sea, wishing she could answer the questions that loomed in her mind. Two strong arms encircled her waist and she accepted them without resistance.

"After only one night of marriage are you considering casting yourself into the sea?" Dane taunted.

"No, just sorting muddled thoughts," she murmured. After a long moment of silence she sighed weakly. "The sea is beautiful at night. I feel as though I could step out on it and walk to the stars." Her gaze lifted skyward, enthralled by the boundless view that lay before her.

"It won't help," he assured her quietly. "You must first decide what you want before you begin your long walk."

A warm tingle skittered across her skin as he spoke in his rich voice. He was again the gentle, understanding man that she had often sought in darkness. Gone was the spiteful tone he had used earlier.

"Don't you ever grow tired of being right about everything?" she quipped, sending him a faint smile.

Dane brushed the back of his hand over her creamy cheek, returning her smile. "I'm not always right, but I have already walked the path which you have begun to tread. Experience is an excellent reference for foresight," he declared philosophically.

Gabe giggled and cocked her head to the side. "Tell me, Captain. Since you profess to be a philosopher and fortuneteller. What do you see in my future?"

With a cunning smile, he traced his fingers down the curve of her neck and then returned his hand to her face, as if he were reading her fortune from her exquisite features. "You're going to fall hopelessly in love with a sea captain. Your heart and soul will no longer be your own."

Gabe leaned back against the taffrail and crossed her feet at the ankles. She scanned the handsome rogue who towered above her. "Perty sure of yerself, Cap'n," she mocked in her boyish tone. "I'd 'ate fer ye to 'old yer breath waitin' fer that to 'appen. Ye might turn blue in the face."

Dane braced his arms on either side of her. "Don't underestimate my powers, my doubtful pigeon," he warned, a wicked flicker darkening his eyes to a hazy shade of indigo blue. "Your fortune has become of interest to me. I am a very determined man and I shall channel my energy to ensure that I keep control of you."

He had gained an insight into her soul after their midnight conversation. There was a way to handle this high-spirited wench and he was hellbent on taming her. She had once had the upper hand, but now he was going to steer her in the direction he wanted her to go.

With wide, searching eyes, Gabe swallowed hard. Suddenly she was fearful of his power over her. Her legs were weak and her heart raced wildly beneath her breasts. He was beckoning her to him and she was raising parted lips to his. Dane lowered his head, his eyes holding her spellbound. He taunted her with light kisses before he pulled her hips to his, letting her feel the bold manliness that yearned to possess her. His tongue teased the recesses of her mouth before his lips made slow descent to the valley between her breasts. Gabe closed her eyes, abandoning all hope. He could make her skin tingle with desire. No woman could resist his skillful ways.

"You're a devil, Captain," she murmured as he unbuttoned her shirt and cupped her breast, teasing its peak to tautness. "I fear my life is being devoured and there will be nothing left of me."

His hand wandered up her neck and lifted her chin so that he could study her face in the moonlight. "Are you really afraid of me, Gabe?" he questioned, his dark brow arching in wry amusement.

"Yes," she answered hastily. "No ... I ..." Brielle shook her head, shattering the spell and quickly set his hands from her. "I don't know. Right now I'm not sure of anything. I have lived in two separate worlds and now I'm not sure to which I really belong. I don't know which of us frightens me the most."

Dane wrapped his arms around her waist and led her to his cabin. He gently unfastened the beggar's garb and pressed her to the bunk. His hands explored her flesh without the rough urgency that he had displayed earlier. His searing kisses traveled to the full crests of her breasts, capturing their peaks to tease them with his tongue. Brielle moaned with pleasure, wishing she had the will to resist his fondling, but knowing that she would surrender just as she always had. When he came to her she opened her thighs to him, soaring to passion's highest pinnacle to remain suspended for that timeless moment where nothing mattered except the security of his arms.

When the *Sea Wind* had docked and the cargo was unloaded, Dane went back to his cabin to find Gabe washing out her spare garb.

"We're going into town," he announced as he poured a basin of water and began shaving the stubble from his face.

"For business or pleasure?" she questioned as she glanced at him.

"Both," he muttered out of the side of his mouth while he continued to shave.

"Can I venture out alone while you're tending to business?"

Dane stopped his chore and peered skeptically at her. "No. I am not turning you loose in Scotland. It might be the last I ever see of you."

"Don't you trust me?" she questioned, arching a delicate brow.

Dane leaned an arm on the edge of the commode and regarded her warily. "You seem to have a knack for attracting trouble, madam. I want you with me every minute so I don't have to worry about you." He wiped his face and strolled over to grab a fresh shirt. "I'm not sure Scotland is ready for a woman

335

like you."

Gabe pulled a face at his broad backside. "I'd rather stay on the ship if I am to be kept waiting all day as I have been in the past." She snorted disgustedly.

"My business won't take long and the pleasure to which I was referring is not what you are insinuating." Dane grabbed his jacket and motioned for her to follow him.

Retrieving her pouch, Gabe hastened to the door and opened it for him, a mocking smile curving her lips. "After ye, Cap'n," she said with an exaggerated bow. "I'll try to be'ave meself, but it ain't goin' to be easy. It ain't me nature to be a perfect gentleman such as yerself."

Dane rolled his eyes and shook his head before nodding to the sailor who strolled down the companionway. "Come along, m'boy."

"Aye, Cap'n." Gabe bit back a snicker and closed the door behind her, following after the captain who walked the hall in measured strides.

Each time Gabe found something interesting she tugged on his arm. She was bubbling with enthusiasm and Dane watched her closely, marveling at another facet of her that he had never seen. After their noon meal, Gabe found a room in which to change and reappeared as a young woman.

Dane stood admiring her with an appreciative eye. "I much prefer you in a dress, madam," he admitted with a rakish smile. "But 'tis difficult to keep my mind on business when you are with me."

Gabe curtsied, allowing him to view the tempting sight that drew his attention. "Shall we go, m'lord?" She placed her hand in the crook of his arm, presenting him with a disarming smile.

After Dane had purchased a gold wedding band for his bride, they visited the merchants whose cargo was to be loaded on the schooner the following day. Each time Gabrielle stopped to admire some item, Dane purchased it for her even though she fiercely protested his extravagance.

Standing outside one of the shops, Gabe struggled with the packages that were draped about her. "This is not necessary, Captain. I have my own clothes at my uncle's home. Now that we are married I can well afford to purchase all that I need or desire."

Dane shrugged nonchalantly. "When we are alone in our cabin, I wish to see my wife, not my cabin boy. Consider these gowns a wedding gift."

Brielle could not suppress the smile that surfaced on her lips as Dane swaggered away, leaving her to follow behind him. He made it difficult to find fault with him, except that he was strikingly handsome, drawing the stares of many women who passed him on the street. Although she fought against it, Dane was burrowing his way into her heart. She didn't want to depend on him, but he was always there with a gentle touch, a reassuring smile, and a protective arm for her to lean on.

Gabe was left to herself that evening while Dane remained on deck. The crew had gone ashore and she was free to do as she pleased. Brielle donned the green velvet gown Dane had purchased for her and thoughtfully studied her reflection in the mirror.

"Is this who I am?" she questioned the image. "The captain's wife? Lady Gabrielle Hampton?" Gabe pulled the pins from her hair, letting the thick mass cascade down her back. "Damn!" The role of the skinny urchin had been easier to play.

Gabe stepped from the yards of velvet and shrugged on her tattered clothes. After pulling the cap down around her ears, she peered up from beneath its brim to view this new image. She was more at ease, but the reflection was sorely lacking. She wrinkled her nose distastefully at the raga-muffin who gazed back at her.

"One ain't much better than the other," she snorted. "Somewhere there 'as to be a 'appy medium. I'd dearly love to find it." A concerned frown gathered on her brows. "I'm goin' to 'ave to light on one or the other and soon or I could end up a pregnant cabin boy. Now that would be interestin' to explain." Her voice took on a sophisticated air. "Why couldn't I have had a simple name? I could have assumed no double identity. But no, I had to be plagued with one that allowed me to flutter back and forth between two different worlds. Now I don't fit into either of them. A misfit," she concluded, "that's what ye are. And jest what the 'ell are ye goin' to do about it?"

Gabe spun on her heels and stalked to the door. She paused to glance over at the mirror that had offered no advice. "Yer a lot of 'elp. Ye jest stand there lookin' at me. The least ye could 'ave done was expressed yer opinion.''

Gabe yanked open the door and jumped, startled when she saw Dane leaning casually against the casing, flashing white teeth and an amused grin at her.

"You and your friend were having an interesting conversation. I wish I could have been here to hear the discussion in its entirety. Tell me Gabe . . . rielle," he drawled. "Did the lad or the lady have the last word?" His brow arched slightly. "Or was it the pregnant cabin boy?"

She blushed crimson red and brushed past him. "S'cuse me, Cap'n. 'Tis a bit stuffy in this dingy 'ole.''

Dane chuckled as he followed Gabe to the deck. They made a strange pair, Dane thought to himself. He was deliberate and Gabe was flighty and unsure of where she was going. He had spent long years in search of his fantasy. He had learned to walk, crawl, and fly despite varying degrees of difficulty. He had found his way in darkness with a small flame to lead his way. He had climbed the tallest mountain to touch the stars, ridden the rough waters, and drifted on peaceful seas. But Gabe had just tasted the sweetness of freedom and had become addicted to it. She was like a small child who had taken her first, unassisted step and was ready to run. She was impatient with time's methodic procedure and searched for quick answers to her questions. She was restless youth tugging at Father Time's robe, urging him to keep her reckless pace. But the old man was not to be rushed.

Dane knew she needed to grow, to learn her own mind. She was not easy to tame and impossible to hold back. He found himself smiling down at her, wondering why he had ever vowed to capture the heart of this misfit. Yes, he mused thoughtfully, she had described herself perfectly. She was a beautiful, uncontrollable misfit. She was a walking contradiction. Occasionally she was the gentle angel who had soothed his troubled dreams. Yet, in the next instant she was the quick-tempered, stubborn waif. That was part of the reason he never seemed to tire of her. She was the woman, the witch, and the waif. Dane cursed himself for becoming involved with her. She was nothing but trouble.

Through the moonlight that splattered on the planks Gabe and Dane walked the deck. The captain strolled in deliberate strides while the waif sauntered in light, springy steps. She paused occasionally and then hurried to catch up, dancing playfully around the captain. And when Dane looked down into those sparkling green eyes he cursed himself again, knowing that she had enchanted him.

Chapter Fourteen

The night before the *Sea Wind* docked in London, Dane opened the door to his quarters to find Gabe in a strange mood. As they sat down to their evening meal, Dane attempted to make conversation, but Gabe peered disinterestedly at him over the rim of her teacup.

"I'd appreciate taking my meal without this idle chatter, Captain," she snapped harshly.

"Pardon me, madam," he drawled, his voice heavily laden with sarcasm. "I didn't realize that I was dining with a foul-tempered twit this evening."

"I am not a twit!" Gabrielle protested as she slammed her cup to the table and bolted from her chair. "Don't ever call me that again."

Dane chuckled at her explosive temper and arched a mocking brow. "If the shoe fits—"

"Just leave me be!" she stormed as her fist hit the table. It hurt like hell, but she never flinched. Dane was unaware of the pain she had inflicted on herself. "You have been smothering me with pleasantries all week. You never criticize me except in your light manner of teasing after I have intentionally tried to irritate you. You never get angry and snap at me. You just keep flashing me those blinding smiles, as if I had just charmed you with some witty remark instead of my insults. Your patience is driving me mad!"

Dane had made her decision difficult. Gabe had tried to instigate arguments with him for the past week, hoping that he, too, would come to the conclusion that they should part company when they returned to England. But Dane had out-guessed her motives and had given her nothing that she had expected from all of her efforts. That had grated on her nerves more than the quarrels that she had anticipated.

Dane rocked back on the legs of his chair and crossed his feet on the edge of the table. Casually sipping his tea, he surveyed her face that was framed in a cape of dark curls. "Please do go on, Gabe. I find your ravings an interesting source of entertainment."

"And that's another thing." She leaned toward him, shaking a slim finger in his face. Her breasts came dangerously close to spilling free from the green velvet and lace. Dane nearly choked on his tea as his gaze rested on this arousing display. "Quit calling me Gabe. My name is Gabrielle. Only my father called me Gabe. I don't want to hear you utter that name again."

With a denying shake of his head, Dane refused her command. "You're still the Gabe I met . . .

although I must admit I look at you in a very different light."

His devouring gaze made her bristle angrily. "Yes, and it can aptly be described as monotonous lust!" she snapped in retort.

"If you had the shape of a cow and the face of a pig you would be spared my appreciative stares." His shoulder lifted in a reckless shrug. "But as luck would have it, you are extremely well-shaped and demand my full attention."

"It would make no difference what shape a woman came in," she countered insultingly. "If she was dressed in petticoats and skirts, she would be susceptible to your leering gazes."

Dane leaned forward, allowing all four legs of his chair to rest on the floor. A wry smile caught one corner of his mouth as he boldly raked Gabe from head to toe. "You wound me to the quick with such slanderous remarks, madam," he mocked dryly. "If I were as voracious in appeasing my appetite for women as you so claim, I would have spent more time in bed than I have on my feet. I can honestly say that has not been the case."

Gabe promptly presented her back to him. Since it was impossible to lure him into a heated argument, she decided to plunge headlong into the subject that had been on her mind. "When we reach London, I'm going to my uncle's to tell him of our marriage. Then I will travel to my own estate," she announced.

"An excellent idea, Gabe," Dane agreed in a bland tone. "I was going to suggest that myself."

Gabe whirled to face him. "You mean you

don't mind?" A hint of disappointment found its way into her voice.

"Not at all, my dear," he replied with a nonchalant shrug. "There is no reason to delay this any longer. Once we arrive in London, I will make the necessary arrangements."

With wide green eyes, Gabrielle watched him rise from his chair and amble toward her. Somewhat flustered by his apparent acceptance of her plans, she opened her mouth to speak, but quickly snapped it shut. She had prepared all of her arguments. Now she had no need of them. The fact that he did not protest rankled her pride more than she wanted to admit. "So you tired of me sooner than you expected," she declared as she studied the opposite wall.

"Not at all, Gabe. I fear you misunderstand." His hand traced a light path from her bare shoulder to the enticing swells of her breasts. "*We* are going to your uncle's house and *we* are traveling to your estate. *You* are not going anywhere without me. I thought I made that clear the night we were married."

"You did, but I never agreed to anything you said then; nor do I now," she informed him, her emerald eyes flickering rebelliously.

"You have attempted to draw me into an argument all week and you have finally hit upon the one subject that will instigate it," he assured her as his hand dropped to his side. "I refuse to allow you to travel alone." Steel-blue eyes locked with defiant green for a long moment.

"We are going our separate ways just as soon as

344

we set foot on solid ground," Gabe insisted, her voice steady and determined.

Dane grabbed her and held her at arm's length, his jaw twitching angrily. "We will travel together and we will live in the same damned house! I will have it no other way!"

"No! I'm traveling alone!"

"You are not!"

Brielle's temper reached its boiling point when Dane gave her a sound shaking. "Let go of me, you dolt! I will not be treated like a child who cannot make her own decisions."

"Then stop acting like one," he growled as his mouth swooped down on hers. His lips devoured hers as his hands slipped beneath the velvet bodice to cup her breast. He clutched her close, allowing no more struggles while his kisses trailed down her neck. As he lifted his head, his eyes held her captive.

"Gabe," he whispered hoarsely, "don't fight me. There are reasons why you cannot be alone, especially now that we are married. It would have been best for you if we hadn't wed and had gone our separate ways, but we both had much to gain from this arrangement. I may have jeopardized your life even though I have given you back your home and your fortune. For once you will have to trust that I know what is best for you. 'Tis too dangerous for you to travel alone."

Her brows furrowed thoughtfully as she studied his solemn expression. She had no idea what he meant, but the seriousness of his gaze told her that he played no games. A hint of a smile touched her lips as she looped her arms around his neck.

"Very well, m'lord. It is as you wish. If you are certain that you have not become bored with me, then let me see some proof of it."

A rakish grin caught one corner of his mouth as he nimbly unfastened her gown. "Isn't it evident in my eyes?" he questioned, his voice like a soft caress. "I am like a starved beast who craves that which he constantly wants, but never truly has. Each morsel curbs the appetite—for a time." His lips brushed against the hollow of her neck and then flitted across her cheek. "Yet, I hunger for your heart and soul, the essence of your being."

Gabe lowered her eyes, her dark lashes sweeping down to protect her from his gaze as he took her chin in his hand. "You ask more than I ever intended to give," she murmured.

"One day you will gladly give it, my lovely witch," he insisted as he pulled the gown from her creamy skin, his eyes eagerly consuming the beauty of her flesh.

As Gabe turned away from his intense gaze, Dane pulled her to him to capture her soft lips. Against her will she surrendered to his passionate kiss, unable to deny the stormy rapture that awaited her. The clash of thunder she heard was her own heart's furious beat pounding in her ears. His experienced touch was a lightning's spark sizzling across her skin, causing her to burn with need, flame with emotion. As Dane pressed her to the bunk, Brielle looked up to him. Fire smoldered in his sapphire eyes; it was as if the devil himself towered over her. And yet, she could not refuse him when his muscled hips parted her thighs. She arched to meet his hard thrusts that carried them both into a churning whirlwind. The world was spinning out of control and Brielle was lost to the tempest of desire that sent logic fleeing from passion's stormy path. Then she was soaring to dizzying heights, content in his strong arms, unable to deny the ecstasy that his love-making brought.

A faint smile skittered across her lips as she brushed her hand across his bronzed cheek. "You're very persuasive, Captain," she whispered quietly. " 'Tis not difficult to understand why you usually get your way."

"Except when it comes to you." Dane returned her lazy smile and brought her fingertips to his lips. "My persuasiveness is an equal match for your stubbornness. But someday I intend to convince you that you can't live without me. And you will come to realize that what you think you're missing by not chasing some distant star is no better than what you can find in my arms. Once you have learned to fly you will become a homing pigeon. You will soar freely among the clouds, yet you will always return to your secure nest."

"Is this to be another lesson in philosophy, m'lord Captain?" she inquired, arching a wary brow.

"No. I'm merely stating fact, m'lady. One day you will see it as truth." When Gabrielle started to interject a remark, Dane pressed his finger to her lips. "Now I plan to fall asleep with my guardian angel watching over me; not that taunting witch."

He hooked his arm around her waist, pulling her tightly against him. "Good night, Gabe," he whispered with a contented sigh.

Brielle smiled to herself as she nestled against his sturdy shoulder. It was difficult to find fault with Dane when she lay content in his arms. He was becoming the dominant force in her life despite her fear of depending on him. Their relationship could never be permanent. In time their passion would die and Dane would tire of her. But for now she would enjoy the tenderness he could offer.

A young boy, standing in a London alleyway, caught Brielle's eye as she and Dane walked their horses down the street. At first glance, Brielle did not recognize him, but as they passed him, she turned in her saddle.

"Sherman?" Brielle questioned.

The lad raised his head when he heard his name. With a delighted squeal, Brielle slid from Blanco's back and hurried toward the urchin. "What are you doing in London?" she queried as she hugged him excitedly.

"I ran off," he answered, holding Brielle close.

Brielle squirmed from his embrace and grabbed his arm, but as she turned, she found Dane towering over her.

"Who is this, Gabe?" Dane questioned impatiently.

"Is there a café near?" she queried in return.

"Right down the street," Dane replied tightly, his gaze sweeping the lad who could do nothing but stare at Gabe.

"Let's go sit and talk," Gabe insisted as she clasped her hand in the crook of Sherman's arm.

"Dane, this is Sherman Brice, the stableboy from Uncle John's who helped me escape. He's my dearest friend," she explained, smiling fondly as they seated themselves at a table. After Dane and the boy had nodded stiffly to each other, Brielle continued, "And this is Dane Hampton, the man I found on the road during the storm." She focused her full attention on Sherman. "Why did you run away?"

"The last time ye came 'ome and then sneaked off again, Lord Jarmon went into a fit of rage, even worse than the time before. The 'ouse servants said 'e 'ad tried to lock ye in yer room again. When 'e found ye gone, 'e came lookin' fer me. 'E whipped me fer 'elpin' ye escape," Sherman muttered, his dark eyes brimmed with hatred.

Brielle reached over to affectionately squeeze his hand. "I'm sorry, Sherm. I should have taken you with me. I should have known that beast would do something like that. He thrives on cruelty."

Sherman shrugged and ducked his head. "When I was able to move about and me back 'ealed, I ran off to London. I found work sweepin' up in one of the shops. It ain't much, but 'tis better than workin' fer Lord Jarmon."

"You're coming with me," Brielle insisted. "If it weren't for you, I would have never managed to escape from that horrible place."

After their meal, Brielle left the two men alone for a few minutes. After a stilted silence, Sherman arched a curious brow.

"Do ye know Gabrielle well, sir?" His attempt at conversation was lacking, but he could think of nothing else to say.

"Well enough to know that she is an unusual little lady," Dane replied, a wry smile slanting across his lips.

"Aye, that she is. She brought the only 'appiness there was at Lord Jarmon's." Sherman's face brightened as pleasant memories of Brielle flashed across his mind.

Dane frowned thoughtfully, studying the lad's love-struck gaze. "I suppose you are infatuated with Gabe."

A sheepish grin settled on Sherman's features. "I know 'tis foolish of me to think she could ever care fer me. But when she's near, I kin do nothin' but dream. She treats me like 'er brother." His shoulder lifted in a reckless shrug. "I guess 'tis better than nothin'."

Dane's countenance became sober. "Sherman, Gabe and I were married a few weeks ago."

"Oh," was all Sherman could manage for the moment. The news was like a blow that knocked the wind out of him. After a long silence he added, "I wish the best fer ye."

A knowing smile grazed Dane's lips. "You will be living at Hampton Estate with us. You will see Gabe often."

Sherman returned the smile, but then it faded. "I know it ain't me place to offer advice, but I think fer ye sake, I'll dare to speak. Gabrielle don't like bein' tied down. She never 'as. Lord Jarmon tried, but ye know 'ow far 'e got with 'er. She's jest like that stallion of 'ers. They're both 'igh-strung. They got to 'ave the freedom to fly when they got the urge. Ye can't 'old either of them back when they want free rein. Even Blanco bends to 'er will more than she bends to 'is.''

Sherman was a very perceptive young man, Dane mused. He must have spent many hours pondering the woman who had stolen his heart at such a tender age. "I see you know her well, Sherman. I appreciate your advice, but I'm well aware of Gabe's need for freedom. I have no intention of treating her the way Jarmon did.''

A relieved smile hovered on his lips before he turned his attention to Gabe who moved toward them.

When they arrived at Lord John's, Sherman took the reins and waited outside while the Hamptons were ushered into the study.

"Well, I see my reward for your return was fruitful.'' Lord John smiled maliciously at the sight of Brielle. "Thank you, Captain Hampton, for bringing my vagabond niece back to me. She has a tendency to come and go as she pleases, despite my effort to control her.'' John roughly grabbed Brielle's arm, clamping his fingers into her flesh.

Gabrielle twisted from his grasp. "Get your hands off me. I no longer have to endure your repulsive touch,'' she hissed, her eyes flaring with contempt.

John's face reddened in rage and embarrassment. "I think perhaps you should wait in the sitting room, Captain. Brielle and I need a moment of privacy." His voice was tight and controlled, but Dane did not mistake the venom in it.

"Gabe is my wife and I have no intention of going anywhere without her." His jaw twitched angrily as his eyes narrowed on Lord John.

"Your wife? You married this tramp, this cheap whore who has slept with every scoundrel between here and London?" he quipped, a menacing sneer curling his lips.

Dane grabbed a handful of John's shirt, lifting the man from the floor. "Gabe is no tramp. From what she has told me about her experiences with you, you should be flogged," he growled between clenched teeth.

"Lies! All lies!" John squawked as he tried to pull away from Dane's iron grip. "Don't you think I would treat my own brother's child fairly?"

"You tried to sell your own daughter to me. Why shouldn't I expect you to do the same with Gabe." Dane thrust the despicable man aside, a dark scowl settling on his face.

"I came for my clothes. When I have them, I will never see you again. That should make both of us extremely happy," Gabe ground out.

A wicked smile caught one corner of John's mouth. "I had them all burned."

"What?" Gabrielle shrieked. "Damn you!" She started for him, her claws bared, ready to scratch out his eyes, but Dane yanked her back beside him.

"Forget it, Gabe. Let's go," Dane ordered,

glaring at John over the top of Gabe's head.

Irate sparks flew from Gabe's eyes while Dane held her in check. "I have one last thing to say to you, *dear Uncle,*" she sneered. "I hope you burn in hell!"

John would have countered her hateful curse, but the deadly gleam in Dane's eyes made him think better of it. He stood frozen to his spot as the couple moved toward the door.

Gabe whirled to face him once more. "Where's Elaine? I want to see her before I go."

"She's not here," John snapped, bitterness lacing his reply.

After Gabe stalked from the house, Dane walked back to Jarmon, his blue eyes cold and unwavering.

Gabe swung up on Blanco's back and dug her heels into his flanks. She flew down the road at breakneck speed, letting the tears flow down her cheeks until her irritation had cooled. She cried, not because Lord Jarmon had spitefully destroyed all of her belongings, but because he had managed to send her into a fit of rage. After spurring Blanco in one last reckless flight, she brought him to a halt. Several plans of revenge came to mind, but all of them would injure Elaine as well. Gabe could never do anything to hurt her cousin. Gabe knew she must be satisfied never having to see John's face again.

When Dane and Sherman came up beside her, a sly smile caught the side of Dane's mouth. "It seems you have had your revenge."

Brielle scoffed bitterly. "I will never have

revenge on that horrid man."

"Elaine found out about the contract John made with Fairleigh. She was furious that her father had tried to sell you off. It seems she followed in your footsteps. Elaine sneaked off to London to live with her mother's sister and has just recently married on her own accord, much to John's dismay. Now he is left with a niece and a daughter who will never again set foot in his empty house."

"He has his just reward," she murmured as she turned Blanco toward her own estate.

As the Hamptons disappeared from sight, John walked away from the window and eased down into his chair. After scribbling a quick note to Fairleigh, his lips curled in a vengeful sneer. Perhaps Gabrielle had managed to best him, but she would not escape unscathed by Fairleigh's wrath, he thought to himself.

Gabrielle's heart swelled with pleasure when she walked up the steps to her home. She moved through the house, touching the furniture, as if she were afraid it was all a dream that would quickly come to an end. It had seemed an eternity since she had been home.

Dane watched Brielle flutter about the servants, warmed by another facet of his lovely wife. Her many moods delighted him. She was a child again, easily responding to the warmth and concern bestowed on her.

*   *   *

When the threesome left Gabe's home they avoided the main road, hoping to bypass trouble. Brielle led them along the path she had discovered while traveling from Dane's home to her uncle's. When they arrived at Hampton Estate they went to the stables to introduce Sherman to the other groomsman and to present Nate with the colt Gabe had brought for him.

Nate came out to greet Gabe, a radiant smile alighting his dark features. It was identical to the one that Dane had seen on Sherman's face. Now he understood the mysterious expressions he had seen glowing in Nate's eyes on several occasions. With a hopeless shake of his head, Dane muttered under his breath. It seemed everything in breeches was in love with his wife; young and old alike, from Sam and Tom to Nate and Sherman. No one was immune to her spell and she frolicked in their hearts, giving her friendship, unconcerned that she could easily devastate each and every one of them.

When the introductions were made Nate received one of Blanco's stud colts. The look on his face brought a warm smile to Gabe's lips. Although he couldn't utter a word, she knew how pleased he was.

After tugging on Gabe's arm, Dane urged her toward the house. At the front door, Higgins awaited with his usual stiff smile. It quickly turned into a gasp of disbelief when he peered into those mischievous green eyes.

"Higgins, I believe you recall meeting Gabe. She is now the lady of Hampton Estate."

Higgins choked and swallowed air as he tried to force words from his mouth. "Your . . . your wife, sir?"

"That's right, Higgins," Brielle assured him, a mocking smile playing on her lips. "And since we are so fond of each other, you may call me Lady Hampton." She stressed her title with the same amount of arrogance that Higgins always displayed toward her.

The servant appeared humbled by the information, but his eyes burned angrily as he bowed before her. "Yes, Lady Hampton."

Once they were in Dane's room, Gabrielle tossed her bag over a chair and lay back on the bed, heaving a tired sigh. It had been a long day and she was just beginning to relax from the tension that had plagued her since her confrontation with John.

Dane's eyes roamed over her, torn between passionate desire and the need to protect her. Now she seemed weak and vulnerable and yet she was untamed, independent, and fearless. When she turned an innocent smile to him, his pensive mood vanished.

"It seems odd to be in your room," she murmured. "I feel I should be dressed as a waif, seeing to your needs."

A rakish smile lifted one corner of his mouth as he swaggered toward her. "You will still be expected to tend my needs." He eased down beside her and leaned back on his elbow, his blue eyes glowing as he reached beneath her gown to caress her thigh. "You may dress, talk, and act as you please while we're here, just as long as you don't neglect your husband."

Brielle looped her arms around his neck, lost to the depth of tenderness she saw in his pools-of-sapphire eyes. "Ye mean I kin run wild jest as long as I keep ye warm at night?" she queried in her boyish tone.

Dane's expression sobered. "I want to see the same sparkle in your eyes that I witnessed while you were at home. I don't want my estate to be your prison, Gabe," he replied, his voice soft and husky.

Gabe drew him to her. "You're very generous, Captain. I suppose you don't want me to throw a tantrum like I did at John's."

Suddenly, Dane drew away, startling her with his abruptness. "Gabe, you must promise me something."

She sat up beside him, a quizzical frown etching her brows. "What's troubling you?"

"If anything should happen to me, do not sell this house. If you don't wish to live here, then at least keep it as it is now, but never sell it. Make an orphanage out of it, a home for wayward children, but don't let it fall into anyone else's hands," he ordered, his eyes mirroring an unexplainable sadness.

With a nod of assent, she placed her hand on his cheek. "Do you know something that I don't? Are you expecting more trouble?"

"I'm only making a grasp in the dark; but yes, I do expect it."

"Who is trying to kill you?" she persisted. When

Dane shook his head she knew he was keeping something from her. "Why can't you tell me?"

"Because I'm not at all sure that my suspicions are correct. Only time can bring out the truth. If what I suspect is true . . ." His voice trailed off into an inaudible whisper and Gabe could not bring herself to press him further. He would refuse to answer.

"We will be traveling to Bristol as soon as possible so that we can settle our affairs. I want to put our legal papers in order."

She nodded in agreement. "Whatever ye say, Cap'n," she taunted, hoping to bring him from his serious mood. "Now, kin we git back to where we were before we began this discussion?"

"An excellent idea, madam." Dane lay back with Gabe in his arms, surprised at her blatant proposal. He usually met with resistance and had to fight his way through a wall of ice to warm her passions. Suddenly she was open and responsive.

He smiled roguishly as he peered into her bewitching face and loosened the ties of her bodice. His skillful caresses took her to the brink of sanity. His mouth covered the peak of her breast, teasing its crest to tautness. And then he clutched her closer, holding her so tightly that she could barely draw a breath. His lips returned to hers and he kissed her passionately. It was a long, drugging kiss that sent her heart running away with itself. Again, his hands took possession of her and she was lost. She was his, a puppet dangling upon a string, moving upon command. Clutching at the rippling muscles of his back, she drew him to her, molding their flesh together. They soared to rapturous heights and Brielle experienced the freedom that only came when she was in his strong arms. The world began and ended in his possessive embrace.

As they lay together in quiet repose, Brielle pulled herself up on his chest and gazed into his handsome face, her breasts pressing wantonly against him. A faint smile glazed her lips as she traced her fingertips over his dark brow.

"I don't think Higgins was overjoyed to learn that I had become your wife."

A broad grin split his rugged face. "I thought perhaps that was the reason you decided to come back with me—to spite the poor man," Dane replied, his voice still heavily laden with passion.

"It would have been a good excuse. I'm ashamed I didn't think of it myself."

"Just why did you come without your usual resistance to all of my requests? Quite honestly, I thought I would have to drag you here, kicking and screaming."

"Of that I'm not certain," she replied, a thoughtful frown furrowing her brow. "Perhaps it was to see if you would be unfaithful to your wife after only a few weeks."

"As of yet, you have given me no cause to search for greener pastures," he answered, shrugging nonchalantly.

"And if I had remained at my estate would you have cleared the fence in haste to find another wench?" she questioned with more hiss in her tone than she had intended.

"Since I have no intention of becoming a monk, I suppose I would have been left with little choice," he said blandly, hoping to annoy her, which, of course, he did.

"Just as I thought," she snapped as she moved away. "I am only convenient. When I'm gone, you will waste no time in replacing me, just as you did before."

Gripping her elbows, Dane pressed her back to his bare chest, a wicked smile curving one corner of his mouth upward. "Could it be that you're jealous? I thought you didn't care what I did or with whom. Wasn't that your plan for our marriage arrangement?"

Attempting to force some commitment from her lips, he had backed her into a corner. But Gabe was stubborn and would only yield slightly. "It was, but I have changed my mind," she defended, her chin tilting defiantly.

"Ah, ha!" he exclaimed, pointing an accusing finger at her. "So at last you have discovered that you can't live without me."

Gabe scoffed at his conclusion. "I didn't say that, Captain. I said I had changed my mind. Perhaps when I become an expert at love-making, then I might wish to venture out on my own as you are fond of doing."

Dane laid his head back on the pillow and chuckled heartily, drawing a bemused frown from Gabe. "When you become an expert, it will be that you have become experienced in satisfying me. If you share your passions with another man, it will not bring you pleasure. Be careful, Gabe. If you stay indefinitely, you may find yourself falling in love with me," he warned, a mocking gleam in his eyes.

Cocking her head to the side, Gabe peered at him in confusion. "What difference would it make whose bed brings me pleasure?"

"If you held another man in your arms, would you expect him to make love to you, just as I have? Would you react to him as you have to me? Take Horace Fairleigh, for instance." Brielle wrinkled her nose at his distasteful suggestion. "Well, he *is* a man. You said all you sought was pleasure," he reminded her. "If another man made love to you exactly as I had, it would be my face that rose before you. If he treated you differently, then you would be comparing the two of us. You could not escape me, my dear. I would be in your thoughts whether you wished it or not. I was the first and I have taught you to satisfy my passions. You will never be able to forget that."

An incredulous laugh burst from her lips. "You have a sly way of twisting logic, making it appear as though your insane ideas were fact."

"One of my unforgettable qualities," he responded, grinning smugly. "And one that will bring a smile to your lips when you are living at Jarmon Estate, wondering what your husband is doing at that moment."

"I think you are trying to confuse me, impairing my sanity. When I have taken leave of my senses, you will lock me in the attic, fill the empty rooms with mistresses, and sell my estate to the highest bidder. You once accused me of driving you insane, but that is *your* deceitful scheme," she concluded, casting him a suspicious glance. "Perhaps that is what you meant when you said we both had something to gain from his marriage arrangement."

"You have found me out," he gasped, feigning dismay. "You are far too clever, madam. I fear my plans are foiled."

"It will be interesting to see which one of us ends up with this vast amount of wealth," she replied, a wicked gleam in her eye.

"Each time I go to sea, I will wonder if you have sold all of my furniture to deposit a handsome sum in your private account."

Brielle propped herself up on an elbow, her gaze solemn. "If you think I'm going to remain here while you go traipsing about, you have lost your feeble mind!" A wrinkled frown gathered on her brows. "I will not sit here twiddling my thumbs for a month at a time while waiting for you to return, especially with Higgins thinking of a way to get his revenge on me."

"I hope you don't think I will allow you to come with me," he choked out. "If I had known you were a woman, you would never have set foot on my schooner."

Her chin tilted to a proud angle as she shot him an indignant glance. "And why not?"

"The *Sea Wind* is a cargo ship, not a pleasure schooner for women passengers," he snorted.

"Then I shall be your cabin boy just as I was before." She lowered her head to muffle his protests with a passionate kiss.

Dane was ready to drop the subject the moment her soft lips melted against his. He was silently laughing at her use of the technique that had been one of his tactics for ending her heated protests. The lovely witch no longer needed an instructor, he mused. She had learned enough to become her own teacher.

Dane pulled her close as a cold chill flew down his spine. He savored the sweetness of her kiss, wishing it would never end. What if he was never allowed to watch her blossom into a woman or win her untamed heart? There was always that foreboding shadow lurking behind him. Dane had begun to put the pieces of the puzzle together. If what he feared was true, he could fall victim to the ruthless scheme. He must find a way to out-maneuver the force that sought to destroy him. He had to confront Saxon as soon as possible.

Dane moved above Gabe, anxious to possess her, forcing the troubled thoughts from his mind. He was lost to the delightful feel of this angel in his arms, an angel who could bring him heaven for a few endless moments.

Chapter Fifteen

As Gabe leaned out the carriage window to plant an affectionate kiss on Sherman's and Nate's cheeks, Dane grumbled under his breath.

"I do wish you would refrain from mauling those livery boys," he chided as he settled himself on the seat.

Her emerald eyes sparkled as she sent Dane a quick glance. "Why, Captain. I do believe you're jealous." She chuckled incredulously. "You? The noble lord and captain whose frivolous wanderings have found you in more ladies' arms on more occasions than any normal man would rightfully expect to be blessed?"

"I am not jealous," Dane snapped defensively. "It just seems cruel that you should tread so carelessly on their young hearts, as if they had no feelings at all. They are both in love with you. Each show of affection strengthens their hopes that you will offer more. Or is that your intention?" He arched a quizzical brow as his gaze swung to Gabe.

Her playful smile vanished as she searched her husband's brooding eyes. He nodded affirmatively to her unspoken question.

"I have witnessed their love-struck gazes. Their young faces mirror their emotions." Dane leaned close, holding her steady stare. "If you would have been more observant, you would have noticed how their faces light up at the mere sight of you."

Gabe's lashes swept down to shield her eyes from his mocking expression. "But I do love them in a special way. They are my friends, my family. They represent a part of me—the Gabe who dressed in tattered clothes and who, in many ways, was like them."

"And do you hold the same affection for them that you do for me?" A ghost of a smile hovered on his lips as he arched a heavy brow.

"No." Her tongue outdistanced her brain and she glanced up to see Dane grinning from ear to ear.

Gabe frowned disconcertedly. He had done it again. He had intentionally forced thoughts into her head and put words into her mouth, hoping to force a commitment.

"Tread gently, my lovely witch," Dane warned. "They are young and you are alluring. Only when they see that you are truly in love with another will they offer you the same type of affection you bring to them."

Gabrielle eased back on the cushioned seat and crossed her arms beneath her breasts, pushing their tempting display upward. She closed her eyes, attempting to destroy the seed that Dane had planted in her mind. He was an expert at giving her food for thought and allowing her time to digest it. The fact that he was manipulating her without force annoyed her.

Clenching his fists in his lap, Dane resisted the temptation to caress the creamy flesh of her breasts. It was not an easy task and he was having one hell of a time diverting his lusty gaze and arousing thoughts.

"Gabe," he muttered quietly, "if you knew what you were doing to me you would be pleased with yourself."

Hearing his muffled utterances, Gabe glanced at Dane who was peering out of the carriage window. Assuming that he was talking to himself, she again nestled in the cushions, leaning against his sturdy shoulder for support. With an affectionate smile, Dane wrapped his arm around her shoulders. With his free hand, Dane touched the pistol that was concealed in his topcoat, assuring himself that it would be easy to reach if he required its services. With Gabe under his wing he had become as protective as a mother hen, he mused. He would never let anything happen to her.

As they entered the café Dane spotted Sylvia Berklin hurrying down the walkway on the opposite boardwalk. Dane's eyes narrowed as he watched her disappear into Saxon's office.

After their meal was served, Dane picked lightly at his food, his mind churning in an attempt to put a few more pieces of the puzzle that engrossed him together.

Gabe peered curiously at him. "What's wrong? Don't you like your meal?"

"It's fine and so am I," Dane assured her as he took up his fork and ate his dinner. He ate only to pacify Gabe for he tasted nothing that he chewed.

When Dane ushered Gabe into the lawyer's office, Saxon displayed a look of surprise.

"Gabrielle, I was concerned about you. I haven't seen or heard from you for some time." Turning to Dane, Saxon extended his hand. "Hello, Dane."

Gabe glanced from one to the other, her brows furrowing bemusedly. "You know each other?"

Dane nodded affirmatively. "Roger manages part of my business ventures," he explained as his gaze swung to Gabe and then back to Saxon. "Gabe and I were married about a month ago."

Saxon's jaw sagged, but he quickly recovered and patted Dane on the back. "You have made an excellent choice." He glanced into Gabrielle's shimmering green eyes that reminded him of those of her father. "I must admit I had given up hope of your finding a woman who would endure your outlandish behavior."

"'Tis difficult, I assure you," Brielle interjected, grinning at Dane's ruffled frown. "But in order to claim my inheritance, I was forced to make the sacrifice."

Roger chuckled, but quickly controlled his mirth when Dane shot him a silencing frown. "Yes, well . . . shall we see to Gabrielle's legal papers?" he offered.

After signing the necessary papers, turning

Jarmon Estate back to Brielle, Dane requested a private conference with his lawyer. Gabe nodded reluctantly and went outside to stroll past the shops. Bored with browsing, she settled herself in the coach and impatiently waited Dane's return. In a quarter of an hour, Dane scooted in beside her and the groomsman headed the carriage toward the Sheffwalls' mansion.

After a few moments of silence Gabe braved her question. "What mysterious business did you and Saxon discuss in my absence?"

Dane grinned wickedly. "I signed some papers giving all I have to you in the event that I am not here to see to things myself. Oh, by the way, I had Roger include a clause saying that you could only inherit my fortune as long as we had shared the same house and a meaningful relationship."

"If that was supposed to amuse me, you failed miserably. I didn't marry you for your inheritance, only for my own. I don't want or need your money," she informed him curtly. Her brows furrowed thoughtfully. "Is that all you discussed? I think there is something you aren't telling me."

"We discussed another matter," he admitted. "But it was a conversation meant to go no further than Saxon's office."

"And as your wife I am not allowed to know?" she quipped, a hint of sarcasm finding its way into her voice. "I thought there were no secrets between husbands and wives."

"Whoever made that ridiculous statement obviously wasn't married," Dane snorted caustically. "Otherwise he wouldn't have uttered such an erroneous comment. And you are correct in this instance, my dear. I can't tell you now, but in time you will know. Have a little patience." Dane placed a fleeting kiss on her unresponsive lips and then reached beneath her chin, forcing her to meet his level gaze. "How long do you intend to pout? If memory serves me correctly I once knew a scrawny little lad who would divulge nothing to me. I don't recall acting like a spoiled child. Instead, I respected his request not to pry. The same was true of the dark angel who crept into my room without ever giving her name or showing her face."

Gabe smiled reluctantly. "All is forgiven. One of my faults is having the curiosity of a cat."

"Thank you, my dear. I appreciate your understanding in this matter." He swept his hat from his head and made a mocking bow from his seated position. "Not only are you the loveliest woman in all of England, but you are the most considerate. I am fortunate to have you as my adoring wife." A devilish grin split his face as he glanced at Gabe.

"Enough of this," she ordered. "What else do you have planned for the day?"

Dane eased back in the seat and crossed his arms on his chest. "We will spend the evening with Nick, unless you have something you wish to do."

"I would like to purchase a few gowns since mine were destroyed," she replied, smiling hopefully.

"'Tis done." Dane leaned out the window and informed the groomsman of the change of plans.

Her purchases made and with the packages piled beside her in the carriage, Gabe became pensively silent. She was apprehensive about meeting Monica, the young woman who would be her rival for Dane's affection.

"Am I to fear having my food poisoned when Monica learns that I have claimed the title she desired?" She raised green eyes to Dane's amused regard.

"I doubt it, but if you become overly suspicious I will be happy to taste the food for you," he mocked dryly.

"Is she the one who possesses the key to your heart?" she inquired, masking her curiosity behind a carefully blank stare.

"My heart is not under lock and key, madam," he replied blandly.

"But isn't she the woman that you—"

"Ah, here we are," Dane interrupted as he leaned out the window, purposely ignoring her remark.

Nick strolled down the steps, anxious to catch a glimpse of the new Lady Hampton. "Dane, 'tis good to see you again," he greeted.

Dane lifted Gabe from the carriage and set her on her feet. Since her back was to Nick, he could only see the shapely figure of the petite woman. Slowly, Gabe turned a mischievous smile to Sheffwall.

"Hello, Nick. I'm glad to see that you are well."

Nicholas' mouth dropped open, his eyes wide in amazement.

"Gabe?" he choked out.

Brielle grinned broadly. "'Tis none other, m'lord."

Nick burst into chuckles. "I didn't know this fetching beauty was staying in my own home. If I had you would have found yourself waiting in line to ask for her hand in marriage," he said, his gaze swinging to Dane. "It seems that Gabe is not the usual lady that I have grown accustomed to meeting."

"Gabe would be insulted if you dared to classify her as typical." Dane glanced down at his lovely wife, a wry smile catching the corner of his mouth.

Brielle fluttered her green eyes and touched her gloved hand to her brow, denying their words. "Why, gentlemen, I am but what you see before you, a gentle maiden who needs a strong arm to lean on and a cup of tea to wash away the dust from the long, tiring trip."

Both men escorted her into the mansion, falling prey to her charade. Gabe played her part, allowing Dane and Nick to treat her as if she were a delicate flower. And to her own amazement, she found herself enjoying their attention.

When Monica joined them for supper, Gabe's fears were put to rest. Monica was delightful company, warm, enthusiastic, and full of life. Gabe was quickly drawn to the blond-haired woman who was only two years her senior.

"Tell me, Dane," Nick began, his brows furrowing curiously. "How long did Gabe travel as your valet before you learned that your bedraggled servant boy was not a lad?"

"What's this?" Monica queried, turning to her brother.

"The last time Dane was here, he traveled with a skinny, little waif. I told you about the lad, remember?" His eyes shifted to Gabe and he smiled fondly. "The Gabe I met was a cocky snip dressed in tattered clothes and a filthy brown cap that he never removed from his head. Now I know why."

Monica focused her attention on Gabe. "You led a double life?" She leaned closer to question her, "Was it exciting? It sounds fascinating."

"It was an experience I'll long remember," Brielle replied, a mischievous smile catching the corner of her mouth.

"I would imagine you were shocked to discover the truth," Nick concluded, sending Dane a quick glance.

"To say the least. We were sailing to Scotland when I realized that my cabin boy was not a boy."

"You mean she actually worked on your schooner?"

"Yes. Only during a storm when she was knocked unconscious did I learn her identity." Dane frowned thoughtfully at Gabe as he continued, "Sometimes I wonder if she would ever have told me the truth if I hadn't found out on my own."

"How marvelous!" Monica breathed, clasping her hands in delight. "Your adventures have captured my interest. Here I've been parading about in coaches, attending balls, and you have had all the fun masquerading as a waif. I feel I've missed out on something."

"Now don't get any crazed ideas, Monica," Nick

warned, his brow furrowing in concern.

Monica waved away his worries with a dainty flick of her wrist. "Don't be silly. Surely you don't think I would dare to try such a thing."

After dinner, Dane and Nick returned to the study to pour themselves a brandy. As they eased into their seats, Gabe questioned them in her cockney accent.

"Is tonight goin' to be a repeat of our last visit 'ere with the duke, Cap'n? If ye two dandies are goin' to clamber up them steps like ye did last time, make sure ye carry a pillow to prevent yer 'ard landin'." Gabe grinned wickedly at Nick's startled expression.

"Did you hear us?" Nick questioned in surprise.

"I'm sure the whole 'ouse 'eard what was goin' on. I was sorry to 'ear you injured yer . . . a . . . pride. I believe that was the term ye used," Gabe retorted, a hint of sarcasm lacing her voice. "Enjoy yerselves, gents, and do try to be quiet when ye make yer way to bed."

Monica had been standing speechless, bewildered by the quick change in voice and character. She found it difficult to believe that it was Gabrielle who spoke. It was little wonder that Dane had been fooled. If Monica hadn't known the truth she could have been deceived just as easily.

Tugging on Gabe's arm, Monica urged her toward the stairs. "We won't wait up for you. Brielle and I will be in my room getting better acquainted. Good night," she called over her shoulder.

Nick and Dane settled themselves in the stuffed

chairs, a full bottle of brandy occupying the position between them. Nick insisted upon hearing the entire escapade from beginning to end. Although Dane omitted the intimate details, Nick was still enthralled by the story.

"I can't believe her uncle would contract her in marriage to Fairleigh," Nick remarked as he swished his brandy around in his glass, watching it splash against the rim. "Fairleigh is demented. Monica said she spent one evening in London trying to stay out of the old buzzard's grasp." Nick chuckled and sadly shook his head. "And the sad part of it is that Horace actually believes that women are charmed by him. Somewhere along the way someone took all of Horace's face cards and left him with a skimpy deck."

"Lord Jarmon has an identical deck," Dane snorted disgustedly. "I'm relieved that Gabe is out from under his wing."

"Is that why you married her?" Nick quipped, arching a taunting brow. "Was it because she saved your life and you felt obligated to free her from Jarmon's clutches?" He chuckled slightly. "Touching, Dane. Your actions speak of a noble gentleman."

Dane's smile vanished. "That is hardly why I married that little misfit, but she only agreed to the ceremony to inherit her own estate. She is stubbornly independent and compromised only to gain her fortune. She doesn't care a fig that I can buy her whatever meets her whim. As a matter of fact, she asks for nothing. When she makes a purchase, she refuses to allow me to pay for it. This afternoon in Roger's office she presented me with a pouch of coins to cover the cost of the gowns that I bought for her in Scotland," he grumbled bitterly.

Nick released an incredulous laugh as he pictured Dane accepting money from his wife. "Don't tell me that you have found a maid who defies you and has not fallen for your charms. How ironic," he managed between chuckles. "You've left a trail of broken hearts, my own sister's included. It seems fitting that you should suffer such a fate." Nick frowned thoughtfully and paused for a moment. "But it seems that Gabe looks to you with something more than gratitude."

With a denying shake of his head, Dane replied, "I do believe the wench has made up her mind never to fall in love, at least not with me. If someone else caught her eye, she would run off with him just to prove that she doesn't need me or my money. I honestly believe that if I told her *not* to take a headlong dive off a cliff she would take a flying leap just to spite me."

"Where's your confidence, man?" Nick queried bewilderedly. "I have never heard you talk like this before."

Dane shrugged and guzzled another swig of brandy before his gaze slid back to Nick. "Shot all to hell, friend," he muttered sullenly. "Shot all to hell since the day that ornery ragamuffin with the dirt-smudged cheeks swaggered into my life and turned the whole damned world upside down."

*   *   *

When Monica had Gabe alone she turned anxious eyes to her. "Where shall we go?"

"Go?" Gabe arched a quizzical brow. "What do you have in mind?"

"I intend to see how the other half lives," Monica informed her.

"Are you serious?" A wry smile surfaced on her lips.

"Of course, I am. Do you want to sit here while those two sops drink themselves into a stupor? They won't even know we've gone."

Gabe grinned wickedly, wheeled toward her room, and held up two ragged suits of clothes that she had in her bag, allowing Monica to inspect them.

"You do come prepared." Monica smirked as she appraised the tattered garb.

"Ye never know when ye might be needin' to travel in disguise, Monty," Gabe insisted in her boyish tone as she tossed the clothes to Monica.

Two shabby waifs sneaked out the back door to find two mounts tethered at the back of the mansion.

"Whose horses?" Gabe questioned as Monica swung up on the bay mare.

"Ours. I sent one of the servants to the stables with a message that we would be riding after dinner."

Gabe shook her head in disbelief and then settled herself on the chestnut gelding. "Shall we go, Monty?"

"Lead the way," Monica suggested, mocking Gabe's nasal accent.

Gabe stopped at the café where she and Dane had eaten lunch and then sauntered inside. Monica attempted to mimic Gabe's boyish walk, delighting in the charade. When the proprietor eyed them warily, Gabe tilted a proud chin and produced several coins, assuring him that she could afford the prices.

Gabe glanced about her and spotted Sylvia Berklin who was sitting with a man at a nearby table. She turned away, hoping she hadn't been recognized. Motioning to Monica, Gabe retreated to the street.

"Why are we leaving?" Monica queried disappointedly.

As the door swung open, Gabe pulled Monica into the alley, and waited until the couple who exited had strolled across the street.

"I didn't want that woman to recognize me," Gabe whispered as she peered around the corner to watch Sylvia and her companion entering the hotel.

When Gabe trotted across the street, Monica followed at her heels. "Now what are we going to do?"

"Follow them," Gabe threw over her shoulder.

Gabe watched the couple enter one of the rooms and then she frowned angrily. Sylvia was draining Dane for sympathy and she had already found another beau to replace the fiancé she had lost five months earlier. Creeping to the door, Gabe leaned close, hoping to hear the conversation, if indeed there would be one.

"How much longer are we going to live in this

rathole? I'm sick to death of it. Nothing has worked out as you planned. I want my own home as you promised," Sylvia whined, her annoying tone grating on Gabe's nerves.

"For God's sake, Sylvia, you sound like my father. Neither of you have any patience," came the man's gruff reply. "By the end of the month what is left of the crates will be stowed away and you will have what you want. Now quit needling me."

When the conversation ended Gabe crept away from the door. There was something familiar about Sylvia's companion. Where had she seen or heard him before? Gabe frowned thoughtfully. For the life of her she couldn't think when and where she had met him.

"Would you mind telling me what is going on?" Monica queried impatiently as she followed Gabe back onto the street.

"I wanted to find out where the wench was staying," she replied absently.

Monica threw up her hands in exasperation. "This is a fine night. I'm playing tag-a-long in your mysterious game and you won't tell me anything."

Two men came toward them and Gabe glanced up, a wry smile lifting one corner of her mouth. "You want adventure, Monty?" Leaning against the supporting post, Gabe eyed the two men. "Where are ye two worthless blokes 'eadin'?"

Monica gasped in alarm when Gabe confronted the burly men. She stepped behind Gabe, shying away from the sailors.

"Well, I'll be damned, Tom, look who we 'ave 'ere. It's Gabe." Sam nudged his friend and they peered at Gabe, frowning curiously. "What the 'ell are ye doin' 'ere?"

"Jest wanderin', same as ye. 'Ow about accompanin' me and me friend to the tavern? Or were ye lookin' fer some other type of entertainment?" Gabe questioned with an impish grin.

The sailors looked over the top of Gabe's head to study the young lad who cowered against the post. Gabe followed their gazes and hastily introduced them.

"This 'ere's Monty." She nodded toward the men. "I met Sam and Tom on me trip to Scotland. They're two of me best friends."

Monty forced a shallow smile and found a little of her courage.

When they were all seated in a dark corner of the pub, Gabe turned a quizzical glance to the sailors. "What are ye doin' in Bristol?"

"Me and Tom signed on with a ship that docked 'ere to collect cargo," Sam explained. "Where's the cap'n? Does 'e know yer out alone?" His brows furrowed accusingly.

Gabe shrugged carelessly. "'E and the Duke of Sheffwall are conversin' over a bottle of brandy," she replied, failing to answer his direct question.

"I met the duke a time or two. Fine gent. The cap'n said 'e 'ad a beauty of a sister, but I never met 'er. Why ain't she entertainin' ye?"

"She is," Gabe assured him, grinning wickedly. Monica shot her a silencing frown, but Gabe continued, "And ye kin judge fer yerself if she's a

379

beauty. She's sittin' across the table from ye."

Sam and Tom shook their heads incredulously as they peered at Monty who managed a sheepish grin.

Tom's eyes narrowed on Gabe. "The cap'n don't know yer out, does 'e?" he questioned suspiciously.

"No, but then I don't tell 'im everythin' I do," Gabe said defensively.

Tom and Sam exchanged glances, knowing Dane would be breathing fire when he discovered that Gabe had sneaked off.

"Paradin' 'round Bristol at night ain't such a good idea," Tom warned with a meaningful frown.

"I'm well armed," Gabe assured him, patting the concealed pistol. "Ye know I kin take care of meself. Besides, with ye two 'ere, I ain't worried."

After an hour the sailors escorted Gabe and Monty to their horses. The foursome halted abruptly when Dane and Nick stalked toward them.

"Damn it, Gabe, just what possessed you to run off without leaving word? We have been looking all over this blessed town for you!" Dane growled as he grabbed her arm, his grip cutting off the circulation.

"I thought you and Nick were too busy to care," she snapped, fire spewing from her eyes. "Besides, you said I could do as I pleased and dress however I wanted."

"While we are home. I said nothing about traipsing all over Bristol at this late hour!" Dane

380

...ntered, his voice carrying a deadly hiss. "I ...ver gave you permission to go out after dark."

"Permission?" she gasped indignantly. "I don't need your consent. I am not your servant. I'm your wife. At least that was the title I thought I had claimed."

Monica moved between them before they came to blows. "It was my idea, Dane. I suggested we go out."

"Damn it, Monica!" Nick snorted angrily. "Have you lost your mind?"

"No," she said flatly. "And quit treating me like a child."

Sam grabbed Dane's shoulder, demanding his attention. "They 'ave bin with us. Ye know I'd never let anythin' 'appen to Gabe."

With a reluctant nod, Dane released his viselike grip on Gabe and wheeled to face the boatswain. "You were there tonight, but what would have happened if you hadn't come along?"

"Nothin', Cap'n," Gabe interjected, her voice rising testily. "I kin take care of meself." She spun away and stormed to her horse before glancing back at the sailors. "Thanks fer the delightful evenin', gents. 'Twas more pleasurable than what me 'usband 'ad planned fer me, which was tuckin' me in a closet while 'e spent the night with a bottle of brandy."

Sam chuckled at Dane's annoyed frown as Gabe and Monica rode away. "Well, Cap'n, it seems ye've got 'old of a 'ellion. Whatever Gabe is, she ain't no average wench. Ye'll 'ave yer 'ands full keepin' 'er in line." Sam leaned closer, his eyes dancing with amusement. "I ain't sure there anyone who kin 'old a rein on 'er, not even ye, Cap'n."

"How well I know," Dane muttered as he watched Gabe disappear into the shadows, just as she had on several occasions.

Sam had hit upon the truth. Gabe was a stubborn, quick-tempered hellion who needed a firm hand when understanding failed. With that new thought milling through his mind, he swung onto his mount.

"Nick, I think we'd better get back. Gabe and I have not finished this conversation. I have a few things more to say to her while the thoughts are still fresh in my mind."

Dane strolled into the study to pour himself a drink. When he went out into the hall, Nick and Monica awaited him with apprehensive stares. His features were chiseled into a determined grimace as he stalked up the steps to his room. He and Gabe were going to come to an understanding. He had pampered her stubbornness to the limits of his patience. By damned, enough was enough!

Gabe sat in her room, rehashing her conversation with Monica as they rode back to the estate.

"I ought to go to my own home and estate and forget about him," Gabe had grumbled sourly.

"Don't be a fool. Dane is a rare man. Don't throw away what you have with him," Monica had warned. "Ever since I was a little girl I have been in love with Dane. But I was never more than just Nick's kid sister. He never took time to see me as a woman. There are many, including myself, who would give anything to have him, Gabe. But you are the one he has chosen. He is a proud man. If you press him too far you may never regain what you have together."

"But I don't know what we have," Gabe groaned in exasperation. "Dane treats me like a child and then in the next breath he tells me to grow up. Besides, you don't know the story of our marriage."

"Whatever the case, I advise you to think twice before you say something you can never take back."

As Dane burst into the room, Gabe's pensive musings scattered. He slammed the door, tossed his coat aside, and wheeled to face her. Gabe eyed him warily, unsure what to expect after his display of temper and a little frightened by the icy glare in his sapphire eyes. She sank down on the edge of the bed and cautiously watched him clasp his hands behind his back and pace the floor.

Dane halted abruptly, glaring into her wide, green eyes. "I have tried to be patient and understanding with you. In the process I have spoiled you to the point that I have given in at almost every confrontation between us."

He paused, expecting her to argue as she usually did, but she just stared at him, waiting for him to come to the point.

"You have been so concerned about your freedom and independence that you failed to consider my feelings. You have humiliated me in front of my friends and goaded my ego without the slightest concern that my heart and pride are not made of rock," he flung at her, his voice crackling with irritation. "You hated your uncle for what he did to you. But tell me, Gabe, have you behaved better?"

"I am as I have always been. I have no intention of changing. I did not force you to marry me. You knew what I was like before the wedding," she responded, her voice rising testily.

"How the hell could I have possibly known what you were really like?" he snorted derisively. "You possess three personalities. I haven't the slightest idea which one of those complex individuals is my wife."

"I would have been content to live as a waif," she persisted, her chin tilting defiantly. "And I find that ragged urchin to my liking."

Dane flung his arms wide in frustration. "Fine, madam. Then why don't you go roam the streets? Live where and how you wish. If you want to return to Sam and Tom, then go. If you want to take up residence at Jarmon Estate, then do it," he bellowed, his tone acid with anger. "But don't expect me to be meek and understanding. I have taken all I can tolerate. If you leave I will search out another woman to appease my desires." He leaned down to Gabe, placing his arms on either side of her hips, his face only inches from hers. "I can only bend so far, Gabe, but I do not intend to break, not for you or anyone else."

A strange emptiness engulfed her as she met his cold glare. He had given her the freedom she thought she wanted, but he had deprived her of the challenge of fighting for it.

Dane pushed away, but stood over her like a looming shadow. "Well, what are you waiting for? Obviously you prefer sneaking out and carousing with sailors to being my devoted wife." Dane spun away, unable to meet her emerald eyes. "You have your precious freedom."

After strolling toward the door, he hesitated, and then turned squarely to face her, as if the distance between them would make his next statement easier to voice. "When I discovered who you were I vowed revenge. I tried to win your love. I wanted you to experience the same feelings that I held in my heart. But it seems I have come up empty-handed for all of my efforts. You were determined not to fall in love with me no matter how I pampered you and catered to your whims. I wanted your love and devotion, but you have none to offer. I have failed miserably where you are concerned."

Dane drew a deep breath and raised his gaze to Gabe's. "I have loved you from the very beginning, but you wouldn't believe it and would never allow me to tell you. I never expected to find someone who could steal my heart the way you did. Now I find that I must swallow my cynical remarks. You were right, I am about to choke on them." A ghost of a smile hovered on his lips as he shifted his weight from one leg to the other. "I have uttered words of love to women in times of passion without meaning what I've said. I have become like the lad who cried 'wolf' once too often. The one time I confessed my deepest feelings, my words fell on deaf ears."

Dropping his head, he studied the carpet beneath his feet, as if something there had suddenly drawn his attention. "I love you, Gabrielle." His eyes rose to fasten on her face. "I love you more than life. I would gladly forfeit it to you if I thought it would help my cause. But I can no longer stand in your way or offer lame excuses to keep us together. You are free to do as you please."

It took Gabe a few moments to find her tongue after his last remarks. "If you truly loved me, you couldn't let me go," she murmured, her voice shaking slightly.

A rueful smile grazed his lips. "It is because I love you as I do that I will not force you to stay against your will. I love you enough to forfeit my happiness so that you can search for what you seek. You cannot understand what I'm saying if you feel nothing for me. You refuse to accept my love and you refuse to share your love with me or anyone else."

Dane moved slowly toward her. "The choice is yours, Gabe. You may go or stay, whatever meets your whim." He reached beneath her chin, raising her face as he bent to touch her soft lips in a strangely gentle kiss.

When he raised his head, his eyes tarried on her mouth, memorizing the gentle curve of her lips. He turned away and crossed the room, leaving her to her decision. The time had come for Gabe to choose between him and her freedom. Casting no glance in her direction, Dane opened the door and then shut it quietly behind him. Gabe listened intently to the sound of his fading footsteps before heaving a sigh.

She sat frozen on the bed, watching the light cast dancing shadows on the wall. Each one of them became a manly form who stared at her from the crevices of darkness. Slowly, she rose and picked up her pouch, stuffing the white gown and plain dress inside. She left behind the belongings that she had purchased after she had met Dane. Dressed in tattered breeches she walked to the terrace, searching the darkness. Even though Dane had professed to love her, doubts still remained. She had known him too well to trust him completely.

Wiping away the tears that clouded her eyes, she swung the bag over her shoulder. After slipping her leg over the railing, she leaned out to grasp the tree branch, carefully making her way to the ground.

Through the eerie shadows she wandered, feeling frightened for the first time. After leaving John's home she had often traveled by night, undaunted by the swaying shadows. But tonight she blanched at the muffled sounds of the wind rustling through the trees.

Gabe paused in front of the tavern in Bristol, hoping Sam and Tom were still there. When she spotted their familiar faces, a relieved smile surfaced on her lips.

"What are ye doin' back 'ere? I thought ye went back to the duke's," Tom questioned as Gabe sank into the chair.

"I did. The cap'n said I could leave if I wanted,

so 'ere I am," she explained, shrugging carelessly. "Do ye need an extra 'and on yer ship?"

Sam's eyes narrowed in a doubtful frown. "Why would ye want to run off? Yer in love with the cap'n. I saw it in yer face the night we stood witness at the ceremony."

"So did I," Tom chided in. "'E thinks the world of ye. The two of ye belong together."

"'Twas all an act," Gabe assured them. "It was a financial arrangement. I thought by now ye 'ad learned that thin's ain't always what they seem."

"'Twas no act," Sam replied soberly. "Yer eyes don't lie. I think ye'd best go back to the cap'n." A faint smile caught one corner of his mouth as he reached over to affectionately squeeze her hand. "Yer a lot of thin's, Gabe, but ye ain't no fool."

Gabe glanced away, unable to meet Sam's level stare. Her cheeks lost all color as she watched Horace Fairleigh stroll over to a table. Her face turned another shade of pale when she recognized the man she had seen earlier with Sylvia.

"I trust the goods will be delivered within the week," Horace stated as he sank down in his chair and motioned for the waitress to bring him an ale.

"And I trust you brought the money tonight," the man replied.

A wry smile slanted across Horace's puffy lips. "Of course, my good man. We made a deal didn't we?"

Gabe turned back to Sam and Tom who were studying her curiously. A rash of questions flew through her mind after hearing part of Horace's conversation.

"Are ye feelin' all right, Gabe?" Sam's brows narrowed in concern.

"Aye," Gabe replied as she rose from her chair and ambled away.

Sam glanced over his shoulder toward the table. Although Fairleigh was facing him, Sam didn't know who he was. The other man had his back to Sam. With a hopeless shrug Sam turned in his chair, still bewildered by Gabe's actions.

"I wonder what got into Gabe?" he mused aloud.

Tom sipped his ale and wiped his mouth on his shirt sleeve. "Damned if I know. Maybe it 'it 'er that she 'ad made a mistake."

Dane had gone downstairs to pour himself another drink, tensely waiting for the sound of the front door opening and closing. Giving her the freedom she desired was the most difficult thing he had done. But if she couldn't be happy with him, he couldn't hold her. Sometimes she behaved as if she cared for him. At other times she left him wondering if it was another of her charades. It was not he who was the rogue, he mused bitterly. Gabe was the one who accepted passion, never allowing a deeper feeling to grow. And to think of the times she had accused *him* of being a scoundrel, he thought to himself. Gabe was far worse. He had fallen in love with a misfit. Nick was right. It was a fitting end. He deserved such punishment.

After a quarter of an hour Dane regained hope since he hadn't heard Gabe leave. Perhaps she was staying. With an anxious smile creasing his lips he went back to his room. His spirits plunged to his boots when he found Gabe's bags lying open. The small pouch she always carried was gone. Dane strolled toward the balcony, his gaze sweeping the darkness. She had left him just as she had come— in the shadows of the night, demanding nothing, taking everything he valued with her.

After closing the door on the woman he had come to love, he stripped from his clothes and climbed into bed. With the aid of the brandy he had consumed, sleep overcame him sooner than he expected, but his dreams were troubled. Again his haunting witch whirled about him, transforming herself into an angel whose comforting arms could dissolve the looming shadows. She bent to kiss him, her innocent smile becoming a jeering snarl, her delicate features shriveling into ghastly lines. Her long, curled claws scraped his chest, tearing his flesh in bloody gashes. Dane cried out in agony, but the spiteful witch cackled and then withdrew until she again became the goddess who hovered just out of his reach.

Dane awoke from his nightmare, finding himself alone, cold, and clammy. There would be many more of these dreams, he mused disconcertedly. Each time he closed his eyes, he would become a haunted man.

"Take care of yourself, my lovely witch. You have taken my heart and soul with you into the darkness. I loved you, Gabe," he whispered to the shadows. "When the sun raises its head tomorrow, there will be no warmth in its light. Only you could make the sun shine. When the dawn comes, I will be like a blind man who sees no difference between the sun and moon."

"You are foolish to entrust your heart to someone who could not even care for her own, Captain," came in a silky whisper from the shadows behind the bed. Brielle moved toward him, warmed by the words she had heard. His quiet confession removed all doubts and her heart swelled with a wild, unfamiliar happiness.

Dane smiled to himself. "I thought I had seen the last of my guardian angel."

Her soft chuckle floated about him as she herself eased down on the edge of the bed. "I was afraid your angel had been transformed into a spiteful witch. I thought perhaps you would be glad to be rid of her."

Gabe swept her cap from her head, letting the dark tendrils cascade about her shoulders. She pressed a tender kiss to his waiting lips, melting to the warmth that encircled her.

"I need both the angel and witch, love. I don't want to survive without either of them," Dane murmured against the corner of her mouth.

"And what of the impetuous lad?" she questioned, a demure smile tracing her lips. "Would you be glad to see him gone? He has brought you much misery."

"I love all three of you." Dane chuckled as he pulled Gabe to him and nuzzled against the sweet fragrance that hovered around her.

"I tried to keep them separate, but none of them can live without the other. They share a common need. The friendless lad desired companionship. The angel sought her own comfort and the spiteful witch wanted to be loved as any other woman. They all found that for which they searched, in you—the friendship, the security, and the love," she explained, her voice cracking with emotion.

Gabrielle raised her head to peer into the handsome face below her. "I do love you, Dane. I think I have since the first time you looked up to me in the storm. Your eyes captivated my heart and touched my soul. I have fought with myself from the beginning." Her lashes swept down, protecting her from his probing gaze. "I suppose I was afraid that you could never love me. I was afraid of being hurt. I had suffered so much at the hands of my uncle." Her eyes raised to meet his, a hint of tears lurking beneath their surfaces. "I find that I can't live without your love. Without it, I am nothing." She traced her fingertips over his bronzed face, touching the lines that could be coarse with anger or soft with tenderness. "I tried to leave you tonight, but all I saw before me was the fearful darkness. Behind me was the dim light that led my way back to your comforting arms."

Dane crushed her to him, seeking her trembling lips, tasting the honeyed sweetness that dreams were made of. "I've waited an eternity to hear those words from you. I had given up all hope when I returned to find you gone," he whispered against her skin. Reaching beneath her chin, he lifted her eyes to his warm gaze. "I love you, Gabe, all of you—the goddess, the sorceress, and even that ornery waif." A wide smile split his face as he wiped the soot from her cheeks. "That is what makes you special. You are ever changing, bringing new life and adventure to each dawning day. Don't leave me again. I would have one hell of a time replacing you."

"I can't leave you." She laughed softly. "You were right. I fell in love with a dashing sea captain and found nothing in my quest that could compare to what I've known with you."

Dane grinned smugly. "It took you long enough to accept the fact. If you had taken the word of experience from the beginning we could have bypassed some rough waters."

"Aye, Cap'n, but 'ow kin ye expect a stubborn misfit to take someone else's advice?" she teased as she unbuttoned her shirt, her emerald eyes flickering seductively. "You have openly admitted that other women have heard your confessions of love. Now, my handsome rogue, convince me that I alone possess the key to your wandering heart." Her expression sobered momentarily, stumbling on a thought. "Just who was that unattainable woman you spoke of? Is she someone from your past, your first love perhaps?"

Dane unfastened the rest of the buttons on her shirt and pulled it from her shoulders, a devilish smile curving his lips. "You really don't know, do you?" When Gabe shook her head, he chuckled lightly. "'Twas my mysterious angel who had no face, no name, and no voice above a whisper. She was the essence of love."

Dane drew her closer, his kiss taking her breath

away with its urgency. His hand cupped her breast, teasing the pink peaks to tautness before his kisses trailed over her flesh, sending ripples of goose pimples dominoing across her skin. Brielle abandoned all restraints, yielding to the delirious sensations that scattered logic. She arched against him, reveling in the rapturous tide that flooded over her. And then she was soaring toward the stars that she had sought so many times before. Tonight she found them within her grasp, touching them one by one for an endless moment.

In the aftermath of love, Dane wrapped his arm across her waist, molding their flesh together. "I love you," he whispered hoarsely. "I hope I have convinced you that there is no other."

A happy smile settled on her delicate features. "I believe you, my love. And I have a confession." She lowered her eyes, her thick lashes gently caressing her cheek. "The night I came to you, requesting that you make love to me, was more from desire than the need to deny the marriage contract to Fairleigh."

"I know," Dane replied, a rakish grin catching one corner of his mouth.

Her brow arched curiously as she peered up at him.

"You were far too passionate to ever convince me that you were . . . how shall I say . . . serving a cause," he teased, playfully flicking her upturned nose.

"I love you," Gabe breathed as she looped her arms about his neck.

"Why don't you snuff out the lantern and prove it all over again," Dane suggested, his hand lightly caressing her bare shoulder.

"And if I cannot convince you?" Her brow arched higher.

"Then you will be allowed every opportunity between now and the light of dawn," he offered, flashing her a devilish grin.

"How very generous of you," Gabe mocked lightly.

"Another of my unforgettable qualities, madam."

When the room was cloaked in darkness Brielle wrapped her arms around his neck, nestling in his tight embrace, offering her love to the only man who could tame her wild heart. Happiness was in his smiles, in the depths of his eyes, in the security of his arms. She had come home where she belonged. Gabe offered herself to him, forgetting about Fairleigh and his companion. All thought escaped her as Dane sent reality fleeing before the passionate fire that consumed her flesh.

Chapter Sixteen

When Gabe's eyes fluttered open, Dane was staring at her, his gaze dancing with amusement. "I had to pinch myself to ensure that this wasn't another dream." He lifted a brown curl from her shoulder and placed a fleeting kiss on the hollow of her neck. "You are all I have ever wanted since the first night you came to me, bringing a contentment I had never experienced."

"That is the most ridiculous statement I have ever heard." Gabe giggled. "You didn't know who I was or what I looked like. How could any sane man profess to love a shadow?"

"The dark enchantress who appeared to me was the woman I now hold in my arms. I knew you long before you understood yourself." Dane propped his head on his hand and smiled contentedly. "For a while I thought I was losing my mind. You almost had me convinced that you were only a dream. Between my haunting nightmares and your mysterious appearances, I could never be sure where reality began and fantasy ended. And yet, I desired you each time you crept in from the shadows."

"If I am to continue to steal from the shadows I will need nourishment," Gabe insisted playfully. "Are you coming?" She rolled away to don her clothes. The temptation to remain alone with Dane was great, but Gabe resisted, knowing that Nick and Monica waited downstairs.

Reluctantly, Dane followed behind her, wishing they could have the day to themselves.

"I'm glad the two of you are still speaking. I didn't want last night's incident on my conscience," Monica teased as she tugged on Gabe's arm, hurrying her to the dining room. "I thought perhaps you were going to spend the day upstairs, locked in your room."

"The thought crossed my mind," Gabe assured her, grinning broadly.

Dane drew an amused chuckle from Nick as he pulled out a chair for Gabe and then sank down beside her.

"My, my. It appears that arguments do wonders for one's marital relationship."

"I'm glad that all is well," Monica bantered as she spread her napkin on her lap. "I was afraid the party would have to be canceled tonight."

A bemused frown gathered on Gabe's brows. "What party?"

Monica glanced bewilderedly at Dane. "Didn't you tell her?"

A sheepish smile bordered Dane's lips. "It slipped my mind."

"I wonder how that could have happened." Nick smirked.

"Would someone please tell me what is going on?" Gabe demanded impatiently.

"We are having a costume ball in honor of your marriage," Monica explained excitedly.

Gabe's gaze swung accusingly to Dane. "I have no costume. What do you expect me to wear, my beggar's garb?"

"I have already selected your costume. I had Monica pick it up for me," Dane replied, a devilish smile creeping to his lips.

"What is it?" Gabe inquired.

"You'll see it later." Dane nodded toward her untouched plate. "I thought you said you were hungry," he reminded her.

"I hope you do not intend to have me dress as Eve," she teased, casting Dane a suspicious glance.

"I would approve of that," Nick interjected, a rakish smile settling on his handsome face.

"I'm sure you would," Dane shot back at him. "I would never let you near her if she wore such scanty attire."

"I am insulted by your lack of confidence in me." Nick snickered. "I thought we were friends."

"I know you too well," Dane retorted, returning Nick's smile. "When beautiful women are nearby, you seem to forget about friendship."

Nick bent his gaze to Dane, arching a mocking brow. "It wasn't too long ago that I would have accused you of the same."

In the privacy of their room, Gabe stripped from

her gown and stepped into her bath. As she leaned back in the tub, a contented sigh escaped her lips, and she envisioned blue eyes smiling tenderly at her.

"Daydreaming, Gabe?" came the amused voice behind her.

Gabrielle sat erect, her gaze sliding to Dane. With a provocative smile she squeezed the sponge, letting the soapy water trickle over her shoulder. "Yes, m'lord. And an enchanting dream it was."

"Oh?" Dane arched a curious brow as he strolled toward her, his hungry gaze raking her shapely form. "Tell me about it."

"No," she replied sweetly, taunting him.

As he leaned on the edge of the tub, Gabe unbuttoned his shirt and slipped her hand against his muscular chest. Dane watched her green eyes sparkle mischievously before he stood up to shed his clothes. He needed no invitation.

Brielle peered quizzically at him. "What are you—" She didn't bother to finish her question as he stepped into the tub. It became obvious what he was doing.

With a playful smile she lathered a sponge and rubbed his chest as he squirmed to settle his long legs on either side of her hips.

"If we decide to make a habit of this remind me to order a larger tub," he commented, a rakish grin catching one corner of his mouth.

"An excellent idea, Cap'n. I no longer 'ave an aversion to bathin'. As a matter of fact, it jest might become one of me favorite pastimes from now on. Perhaps ye could sell yer schooner and we could sail away each night in our own tub," she teased.

Dane suddenly became serious. "I have considered selling the *Sea Wind*."

"Why?" she questioned as she began scrubbing his chest, seemingly intent on her chore.

As he trickled water down her arm, Dane gazed steadily at her. "I don't want us to be apart. Besides," he added, shrugging nonchalantly, "I have my own sea nymph. Why should I search out what I already possess?"

"I thought you loved the sea. How could you give up your voyages?"

"Why did you come to live with me instead of staying at your own home after all you went through to obtain it?" he countered.

Gabe settled back in the tub, studying him thoughtfully. "'Tis your decision, m'lord. Do with it what you wish."

"I rather thought the idea of selling it would please you since you cannot accompany me."

"What concerns me most is coming and going to London; not the time you spend on board." She paused a moment before her eyes glowed like priceless emeralds. "I think I have the perfect solution."

"Perfect solution?" His brows furrowed skeptically.

Gabe looped her arms around his neck, her face only inches from his. "Keep your schooner and take me with you."

His jaw set determinedly. "No."

"Well, that's a fine attitude to take toward the person who saved yer stubborn 'ide more times than I care to count, Cap'n," she snapped indignantly. "'Tis a small request and ye act like I've asked ye—"

"Enough, Gabe. Don't start that again. God knows I've heard it enough already," he snorted derisively.

Her chin tilted rebelliously. "I'll follow you."

"I'll bind and gag you and let Higgins untie you after I'm gone," he threatened. "As well as you and Higgins get along, you never know how much time might pass before he decides to release you."

"Nate and Sherman would come to my aid. You won't leave me behind."

Dane heaved a despairing sigh. He could never do that to her. "All right, Gabe. I yield."

"You mean I can go?" she queried, her voice crackling with enthusiasm. When he nodded affirmatively, she fell into his arms, smothering him with affection. "Thanks, Cap'n. I won't cause ye no trouble. I promise."

"I doubt that, but I suppose I can endure your antics as long as I have a warm, willing wench in my bed."

Dane cursed himself for giving in, but she was impossible to refuse. If his past record was any indication of the future, she would have him twisted around her little finger so tightly that he could barely breathe. And the sad thing was he did not care. There was no other place he'd rather be.

"Madam, I fear we have tarried too long at sea. The guests will be arriving and it will be difficult to explain why we both look like shriveled prunes." He stepped out and grabbed Gabe's towel, leaving her to drip across the carpet with no covering.

"Where is my costume?" she questioned as she shivered and reached for his towel.

"Monica will bring it," he replied as he strolled to the wardrobe closet to grab his costume.

Gabe giggled as he drew it up in front of himself. "You'll make the perfect pirate," she assured him before a knock at the door interrupted her.

"I brought your costume, Gabrielle," Monica called from the hall.

"Come in," Gabe requested, wrapping the towel about her.

Dane dived for the bed and crawled beneath the quilts. He cast Gabe an annoyed glare, but she shrugged it off, grinning wickedly.

Monica rushed into the room carrying the costume, but she halted abruptly when she saw Dane lying bare-chested in bed. "My goodness, have I interrupted?" she queried, chuckling amusedly.

"No, but if you had come in a moment earlier you might have seen the captain out of uniform," Gabe smirked as she sent Dane a quick glance.

Dane grumbled under his breath about being bedfast.

"The guests should be arriving about eight o'clock," Monica called over her shoulder as she swept from the room.

Dane threw back the quilts and grabbed Gabe's towel, drawing her down on the bed. "Would you have cared if Monica had seen me in the raw?" he quipped gruffly.

"Would you have cared? I never considered you the modest type."

"Hell, yes!" he snorted indignantly. "I do not intend to be put on display for the world to see."

"Now, don't git yer feathers ruffled, Cap'n," she taunted, mischievousness glistening in her emerald eyes. "No 'arm done. I jest wanted to see 'ow fast ye could move if ye were forced to it."

A reluctant smile found its way to his lips. Damn, but she was an ornery vixen. "Remind me to wring your neck later. We don't have time right now or I would see to it immediately."

Dressed in her gown, Gabe modeled her costume for Dane. "Does it meet with your approval, m'lord, pirate?" she queried, arching a delicate brow.

Dane's eyes flickered down her alluring form and he smiled appreciatively. The snug gown with the low, scooped bodice had not seemed so daring when Monica had modeled it for him. Gabe filled the dress to overflowing. The high-collared cape was pulled back over her shoulders, flowing down in gentle folds of majestic simplicity, allowing the trimness of her waist to be displayed, along with every curve and swell she possessed. Her hair was a mass of silky curls from which a few tendrils escaped to dangle about her face. The effect of the gown was as he had anticipated. Brielle was an enticing sorceress. No one could resist her.

Dane sauntered toward her, his gaze hungrily

raking her. "I fear my friends will be sorely tempted, my enchanting wife," he murmured huskily.

Gabrielle curled her finger around the leather jerkin and pulled the dashing pirate close. "And you will not have to steal from the ladies, m'lord. I fear they may willingly yield any treasure that you desire. See that you do not become greedy or you may find yourself stewing in a witch's kettle," she warned.

Feigning alarm, Dane retreated and withdrew his sword. His attention was quickly drawn to slim ankles and then to a shapely thigh as the black, sequined gown rose to reveal a silver dagger stashed in her garter. Before he could drag his eyes from this display, he found the blade lying against his neck.

"Touché, my wicked witch," Dane whispered as he drew her to him. "Your point is well taken. I will steer clear of all other women. I have found my valued treasure."

"See that you do, m'lord pirate. The fires of hell cannot hold a candle to a witch's fury," she warned, her brows furrowing slightly.

"Do not lightly dismiss a pirate's wrath," he countered as he nibbled at one corner of her mouth. "I will have you burned at the stake if another man lays a hand on you."

A devilish grin spread across her face as she tested the point of the dagger. "Only a fool would tamper with this witch."

Dane placed a fleeting kiss on her cheek and then drew Gabe into the hall. As they walked downstairs, Nick glanced up at them, his eyes lingering on Gabe's alluring costume.

"If all witches were as tempting as this one, I would sell my soul for one dance," Nick assured Dane.

"Your flattery is accepted for what it is worth, sir. Very little," Gabe remarked, her angelic smile contrasting her words.

"Don't stand too close to this vixen," Dane interjected, his gaze swinging to Nick. "She has a razor-sharp tongue and claws to match."

"I'll take my life in my hands." Nick clasped Gabe's elbow and led her to the ballroom. As he drew her into his arms, a warm smile grazed his lips. "Forgive me, Gabe. I have a weakness for beautiful women. And you are one of the fortunate."

Gabe arched a quizzical brow. "How so, m'lord?"

"Your husband is an exceptional man. Never forget that. He can offer you the world."

"I have become aware of his endearing qualities," she assured him, a faint smile playing on her lips.

When the music ended Nick led her across the room. Many pairs of eyes were on Gabe, but she was not aware of it. When she caught sight of Dane, her gaze narrowed in annoyance. Sylvia Berklin stood beside him, dressed in a gown that fit as tightly as her skin. Although the Grecian goddess wore a mask, Gabe recognized her by the nasal voice that grated on her nerves.

Dane noted the wicked gleam in Gabe's eyes.

Her mask did little to disguise her irritation. "You remember Sylvia, don't you, my dear?" he questioned, wrapping a possessive arm around Gabe's waist.

"Of course, Captain," she replied with a pretentious smile. "'Ow are ye, Sylvia? 'Tis a pleasure to see ye again."

Sylvia's mouth dropped open as she met the bright, emerald eyes and listened to the cockney accent.

"Why, Dane. How did you ever manage to turn that disgusting urchin into an attractive woman? Only you could work that magic." Her gaze slid over Gabe, a mocking smile catching one corner of her mouth. "But of course with Dane's reputation with women, it probably took little effort."

As she had at Hampton Estate, Gabe again experienced an urge to slap the arrogant look off Sylvia's face. Holding a tight rein on her temper, Gabe produced a sarcastic smile. "As the waif I was allowed to do what a gently bred lady could not have done. My only regret is that I didn't rub those tarts in your face when I had the chance. I would find you more appealing with blackberries smeared all over your milky-white complexion."

Sylvia gasped at Gabe's snide remark. "Really, Dane, are you going to allow her to talk to me that way?"

"I will talk to you however I wish," Gabe snapped before Dane could retort. "You may have fooled Dane with your *own* charade, but I know what you are." She grabbed Sylvia's arm and pulled her away from Nick and Dane. "I have a few things to say to you in private."

"Let go of me," she hissed.

"Unless you want the hand that feeds you cut off at the elbow, you had better curb your tongue," Gabe warned, her gaze pricking Sylvia like sharp-edged daggers.

"What are you talking about?" she queried as she glanced down to see the red fingerprints Gabe had left on her arm.

"Do you think Dane will go on supplying you with funds when he learns that you are living with some rogue at the hotel? I think not," she added with a caustic smirk. "You have played on his sympathy long enough."

"How do you know that?" Sylvia questioned, the color seeping from her cheeks.

"I followed you last night to hear your conversation. Tell me, Sylvia, did you bring your lover with you tonight? I'm sure Dane would like to meet him." She glanced about her, wondering if he were indeed at the ball.

Sylvia's eyes darted frantically. "What do you want from me?" Her pale skin was turning whiter by the second.

"Your head on a platter would be gratifying, but I'll settle for less," Gabe mocked dryly. "Stay away from Dane and me. And when you find it necessary to indulge in conversation, try to act like the proper lady you portray. I played the role of an urchin more convincingly than you masquerade as an aristocrat." Her eyes narrowed to cold, green chips. "Dane is blinded by guilt and he fails to see you for what you are. If you come begging to him again, I will ensure that he knows the truth about you."

Gabe forced a shallow smile. "It was charming to see you again. I do hope you enjoy the evening—at Dane's expense." She paused to glance back at Sylvia's distraught expression. "Be sure to say hello to your lover for me."

As Gabe sauntered away, Sylvia disappeared into the crowd. "Dane's wife knows about us," she whispered to a bandit dressed in black.

When they were alone on the terrace, Eric questioned her accusingly, "What did you tell her about us?"

"Nothing! I said nothing." Her voice cracked in panic. "She followed us from the café and listened outside our door. What are we going to do? She will spoil everything."

"Calm yourself," Eric ordered curtly. "She doesn't know who I am. We have nothing to fear. Just keep your distance and give her no cause to tell Dane about us."

He smiled into Sylvia's alarmed face. "Easy, love. Don't fall apart on me." The outlaw bent to press a kiss to her trembling lips. "Go back inside and pretend nothing has happened."

"I'll try, but that wench is unnerving. She eyes me as if she were reading my very thoughts."

"I'll handle her. I want to have a closer look at Lady Hampton."

"Not *too* close, my love," Sylvia warned, a hint of jealousy finding its way into her voice.

As Gabe moved across the floor, a timid voice

drew her attention. She turned to see her cousin coming toward her, her face so tanned and full of life that Gabe marveled at the change.

"Elaine, you look radiant!" she breathed as she hugged her close.

"I was afraid you wouldn't speak to me after what Papa did to you," she murmured.

"My grievances were never with you," Gabe assured her, wiping away a tear. "Where is your husband? I want to meet the man who has put such sparkle into your eyes."

Elaine led her to Jason and quickly introduced them. Gabe was impressed with the man and his affection for Elaine. Dane joined them and was introduced. Then he led Gabe to the dance floor. As she nestled in his protective arms, she murmured, "Elaine told me that you had written to invite her to the ball. Thank you."

"I thought you might like to see if all was well with her," he replied, placing a kiss on her cheek. "Tell me what you said to Sylvia. I've been dying of curiosity. I thought you had said enough before you dragged her out of earshot."

"There were several points to be made to that pretentious twit," Gabe answered, shrugging evasively. "I prefer to discuss my handsome pirate. 'Tis far more pleasant than dwelling on that annoying wench."

Feeling a tap on her shoulder, Gabe glanced back to see Monica standing behind her.

"Really, Gabe," she chided playfully. "You are much too possessive. Let the rest of us dance with this handsome pirate."

Brielle stepped from Dane's encircling arms and curtsied gracefully. A hint of a smile surfaced as she eyed the gypsy with the sandy-blond hair flowing down her back. "Forgive me for being so demanding of my husband."

She strolled to the refreshment table while Dane and Monica danced. A hushed voice came from behind her, startling her with its familiarity.

"May I dance with such a bewitching lady?" Eric questioned.

Gabe spun to face the masked outlaw. "I thought to see you hiding behind Sylvia's skirts," she mocked dryly.

The bandit flinched at her biting remark. "You, Lady Hampton, are stunning, but vicious."

"I suppose you searched me out to discover just how much I know about you and Sylvia," she concluded, taking a bold step forward.

"And just how much do you know?"

A wry smile creased Gabe's lips. "Enough to realize that you and Sylvia are leeches. There will be no more funds from Dane."

With a low growl, the thief spun on his heels, but Gabe's wicked chuckle brought him to a halt.

"Your choice of costumes is appropriate. But if you could have come as a viper, crawling on your belly, it would have suited you just as well."

As Eric stalked away, Gabe frowned thoughtfully. Where had she met that man? It nagged at the corners of her mind, but she had no time to ponder the question because another gentleman requested a dance with her. When the music ended Gabe walked away but she froze in her tracks when she saw Horace Fairleigh's chalky-white face twisted in a menacing smile.

"Brielle, I would like a word with you."

Before she could refuse, Horace clamped his bony fingers around her arm and whisked her out to the terrace.

"Let go of me," she spat as she jerked from his grasp.

"You have made a fool of me, you little bitch. No one does that to the Duke of Fairleigh and remains unscathed. Do you understand me, Brielle?" he sneered venomously, his dark brows forming a hard line over his deep-set eyes. "You have married Hampton, but I intend to extract my revenge by sampling what was rightfully mine."

His hand snaked out to yank her to him; his lips cruelly swooped down upon hers. Brielle struggled, repulsed by the feel of his mouth devouring hers. As she squirmed away, Horace crushed her to him again, his hands biting into her waist.

"You may be the first woman to be raped at her own wedding celebration," he threatened as his hand dipped beneath her bodice.

Her scream was drowned in another hungry kiss, but it only lasted an instant. An iron grip clamped onto Horace's shoulder, wheeling him around to face Dane's murderous glare. Before Horace could defend himself, Dane planted a fist on his jaw. Horace stumbled back against the terrace rail only to find a second blow coming at him with incredible speed. As he crumbled to the floor he looked up through a myriad of stars to see

Dane towering over him.

"As usual, you have come uninvited, Fairleigh," Dane hissed at him. "You are not welcome in Sheffwall's home, or in mine." Dane moved a step closer, blue fire flashing in his eyes. "And if you ever touch my wife again . . ." His voice became a harsh, gritted growl. "You may as well sign your own death certificate, Fairleigh, because you will never escape alive."

Dane wheeled away, wrapped a protective arm around Brielle, and ushered her back inside.

Horace groaned in agony as he fought his way to his feet. He propped himself against the rail and wiped the blood from the corner of his mouth. An amused chortle from the shadows caused him to frown angrily.

"I was beginning to wonder if you would live long enough to meet me tonight," Eric taunted as he swaggered forward.

Fairleigh snorted and then carefully examined his bruised jaw with his fingertips. After a long moment, he reached into his coat to extract a pouch of coins. "Get rid of them—both of them," he hissed. "No one humiliates me, threatens me, and lives to brag about it."

Eric grinned at Fairleigh's vengeful snarl as he accepted the pouch. "With pleasure, your lordship . . . with pleasure."

The following morning the Hamptons and Sheffwalls decided to travel to Hampton Estate to spend a few days in the country. When both carriages were loaded, they rumbled down the

412

path, unaware that they were being watched from the underbrush. Another attempt had been thwarted, this time by the presence of the Sheff-walls.

"I'll give you one more week, Eric. We have wasted too much time. I'm tired of your games," Gavin growled at his son. "No more of your empty promises. At the end of the week I will take matters into my own hands." He whirled his steed and darted across the road, leaving Eric alone in the brush.

"Damn you, old man," Eric muttered. "Your impatience will only bring us trouble."

Eric moved from cover, continuing at a slower pace than his father. Gavin had always been there to criticize every move he made. It had been that way all of his life, he thought bitterly.

Chapter Seventeen

When Gabe and Monica had ridden across the meadow, they paused by the bluff that jutted out over the sea. After an hour, Monica decided to return to the house, but Gabe was appreciative of the setting and was in no hurry to leave. Although Monica urged her to ride back with her, Gabe refused, saying she would return before breakfast.

Gabe had not been able to ponder the events of the past week until that morning. Sylvia was using Dane to supply her with funds while she and her lover lived as noble parasites, feasting on Dane's sympathy and guilt. Should she tell him about Sylvia? Would it matter that Sylvia had found someone to take his brother's place?

There was something about the masked outlaw that nagged at her. She should have known who he was. It seemed the truth was staring her in the face, but she couldn't grasp it. Something in his eyes seemed familiar.

Her gaze slid to the ragged rocks where a broken

crate caught her eye. She peered intently at it, wondering if she had failed to notice it before. Filled with curiosity, she made her way around the slope until she found a tedious path along the moss-covered boulders where the wooden slats of the crate lay scattered. She glanced up to see an opening in the rock cliff.

Gabe discovered a large cavern that was camouflaged by the bluff. Inside she found several crates of cloth, wine, and other dry goods. Her brow furrowed, remembering the conversation she had overheard between Sylvia and her companion.

"I see the inquisitive Lady Hampton has discovered the storehouse," came a hushed voice that echoed about the cold walls.

Gabe whirled to face the same man she had seen with Sylvia. Eric strolled forward, his lusty gaze sliding over her.

"I approve of your attire. Your tight breeches and shirt are much more appealing than those baggy clothes you wore when you first came here." A devilish grin parted his lips. "But they still do not compare with the seductive gown you wore at Sheffwall's ball."

For the most part, Gabe was unaffected by his bold regard. She was more concerned about how this man had come to be there.

"I can see why Dane is so taken with you. I'm sure you have a great deal to offer," he breathed as he sauntered closer.

Her chin tilted to a proud angle until she noticed the jagged scar on the side of his neck. The scar! Sam had said he knew a man who carried a silver dagger and that he had left a scar on the man's neck. The dagger belonged to this man. Sylvia's lover had attempted to kill Dane. That was what was familiar about him: the shape of his face, his dark brows, the set of his jaw. He was the man wearing the brimmed hat who had thrown the dagger! But there was something else. It was his eyes. What was there about his eyes? Who was he? Her mind raced in frantic thought as she took a cautious step back.

"Why have you brought these things here?" she asked in a voice that didn't sound like her own. Had she said that?

Eric shrugged carelessly. "Because no one knows about this cave. Dane was always standing on the bluff, staring out at the sea. He never explored the rocks. What better place to stash the goods than right under his nose?"

Brielle's eyes narrowed in a confused frown. "Who are you?"

"Pardon my manners, my dear," he retorted, bowing mockingly. "The name is Eric Dristol." When her expression didn't change, a wry smile grazed his lips. "I see you don't recognize the name. I'm disappointed Dane didn't tell you about me. He must have been so entranced by you that he could think of nothing else." His hazel eyes flared with renewed desire. "Not that I blame him."

Gabe continued to stare at him, a bemused frown gathering on her brow. "You have some connection with Fairleigh and you have tried to murder Dane. You're a seaman who has had at least one confrontation with Sam." She nodded toward the scar on his neck. At her reminder Eric touched his fingers to it and his eyes burned angrily. "And you are Sylvia's lover," she finished assuming a more bold attitude than she felt.

"You are very perceptive, but you have missed the most important point." He moved steadily toward her, a devilish grin slanting across his mouth. "I'm Dane's stepbrother."

"His stepbrother?" she repeated incredulously.

Suddenly, it all tied together in a knot that choked her breath. Eric wanted Dane's fortune. He kept close tabs on Dane and used Sylvia to pry out information.

"I see it has become clear," Eric remarked with an amused chortle. "A rather clever scheme, don't you think?" As Gabe backed against the crates he strolled toward her. "But I cannot take full credit. Actually, my father was lost at sea and returned. It was his idea."

"So you return from the dead after you murder your brother and stake claim to his inheritance," she concluded, wishing she were home, nestling in Dane's protective arms.

"Precisely, my dear. I had the cargo put aboard the smaller boats before burning the schooner. We sell a little of the merchandise to the Duke of Fairleigh and with Dane's generous contributions we have managed quite well," he remarked haughtily.

"How is it no one recognized you in Bristol?" she questioned curiously.

"I'm originally from London. Only one man in Bristol knows who I am and I have been careful not to confront him." Eric again raked Gabe's shapely form with a lusty stare. "'Tis a pity you had to marry my stepbrother and endanger your own life. It was bad enough when you played the urchin who kept Dane from catastrophe. Now you pose an ever greater threat to our plan."

Eric moved a step closer, his hazel eyes cold and unwavering. "No doubt Dane has made you the beneficiary of his estate."

Gabe stood as still as a stone wall, not bothering to affirm his statement. Eric brushed the back of his hand over her cheek, but she blanched at his touch, repulsion mirrored in her eyes.

"You're far too lovely to dismiss with a pistol or dagger. Perhaps you can persuade me to spare you even though Fairleigh has put a price on your head." He braced his arms on either side of Gabe, his gaze flickering over her, his face close to hers. "Dane would never have given up his many lovers if you had not satisfied him more than the others. I think we could strike a bargain, you and I."

Gabe ducked under his arms, but Eric pounced upon her, forcing her against the wall. As he pressed her to the floor she struggled against his bold caresses, but he easily overpowered her. Gabe released an agonizing scream, knowing that it would serve no other purpose than to vocalize her dread anticipation of what was to come.

"Don't be afraid, my sweet," he whispered breathlessly. "Don't make me hurt you. You cannot escape me. I will have you just as surely as I will take Dane's fortune."

All the words Dane had uttered that first night

she had surrendered to him came rushing at her. All she could think of was Dane. Eric's caresses and kisses brought a wave of nausea flooding over her. She writhed and squirmed beneath him, squeezing her eyes shut in the hope of blocking out what was happening.

Monica strolled into the house and smiled as Nick and Dane descended the steps. "So you finally decided to rouse," she mocked. "If you two hadn't been down in the study wallowing in brandy until all hours of the night, you could have enjoyed the morning by riding with Gabe and me."

"Where is Gabe?" Dane questioned absently as they strolled into the dining room for breakfast.

"She said she would be along in a few minutes. I left her at the bluff," Monica replied as Dane drew out her chair.

After several minutes of waiting for Higgins to serve them, Dane went into the kitchen.

"Where is Higgins this morning?" he questioned Liz.

"I don't know sir. I have seen nothing of him." She set the teapot and cups on the tray and entered the dining room while Dane held the door for her.

A loud rap on the door sent Dane stalking to the entryway, grumbling because Higgins had failed to heed his duties.

"This message is from Mr. Saxon. 'Tis for Lord Hampton," the young lad announced as he extended the envelope to Dane.

His eyes narrowed into hard slits after he had

read the letter. Roger had followed Sylvia to see if it was Eric who had returned from the dead to threaten Dane's life.

"I'm sorry, Lord Hampton," Higgins apologized as he rushed forward. "I was visiting with the servants at the stable and didn't realize the hour was so late."

"Just serve the breakfast. My guests are waiting," Dane replied, preoccupied in thought.

Although Dane seated himself beside Nick, he was restless. The thought of Eric lurking about the area made him uneasy, especially with Gabe riding alone.

"I think I'll go fetch Gabe," Dane said as he rose from the table. "You two go ahead without me."

"Don't you think she can take care of herself?" Nick teased, a lopsided grin catching one side of his mouth.

Dane paused and turned a solemn expression to Sheffwall, holding the letter up in his hand. "This note from Roger confirms what we discussed last night, Nick. Knowing the truth leaves me wary about Gabe being out alone."

Nick's face paled as Dane wheeled around and exited from the room.

"Confirms what?" Monica queried, a bemused frown gathering on her brows. "What is he talking about?"

"It seems Dane's stepbrother, Eric, didn't die at sea. He has attempted to kill Dane several times the past few months. Now that Gabe and Dane are married, he cannot claim the fortune until he has disposed of both of them."

Monica stared at Nick in alarm and then scrambled from her chair. "I wish someone would have told me. I would never have left Gabe alone."

Nick was one step behind her as she rushed to the door.

Dane's heart stopped when he saw Blanco grazing on the slope. There was no sign of Gabe and he dismounted, rushing to the cliff to see if she had met with the same fate she had suffered earlier. As he peered over the edge, he breathed a heavy sigh of relief when he saw no mangled body below him. He scanned the rocks and noticed a small skiff tied to the boulder. At the sound of a muffled shriek he jumped to Sultan's back and galloped down the hill. He made his way by foot along the same treacherous path that Gabe had taken.

Gabe struggled against Eric as he pulled at her clothes. When she was able to bend her knee, she grasped the dagger that was tucked in her boot and with one, fluid movement retrieved it and thrust it into Eric's back.

Dane appeared at the cave entrance in time to hear Eric's blood-curdling scream. He rushed forward to find Gabe pinned beneath Eric's slumped body. As he turned his stepbrother to his side, Gabe scooted away, clutching her torn shirt about her. Dane turned a concerned frown to her, assuring himself that she was unharmed before focusing his attention on Eric.

"Why?" he breathed, his voice quivering with tortured confusion. "Half of everything I owned was yours. Why, Eric? You set me up with that woman in London. She drugged my drinks, didn't she? Now you have tried to take my wife. Why have you become so envious of all that is mine? What have I done to make you despise me?" The questions came out in a rush, releasing the troubled thoughts that had plagued him.

Eric looked up, his hazel eyes dulled with pain. "Sylvia and my father weren't satisfied with half," he managed to choke out. "They wanted it all. I was never as strong as you, Dane. I gave in to their scheme. Perhaps that is why I never succeeded in killing you. My heart wasn't in it. But your wife . . ." Eric rolled his head to the side to see Gabe cowering behind Dane. "She is too lovely to ignore." A rueful smile touched his lips as his gaze swung back to Dane. "You can't blame me for wanting her. I . . ." His head tumbled against Dane's shoulder.

Dane frantically shook him, trying to bring him to consciousness. "Where is your father, Eric. Damn it, answer me!"

"Here, Hampton," came a taunting sneer from the front of the cave.

Gabe and Dane glanced up to see Higgins standing before them, holding a pistol aimed in their direction.

"You?" Dane gasped in amazement.

A jeering grin curled Higgins' lips as he nodded affirmatively, his hazel eyes dancing in demented amusement. "The name is Gavin Dristol. My ship went down in a storm at sea, but I survived. I spent almost four years in the colonies, not knowing who I was or where I belonged. I took the name of Benjamin Higgins. 'Twas as good as any other," he added, shrugging recklessly. "I finally regained bits and pieces of my memory. When I returned to England I found that Alicia had married your father."

Higgins took a step toward them, continuing his explanation. "I tried to persuade Alicia to run away with me, but she had fallen in love with your father. He had everything to offer and I had nothing," he hissed as painful memories flashed through his mind. "When they left for Bristol to dissolve Alicia's marriage to me they met with an accident." Higgins chortled maliciously. "'Twas no accident. I forced them off the road, their carriage overturned, and that was the end of it. They both got their just reward."

Higgins squinted down the barrel of his pistol. "And now to put an end to you once and for all. You'll be first, you little bitch," he sneered at Gabe. "I tried to get rid of you while you were disguised as that disgusting waif, but you were fortunate. This time there will be no mistake."

"You have nothing to gain now," Dane barked, drawing Higgins' attention. "Without Eric, you cannot collect my fortune."

"'Tis no matter. Putting an end to the last of the Hamptons is a pleasure in itself. Your family took all I ever wanted . . . Alicia. Nothing matters now except extracting my revenge."

"Don't be a fool, Higgins. You will never escape

alive," Dane insisted as he clutched Gabe to him.

"It doesn't matter I tell you!" Higgins growled venomously.

Eric had regained consciousness in time to hear his father confess to having killed Alicia. His mouth twisted in hatred as he groped for his pistol. With his last bit of strength, he aimed the weapon at his father.

"This is for my mother," Eric ground out in forced breaths.

Higgins' eyes widened when he saw the deadly gleam in Eric's gaze. "No! I'm your father. Your mother was a liar and a cheat. She deserved to die. All she cared about was Hampton's money."

"Lord Hampton was more of a father to me than you ever were," Eric choked in a seething rage.

When Higgins heard the click of Eric's weapon, he turned his own pistol on his son. "Don't force me to do it, Eric. Don't be a fool."

The cave exploded with the sound of a pistol firing. Gabe and Dane peered up to see Higgins clutch his chest. When Higgins had fallen face down, another echo shattered the silence.

"Forgive me, Dane," Eric whispered hoarsely as the pistol fell from his hand and a lifeless glaze covered his eyes.

With a muffled shriek, Gabe buried her head on Dane's shoulder. She was sickened by the devastating scene, the images coming at her from the darkness. Tears rolled down her cheeks as she sobbed hysterically. The incidents appeared again and again. No matter how hard she tried she could not shut the visions out. She had taken a man's life and watched another die.

Dane nuzzled his chin against the top of Gabe's head, his own eyes clouding with tears. Eric had been pushed into something that he was not strong enough to resist. Dane could feel nothing but pity for him. And yet, Eric had saved their lives with his last bit of strength. His gaze swung back to Eric, his heart aching with a strange, overwhelming sadness.

"I do forgive you, Eric," he murmured. "I only wish I could have had the chance to tell you."

Chapter Eighteen

The following month was one of strained emotions. Gabe had difficulty putting the past behind her. Her days were filled with troubled musings and her nights were haunted by nightmares.

Awakening early after another sleepless night, she gazed ruefully at Dane's tired, drawn face. He seemed like a child lying beside her so calm and still. He had been her strength. They had exchanged roles, she thought to herself. Dane had become her angel of mercy, comforting her when she awoke in the darkness. His reassuring voice and protective arms had sheltered her from her fretful dreams.

After easing from his side, Gabe dressed in her tattered shirt, jerking, and cap. When she strolled into the stable, Nate and Sherman eyed her warily. Why had she assumed her role of the lad? they wondered. Did she intend to run away?

"Well, don't jest stand there gawkin'. Git me my 'orse," she ordered with a cocky grin catching one corner of her mouth.

"Would ye be wantin' some company?" Sherman inquired for both of them.

"I want to be alone," she explained, her smile fading.

"Yer coming back, ain't ye?" Sherman asked, a hint of apprehension in his voice.

"I'll be back." Gabe swung into the saddle and reined toward the meadow. When she dug her heels into Blanco's ribs he lunged forward, stretching into a reckless gallop.

Sherman grinned at Nate as they watched Gabe disappear through the trees. "Now that looks like the Gabe I used to know, flyin' wild and free on that white stallion of 'ers. Ain't it a glorious sight?"

Nate nodded before they turned back to their chores.

When Gabe brought Blanco to a halt at the top of the bluff, she slid from his back. Her eyes lifted to the sea, determined to find tranquility there once again. She stood watching the gulls dip and dive in effortless aerial maneuvers and then she finally braved looking down at the rocks. A flash of pain tore her heart.

She had not ridden to the bluff since that day she and Dane had confronted Higgins. Dane had urged her to do so, but her haven had become a haunting reminder that she had taken a man's life, a man whom Dane could not bring himself to despise after all that had happened. Gabe had watched Eric die after he had managed to spare her life.

Gabe had come to the cliff to face her emotions, determined to overcome her fears and put her ghosts to rest. She stood facing the wind, inhaling the fresh air. It would take time, but she would put the past behind her.

Dane stood watching the trim silhouette on the hill; his spirits soared with the gulls that glided above him. Gabe was home again. The lone, wandering waif who was just passing through had stayed to claim his heart and soul. Now she reminded him of the determined urchin who had once brightened his life. Yet, she had become so much more. She was his reason for being.

Gabe felt Dane's presence behind her, as if he had called out to her. She glanced over her shoulder, an impish grin settling on her delicate features. The sparkle in her emerald eyes dissolved the weariness in his face.

Gabe strutted toward him, her smile splitting her face. "What's a matter, Cap'n? Did ye miss 'avin' me 'round? Ye couldn't stand that dreary old 'ouse with all that peace and quiet, could ye?"

Dane rolled his eyes and snorted derisively. "Lord, I should have stayed in bed," he muttered.

"Ye should 'ave," she agreed. "Lords and dukes ain't s'posed to rise before noon."

Dane hooked his arm about her. "Haven't you plagued me long enough with that charade?"

Gabe tossed her cap over the bluff and then

428

focused her attention on the captivating blue eyes that watched her intently. She tossed her head, allowing a cape of brown curls to tumble about her shoulders. "Would you prefer the witch?"

A wry smile found its way to his lips as he studied the mischievous gleam in her eyes. "No, that is not what I had in mind either."

Gabe looped her arms over his shoulders and raised parted lips to his kiss. "Is this better, m'lord?" she whispered.

"Mmmmm. Yes," he murmured against her mouth.

Her fingers worked the buttons of his shirt; her hands roamed over the dark furring on his chest.

His brow arched as he watched the provocative smile on her lips. "Do you intend to seduce me right here with the world as witness?" The thought was appealing.

"Can you think of a better place?" she countered as she slid the shirt from his shoulders.

Dane lost all playfulness as he drew her down beside him in the grass. "Come to think of it, no." His lips slanted across hers, tasting the sweetness of her response.

"Love me now and forever, Dane," she requested breathlessly. "I want nothing more."

Dane smiled tenderly as he gazed into the lovely face that had once haunted his dreams. "I have from the moment you first came to me. I always will."

As their breaths intermingled, sea gulls winged their way above the water's surface. A lone eagle spread his wings and took to the sky, soaring effortlessly above them all. He circled and spiraled, casting a single shadow before he disappeared among the clouds. Perhaps he would reach rapture's lofty pedestal and alight, content to remain forever watching the emerald sea blend with the sapphire sky.

THE BEST IN HISTORICAL ROMANCE
by Sylvie F. Sommerfield

CHERISH ME, EMBRACE ME   (1199, $3.75)

Lovely, raven-haired Abby vowed she'd never let a Yankee run her plantation or her life. But once she felt the exquisite ecstasy of Alexander's demanding lips, she desired only him!

SAVAGE RAPTURE   (1085, $3.50)

Beautiful Snow Blossom waited years for the return of Cade, the handsome halfbreed who had made her a prisoner of his passion. And when Cade finally rides back into the Cheyenne camp, she vows to make him a captive of her heart!

REBEL PRIDE   (1084, $3.25)

The Jemmisons and the Forresters were happy to wed their children —and by doing so, unite their plantations. But Holly Jemmison's heart cries out for the roguish Adam Gilcrest. She dare not defy her family; does she dare defy her heart?

TAMARA'S ECSTASY   (998, $3.50)

Tamara knew it was foolish to give her heart to a sailor. But she was a victim of her own desire. Lost in a sea of passion, she ached for his magic touch—and would do anything for it!

DEANNA'S DESIRE   (906, $3.50)

Amidst the storm of the American Revolution, Matt and Deanna meet—and fall in love. And bound by passion, they risk everything to keep that love alive!

Available wherever paperbacks are sold, or order direct from the Publisher. Send cover price plus 50¢ per copy for mailing and handling to Zebra Books, 475 Park Avenue South, New York, N.Y. 10016. DO NOT SEND CASH.